Stranded

by

F. S. Winstanley

Volume 3
The third book in the trilogy of
the life and times of George Eefamy

May 2007

Published by
F S Winstanley
7a Blakeley Brow, Raby Mere, Wirral. CH63 0PS
Tel/Fax 0151-334 7085

Printed by Gorman, Shorrock & Davies

I must thank Doreen and Rob Mosedale who have been extremely patient with me as I worked my way through five or was it six proof-readings. My wife Lorna has supported me right through this long and often dismaying set of hurdles that one has to jump to have a book published. Linghams the Booksellers on the Wirral have given me confidence and I am grateful to them for their help.

The picture of the horse on the cover was loaned to me by the Oakwood Animal Sanctuary. They are a charity and if you feel inclined to support them you can write to them at Oakwood Animal Sanctuary, Thornton Common Road, Thornton Hough, Wirral or ring them on 0151-334 6665. Like all animal sanctuaries they never say "No", as they really have more animals than their funds can cope with. If you can help they will use the gift wisely.

F S Winstanley

CHAPTERS

Foreword

Foreword

This is Volume III and IV in one cover. After taking advice I decided that rather than issue two books of about 170 pages it would be a better read to combine them into one book.

Volume I and Volume II have resulted in a lot of encouraging letters and I quote some of them, below and inside. I am told by people in the Publishing business that self-publishing is not a good thing to do, but the following authors all tried it:- Horace Walpole, Balzac, Whitman, Virginia Woolf, Gertrude Stein, Galsworthy, Kipling, Beatrix Potter, Lord Byron, Zane Grey, D H Lawrence, James Joyce and William Blake.

Extracts from readers who were moved to write to me are as follows:-
"I passed the book around to three friends and everyone agreed it was very enjoyable."

"I have read and enjoyed your latest novel 'Blue Sailing'. I feel I should tell you what impressed me about the book. You must have researched the naval topic thoroughly to have captured the spirit of the theme, and the fascinating knowledge of ports and cargoes. In addition you have succeeded in keeping two stories going at the same time; what is happening on board ship, and the interplay of the strong characters on land. I look forward to seeing your next novel."

"I have just finished reading 'Number Eighteen', and write to say what a pleasure it was. I am looking forward to the next volume."

"'Blue Sailing' is now my bedtime reading, and I am so enjoying it, my bedside light goes out later than usual."

"Thank you for sending me your book. I sat down and read it from cover to cover. Allow me to compliment you on your beautifully clear and direct style."

"Many thanks for your splendid novel 'Blue Sailing'. It is a great feat to have written such a gripping book."

I also had a lovely review from June Lancelyn Green in the 'Champion' magazine where she says "I read it on holiday and did not want to put it down – this is a great story telling and with plot and characters interesting one wishes to finish the book and read the others."

CHAPTER 1

Expensive Confusion

Mr Penaluna and Mr Fothergill came up from Poole by train. They had used the journey to discuss the war, what it might mean for the country and more pertinently what it could mean in terms of business for Mr Penaluna's ship. They arrived at Waterloo Station and took a cab across London to Tilbury, a journey of about fifteen miles. The cabby was surprised and said so, "Blimey Govnor, I hav'nt been that far out of town, not in years."

Mr Penaluna passed him half a sovereign. "There's another half for you later, but stop at a good Inn halfway there, and we'll all have a meal together."

"Proper gent you are Sir, and no mistake, I knows just the place where they does boiled beef and they brews all their own too."

"Will it be as good as your young Cook's meal I wonder?" Mr Fothergill enquired of Mr Penaluna, remembering the lamb chops followed by brisket slices.

"I doubt it very much, but it will be welcome for all that."

Evidence of the Boer War was everywhere: as they passed through London's East End: there were hundreds of soldiers, some being marched complete with Band. Some making their own way to the Docks. Huge numbers of horse drawn carts and just the occasional steam driven one, all heavily sheeted up, were on the move. Crowds of people cheered the soldiers and waved flags – our gallant lads were going to some part of the Empire and they would show 'em what is what. It was not going to be quite so easy – in the end it took a quarter of a million soldiers and Kitchener, to win a not so decisive victory.

Traffic began to thin out as they passed Beckton and so the cabby was able to maintain a nice steady trot via Thurrock. The two hour journey afforded Mr Penaluna and Mr Fothergill an opportunity to discuss the business matters which lay ahead and both took advantage of the gentle swaying movement of the cab to enjoy a doze for half an hour. The next thing they were aware of was the cabby opening his little hatch to announce that they were in Tilbury.

"Find a soldier or a sailor and we'll ask where the offices are" Mr Penaluna shouted sleepily.

A stiff bristling efficient Sergeant helped them out, and they were shown into offices where queues of people were waiting – they were all ship owners or agents looking for work. After about an hour, a clerk came out and addressed the fifty or so applicants. "We can't see anyone else today, and we are due to close the office at six o'clock. If you could come back tomorrow, we will make a fresh start then."

Murmurs rose to shouting and the clerk began to look quite scared.

"Yes we understand, gentlemen, but we do have homes to go to and we have had a busy day."

Mr Penaluna deliberately did not make for the exit, instead he feigned courtesy and allowed everyone else to leave before him. When he was the only one left, he advanced to the clerk offered him his hand, in which was concealed a tiny purse containing five sovereigns.

"Penaluna's the name," he said. "I would like an early appointment if that is possible – remember the name Penaluna."

The clerk's fingers tightened around the gift "Yes – I'll remember – be here at nine o'clock and I'll see what I can do."

Mr Penaluna was wearing his hat, and as he parted, he turned and said with a laugh "If you can't remember the name, make a mental note of the hat."

The next morning Mr Penaluna presented himself at the Government office at 9 am. At ten minutes past the clerk came out to begin the day's work and called for "Mr Pennysoona." It was near enough, Mr Penaluna was in with a chance of securing very lucrative work. He took Mr Fothergill in with him. He would make the main decisions himself, but Mr. Fothergill was invaluable when it came to the minutiae. Firstly he was asked about the size of his vessel, and how long he thought a passage to Cape Town would take. Mr Penaluna's answers were satisfactory. Now came the questions about what could be carried. Mr Penaluna did not want live ammunition nor horses. He was offered troops, how many did he think he could accommodate and feed? The journey from Southampton to Cape Town is over 6000 miles, given fair winds Mr Penaluna thought seven weeks would suffice. He made this point "I think I could take two hundred and their equipment and tents. Two hundred men would need to be fed for seven weeks, the food needed would weigh say twenty tons and there would have to be field kitchens lifted on board." The men giving out the contracts looked at each other, they realised that they were dealing with someone who was one step ahead all the time. Mr Penaluna continued "My decks are of teak and would need to be protected – field kitchens can be very dangerous pieces of equipment, especially in heavy seas."

"How could that be done – the protecting of the deck I mean?" the Chairman asked.

"Railway sleepers lashed together with rope to make a platform" came the prompt answer.

"We would need you to be in Tilbury by the sixth of next month, can that be done?"

Mr Fothergill joined in the discussion at this point "Does that mean we are paid from the sixth or are we paid from the date we are loaded?"

"Why do you ask that?"

"Because, if the ship is late leaving Tilbury, through no fault of ours, it is dead time for us, and we will be paying wages to a crew of thirty or more for nothing." Mr Penaluna nodded approval and congratulated himself for bringing Mr Fothergill along.

"You will be paid for the journey to Cape Town, plus £20 per day for every day – every full day, you are kept waiting."

"And for any damage caused by soldiers to my ship?"

The Chairman looked up at Mr Penaluna enquiringly.

"I do know Sir, that army men can be rowdy, there will be little to do on board for seven weeks, fights could break out."

"Yes I'm sure that is all correct, but there will be Sergeants and Officers on board – it will be up to them to maintain discipline, but claims for damage will be studied – I do not say sympathetically, but they will be dealt with."

Mr Penaluna was asked to sign, instructed to be in Tilbury by the sixth of next month at the latest and to leave an address for documents to be posted to.

A jubilant Mr Penaluna came out of the meeting and said to Mr Fothergill "We will walk round Tilbury Docks now and see what's what."

They walked through busy streets, cluttered with Army wagons, horses, hordes of soldiers and just what Mr Penaluna was looking for – confusion. They arrived at the Docks and saw again exactly what Mr Penaluna was hoping for – hopeless congestion. Ships were docked everywhere three and four deep. Mr Penaluna stopped one sea faring man who was first officer on a large steamer – he pointed to the confusion, "Is it always like this?"

"It is – we've been here for ten days and we can't get near the wharf– now we hear all the food we were booked to take has gone off in the warehouse, it wasn't stored properly, and we've been put back two weeks."

"Thank you very much" Mr Penaluna said. Then he turned to Mr Fothergill "Come on I'll treat you to a good dinner – I reckon we have made three or four hundred pounds this morning – we'll never be away from here on the sixth – nor the sixth of next months either - £20 a day for nothing.

"The whole place is a shambles," Mr Fothergill said.

"We haven't had a war since the Crimea and that's over forty years ago, so there is not the necessary experience among the Government officials to run it properly – we'll make a fortune out of this – let's find some good lamb chops and a bottle or two of claret."

The next day Mr Penaluna and Mr Fothergill made the journey by train back to Plymouth, only 'Chips', 'Sails' and Bo'sun were on board. Mr Penaluna checked that everything was in order, and with three such reliable custodians it was bound to be, and he went off into Plymouth in search of food, wine and female company. The next day he contacted Mr Baguly and Mr Strange, and asked them to round up the crew, and make ready to leave Plymouth for Tilbury.

George had enjoyed his few days at No 18, but now he was ready to leave. Clarissa had given up even mentioning the possibility of his accepting permanent work ashore, though George was very happy to work in the stables, or help Tom with deliveries. George always spent time in the kitchen with Polly and Rose, firstly because he was happy in their company but also because he felt he had much to learn in matters culinary and this was the place to extend his knowledge.

Mr Baguly called at George's home to request his presence on the 'North Star', and he was invited in to meet everyone and to enjoy two or three of Polly's scones and a pint pot of tea. George's reception of the news about a trip to South Africa was quite different from everyone else's – he couldn't wait to be off – but they all acknowledged that George would not be happy with any other work, and they were all sure that, having met Mr Baguly, George was in good hands.

Three days later George left No 18 with his rucksack and some additional parcels specially made up by Polly and Rose: a large fruit cake, apples, pears and oranges and a pound of treacle toffee, which would have made a heavy burden had the knowledge of the precise contents not rendered them almost weightless. Humpage arrived with Mrs Humpage plus three little ones. Bo'sun, again a man of mystery, came with a very prosperous buxom lady, who was obviously very sorry to release him. Sweeting arrived with his brother, Matthew and Oliver came with their respective parents. All were welcomed aboard by Mr Penaluna. He had arranged with a local inn-keeper for a selection of suitable refreshments to be laid out in his saloon, the ladies were greatly impressed with the Karelia Birch panelling and furniture, and this pleased Mr Penaluna who was very proud of his ship. Steward kept a wary eye on exactly who was, and who was not, allowed into the sanctum, Radford was amongst those proscribed, as was Hazel, though refreshments were available to all, and after a pint or two of cider the rebuff was soon forgotten – Radford was hardened to it anyway having spent most of his lifetime being rejected by someone on some pretext or other.

At the appointed time, actually dictated by the arrival of the tug, farewells were said or sobbed. George came to the portside rail in his 'whites' and there were the six ladies in his life all waving furiously, Tom was there too, standing with Rose. The commands began to be rapped out which meant such sharply contrasted things: to Mrs Humpage it meant that she would not see her husband for at least three months. To George it indicated that they were off on a journey of twelve or thirteen thousand miles, they would go south of the Equator and arrive in Africa. To Mr Penaluna it was the start of a period of financial risk and perhaps more importantly a wonderful opportunity to let the 'North Star' show those steamers what a real ship could do. And to a plump prosperous looking lady it was the beginning of a period of chilly nights with no one to cuddle up to - unless that is, she found a replacement for Bo'sun.

Mr Baguly took charge, Mr Penaluna stood on the poop deck, resplendent in hat and coat.

"Make fast the hawser – look lively." "Let go for'ard. Let go aft." Splash followed splash, as the ropes hit the water.

"Easy now – handsomely does it lads."

The tug took up the slack and the 'North Star' was eased away from the dock – she looked wonderful, her cream shone in the sun and the new red Plimsoll line made a striking contrast. Mr Penaluna's pennants were flying on the main mast also she flew a union jack and a red ensign, Mr Penaluna was thoroughly, eccentrically British. He made up his own rules.

There was little to do until they were clear of the Eddystone lighthouse, so most of the crew stayed on the port side waving until even the most enthusiastic had to admit that everyone was out of sight. No one was more gentle and understanding than Mr Baguly until that point was reached, then suddenly his tone of voice changed.

"Right. T'gallants and Royals at the ready, up you go." The men climbed rapidly up to their posts, over one hundred feet above the deck.

"Wait for the word."

They knew the routine but Mr Baguly had to have his moment of glory. He signalled to the tug to release the hawser.

"Bring the hawser to us lads."

"T'gallants and Royals now."

"Sheet home." "How is she Humpage?"

"With this wind, I think the spanker would help Sir." Mr Baguly looked round towards the Napoleon like figure on the poop deck – he received the Emperor's nod. The men knew he would and they were standing ready to do Mr Baguly's bidding. Two minutes later he shouted to Humpage "How is she now?" Humpage began to sing by way of response and others joined in, some breathlessly; the towing hawser took a deal of puff to get it stowed properly. Mr Penaluna surveyed his ship, heard the song and the rhythmic slap on the water of her bows. George stood by the rail, thirty years Mr Penaluna's junior but enjoying exactly the same sense of possession and revelling in the music of the sailors and of the sea.

Steward went to the galley and told George to prepare coffee, and to make a start on dinner. Radford made a rude sign as Steward left the galley.

"We don't need the likes of him a tellin' us 'ow to run the galley." George agreed. The fires were well and truly hot and a beef pie with a deep suet crust was well on the way. George took his coffee, once everyone was served, to the rail,

In his other hand was a large slice of Polly's fruit cake. Radford's hands were similarly encumbered, as were Hazel's, at this rate the cake would not last long, but the total enjoyment generated would be considerable. As far as George was concerned this was not HIS cake, it was a cake for all to enjoy. George was daydreaming, when he suddenly heard Mr Baguly bellow "Main courses."

"Main courses" came the echo from above.

"Sheet home."

They were now out in the English Channel with a brisk wind blowing away from France. Mr Penaluna was determined to try out the 'North Star'.

"Overhaul the buntlines and the leach lines."

"Hook on the chain fore tack."

Her lee rails were hissing off through the sea, the main deck was awash, all the sails except those on the jib were full and pulling.

"Trim the lee fore brace," bellowed Mr Baguly.

"Sheet home main topsail."

Mr Baguly and Mr Penaluna were now fine tuning the sails to get the best possible results.

"Wire back stays do you think Mr Baguly?" Mr Penaluna asked as he was saw the top masts flexing.

"Brace up lads" Mr Baguly roared by way of response. "And the jib sails Sir?"

"No leave her now Mr Baguly and we'll heave the log."

Sweeting and Bo'sun were nearby as Mr Baguly shouted "Heave the log."

Over the side went the leather cup followed by the white cloth. "Turn" snapped Mr Baguly. "Turn" responded Sweeting as he turned over the glass. In fourteen seconds the last of the sand ran out and Sweeting shouted 'Stop'. "Thirteen knots," Bo'sun shouted. "I thought so" Mr Penaluna said calmly, he had been standing near so as to witness the operation. "So we will try all the jib sails now if you please Mr Baguly."

"You heard lads, jib sails now, jump to it."

"Did you hear that Humpage?" Mr Penaluna called to his faithful helmsman.

"I did Sir – thank you, we'll try it, but we might have to brail in the head of the spanker or she might move to windward."

Mr Penaluna looked at Mr Baguly. A knowing look it was, Mr Baguly nodded and said "That Humpage has hands so delicate he should take up embroidery."

"Good man on the wheel though – best I've ever known." Mr Penaluna said. The 'North Star' plunged forward, fully rigged now, the sails blown dry and creamy white, the ropes and shrouds singing triumphantly. Mr Penaluna spotted George hurling some waste to leeward. "Mr Eefamy – coffee and a ham sandwich would not go amiss – for me and Mr Baguly.

"Aye Aye Sir – five minutes."

"Right Bo'sun – strike four bells. That'll do starboard watch, relieve the wheel."

The rest of the trip to Tilbury was uneventful until they actually reached the docks. They were towed in with the seventy foot jib safely withdrawn and stowed on deck. Ships of all colours, sizes and origins were everywhere. Mr Penaluna's papers told him which dock to go to, but the chances of finding space there were nil. Mr Baguly could not understand it; he was a simple man and he thought Government officials knew exactly what they were doing, he was about to find out that they did not. The pilot and the tug skipper eventually towed, and then nudged them into a favourable position, where they were only two ships away from the dock. Always a courteous man Mr Penaluna climbed on board the ship next to his to ask if he could throw some ropes across and lash the two ships together. The Captain came out of his quarters to greet Mr Penaluna. They had met before as able bodied seamen sailing out of Plymouth. Mr Makepeace had reluctantly turned to steam.

"I was offered a small steamer ten years ago, complete with a good crew. Now I have this one, 4000 tons and a very seaworthy vessel, so I can't grumble." "Is this yours?" Mr Makepeace said pointing to the 'North Star'. "Isn't she a beauty – how did you manage that? She must have cost a pretty penny."

"Same way your owner bought yours – some good management, a bit of cheek and a lot of luck," Mr

Penaluna said modestly. "Are you waiting to go to Cape Town?"

"Yes I've got my papers but I can't get near – someone said our stuff is available and I have tried to rig up cranes so I can swing my load right over that ship which is right next to the dock, but he won't hear of it – says all the ropes will get tangled and all the bales will land smack on his rails, rigging or companion ways."

"So we are here for a few days then" observed Mr Penaluna.

"Looks like it – they just do not seem to know what to do next."

"Ah well I'll let my crew loose on Tilbury and then I'll study my charts while it is all nice and quiet. Have you sailed to Cape Town before?"

"Yes, three times and always in a four master, once you are south of the Equator, we found winds by sailing nearer land, no point in calling in at Ascension Island, or St Helena unless you really have to. We didn't exactly hug the coast, because there are some very rough characters still living on the west coast of Africa. We have given up having slaves, but they haven't and given a chance, they'll take your ship and sell you and your men into slavery."

Mr Penaluna bore in mind his narrow escape in the Mediterranean Sea and thanked Mr Makepeace for his advice. Permission was given to lash the two ships together, and Mr Penaluna passed Mr Baguly the message. He then went in search of George. He was writing home to say where he was when Mr Penaluna came into his cabin.

"We are going to be here for a week or two Mr Eefamy, so I suggest you go ashore, when it is convenient, don't rush your letter, and try to find a good butcher and some fresh vegetables, bread – well, you know better than I do. So you can cook for us while we wait the Army's pleasure."

CHAPTER 2

Clarissa Pays a Visit

George's letter was received at No 18 four days later, Clarissa decided she would go to London, because she had some business there, and then make her way out to Tilbury by cab. She felt confident that she could leave the paperwork to Thurza, who was proving to be a real asset in her office. She enquired at two or three shipping agents as to how she could locate George's ship and eventually decided to walk around the docks until she found the 'North Star' with its distinctive cream hull. After half an hour or so she found the ship but could see no way to it, as two other ships were between it and the dockside. Clarissa was a lively lady but she did not fancy climbing across two ships to arrive at her destination. She found a small rowing boat, the owner of which was looking for employment. Usually his job was to carry provisions to ships, but he said that for two shillings he would row Clarissa out to the far side of the 'North Star', where she would be able to climb up on to the ship. The oarsman was skilled at his trade and in ten minutes he had positioned his little boat exactly beneath a set of wooden ladders which were screwed to the hull of the ship. He held his boat steady and Clarissa made a grab for the ladder, she was soon at the top. Now came the tricky bit: how to actually climb over the rail onto the ship whilst retaining a hold on one's handbag and hat. She threw caution and her two impedimenta to the winds and using both hands, climbed over and arrived on the deck, where she was met by Mr Penaluna who had witnessed this invasion with some amusement. He said, picking up the gaily bedecked hat and the handbag, "I don't recall that these belong to any member of my crew, so I think they must be yours."

"Yes they are – I've come to see George – is it alright – am I intruding?"

"You certainly came aboard like a pirate, but you are a very welcome intruder – George has just gone ashore looking for provisions, but he'll be back in half an hour or so, can I offer you some tea?"

Clarissa had now regained her composure along with her hat and bag. "Yes that would be nice, and may I walk round and see where George lives?"

"Of course – I'll contact Steward first, and arrange for tea, then I'll show you around."

Mr Penaluna left no detail unexplained as he took his guest around his ship. Thanks to Hazel's bullying ways it was even possible to go in the men's cabins and be proud of the tidiness. George and Radford always kept the galley very clean, the companion ways were swept every day, and the beautiful teak decks and handrails were immaculate. Clarissa was impressed. She insisted upon well ordered places of work on her own premises, so she knew that efficiency such as this was not arrived at easily.

But her appreciation of the 'North Star' turned to amazement when Mr Penaluna ushered her into his quarters. She had never seen Karelia Birch in any form before, and now she was surrounded by it – it was a completely new and astounding experience for her, as indeed was the tea tray which Steward brought in. A very rare visitor to Mr Penaluna's table was his set of Beleek china tea cups and saucers, of which he was both proud and apprehensive: the china used was paper thin, translucent and of a pale pink hue which added to the feeling of fragility. He had shipped a large quantity of this china from Northern Ireland, where it is made, to Germany, fifteen years ago, and the manufacturers were so delighted with Mr Penaluna's success in taking a large quantity on such a perilous journey with no breakages at all, that they presented him with a full tea service as a bonus. Mr Penaluna remembered the trip very well, it had taken place in June and they had the most idyllic sea journey imaginable: the weather was warm, and the westerlies took them down through the Irish Sea, into the English Channel and gently wafted them up to Hamburg. It took weeks because they never exceeded five knots on the fifteen hundred mile trip, and sometimes they were barely doing enough to have steering way, but it was a wonderful sea journey. The men had little to do, trimming the sails was rarely necessary, so they danced, sang and slept. The system of four hours on and four hours off was discontinued, and it was a three week long holiday. Mr Penaluna could not recall any similar trip in his thirty years at sea. And now the delicate tea cups were poised between him and a beautiful woman – Mr Penaluna was a happy man.

"These are lovely cups and saucers," Clarissa said, thus adding to Mr Penaluna's pleasure in owning them. "I am in the ceramics business," she continued, "so I am acquainted with the difficulties." She picked up a cup and held it to the light. "The wastage must be terrific."

"Wastage – what's that? Mr Penaluna asked.

"All pots of any kind have to be fired in a kiln at very high temperatures – some do not come out of the kiln as we would like them to – cracked or misshapen – our percentage is quite small, but with this I would not be surprised if as many as thirty per cent were faulty."

"Could they be sold as seconds?" Mr Penaluna asked, trying to make an intelligent contribution to the conversation, when his thoughts were completely occupied by just how attractive Clarissa was.

"Yes we can sell 'seconds' as little gifts at holiday resorts, but anyone who has aspirations which reach as far as Beleek would not settle for 'seconds'." She raised the now empty cup to the light and added "And yours are really top quality – I envy you – they are very beautiful."

"Ah – I think I hear Mr Eefamy whistling, he must be back – we'll go and give him a surprise."

Clarissa enfolded George into her arms, (Mr Penaluna wished he were the recipient of such a welcome) and the three of them discussed how to proceed towards a meal. They were effectively marooned on board ship. They were two full sized ships away from the dock. The man

who had rowed Clarissa out was gone. There was nothing for it but to wait and see what George could produce.

"I'll do lamb chops" George volunteered. "They are Mr Penaluna's favourite and I know you like them too, Mama – so give me an hour, and I'll have it ready."

Mr Penaluna steered Clarissa back to his saloon, and George began to prepare the evening meal. When the food was ready George brought in a tray with two plates of chops and a large tureen with enough vegetables for two.

"Please bring your own meal in George" Mr Penaluna said. "I hate to think of anyone eating alone." Clarissa was very pleased to hear this, it all confirmed for her what George put in his letters home; this was indeed a family ship. As soon as the very convivial meal was over George collected up the trays and announced that he had a lot to do stowing away the provisions he had just bought. Mr Penaluna suggested a stroll on the deck, Clarissa agreed. They went up on deck, Mr Penaluna carrying two good sized glasses of wine.

"This place looks as if they do not know what they are doing" Clarissa said, having surveyed the vast numbers of ships awaiting cargoes.

"These sort of jobs require co-ordination Ma'am" Mr Penaluna said. "And that is one quality the Commissariat just haven't got." "They told us all to be here by the sixth – I've seen the papers issued to other skippers – it is ridiculous and quite unworkable." Mr Penaluna went on to explain about the clauses in the agreements about delays.

"So you are being paid waiting time?" Clarissa said.

"Exactly that. We are being paid for doing nothing."

"Very nice too – we all pay taxes, and this is what they do with it."

"Never mind Ma'am – it's a lovely evening and this wine is especially good." The taste of wine for Mr Penaluna varied immensely according to the company with whom he shared it. The same wine yesterday was 'acceptable', today it was 'especially good'.

A quizzical expression alighted upon Clarissa's face. Mr Penaluna, very much aware and in tune with his guest, said "Was there something Ma'am?"

"Two things actually: please don't call me Ma'am, my name is Clarissa."

"And secondly?"

"Secondly – how do I get off your ship tonight? – it is going dark, the man with the little boat is no doubt at home with his wife."

"Or in a pub."

"Yes, or in a pub" Clarissa laughingly agreed. "But he certainly isn't here, and we are two ships away from the dock."

"I have it Ma'am – err Clarissa – you must stay on the ship and have my cabin – the bed is very comfortable, and I will sleep in Mr Baguly's quarters, and in the morning you will breakfast with us, and I'll send George in search of a bum-boat – a slightly inelegant expression, but the correct one nevertheless – how does that sound?"

"Very acceptable – perhaps we should salute the decision with another glass of this excellent wine."

"Certainly Clarissa – pray follow me back to my saloon and we'll break open a new bottle."

They enjoyed their second glass and their third, then Mr Penaluna said "I'll leave you now Clarissa, you will find all the usual offices through there," indicating a door which led through to his bathroom. And with that he walked towards the door. His hand was on the door knob when he felt Clarissa's hand on his, preventing him from turning the handle.

"I think we could both manage very well in here – don't you?"

"Beautifully my dear, beautifully" gasped Mr Penaluna as he slid the bolt in place, to secure their privacy.

Mr Penaluna rose next morning quite early, looked at the lovely Clarissa in HIS bed, and kissed her gently. She swatted at him as though he were a fly, and she turned over revealing her flawless shoulders and back. Mr Penaluna went in search of George, he didn't want George to know of this little interlude. He found him in his galley whistling and cooking bacon and eggs – the smell of coffee seemed especially alluring this particular morning as indeed did everything – the sky was bluer, the sun was warmer, the bacon smelt better. His senses were not merely aroused, they were renewed.

"I'll take your mother some breakfast George, I let her have my cabin – I expect she slept well enough in there."

"Yes I'm sure she did – she usually does sleep well – she likes the bacon crispy, so I'll leave it for a minute. Will she be able to leave today? – I expect I could find a bum-boat." George was not worldly wise – he suspected nothing.

"We'll see what happens, she might like another of your meals – she likes good food."

"Well here's her's now Sir, and I'll have yours ready as soon as I can."

It was a lovely warm day, just the three of them were on the ship, but at midday a tug came alongside and told Mr Penaluna of a space next to the dock, he could secure it for him for £10. Here was a quandary for Mr Penaluna: the last thing he wanted to do was to part from Clarissa so soon, but he had to display enthusiasm for the move to the dockside. He went down on to the tug boat, paid the man £20 to keep the place for him by docking his tug at the spot – and to return tomorrow to do the job. Everybody was happy: George had his mother's company, Mr Penaluna had the prospect of a dockside mooring and another night with Clarissa – he felt as if the Boer War was of terrific benefit to him. As Mr Penaluna was descending into the tug the skipper made a very acute observation. "Do you see those plugs which have been knocked in two feet above the Plimsoll line?" No – Mr Penaluna had to admit he had never noticed them – they fitted so tightly and had about six coats of paint on them. "Well" continued the tug skipper "I think this ship carried sweeps at some time in the past, so she must have been on the tea-run, and if she was caught in the doldrums the plugs would be knocked out and the sweeps – look there are six plugs – so six sweeps each side and two or three boats out at the front pulling – the skipper could go looking for a breeze."

"I am indebted to you – I am going well south of the Equator and sweeps could prove to be very useful."

"They used to use sweeps on men of war in Nelson's days, so they must work and frigates was very heavy ships – full of cannon and hundreds of tons of supplies, water etc for four hundred men."

"Yes, I'll look around the chandlers and see if I can buy some – I'll take my carpenter with me he'll know what to look for."

Sweeps were oars about thirty feet long and if used skilfully, with five men per oar, they could move a big vessel out of the calm water and into breezes.

Next morning the tug came alongside, George was sent off to the local Inns and boarding houses to rouse out Mr Baguly and enough of the men to effect the move. Clarissa stayed on board and was able to watch a very different side of Mr Penaluna's character. His orders were succinct, clear and precise, and in two hours, the 'North Star' was repositioned near the dock. Clarissa left in a far more dignified way than she had embarked, and waved and blew kisses as the cab drove away. George was sure they were for him. Mr Penaluna stood with his arm around George's shoulders and hoped they were for him. They were for both of them, but only Clarissa knew the exact proportions.

Now Mr Penaluna's ship was ready for loading and ideally positioned. A Major in the Lancashire Fusiliers came to see Mr Penaluna and to acquaint him with the fact that 200 of his men, plus officers and NCOs would be arriving in the next four days, and he wished to see (quite rightly) how they would be accommodated. This was a big roomy ship, but 230 people plus all their gear take up a lot of space. In order to make sure that things went well from the start, Mr Penaluna had arranged that Mr Baguly and Sweeting would vacate their cabins and move into a 'double' that was not being used. Thus ensuring that the Commanding Officer and his deputy had some privacy. The Major was impressed with his cabin (all cleaned up and polished by Hazel), then Mr Penaluna took him to his saloon for a drink, and not inadvertently, to make it quite clear exactly who was in charge on the 'North Star'. The Major got the drink and the message.

"If you do need my saloon for important meetings with your fellow officers or for disciplinary reasons – naturally by prior arrangement, I shall be happy to make it available for you." The Major thanked Mr Penaluna and set off to make arrangements for the field kitchens to be delivered. Mr Penaluna took 'Chips' around the various ships' chandlers in search of railway sleepers and sweeps. They had the dimension of the field kitchens and there were to be five installed on his ship, so he knew how many sleepers would be needed. The chandler had no sweeps, and said they were not much used now and recommended a visit to Deptford further up the Thames towards Central London where Mr Penaluna might find some in a breaker's yard. Small steam ferries plied up and down the Thames, so it was not difficult to find one which went past Deptford and two half crowns ensured that the ferry for once, would actually stop at Deptford.

The breaker's yard was indeed a sad sight for Mr Penaluna. Huge naval ships like the 'Fighting Temeraire' in Turner's painting were everywhere all looking forlorn, neglected and pitiful. The boss was a hearty Irishman who loved his work and had no sentiment.

"Yes we have sweeps, they were often used on ships like this – they had a crew of 700 so there were plenty of men to go on the oars – most I've got are about 40 feet long but you can saw off what you don't want – better too long than too short."

He then set off at a brisk pace with Mr Penaluna just behind him. It was a ship's charnel house: they were surrounded by maritime devastation; rotting timber and ropes, musty canvas and huge rusty cast iron brackets and fixings. The Irishman knew exactly where he was going and he led Mr Penaluna into a long shed where order and tidiness prevailed: the really worthwhile items from the rotting hulks were put away ready for sale. Well made helms, capstans, doors, panels for cabins, complete galleys, ship's furniture, tables, cots, steps, all lined up waiting for new homes. The sweeps were on trestles. "One pound each – pick any you like – how many do you need?"

"Twelve" Mr Penaluna said monosyllabically – he was still bemused and sad, looking at all this high endeavour reduced to scrap.

"I'll charge for twelve but take fifteen then you have three spares."

"Can you arrange transport for me?"

"That's easy come with me – Fred," he called to one of his men, "bring fifteen sweeps to the riverside." He led Mr Penaluna to the riverside and picked up a large green flag. He waited until a steam driven tug came into view going down river with a barge in tow. He waved to the tug skipper who signalled that he had received the message, and he moved towards the riverside. The sweeps were loaded on to the barge, Mr Penaluna jumped on to the tug and they were away. Mr Penaluna looked back as one of the masts of a huge superannuated battleship came crashing down, felled, just as oaks had been felled a hundred years before in order to build what was now a wreck. The first felling led to a hundred years of desperate situations, glory, hair-raising escapes, ceremony, victory and the taking of lucrative prizes. The second felling would result in tons of firewood being hauled around London streets, to be sold off at sixpence a sackfull. Mr Penaluna hated the passing of the sailing ship, upon which man pitted his wits against nature's unpredictability, it was too easy to conquer the seas with steam, it was not a contest to which Mr Penaluna ever intended to be a party.

Mr Penaluna by dint of persuasion and bribery had his sweeps delivered to the 'North Star', and he took 'Chips' over the side with him to look at the plugs.

"They can be knocked out from inside the ship, I'll knock a six inch nail into each one, so we can tie some strong thread to it before we knock it, otherwise, once the plug is knocked out but if we"-

"Yes, yes I follow, Mr Penaluna said. "We don't want to lose the plugs, somehow those sweeps are going to have to be stowed away – have a word with Bo'sun." By this time the ill-tempered 'Chips' was climbing back on to the ship muttering about how many jobs he was expected to do, and for what little thanks or reward.

The sleepers were in place now on the decks, ready for the field kitchens to arrive, and some of the soldiers had also made themselves at home on board the 'North Star'. It was not among Mr Penaluna's plans nor in his contracts that he should feed the soldiers, so he insisted that the field kitchens be used immediately. The men said they were not cooks and didn't know how to manage them.

"I'll soon arrange tuition," Mr Penaluna said, and he went in search of George and Radford. Next he buttonholed the Major who was on and off the ship everyday.

"I don't mind arranging for your men to be shown how to use a field kitchen, but have you arranged for enough wood to be brought on board for say seven weeks sailing?" No, the Major hadn't, he summoned one of his Lieutenants, who was in charge of stoves – a mere lad of 18 or 19. "Sorry Sir, I've ordered all the food but no one mentioned fuel."

"Right. Now get your head together with the ship's cook and come up with some calculations, we still have time."

Mr Penaluna thought how young and inexperienced the lad looked to be going thousands of miles to fight a war.

The soldiers began to arrive in larger numbers, one day over one hundred were marched to the docks, and they arrived with a shattering "Halt" by the 'North Star'. The Sergeant Major in charge came on board with a lot of stamping, spluttering and saluting. The men had marched eighteen miles with their gear, they were tired, hungry and thirsty, and there were over a hundred of them. Mr Penaluna decided to act on their behalf to show good will and to get the relationship off to a good start. They were all going to share this ship for seven weeks, so no point in looking for bother – bother would come anyway with so many people in close proximity.

"I'll have my cook and his assistant make tea and soup for the men," he said to the Major. "Steward, ask Mr Eefamy and Radford to come here."

George appeared five minutes later with Radford, both were immaculately turned out in pristine 'whites'. The Major was impressed. Mr Penaluna said "Mr Eefamy, please choose five or six soldiers to help you, light the field kitchens, prepare soup for one hundred and in the meantime ask Mr Radford to make enough tea for all the men - their kettles and teapots – but on our galleys, quick as you can." He then said to the Steward "Take Bo'sun and two men and buy fifty good loaves – these men need feeding." The soldiers heard all this and cheered. The Sergeant Major called them to order and one hundred now smiling soldiers came on board, for most of them it was the first time they had ever been on a ship – today and the next few weeks were going to be a real experience for them all.

George's willingness and adaptability were invaluable in the next two or three days. There were problems everyday: the fires would not light, the army cooks had forgotten to soak the peas overnight, where could they dispose of all the rubbish, the officers were used to nice plates and cutlery could they borrow some until theirs arrived. George was already old headed enough to recruit Mr Strange in all these matters, and he made a list of everything on loan and obtained a signature.

When the main body of men had been on board for two days Mr Penaluna asked to see Major Strudwick and his Captain. "We must get underway as soon as we can," Mr Penaluna said. "Your men are already uneasy and the problems will build – I would like to leave tomorrow."

"All our men are not here yet and they are not expected until next week."

"Please telegraph your camp and have the men put on a train today – I can see this ship being a home for malcontents unless we get underway – I can feel the tension building – the sea air will settle all that – I want to leave Tilbury tomorrow and I am going ashore now to seek the necessary authority to leave tomorrow – there is a tide in the afternoon which will take us out nicely."

Major Strudwick was a peace-time soldier with no active service and no really useful experience to help him cope with emergencies. To him being in the Army had been a wonderful opportunity to meet hearty chaps in the Officer's Mess, play billiards, go riding. True enough there were parades and that sort of thing, but usually one could wriggle out of one parade in every two, on some pretext or other, but this chappie Penaluna was something new in Major Strudwick's experience. He went ashore with his Captain/Adjutant to send the telegram to the Barracks at Bury which read "Entrain balance of men today – sailing tomorrow." It ruffled a few feathers but the men were on a train from Manchester to London within six hours.

"Is everyone on board and settled Major?"

"Yes, they are, the platoon commanders have checked, we are one man missing, and we have to assume that he is a deserter."

"Very well. Do you think all the officers and the Regimental Sergeant Major could meet in my saloon in twenty minutes time? I want to outline the procedure for setting sail."

"Yes – I will arrange that – thank you Mr Penaluna."

The gathering could not fail to be impressed with Mr Penaluna's saloon. The large table was bedecked with a snow white table on which was laid out the most enticing looking buffet imaginable. Also there was a good selection of wines and spirits. George in his 'whites' and Steward wearing his navy blue coat were in attendance. Radford was not acceptable in polite company.

"Now gentlemen this will not take long" began Mr Penaluna. "We are due to be towed down the Thames at four o'clock this afternoon. We do not need the decks whilst we are being towed, so the men can gather on the portside of the ship to wave and shout 'goodbye' to loved ones etc. But once we are past Sheerness, my men must have full access to the decks, and gradually as our sea voyage progresses you will see why – there are about thirty miles of rope on this ship, and with these ropes we control this 1000 ton monster, and with luck, and the skill of my men, we will take you all safely to South Africa. It is not a prison ship and your men must have fresh air and exercise, so we will have to work together to ensure that when it is essential my men must have full access to the decks, and when the decks are free your men can come up from below and enjoy the fresh air. So what I am saying gentlemen is that we must live and work and where possible take pleasure, on a give and take basis and with good will. And to carry on with the theme of goodwill my cook Mr Eefamy and Steward (who apparently had no name) will assist you with these refreshments."

"A moment please – if I may," Major Standwick began. "We are very much aware that we are lucky to be on such a fine ship, and I can assure you Mr Penaluna that I, and my fellow officers will do all we can to pursue the idea of goodwill." This was followed by a chorus of 'Hear, Hear'. Mr Penaluna and the Major shook hands and George's buffet was enthusiastically destroyed in the next fifteen minutes and many of Steward's bottles of best were assiduously emptied.

CHAPTER 3

The Journey to South Africa

The tug came alongside and the hawser was attached. The 'North Star' assumed a slight slope towards land as all the men, sailors and soldiers alike, stood waving. Hundreds of patriotic Londoners waved flags and Mr Penaluna stood on the poop deck in all his finery, smiling to himself – he knew this was no picnic and he had a very prescient notion that the campaign in South Africa would be even worse.

Very slowly and with infinite care, the tug skipper, Humpage, with Mr Penaluna in close attendance, threaded the 'North Star' through dozens of ships and out into the river proper. The noise was deafening, military bands playing stirring tunes, steamers hooted, whistled and generally let off steam. The huge crowd roared and wailed according to their respective disposition, or loss. Two hours later the tug was ready to cast off the hawser, there was a good wind blowing from the east. Mr Penaluna and Mr Baguly looked up to see the masthead teams were in place for the Royals and Top Gallants. Mr Penaluna sent Sweeting to the Major to ask him to get his men below and to say Mr Penaluna would be obliged if he, the Major, would kindly join him on the poop deck.

At the moment the tug dropped the hawser into the sea, the orders were rapped out, and echoed from above. The sails were unfurled, they filled, the power of the wind was harnessed and the hitherto silent rigging growled, groaned and squeaked as it took the strain. The Major noted how Mr Baguly sought Mr Penaluna's permission to move to the next procedure merely by glancing at Mr Penaluna and receiving a nod. The orders ceased, the men descended from their lofty places of employment and alighted on the deck like ballet dancers, exulting in their own fitness and dexterity. The 'North Star' went over at an angle, her lee rails and chains hissing through the water. They were on their way to South Africa.

The fight started because two soldiers could not agree about the amount of space allotted to them. It was a bloody affair, and gradually it became more wide spread. Three or four of their mates tried to separate them, they received blows and gradually more and more became involved. The Sergeant Major could not be heard, so he told the bugler to sound the charge and gradually order was restored. On deck it was a beautiful day, on the starboard side were the gentle fields and slopes of Devon, gulls were wheeling and crying overhead and it was the ideal day to get all the soldiers on deck, do some exercises and let the wrath ebb away. There were a few black eyes and bloodied noses, but no hard feeling and the field kitchens offered tea or coffee. The soldiers mixed with the sailors, some of the former wanted to try their hand at going aloft. Mr Baguly was consulted, he in turn spoke to the Sergeant Major and permission was granted for four of the soldiers to go up the shrouds, closely supervised by a sailor. Mr Penaluna watched and nodded his approval, bonding was taking place and anything which led to a reduction in friction was a good thing. One young soldier made it to the cross trees, looked down and froze. His mates descended successfully, but he was still up there eighty feet above the deck. Mr Baguly moved across to the helm and took over from Humpage. "Go and get him Humpage." Mr Penaluna said "Be gentle with him."

Humpage went up the eighty feet in seconds, put the lad over his shoulder came down slowly, and handed the limp parcel over to his mates, one of whom went in search of a reviving cup of tea. Mr Penaluna and the Major looked on and smiled approval. Things were working out very well.

As they passed the Isles of Scilly the weight of spectators caused the ship to straighten and level out. They were all looking at the wonderful patches of colour, orange, pink, blue, yellow and red. Mr Penaluna explained that one of their main ways to earn a living was to grow flowers, which were cut and bunched every day and sent up to London, Bristol and Southampton by early morning train, to be sold in the florists shops in the large cities.

The passage so far had been ideal, a good breeze from the east had taken the 'North Star' down the English Channel in two days. As they met the Atlantic, Mr Penaluna and his men had to have full use of the decks, conditions were about to alter, the holiday was over and the battle was about to begin. The Bay of Biscay can be warm days, gentle winds and basking whales, but this was not how it was. A North wind disturbed the surface of sea, and brought with it cold temperatures and an irritating unpredictability. Mr Baguly had no sooner trimmed the sails, than Humpage was shouting for the spanker to be brailed in or could the forestay sail be tried. "She will not stay on course, she's moved off two points already," Humpage shouted. Mr Penaluna knew this could happen, every ship reacts slightly differently, and a refined aristocratic lady like the 'North Star' would take a long time to fathom. Mr Baguly looked to Mr Penaluna for guidance. "Try all four of the jib sails – and if it is not quite right, take 'em off one at a time." That was Mr Penaluna's advice. He stood on his poop deck, with the Major by his side, this was now a daily routine. Steward arrived with two mugs of tea, and freshly made scones. George's speciality was cheese scones – Mr Penaluna loved them, and though they were new to Major Strudwick he was beginning to acquire a taste for them.

George's source of information as to how to bake scones was Polly, back at No 18 and just as the north wind decided to try Mr Baguly's patience a delivery van arrived at No 18 with a very large but curiously light weight parcel addressed to 'Clarissa Eefamy." It was brought inside by Rose and Polly and placed on the kitchen table.

"Better not open it," Polly said, despite the fact that her inclinations were diametrically opposed to that opinion. Polly loved parcels.

"No, we won't – Mistress will be home soon – it must be a surprise."

"Shouldn't think so," Polly said. "It'll be something she had ordered – it's come from London."

Polly spent most of the rest of the day, glancing at the parcel, and at last her ordeal was over or nearly so. Ann and Caroline came home with Marie.

"I do hope Mrs Eefamy isn't late," Polly said, hinting that the meal might be delayed but really her impatience was ill concealed and contagious. The girls were just about to take a pair of scissors and begin cutting open the parcel when the lady of the house arrived home.

"Is this for me?" Clarissa said. She looked at the labels. "It is for me – I haven't ordered anything."

"Should I open it Ma'am?" Polly asked desperately.

"Yes do – I'll take my coat and hat off."

The parcel was opened and on top of the contents was an ornate card of heavy calendered paper with artificial roses surrounding the words "From an admirer." Clarissa picked up the card, and passed it to Ann or would have done had Polly's inquisitive hand not intercepted it. "From an admirer – it says Ma'am."

"Yes I know Polly, I read it."

"But who Ma'am, who?"

"I don't know – we will unpack the parcel perhaps the answer lies in there."

The parcel seemed to be almost entirely composed of tissue paper, but cuddled in there, were cups and saucers and gradually they were revealed. Clarissa placed them carefully, piece by piece on the sideboard.

"Oh! They are lovely Mama," Ann cried. "Who are they from?"

"They are from Mr Penaluna – George's Captain. I told you I have visited George on his ship, we had tea out of them, and the dear man has sent them as a present."

"He must have enjoyed meeting you then Ma'am," Rose said.

"Yes I rather think he did," Clarissa said with a far away look in her eyes. "I rather think he did. Well Polly what's for tea – I expect we are all ready for it – what's it to be?"

"Sausages Ma'am, potatoes mashed with parsnips, onion gravy and grilled mushrooms."

"Well that sounds just fine to me and I hope George and Mr Penaluna are having something equally tasty." Cruel fate had decreed that they were not having the same. Fires are damped down when seas are rough and the food becomes plainer and plainer. George had by this time sufficient experience to be one step ahead and he had advised the Army cooks to be prepared.

"Have plenty of fresh bread or cold duff to hand, because when it is really rough pans can go flying all over the place." George had bacon to go between his slices of duff, the Army had to make do with bully beef, but the healthy appetites engendered by sea air are not fussy and the sandwiches went down a treat. Trouble was they came up just as quickly and what ensued was the Army's first lesson seamanship. Some of the soldiers who felt queasy dashed for the nearest side of the ship. If they chose the lee side they were safe but the wind-ward side was more capricious and it blew the vomit back in the face of its originator or it decorated someone standing close by. The seamen ran around with buckets and mops, clearing up the mess which had been accurately forecast by the Bo'sun, and the ship was quickly put to rights, but not so the clothes which had been spattered.

Laundry was a problem. The soldiers in the main were not all that bothered, at home they bathed regularly once a week or once a fortnight and changed all their clothes at a similar interval. But regular changes of clothing and socks were part of Army regulations, and with over 250 people on board a ship this did present problems. Major Strudwick and his Adjutant came to Mr Penaluna's saloon with this problem one morning. Mr Penaluna noticed that they usually turned up for a meeting at coffee time or in the afternoon when scones were likely to be on offer. "Come in gentlemen, do sit down." "Steward we have guests, tea and toast perhaps?" "Now what can I do for you gentlemen?"

"I think we are in a spot of trouble with a build up of soiled clothes – I do apologise for my men being so sick all over the ship, but a lot of it went on their clothes and we are way behind with the laundry work."

"Don't worry about anyone being sick, we are used to that. Nelson was sick every time he went to sea. We are running down towards warmer weather and because we are in the Atlantic it often rains. You see we need fresh water, we are surrounded by the stuff but salt water is no use for washing clothes. So I will get a big sail rigged up to catch the rain and we can run it off into casks and then it becomes available for washing, indeed when it gets really warm, we'll fix it up so the men can actually bathe. Just give me a few more days to make a southing and it will be warm."

"That is very good news isn't it Mr Place?" Major Studwick said, addressing his Adjutant.

"Yes it is Sir – I must say, inspecting the men's quarters has been something of a trial because of the smells."

"Good job we didn't agree to take horses as well," said Mr Penaluna trying to bring a little humour into the discussion.

"They are taking thousands of first class Irish hunters to Africa," the Major said. "Precious few will ever see the green fields of Ireland again I'm afraid."

"Nasty business war, Mr Penaluna said. "Never does anyone any good." Steward was still in attendance and he thought, "No, never does anyone any good – except shipowners."

George spent as much time as he could spare (he was cook to over thirty men and Hazel) with the Army cooks, and they did learn to make duff. Their biggest difficulty was holding pans in place when the sea was choppy. George showed them how his galley stoves were equipped with fiddles to keep his pans in place, he took 'Chips' with him to see if he could devise a method of keeping the Army pans steady on their field kitchens. 'Chips' made carefully measured frames of hardwood which worked very well. The Army cooks were grateful and this led to more rapport aboard the ship. They swopped recipes too and this led to corned beef hash becoming part of George's repertoire.

The ship continued its southing leaving Spain behind and heading for really warm weather. As promised Mr Penaluna rigged up main sails to catch the rain and clothes washing became a daily job. Clothes drying took no more than an hour or two, so another problem was solved.

Hazel carried on her work in being general charlady to Mr Penaluna and the crew. She did all the cleaning and laundering and had volunteered to look after the officers and the Regimental Sergeant Major, performing similar duties. She had asked Mr Penaluna's advice about this and he told Hazel to ask for two shillings per week per person for this favour. It had not occurred to Hazel to try to make money out of it, but so far as turning an honest shilling was concerned, everyone could learn from Mr Penaluna. She also helped sometimes in the galley though she took up as much room in that crowded space as both George and Radford put together. So she was very visible on the ship – the only woman amongst 250 men. She spent a lot of her waking hours bent over dolly tubs or reaching up to peg out clothes and such female attributes as she had, and goodness knows they were illusive if not actually chimeric, were shown off. As Mr Baguly had predicted all, women, no matter how lacking in feminine beauty, do gradually become more attractive after the absence of any comparisons, and quite a few of the soldiers had begun to cast admiring glances her way. It was known that she was the 'friend' of the tiny, spindly weakling, Radford, so no opposition there. The men had not much else to think about all day, and four of them hatched a plot to catch Hazel whilst she was attending to one of the cabins and take her – they assumed for some reason that she would be grateful. So they waited for their opportunity and one specially sunny day when everyone was on deck except Hazel, who was tidying one of the officer's cabins, the four conspirators went to look for their prey. They went into the tiny cabin and confronted Hazel.

"What are you lot after?" she said. One of the men put the catch on the door and they all began to drop their trousers.

"You wouldn't want me – I've got the pox," lied Hazel.

"So have we, so it makes no odds," a great beefy lance corporal said.

"I reckon I can take you lot on anyway" Hazel said – she started to fight and scream. The four men clawed at her, but what they had not reckoned on was the galley was very close to the cabins. George was aft taking coffee to Mr Penaluna. Radford was in the galley alone. He hard the screams, picked up a twelve-inch carving knife and went to the rescue. The fight was going the men's way until Hazel battled towards the door and released the catch. Radford came in like D'Artagnon, he stabbed one of the men and slashed another, a third made a grab at him and lost half his hand. Hazel had the fourth in a grip which left him exactly where his ambitions had led him, with his face between her magnificent breasts – the trouble was that she was suffocating him and she knew it. She felt him go limp and she dropped him on the floor and walked on him to get to the other, but the fight was over and Mr Baguly was at the door, looking fierce and powerful. This cabin door had a bolt on the outside, he shut it firmly and took Radford and Hazel on deck to find Mr Penaluna. They were both shaken and terribly frightened but they were unharmed. Mr Baguly took the knife from Radford and related what he had seen to Mr Penaluna. Major Strudwick was near enough to hear, and he sent his Sergeant Major to examine the cabin and to report back to him. He tried to put into words his apologies, but Mr Penaluna stopped him. "Let us find out exactly what has happened, then we will know how to put it right - go to the galley you two, tell Steward to use some of my brandy and make yourselves a good reviving mug of coffee."

The Sergeant Major opened the cabin door, it was like a slaughter house; the man who had lost half his hand held up the bleeding stump, one man was lying on the floor, blood oozing from a huge wound in his shoulder, another had a cut downwards across his forehead and right across his face so the flesh hung from his face like a flap, the fourth who had suffered from Hazel's vice like grip, was still on the floor coughing and spluttering.

"You lot – you've disgraced us all – don't wag your bleeding hand at me – looking for sympathy, you got what you deserved, and there's more to come, the Army 'as ways of dealing with scum like you."

"We'll need help – get the doctor Sarge."

"I have to report back to Major Strudwick first, and I shall take my time doing it – with luck two or three of you bastards will have bled to death by the time I arrange for the doctor to come – if I even bother to tell 'im."

The Sergeant Major locked the four men in the cabin, and went to report the shabby business to his Major. Grudgingly and after a delay he did admit the doctor was needed. But for two of the men he wasn't. The other two, the one whose hand was halved and the one on the floor, he helped, but they spent the rest of the trip on bread and water chained in the fo'c'sle.

Mr Penaluna called Major Strudwick into his cabin where drinks were laid out – this was for him a very awkward situation – he had been hired, and was being very well paid, to transport the British Army to South Africa, not to slaughter it. Major Strudwick began by saying it was all the fault of his men. "Four men without trousers, fighting with a woman in a cabin, the evidence is overwhelming and I do not blame your man Radford at all. Any man would have done the same thing – probably not as well as he did it." The Major took a sip of his drink – it was Mr Penaluna's best claret, Mr Penaluna thanked the Major for his generous acceptance of the circumstances. "How are you going to square this with your Headquarters?" Mr Penaluna asked.

"Captain Place is my Paymaster as well as my Adjutant and he advises that when we arrive in South Africa we must account for them saying 'lost at sea'."

"If the confusion in Cape Town is anything like it was at Tilbury, I don't suppose anyone will bother about two men," Mr Penaluna postulated.

"You are probably right – I do know at least sixty ships left for South Africa the same weeks as ours, so yes, confusion will, I think, help to conceal this unfortunate incident."

"And the two men in irons. What is to happen to them?" Mr Penaluna asked.

"They will be put on a ship which is returning to England, and kept in confinement until I know exactly when the ship is leaving."

"So you do not intend to proceed against Radford for excessive use of force?"

"No I do not – my private opinion is that he acted honourably and was within his rights."

"Another glass of this claret – perhaps? I bought it in La Rochelle last year, I've never tasted its equal."

"Yes please – we never had anything to touch it in the Officer's Mess, sherry or port could be had, but nothing like this."

Mr Penaluna leaned over towards the Major and filled his glass. The day had ended quite well after all.

The 'North Star' was now off the north coast of Africa, it was becoming warmer every day. Some of the men asked if they could sleep on deck – Mr Penaluna had no objections to this provided that they removed their bed and bedding by 6 am. He added a warning that sleeping on deck was lovely on fine warm nights, but to cover up one's face was essential when it was a full moon, as the light from the full moon in tropical latitudes did have decidedly dangerous results to health. He would not elaborate but the emphasis he placed upon this point became firmly fixed in the soldiers' mind. There was no need to mention the dire consequences to the sailors –

they already knew. At 6 am he expected to be able to unreef extra sails and try to 'crack on' and his men needed unimpeded access to the ropes, shrouds and rigging. On two occasions two hundred men awoke soaking wet, but no one bothered because two hours after sun up they were all dry again.

George was now fully skilled as a ship's cook, and he knew exactly how much time he had to spare, and it was not much. But very early in the morning there was usually half an hour he could call his own. The days when he was part of the crew were not so far in the past and he still knew how to climb the rigging right to the top of the main mast, 150 feet above the deck. He used to take his breakfast up there with him. It was two thin slices of duff and about five slices of crispy bacon made into a sandwich. He was working on the idea of taking a mug of tea up there with him (he still had his father's cup which he had taken from No 18, the day he walked to Southampton). He would stand right at the truck with him arm round the mast and look around. From that height the horizon is stretched to about twenty-five miles, so he was master of about five hundred square miles of ocean. The end of the night was mysterious, the stars began to shyly hide their beauty as the confident sun gained strength. The sea acquired a deep purple hue, and occasionally phosphorescent lights would appear spasmodically and to no known pattern. Soft colours appeared in the sky; peach, yellow and the palest pink, and small breakers on the sea's surface added a touch of white and cream to nature's already generous palette.

Suddenly a blaze of light, as the tiny orange parabola peeped over the horizon. The light had travelled ninety million miles but such is its impatience with darkness that in less than a second the gloom was vanquished, the colours intensified and the darkness is sent scurrying westwards defeated once again. The sea nearest to the sunrise took on the colour of deep red pansies, just for a few seconds – this was a moment George did not want to miss. Once he had seen the colours (they were different every morning) he reached in his pocket: his eyes had feasted, now his mouth began its treat.

He took a huge bite and immediately wanted to shout. He delayed for a second to adjust the food. "Sail oh" he managed chokingly. "Where away?" came the answer from below. "On the lee bow." It was a four masted ship with topsails and t'gallants, she was just above the horizon. The sun was behind her and she presented a black silhouette. She was coming towards them. As she came nearer it could be seen that she was a full rigged ship, with a dark green hull and white spars. Mr Penaluna saw her at great distance and said confidently "She is 'The Patriarch'." It was a lovely morning and 'The Patriarch' was going to enjoy the luxury of an audience of over 250 as she sailed by. Her tapering towers of sails were immaculate, the yards were precisely trimmed and parallel, every sheet was home, every sail flat, taut, not a wrinkle to be seen and as she cut through the sea she cast a snow white wave either side of her bow.

Mr Penaluna shouted "Bring out the flags," and he started to thumb through the Signal Book. Mr Penaluna signalled 'London'. The answer came back 'New Zealand'. Up went flags to say '23', meaning, days out of London. Their answer came '70'. The two ships were now passing each other – their crew of 40 raised their hats and cheered and received a vociferous response from 290 English throats. Next Mr Penaluna asked for T.D.L. "I wish you a pleasant passage" and the answer came X.O.R. "Thank you". Then they dipped their ensign three times for "Farewell."

"Well done lads," Mr Penaluna said to his apprentices – they had expertly and quickly used the correct flags. It had been a busy five minutes, and one that they would never forget. The seamen immediately began to discuss the way the ship was rigged and how she had been handled. What George had seen that morning, the wonderful multi-coloured sunrise, followed by the stately beauty of 'The Patriarch' made a tremendous and lasting impression. He was a sensitive boy, aware and appreciative of beauty, but he could not discuss beauty with his shipmates, the word was only used to describe a woman, a meal, tobacco or beer.

The southing continued, usually at the rate of one hundred or one hundred and thirty miles per twenty-four hours. They reached the Equator on a day when there was very little wind and the 'North Star' was really doing nothing more than drifting with any current there happened to be. The soldiers were not aware of the importance of crossing the line and knew little if anything behind the reasoning, when the spare main sail was rigged up as a bathing pool and the pumps were manned to fill it up with sea water. At midday Buckley a seamen of vast experience and even bigger girth, suddenly appeared from over the side with his 'wife'. The latter was a one eyed bald headed toothless assistant to 'Chips' named Wolfe – he wore a wig, extravagant make-up, a gaudy red dress and two very large grapefruits were tucked into his bodice in more or less the right place to affirm his femininity. Buckley was wielding a ten foot trident, he announced in a broad west-country accent that he was Neptune and this 'ere was his beautiful wife. He continued "Do you lot know of any varmints and criminals what is trying to invade my territory,'cos if there is any, I likes to be sure they are clean." Three seamen who had been South before dragged out Oliver, Matthew and George and offered them up as sacrifices. One by one they were held in a chair and lavishly soaped and lathered, any attempt to speak was thwarted by a mouthful of soap-suds. "What is the best way to make sure my territory is kept clean?" Neptune asked. "Drown him" came the chorus from 200 throats. One by one the three lads were lathered and hurled into the sail, which was now three feet deep in sea-water. Willing hands dragged the villains and varmints out of the water. No harm done, they would be dry in an hour and now they were initiated. Neptune turned his attention to the army. Mr Penaluna had warned the Major, so he was wearing his oldest uniform as was Captain Place. It is to their credit that they both joined in and it greatly added to the merriment, as their own men flung them into the water. Then Neptune decided that ALL the soldiers were filthy, flea ridden and lousy (not that far from the truth) and they all got dumped in eight or ten at a time.

Mr Penaluna decided to continue the celebrations by giving a 'main brace' to everyone on board and then to everyone's surprise stepped up on a bench and started up a sing song. Some of the sailors and quite a few of the soldiers had a tolerable mastery of a musical instrument and so there was this most unusual set of circumstances: over 200 men, on their way to fight a war, adrift in the South Atlantic on an outmoded clipper, all singing their hearts out with no audience within a hundred miles of them. The sun was directly above, it was roasting hot, but the concert lasted for about half an hour, by which time they had run out of energy and repertoire. The great sail was emptied and Mr Penaluna had 'Chips' go over side to attach strong twine to the plugs. He then told Bo'sun to put the chickens out of the boats and have them lowered into the sea. Mr Penaluna was going to try to get them out of the doldrums. The plugs were knocked out and carefully put away so that 'Chips' knew exactly which plug belonged to which hole. The sweeps were put in place, Sweeting went forrard in charge of the two boats. Mr Penaluna asked the Major if his men could help: it needed five men per sweep, so there was one sailor and four soldiers to each oar. Thirty men on each side operating six sweeps and eight men in each long boat. Could a total of seventy-six men pull the 'North Star'? Mr Penaluna was sure they could – it was all a matter of timing.

Firstly Mr Penaluna signalled to Sweeting to make sure the ropes were tight. Then he signalled to the 'Captains' of each team on the sweeps to begin. At first the rowing was ragged and lacked any synchronisation, but gradually it all improved and a great shout went up and she actually moved. "Reef up all the sails please Mr Baguly," Mr Penaluna said. "But keep the teams up there and if we catch wind they can drop the Royals and the Top gallants."

Mr Penaluna decided twenty minutes for each team was enough and there was no shortage of volunteers. The Major, the Captain and the Regimental Sergeant Major came forward, as did Mr Penaluna, Mr Baguly, even George and Oliver took their turns. Once the ship was underway it was not difficult to keep her moving, but the amount of sheer strength required to change the 'North Star' from stillness to motion was terrific, the total weight of ship plus cargo was about 1500 tons, but they did manage it and with Mr Penaluna's organising skill they kept her going, not by changing the teams all at once but by changing just one sweep at a time. True the ship veered slightly in the change over, but they were in search of a breeze not navigational accuracy. The cutter and the jolly boat offered a different kind of problem, but Mr Penaluna solved this by putting two teams in each boat, so that as one team was resting the other was pulling, but it was hard for them: they were exposed to the full rays of the sun. Sailors only were employed in the boats and they were semi–pachyderms thanks to their years at sea.

Sometimes a shy deceiving breeze would cause the reefed up sails to idly flap but no real wind came along and they did not find one, so after two hours Mr Penaluna decided that was enough for one day, and he called the two boats back and told 'Chips' to knock in all the plugs, stow the sweeps on deck and they would try again tomorrow.

"I had heard about the doldrums," Major Strudwick said. "But I had no idea they could keep us fastened up for a full day."

"I have known it to last ten or even twelve days," Mr Penaluna said. "In some areas these are known as the horse latitudes, because horses take a lot of water daily and if the stay in the doldrums was too long they would have to kill any horses on board and throw the carcases overboard."

"You paint a gloomy picture Mr Penaluna," Major Strudwick said.

"I'm sorry, I didn't mean to, I am sure if we try again tomorrow, perhaps very early in the morning and again in the evening, we should be more lucky. But we will avoid the mid-day period, it is too hard on the men."

And so the urgent call to arms, to save the Empire and to put the enemy to flight received a setback. The sea all around the ship was flat and still. They were surrounded by the garbage they had thrown overboard. Only George was enjoying this experience: it was new to him and since he enjoyed EVERYTHING about the sea, this was yet another thing to be relished. He had the next meal under control – it was salt pork, suitably steeped for twenty-four hours to soak out the worst of salt, peas – dried ones of course but again steeped and allowed to rise to more or less their original shape and colour and for the last hour he would add potatoes to the stew. Mr Penaluna's more refined palette would be caressed with a four egg omelette filled with crispy bacon. George himself was having his evening meal as he learned against the taff rail, looking behind him where the wake should have been, with a huge bacon sandwich in one hand and his father's rose covered mug in the other. Soldiers were clustered there also, George was well respected by all on board as a hard working member of the crew. He did receive a bit of ribbing about the size of the sandwich but he was allowed to enjoy it without any undue interference.

The smells of the evening meals hung about the ship: George's pork mixed with the five field kitchens. They were all doing corned-beef hash, the men's top favourite, the smell of coffee also played its part and with no breeze at all to move them on, the appetizing odours became stronger every minute. The soldiers had rigged up makeshift tables and ate on deck. Mr Penaluna did not like all the untidiness which resulted, but eating below was difficult, so he just had a word with Bo'sun about holy stoning his precious teak decks to preserve their beauty. This was not a time for niggling about small matters, the doldrums with temperatures of 120∫F are not the place for arguments, more a time for 'laissez faire' and that is exactly the attitude Mr Penaluna took.

Next morning as the sun rose in the East, Mr Penaluna's first team on the sweeps was ready, the cutter and the jolly boat were out at the front and just as the sun rose to mock their puny efforts the seventy plus men began to heave and strain. She moved, and gradually they left yesterday's detritus behind, no wake formed, no waves curled away from the bows, but she moved. A great cheer went up, this heartened the men and they pulled mightily. The wind remained shy, the sails and ropes hung loose. Two hours later with the sun well up in the merciless clear blue sky Mr Penaluna cried "Halt." It was enough, they had travelled perhaps two miles, but they had not found wind, what they had found was unison: they were now skilled in the matter of sweeps and the more optimistic of the becalmed were sure that tonight would do it.

During the day Mr Penaluna had 'Sails' and Bo'sun rig up shelters using the spare sails so the crew and the soldiers could find some respite from the sun. Some squabbles arose because of gambling but it was not a situation which was beyond the combined powers of Mr Baguly and the Sergeant Major and good behaviour was soon restored. They became eager to try the sweeps again, the novelty of lounging about in the warmth had worn thin. Half an hour before Mr Penaluna would have advised it, the wishes of the rowers prevailed and the two boats each with two teams were sent ahead. The sweeps were ready and the men were eager, they soon had the 'North Star' going forward. Mr Penaluna asked Mr Baguly to ensure that the men were aloft, ready to drop the sails should a breeze come. They were moving but it profited them little, and the changeover took place and a fresh team put their backs into it.

"Sail away." came the call form the main mast.

Port bow – three points."

"They must have found some wind," Mr Penaluna said. "Humpage," Mr Penaluna continued loudly, "Humpage – head for that sail."

Mr Baguly went down to the men on the sweeps, "There is a sail about ten miles off – it must have found a breeze." A cheer went up and the sweeps were handled with renewed vigour.

George was in his cabin, writing home. He heard the rumpus about the sail and decided to finish his letter off. If the approaching ship was bound for England his letter could be on its way in a few hours. Mr Baguly passed the word to Captain Place that if this was an English ship, arrangements could easily be made to pass a parcel of letters across. 'Sails' grumbling all the time, hurriedly prepared a canvas bag and eighty letters were tucked into it ready for transferring across. As the ship came nearer – still under sail, a wind or at any rate a gentle zephyr wafted across the 'North Star'. The men roared their approval. It was indeed an English ship bound for London. Mr Penaluna ordered the sweeps to be brought back to the deck, and the 'North Star' wallowed for half and hour until the 'Newcastle' approached with very little way. Mr Penaluna told Mr Baguly to get all the sweeps to one side to hold off the 'Newcastle', just in case they drifted together. Then he called to the skipper – "Where are you bound for?"

"London – out of Shanghai." came the reply.

"The South Africa War has started we are taking troops to Cape Town," Mr Penaluna shouted. "Where did you find the wind?"

"Just south of here – good easterlies, should give you four or five knots." "Have you any mail for us to take back?"

"Yes – coming over." Mr Penaluna nodded to Matthew who threw the canvas bag forty or fifty feet, it landed safely and was held aloft by the skipper. "We'll look after them."

"Many thanks – safe voyage." Mr Penaluna shouted.

"Yes safe voyage to you."

The soldiers and the crew crowded to the port side shouting and waving. The mast hands of the 'Newcastle' at a signal, dropped their sails. Commands were given and she crawled away.

"Main courses please Mr Baguly." Mr Penaluna said.

Mr Penaluna walked solemnly back to the poop deck – his hands clasped behind him. Mr Baguly was amongst the crew, giving orders. The 'North Star' was about to become a sailing ship again – the God given invisible fuel had arrived. The sails filled out. Mr Penaluna looked round to see Humpage at the wheel, with a smile on his face a yard wide. The Major joined Mr Penaluna. They stood together silently – both glad that the doldrums were past but apprehensive about what lay ahead.

CHAPTER 4

Confusion Again

Six days later they arrived at Cape Town. The confusion at Tilbury had transferred to this new location; Cape Town was a forest of masts and funnels. Beyond the masts and the town was Table Mountain – 3000 feet high and perfectly flat and over ten miles in length, a hugely impressive sight. The smaller Lion Mountain lay between it and Cape Town – the two hundred soldiers and the 'North Star's' crew gathered on deck and were filled with anticipation by their first sight of Africa. Mr Penaluna was not at all impressed, his first priority was to allow the military personnel to disembark, so he could look around for a return cargo and be back in London as soon as possible. Mr Penaluna hailed a passing steam tug. "What chance of getting in? he shouted.

"How long have your got? came the reply, then the tug skipper added "Some of 'em have been here two weeks."

"Come on board and have a drink with us," Mr Penaluna suggested. Never one to refuse such a generous offer the tug skipper drew near and Bo'sun and a couple of seamen made the tug fast.

"Come into my cabin – have you eaten?" Mr Penaluna said.

"I could use a bit of something," came the not entirely unexpected reply.

"Steward" Mr Penaluna called. "Ask Mr Baguly to step this way please and tell young George there are three of us for breakfast." "Perhaps a whiskey first Skipper?" the courteous Mr Penaluna said.

"Well yes that sounds about right," the tug skipper was beginning to enjoy his morning.

Mr Penaluna, Mr Baguly and the tug skipper got round the table and started to look at detailed maps of the immediate area.

"This part is full up" the tug skipper said pointing to the Alfred and the Victoria basins, "in fact so much stuff has arrived that the railway can't cope with it," he continued.

"So the warehouses are all full?" queried Mr Penaluna.

"That is right. Some of the equipment has been left out in the rain and been spoiled, food is going off, horses are starving, and the men are living in tents pitched on railway sidings."

"It was just the same in London," Mr Baguly said. "How can they win a war if they can't organise a proper transport system?"

"Ah! Here's my cook – what have your there for us Mr Eefamy?"

"I thought fried eggs on toast Sir – is that alright?"

Mr Penaluna looked to his guest and Mr Baguly for approval. Smiles were the only answer George needed.

"Yes that would be most welcome, and tell Steward to hurry along some coffee."

Steward hated to be told what to do by anybody and certainly not by George. George knew that, and so he suggested that Steward might like to take some coffee to Mr Penaluna's saloon.

Once breakfast was over Mr Penaluna rang and asked Steward to remove the plates – they needed the table to study maps. The tug skipper went back to his boat and brought more, and together they studied the various possibilities. Mr Penaluna decided that the tug skipper's idea of going round to Simon's Town might be the best solution. It was about sixty miles and because the winds were still very light he would have to be towed, but even that would be cheaper than just waiting his term at Cape Town. Mr Penaluna paid the tug skipper five sovereigns for his time and trouble, and asked him for a lift right into the docks so he could enquire what the authorities had in mind. An hour later Mr Penaluna was ashore and asking for directions to the Harbour Master's offices. There he was told that the Military were running everything, and so he would need to see them – they had offices in Darling Street and in the Castle.

Mr Penaluna left the Harbour Master and walked along the Esplanade. The 'waiting time' arranged by Mr Forthergill at the initial meeting in London some weeks ago applied to this end of the journey also. Mr Penaluna jingled his money in his pocket as he walked along, he could see the 'North Star anchored three miles out and he comforted himself with the thought that he was earning money even though the 'North Star' was not moving and he was walking along with the warm sun on his back. He made enquiries at the Castle. When asked what his cargo was he replied "Men – over 200 of them." A very flustered young officer who was obviously out of his depth asked Mr Penaluna if he had any solution.

"I have been here for only one day, so I can't be expected to understand the situation, but my tug skipper reckons Simon's Town would be a good place to disembark the men – what do you think?"

The young officer saw the chance of moving one ship out of his area and took it – "Yes I agree – there are good rail links there."

"Fine, I'll take my ship there, but I want a signed note from you on official paper, and the extra time going there will have to be classed as waiting time." Mr Penaluna said. The young man did not really understand the significance of 'waiting time', nor did he care. He passed a blank sheet of headed notepaper to Mr Penaluna and said "Put on there what you think you will need by way of authorisation and I will sign it." He then turned to another sea captain, one of many waiting in line, to see what he wanted. Mr Penaluna wrote out his document in his finest copperplate and the officer signed it unread. There was an official stamp on the desk, so Mr Penaluna helped himself and banged the stamp right next to the signature. He then appropriated a suitably sized envelope, tucked the letter inside and carefully stowed it away in his inside pocket.

He then made his way to the docks, found a bum-boat and asked to be rowed out to his ship. He brought Mr Baguly up to date with what he was trying to arrange and asked Mr Baguly to be prepared to make a signal with flags – this would be to indicate to the tug boat owner that they were ready for a tow to Simon's Town. He then climbed down into the bum-boat – the owner knew the tug boat owner in question and Mr Penaluna was able to leave a message regarding the tow to Simon's Town.

He felt he had done a good morning's work and went off in search of a suitably good lunch. He found a likely looking hotel and wandered into the dining room. It was an expensive place and as such places do, it kept out the riff-raff. High ranking officers, civil servants and a few sea captains were the only clients. Mr Penaluna felt quite at home in such company and he joined a table which had just one chair vacant. He was made welcome and soon fell into conversation or at any rate started to listen and learn. A fellow skipper asked about Mr Penaluna's ship.

"She's a brigantine about 900 tons, fast, seaworthy and I would describe her as clever," Mr Penaluna said.

You sailing ship chaps do have some quaint expressions for your ships I must say – clever – how can a ship be clever?"

Mr Penaluna replied to everyone's amusement "Well she was clever enough to choose me as her owner." "Have a drink with me," the friendly skipper said. Mr Penaluna was in good company. His ears were pricked for information, and there was a lot to be had. He learned that some of the Boers who had been captured and might prove troublesome if they remained in captivity, were going to be transported to Tristan-de Cunha or St Helena, no one was quite sure which. This was just the sort of job Mr Penaluna was looking for. Also it was strongly rumoured that a large number of volunteers in Canada, Australia, and New Zealand were awaiting passage to South Africa. Mr Penaluna was delighted, there was business to be done, but he was always a man to savour the moment and he signalled to a waiter that all their glasses were empty and could something be done about that.

The vital piece of information which Mr Penaluna was able to take away from his carousal was the name of the Colonel who was allocating the jobs. He was situated in an office on Darling Street. He made enquiries from soldiers who were to be seen everywhere and he was soon in an anti-room waiting to see Colonel Waterson. He was a very harassed man and had not much time to spare. Mr Penaluna was aware of this and was determined to use this to his own advantage.

"I have brought men here, I am at Simons Town, the soldiers are disembarking and if you have people in New Zealand waiting to come here, I can be away within a week. It will ease the confusion in the docks area and I'll be back within a few weeks with more men."

Colonel Waterson eyed his man up, he liked the look of Mr Penaluna and reckoned he was a good judge of character, he turned to the young officer who was acting as his assistant, "Provide Mr Penaluna with the authorisation for a trip to New Zealand to bring 300 men back by the quickest means possible."

"I brought out 200 on this trip – I think I could manage 250 but 300 would be uncomfortable, I think."

"What do you think it's like here?" "Do you call this comfort?" the Colonel said irascibly.

"Very good Sir – 300 it is," Mr Penaluna answered humbly, whilst thinking to himself that New Zealand was a long way away and from what he already knew of colonial people they were pretty easy going, so he would sort out the numbers at the other end. He looked at his papers, hurriedly prepared by the young officer, thanked them and tucked his precious documents into his inside pocket. His next job was to find a cargo needing to go to New Zealand, he did not want to be in ballast – no money to be made by going down that road. His agents in England had provided him with one or two names, but he was in no hurry, his day had gone well, so he walked along the Esplanade Drive, and from there he could look along towards the two basins where scores of ships were waiting. He went over in his mind what all this was costing in terms of money and what it would cost in lives once the war really started. Some of the arguments were about the vote; who could and who could not vote. How long a person had to be in South Africa before he was entitled to vote, but some argued it was about land. Why fall out about land, Mr Penaluna thought. God knows there is enough of it here, what most people regarded as South Africa offered one and a half million square miles of land. No, Mr Penaluna was old enough and he had travelled the world – he knew what the war was about, it was all about money. South Africa was rich in gold, diamonds and labour. If you were not English and many of the people living in that area were Dutch or German, you used slaves. England had abolished slavery sixty years before, but the Dutch and Germans ran their farms and mines with slave labour, and they had no intentions of giving that up. To those who used black slaves they were a lower species, not worthy of consideration as human beings, and the wealth, comfort and life style of many people in South Africa depended upon free labour – they were not going to give it up to suit the English. And the English – they were out there with their enormous army to protect the gold and diamond mines and to ensure that the pink portions of the world's maps remained pink. They had put down the Indian Mutiny and they intended to do the same in South Africa. Their representative, appointed by Mr Chamberlain was Milner, an inflexible person who was determined to establish the rule of law as he saw it. Mr Penaluna had picked up all these shreds of information and he mulled them over as he strolled along looking for one of the addresses given to him by Fothergill and Jones. He was not the sort of person who wanted to become deeply involved in politics, he knew that world events were too big for him to reshape, he just wanted to sail his ship, make a living and live his own life. His philosophy was that he did the best he could to help anyone and he tried to conduct his affairs honestly, but the real world was a hard place and so he just wanted to get on with his own affairs. South Africa offered opportunities and as he approached his destination he had philosophised enough for one day. Now he wanted to secure some business. He was made welcome in the offices of Holt and Wellard, coffee was brought in and everything was very business like.

"I am under orders to go to New Zealand soon," Mr Penaluna began. "But I do not want to go in ballast – so I am looking for a cargo of about 800 tons, what is there?" "Have your any suggestions?"

Mr Wellard said "We have instruction for a very large consignment of leather to Australia, of course we know that is 2000 miles short of New Zealand but the price is good, it is a valuable cargo."

"What is a good price?" Mr Penaluna asked. "I like to talk in terms of £4 for fifty cubic feet – but what does fifty cubic feet of leather weigh?"

"Well fifty cubic feet of leather would be about five and a half tons."

"And you have eight hundred tons to move?"

"That is right, at fifteen shillings per ton."

"I would want £1,000 for that job. Because I know leather can smell, and I have to bring a human cargo back. So once I'm in New Zealand it will take me at least a week to make my ship habitable again."

Mr Wellard said "The price of leather on the open market will not stand £1 per ton. It can't be done."

"The trip is over 8000 miles – that will take eight or nine weeks. I have a crew of over thirty to pay. You reckon that up. Thirty men's wages for eight weeks comes to over £200 for a start and I have to feed 'em as well."

Mr Penaluna made what he thought was a good case but it profited him nothing.

"That is the offer – the harbour is full of ships and we shall have to move the leather for you if you are in Simons Bay."

"Right I'll take it – fifteen shillings a ton. Have the papers prepared and I'll send my clerk to collect them, in two or three days time."

"What is the name of your ship – we need it for the Bills of Lading?"

"Yes of course – I am Captain Penaluna and my ship is the 'North Star'."

"Good day Captain Penaluna."

"Good day gentlemen."

Mr Penaluna then walked back to the hotel where he had dined and booked himself in for the night. He rose next morning, treated himself to a breakfast of steak and eggs, then made his way to the goods yard belonging to the railway. It was about twenty five miles back to Simons Town and he reckoned he would like to go by train, either as a passenger or if they didn't run passenger trains, he thought he would ask for a lift on a goods train. The latter method was the only solution as it turned out. He combated the initial refusal by the driver with two English half-crowns, and climbed onto an open truck from there he enjoyed the fresh air and the lovely views over False Bay. He arrived in Simons Town and quickly found the 'North Star' looking quite splendid. Mr Baguly and Bo'sun had mustered all hands and everywhere shone. "Well done Mr Baguly," Mr Penaluna said, "She looks beautiful." The crew were all on deck enjoying the sunshine, and the soldiers had gone.

"Not all the credit is due to me Sir," Mr Baguly said generously. "The lads all worked hard." Mr Penaluna nodded and smiled his appreciation but sensed that there was a revelation about to be made. "Well it's like this Skipper," Mr Baguly began falteringly. "Do you see them three ships about half a mile away?" Mr Baguly pointed to three huge hulls anchored in the bay. "Well they are prison ships – not for criminals but for prisoners of war."

"Yes I see them – carry on," Mr Penaluna said.

"Well it's like this you see Skipper," Mr Baguly began to move his weight from one leg to another. "Two of 'em escaped and climbed on board at night, we have 'em safe, but I didn't know what to do about it – they are so young, but really they are escaped prisoners." That was a very long speech for Mr Baguly and he was quite exhausted.

"Well first of all I'm hungry," Mr Penaluna said. "And I don't think very well when I'm hungry – so what do you suggest Mr Eefamy?"

"I think we should keep them and look after them like you did me Sir."

"When I said what do you suggest I meant what are you going to cook for me." Everyone began to laugh at George's discomfiture.

"Sorry Sir I thought-"

"Yes I know what you thought and you are probably right, but just now I want food – so what do you suggest?"

"Bacon and eggs with fried bread and a large jug of coffee Sir."

"Right – three eggs and no more, and extra coffee for Mr Baguly and perhaps a sandwich, we have to decide a few things. Where are the two run-aways?"

"Locked in Bo'sun's cabin Sir," Mr Baguly said.

"Are they fed and clothed?"

"Yes Sir."

"Good. Stay here Mr Baguly and then we'll see what's what."

Mr Penaluna's cabin was soon visited by Steward who had Mr Penaluna's meal under a snow-white cloth. The coffee smelt wonderful but as with all coffee, even the best, it never quite lives up to the expectation which its aroma has aroused. Bacon does however, and Mr Penaluna paid it full attention. Mr Baguly's sandwich was his favourite, corned beef with thick slices of raw onion. As soon as their appetites were partially satisfied, Mr Penaluna began "Just how young are these two people?"

"I would say seventeen and fifteen," Mr Baguly said.

"And they were prisoners?"

"That's right – they were part of a Boer warring party, captured after a battle. They seem to be a rough, hardy pair – well, they swam the half mile from the prison ship, but I didn't want to turn them away and I didn't want to report them."

"Well we are not part of the war – I don't agree with wars – ring for Steward and tell him to bring them in here. Oh! and tell Steward to bring more coffee and two more mugs."

Mr Baguly conveyed these messages. Steward grumbled, "Why should I be expected to wait on escaped prisoners – I'd throw them back in and let 'em swim for it."

"You missed your way Steward," Mr Penaluna said. "With such generosity of spirit you should have entered the medical profession."

Steward just grunted and five minutes later returned with the coffee and the two young people.

"Come in and sit down – would you like coffee?" The two escapees were very fit, healthy out door types, they looked uneasy and were no doubt wondering what was to become of them. Mr Penaluna continued "Do you know where your parents are?"

"They are both dead – killed by some black men who came to our home late one night – that's why we joined the Boer army, our house was burned down."

Mr Penaluna looked at Mr Baguly, who was visibly moved

"We think we are going to Australia and New Zealand in a week or ten days time – if you would like it, you can be part of the crew – you'd be safe – or as safe as anybody is out at sea, and of course, well fed."

The two looked at each other, and then at their two hosts: the avuncular Mr Baguly and the friendly Mr Penaluna. They both nodded and said "Yes, we'll be part of your crew, but we know nothing about ships."

"Don't worry Mr Baguly and Bo'sun are good teachers, we are a bit short handed and we will find the right kind of work for you. You are now part of the crew."

"Mr Baguly, ask Mr Strange to enter them into the books as apprentices at £1 per month starting pay today." He nodded to the pair of newcomers and said "You may go."

Once they had gone he indicated to Mr Baguly that he might leave also, just before he left he said to Mr Baguly, "By the way Mr Baguly you have a new problem."

"Oh" what's that Sir?"

"The younger of the two is a girl."

"Never" Mr Baguly said. "Are you sure Sir?"

"Never more so – tell Hazel to look after her, and tell her brother to come back in here."

The young man went back into Mr Penaluna's saloon. "I think you know what I am going to say – you are responsible for your sister – this is almost an all man crew, and you know what that means. Mr Baguly will do his best to maintain discipline but really it is up to you – she is very young and you must be her father now as well as her brother."

"Thank you Sir – you are a good man."

"Not all Englishmen are as bad as you think we are – I think we will get on fine. Do your work, learn about how a ship is run and you'll be far better off than fighting a war – nobody ever wins a war – often people lose wars but there are never any winners."

"Thank you Sir and thanks again for taking us in – it was terrible in that ship – it stank and I was terrified what would have happened if they had found out that there was a girl on board."

"Well you are safe now – what's your name?"

"Pieters Sir – Jan Pieters and my sister is Tiana."

"Very good – I'll remember. You may go now." Mr Penaluna then mumbled to himself "More problems."

Two days later Mr Penaluna despatched the far from enthusiastic Mr Strange to Cape Town, to sort out the paperwork for the leather they were going to ship to Adelaide. Mr Penaluna told Mr Strange what the deal was, and also told him to ensure that the documents clearly stated 'tanned and cured leather'. Leather not properly treated can contain a lot of fat and 800 tons of putrid fat on board was not Mr. Penaluna's idea of suitable cargo. The grumbling Mr Strange set off on a goods train to Cape Town, with some cash for expenses and was told to be back in two days. Two days later a very dishevelled Mr Strange returned to the 'North Star'. All the hotels were full of soldiers and he had slept rough, the food obtainable was dreadful and so on.

"Never mind all that," Mr Penaluna said. "Let me see the papers." Mr Strange handed over a large envelope with all the documents inside. "Ah, good it does say tanned and cured, so we'll see what they send."

Mr Strange said, "They told me to expect train loads from today but couldn't say exactly when, because the Army kept requisitioning the engine."

"Anyway, well done Mr Strange – see young Mr Eefamy now, I'm sure he'll find something tasty for you, then have a bath and a change of linen. You'll feel like a new man."

"I'll never feel like a new man Mr Penaluna," said Mr Strange – as ever, he was tireless in his pursuit of pessimism.

Jan and Tiana Pieters were quickly accepted as part of the crew. Bo'sun at first wanted to sort out light duties for Tiana, but no, that would not do, she wanted to climb the rigging and learn about the sails, so the brother and sister worked together. Jan was only seventeen but he was big and tough. He had always lived a hard life and was quite capable of looking after himself and his sister. The crew quickly realised this, and everything settled down.

The leather began to arrive. It would require manhandling. It was tied into one hundred weight bundles, and though the train ran into the docks area, it could not get near to the 'North Star' and it was still about one hundred yards away. Mr Penaluna's paperwork did not cover for this sort of handling, so even before the job started he instructed Mr Strange to keep an accurate list of who did the work and for how many hours. His men were sailors not stevedores. Someone would have to pay.

Three local men who had small carts and ponies came around in search of work and soon they were operating a regular system of delivering the bundles of leather to the 'North Star. The hatches were open, and the bundles could be dropped into the hold and packed away. A few bundles were left on the train because Mr Baguly spotted that they contained hides which were oozing some noxious substance, so they were rejected. It was four days before the train driver said "That's it – you've got it all now." Mr Penaluna thanked him and passed him and his fireman a bottle of rum each. Then he went in search of a tugboat. No easy task; they were all busy around the Cape Town docks dealing with scores of English ships. He looked at the problem and finally decided that with a brisk wind from the west, he could make it out into False Bay unaided. He put it to Mr Baguly and Bo'sun that the cutter and the jolly boat, suitably manned could get her away from the wharf and with t'gallants and royals at the ready, they should take her out. They decided to try. Twelve men went into the cutter and six into the jolly boat. That was eighteen out of his crew of thirtyfive. Mr Penaluna took the wheel. Mr Baguly and Bo'sun were part of the rowing crews, and the rest of the men were right up at the top of the main and fore masts, ready to release the sails just as soon as the word came.

"Let go for'ard," Mr Penaluna called.

"Let go aft." George and Radford had been recruited for the aft ropes.

"Heave on it lads" Mr Penaluna shouted, as the men in boats put their backs into the job. Very slowly, inches at a time, the bows came away form the dockside, the water was a little choppy and though Mr Penaluna had chosen an outgoing tide for his experiment, she could still be thrust back with disastrous results.

"Sails away" Mr Penaluna sang out.

"Sails away" came the response.

"Sheet home."

"Sheet home for Australia" the men aloft shouted. The men below were on the halyards.

"Wait now, men" Mr Penaluna called. "Let's not leave the rowers in Africa."

"We can manage without them lot" Radford said.

"Keep the rope tight in the cutter – keep pulling. Humpage, rig up the davits ready for the jolly boat." "No more sails yet" Mr Penaluna called to the men aloft. "But stay ready."

Bo'sun and his team brought the jolly boat to the side and clambered aboard. By now they were fifty yards out and feeling safer, so long as the breeze stayed steady she would be gradually pushed away from danger, but too much speed and they would over run the cutter, and start to drag it along. Timing and judgement were vital. Mr Penaluna was tense and concentrating but confident.

"Foremast t'gallant now" Mr Penaluna called, this gave the 'North Star' just a little more way. The tide was causing the ship to bob up and down and Mr Penaluna suspected that she might be drifting back a little. A ship without way is a clumsy thing, but given a little forward movement and a good man on the wheel then she becomes biddable again. There was no wake, but she was holding her own.

"Bo'sun" Mr Penaluna called. "We have her, now tell Mr Baguly to get back on board." It was a tricky moment: would she still go forward without the cutter towing? The exact time the towing rope went slack Mr Penaluna called out "Royals now lads – look lively." The sails filled out, and suddenly the 'North Star' became the graceful creation she was intended to be.

"Take the tow rope to aft" Mr Penaluna called. Now the cutter was being towed, the 'North Star' was off and Mr Penaluna moved all his spare men onto the tow rope. He was now 500 yards from the docks, and safely out.

"Haul her in lads – don't let's leave Mr Baguly behind."
This suggestion was met with a derisive response, but
very willing hands moved to the rope and hauled the cutter
in.

"Go to the wheel" Mr Penaluna shouted to Humpage.
"Keep her full and by – and watch out for those prison
ships."

"The spanker?" Mr Baguly asked.

"Yes please Mr Baguly and the foresails, we are
underway now lads – well done. Where's Mr Eefamy?
Ah! There you are – right, it's large bacon sandwiches all
round. Steward, a good tot of rum would be appreciated.
How does she feel Humpage?"

"As happy as a bride on her wedding day – Sir."

Mr Penaluna smiled at that fanciful response and
thought to himself, incorrigible romantic that he was.
"And I've saved myself fifty pounds."

CHAPTER 5

Across the Pacific

They were just to the east of the Cape of Good Hope and heading down to Quion Point and Cape Agulhas, the wind was from the west and they were making a good seven knots. This area can be stormy, nothing like rounding the Horn at the tip of South America, but it can be rough. At this point they found the Indian Ocean to be warm and hospitable. Mr Penaluna hoped it would continue to make them welcome. The Indian Ocean is a vast expanse, he would have to travel at least 8000 miles before any land came into view. He had provisioned the ship for a three month trip and as soon as the fresh vegetables and the sacks of potatoes were used up, it would be salt pork and peas almost every meal. They had about thirty chickens on board, so eggs could go into George's famous duff and Mr Penaluna had bought six goats – he liked milk in his early morning coffee, and goat's meat was tasty enough if cooked in stews. There was horsemeat too, prime stuff not the flesh of old knackers yard victims. The meat was available because the horses brought out from England in huge numbers would not, could not eat the tough native grasses of South Africa. They were Irish hunters, thought quite correctly to be far faster than the Boer's ponies. But what had not been taken into consideration was the fact that they had been brought up on lush, often rained upon, Irish meadows, and a nice bucket of oats each day. In South Africa the grazing was dry and tough, the native ponies thrived on it, but the thoroughbreds didn't and had to be killed (and eaten) in their hundreds. This was a problem for George, could he produce tasty food from horsemeat – he had three months practice ahead of him.

George had taken to writing home every day, by noting down interesting and amusing things which happened. He would not be able to despatch his present opus until he reached Australia so it would be quite an epic affair. He managed to get one off during their week long stay in South Africa, because ships were leaving for England every day and Mr Strange had dropped George's letter off during his visit to Holt and Wellards' offices, with a request that all the letters – Bo'sun's, Mr Baguly's, Humpage's etc all be put on a ship which was Southampton bound if at all possible.

Dear All (George's long letter began)

We are now just one day out from South Africa and we are travelling at seven knots. (about 8 miles per hour) due east towards Australia. We will not see land until we have travelled for at least 8000 miles, and then Australia (which is the biggest island in the World – or so Mr Baguly tells me) is 4000 miles across. We have to deliver 800 tons of leather to Adelaide and then we are going to New

Zealand, another 2000 miles, to take soldiers to South Africa.

Two escaped prisoners swam from Prison ships to ours' and Mr Penaluna has let them stay and in fact made them welcome (as he did me) and one of them is a girl, named Tiana, she is about fifteen, same age as me. It is lovely and warm for this journey and it will be all the way because we do not have to go south towards the South Pole. We spend each afternoon on deck, sometimes we bring our mattresses on deck and find a shady spot where we can sleep for an hour or two. Life is very leisurely on a trip like this, provided we do not have storms, at the moment the wind is in the right quarter for us and this makes life very easy.

Others were writing letters too, some were just sleeping. Jan and Tiana Pieters spent as much time as they could up the masts with Sweeting because they wanted to become as efficient as possible with their duties, so they were learning how to reef up sails correctly, what buntlines were for exactly – they were quick learners and Sweeting was a good teacher. Even up there, one hundred feet above the deck there was still time to look around and enjoy the gentle climate and the wide expanse of sea. Sweeting's view from one hundred feet up the mast covered a huge area and visibility could not have been better – he spotted dolphins and he shouted 'Dolphin'. Humpage asked Mr Baguly if he could take time off to try to catch some – they are a very tasty alternative to salt pork and salt horse. Mr Baguly agreed and Humpage went off to make up his fishing tackle. He decided to occupy the end of the jib boom and he concealed the hook with a piece of white cloth. He played his (to dolphins) tempting morsel just above the surface of the water, it was a very disturbed surface, as the bows were cutting through the water at nine or ten knots and there was a brisk wind blowing. So the bait jumped and danced, Humpage added to the gyrations by flicking his wrist, causing the cloth to leap and fly. Thirty or forty dolphin were in the school, and they were fascinated. Flying fish joined the race and the dolphins began to pick off the flying fish one by one, until one of their number made a fatal error, and Humpage had him writhing on his line. He weighed about 40 lbs and such was his strength he nearly had his captor in the sea with him. But Humpage held on and dropped him into the nets which hung from the boom. George came to the side rail to watch, he had heard about the colours, and saw that they were very beautiful creatures: near the surface their backs were bright green, and as they went down it changed to olive green and then deep blue and finally a royal purple. They twisted and turned as they strove to catch the flying fish, with flashes of yellow and silver on their flanks. Occasionally one would leap out of the water and catch a flying fish in midair like an athletic slip fielder at cricket. Suddenly as if by a pre arranged signal the whole school went into the depths, the water was so clear that they could be seen quite clearly, though they were fifty feet down. Then they came up together and leapt at their intended victims, but one of their number miscalculated and Humpage had another one hooked.

Sweeting came down from the mast and copied Humpage's tackle, soon he too was bringing dolphin onto the deck. They stopped at six and Bo'sun who was vastly experienced in these matters began to cut them up – all the innards he threw to the chickens and the unwanted parts he heaved overboard. In the process he had made a terrible mess on Mr Penaluna's beautiful teak deck, but the pumps and holy stones soon had it all to rights.

Later that evening George continued his letter.

We caught six dolphin today, the weights varied between 25lbs and 40 lbs. So we had fish and roast potatoes for tea. I have never cooked dolphin before but Bo'sun told me to cut it into slices one inch thick and fry it in suet with just a little salt and pepper. Mr Penaluna (our Skipper) usually likes something different, so I put two poached eggs on his slice of fried dolphin and he liked it. There is plenty left over for tomorrow so I am going to make two really big fish pies – there are thirty seven of us now, so big really does mean big, and I must remember to put about 15 lbs of dried peas to soak before I go to bed tonight – I have tried to cook them unsoaked, but the men say they are like bullets.

The voyage continued week after week. Usually they logged 100 or 120 miles in twenty four hours. 700 or 800 miles per week, out of a journey 8000 miles. The crew had little to do, Mr Penaluna knew that there was little they could do to 'crack on', but if he had the feeling the day ahead was going to be reliable, he would suggest to Mr Baguly that they used the studding sails, it was good practice for the mast crews and it did add a knot or two to their speed. Mr Penaluna also used their long uneventful days to teach navigation to Oliver and Matthew and the two new members of the crew, Jan and Tiana. He asked 'Chips' to rig up a canopy so they could work in the shade and he made sure that the man on the wheel kept an accurate record on a blackboard of their course. He had the four apprentices heaving the log every hour to check their speed, and he was able to take them through the procedures for dead reckoning. It was a two hour session of hard work – usually broken up by George's arrival with coffee and freshly made scones. The butter had long since been consumed, but a little cheese grated into the scone mixture made them very acceptable.

The men played their flutes and penny whistles in the evenings, there would be some dancing in which Tiana and Hazel would join. Then a few songs and off to bed apart from those on watch. The four on and four off system was dispensed with and they did eight hour shifts, so they could have a really good sleep, when it was their turn. The men on watch overnight usually sent two of their squad right up the main mast to maintain look out, and to keep each other awake. Coffee was left for them on the stove, it became increasingly stewed if it was kept on the top or it became cold if it was taken off, left over scones and duff were lying handy, and so the overnight watch chatted, drank and munched their way through their duties. No one dared risk a doze because, either Mr Penaluna or Mr Baguly, invariably took a stroll at two or three in the morning. They would have a friendly word with the lookouts. No they hadn't seen anything – not surprising in an ocean covering about ten million square miles. In the morning the sun would peep up. It was good light in minutes. Fresh coffee was on the go. George and Radford were at work, sometimes bacon could be sensed, or maybe just toasted duff would give off a scorched but not unattractive scent. Porridge was made, perhaps, a little honey to go with it. Steward was shouting that Mr Penaluna was up and ready for his breakfast (goat's milk in his porridge) and poached eggs on toast to follow – another day had begun.

Mr Penaluna and his first mate Mr Baguly spent a lot of time studying charts; the journey from Adelaide to New Zealand was occupying them for much of the time: should they go south or would it be easier to go between the North and South island? They could go round Cape Farewell, pass Wellington to the east and travel down to Christchurch. It was the small port of Lyttelton which was their ultimate destination ten miles south of Christchurch. They did weigh up the possibility of going via the southern most tip of New Zealand via the Foreaux Straits and up the east coast of South Island, Mr Penaluna decided it would be further and much colder. But for the time being it was simply a case of trying to 'crack-on', and coaxing a few extra knots out of the 'North Star' so that the log book might read 150 miles covered in twenty four hours instead of 120.

George kept up with his letter, which by now ran to many pages, but so little happened that he despaired of having anything really interesting to write about. This was not because he was bored, he was in fact enjoying the 8000 miles journey very much, but the love of the sea, the tranquil days and nights, the beauty and wonder of being transported amidst a 150 foot cloud of canvas, these were pleasures beyond his meagre vocabulary. He was sensitive and appreciative enough to enjoy them but his powers of expression were not sufficiently sophisticated to allow him to put his feelings onto paper. So his near ecstasy came out on paper as 'another lovely day' or 'yesterday we covered 140 miles'. His innermost feelings were actually of complete happiness – a rare commodity indeed.

Mr Penaluna sent for George and Steward one morning and gave them notice that in four days time it was Mr Baguly fortieth birthday – the big question was, how could they salute it with a really good dinner?

Mr Penaluna started off the suggestions. "I think goat cooks quite well does it not Mr Eefamy?"

"I think it is like mutton Sir, I would perhaps give it an extra hour just to be on the safe side."

Mr Penaluna salivated at the prospect of meat cooked for an extra hour, he loved rich gravy. Steward for once shed his sour demeanour and volunteered that he had a sack of good firm potatoes or two put aside, and some onions.

"Will it be roast potatoes and onions then, Mr Eefamy?" asked Mr Penaluna eagerly.

"Yes of course Sir, they are no trouble."

"Not to you perhaps, but I fear it is all a mystery to me, and now Steward have you still a case or two of the claret I bought in La Rochelle?"

"Yes Sir, twelve or fourteen cases I think, and plenty of the ordinary stuff for the crew."

"Ah well" said Mr Penaluna rubbing his hands together, "Things are coming together nicely – and for pudding?" Mr Penaluna's face was now glowing with anticipation.

"We have some tinned plums. So plum duff, with real custard – how would that be?" George added.

"Real custard – what is real custard?" Mr Penaluna queried.

"It is made with milk – from the goats and eggs and just a little sugar."

Mr Penaluna nodded his approval.

"And cheese to follow – I would hope for cheese, with those biscuits you make yourself Mr Eefamy – not ship's biscuits you know for Mr Baguly's fortieth birthday."

"When is the birthday?" George asked, beginning to worry about preparation time.

"Four days off yet – plenty of time."

"We'll have to kill the goats today" Steward said. "Me and Bo'sun will do it."

"Don't pick old tough ones Steward," Mr Penaluna advised. "Take two youngish ones – next time we provision the ship – in New Zealand perhaps, I'll buy five or six sheep and some pigs – this is a big ship we have plenty of room to house them, and fresh meat is the thing. Thank you gentlemen, you have put my mind at rest. Friday is the big day and I would suggest dinner at five in the afternoon, it's going a little bit cooler then. Can we keep this a secret from Mr Baguly – will you please try – I would like to surprise him if I can."

Steward and George left Mr Penaluna's saloon together. George asked if he could see the potatoes and onions Steward had mentioned. "I would like to be quite sure – not that I am doubting your word," George added. "Just for my own peace of mind." Steward resumed his normal grumpy manner but he did display his wares and George approved.

George returned to his galley and told Radford about the impending festivities. "We must gather up all the eggs, - don't miss any, and keep all the goat's milk, we will need it for custard."

"How about the liver?" Radford asked.

"Liver, what liver?"

"Why the goat's liver o'course – do you mind when you cooked brisket for the crew once before, you bought liver for me – I can taste it now."

"Right – I can promise you will have some liver – now let's tidy up here and make some special biscuits to eat with cheese."

"Cheese – who said cheese?" Hazel had just arrived, to see what her 'beloved' was doing.

"They are going to have a special dinner for Mr Baguly's birthday and we have to do everything special" Radford said.

"And it is a secret – don't tell anyone Hazel – Mr Penaluna did ask us to keep it as a surprise." George emphasised this as much as he could.

"What are you going to cook?" Hazel asked.

"Two goats." George said.

"He'll know then won't he – he'll be able to smell the roasting joints."

"I don't think he'll cotton on, birthdays aren't really important to him, so let's try to make it a surprise."

The great day came, George recruited Hazel to help Radford prepare the vegetables, and the menu was indeed as outlined in Mr Penaluna's saloon four days before. George continued his letter after the party was over:-

Today is Mr Baguly's birthday – his fortieth and Mr Penaluna decided to give him a surprise dinner. The table was laid out in Mr Penaluna's saloon so it looked as if Royalty was expected. The weather was fine, we had a steady wind all day, but it was ideal for working in – 'Chips' has taken my galley doors off – just for now – so a breeze can blow through. The menu was as below

Meat Soup
Roast Goat with potatoes and onions
Plum Pudding with Egg Custard
Strong Cheese with home made biscuits
Port Wine
Coffee & Dates

Mr Penaluna invited Mr Baguly (of course) Bo'sun, Sweeting, all the apprentices, there are now four of them, two are the escaped prisoners who swam from the prison ship – I can't remember if I told you about them in a previous letter and Mr Strange, who now calls himself the Purser – tho' Mr Penaluna himself is really in charge. Wine was served all through the meal. Steward said that Mr Penaluna and Mr Baguly must have had two full bottles EACH, and port wine with the cheese. Yet it had no effect on them at all. Sweeting and Mr Strange were a bit tiddly. The apprentices had one glass of beer each and then just ginger beer.

I also cooked for the crew, they like stews, fresh bread and peas – it has to be peas with every meal. Mr Penaluna provided lots of wine and beer – I had some too, but only one glassful. For pudding I did two enormous plum duffs and it all disappeared. My faithful helper, Radford, had goat's liver – I fried it with onions – just like Polly showed me – and he thought it was lovely. Later in the evening the crew became very drunk – everyone of them, so there was no one to sail the ship. Mr Penaluna who knows all about these things said nothing. He manned the wheel and Mr Baguly and Bo'sun acted as lookouts and took over on the wheel now and again, to give Mr Penaluna a rest. Most of the men did not go to bed at all, they just collapsed on deck and went fast asleep. Some of them made very peculiar snoring noises and in the morning they were a few very sore heads – especially when Mr Baguly and Bo'sun started shouting orders. I made strong coffee for everybody and bacon sandwiches for myself –

I usually eat my breakfast 100 foot up the main mast. It tastes wonderful up there. The views are beautiful – sometimes I see dolphins, leaping and playing as they go along. I see whales too and sharks and sometimes another ship, usually it is a long way off, twenty miles or so. I am still trying to think of a way to bring a cup of tea or coffee up here to have with my breakfast, but I haven't managed it yet. I will add to this letter as soon as I have anything interesting to tell you and I will send it from Australia. Mr Baguly reckons it takes a steam ship about eight weeks to travel from Australia to England. We are going to carry on to New Zealand, then back to South Africa, and then, probably, back to England for more soldiers, so I don't think I'll be home at No 18 with you for another six months.

A tug boat was sailing off the North coast of Kangaroo Island looking for work when the 'North Star' arrived. It is a sixty mile tow into Adelaide, but Mr Penaluna had heard of ships being betrayed in this stretch of water and so he went for the easy but expensive option of being towed into Adelaide harbour. It was not a very busy place and three days later they were rid of the leather. Mr Penaluna had not wasted the days; he went round all the agents looking for something, anything he could take to New Zealand. He did not enjoy travelling in ballast. It cost money to ballast a ship and then there was the problem of what to do with it once a new cargo had been found. Three hundred tons of rock is not an easy item to sell, so usually the ship owner wishing to discharge this amount of ballast was charged for it, only to hear a week later that his 'unwanted' rock had been sold on to another ship. No, by far the best way was to find a good cargo, and Mr Penaluna was busy doing just that. He called into four or five agents without luck and enquired at the last one which hotel was recommended for a good meal. The George Hotel was mentioned and he made his way there just in time for lunch. Mr Baguly happened to be walking by just as Mr Penaluna reached the front door of the hotel.

"Well met Mr Baguly – I am about to sample Australian hospitality, do join me."

"I was feeling a bit peckish Sir, so I will gladly accept your invitation."

They went in together to enquire what was on offer. 'Steak' they were told. 'Steak and eggs, steak and onions, or just plain steak'.

"Steak and onions sounds fine to me what you say Mr Baguly?"

"Can't think of anything I would prefer Sir – thank you very much." So it was soon settled.

"Have you a cargo in mind Sir, to take to New Zealand?"

"No luck yet Mr Baguly, but this lunch will renew my energy and I shall continue after our Australian steak."

The steak arrived, it was enormous, enough for four or five people.

"I've never seen that amount of meat on one plate before Sir."

Mr Penaluna said "I reckon a good vet could get this back on its feet. Let's see what it tastes like."

It proved to be more than satisfactory, though both were defeated and they apologised to the waiter for their failure to do justice to the meal. The waiter was Irish and he told them that Australians usually gave English customers too much just to have the pleasure of seeing them defeated. Mr Penaluna was tempted to launch another assault, but decided that enough was enough and he conceded defeat.

Walking around Adelaide in the afternoon Mr Penaluna and Mr Baguly saw an Australian Government office and decided to enquire if they could put them in the way of any business. The building was a typical colonial pile of the type designed by Rattenbury, one section displayed the notice 'Shipping and Transport' so Mr Penaluna knocked on the door and was asked to enter. The occupant of the office was a high ranking Australian civil servant and he indicted that the two seafarers should be seated. He carried on signing papers and shuffling through files for about twenty minutes. Mr Penaluna was a man of unfailing courtesy and he would not have treated his most junior apprentice in this way. At last Mr Penaluna received the question "What can I do for you?"

"We are here on British Government business" Mr Penaluna began. "We have unloaded here and we are looking for cargo to take to New Zealand."

"Why New Zealand?" the official asked.

"Because we are taking New Zealand military personnel, volunteers, back to South Africa."

"I see – well we may be able to find a cargo – I will have to fill in a form – excuse me for a minute, I'll go and get one."

Twenty minutes later, and without an apology for the delay the official returned and began asking the questions which would enable him to fill in the form.

"Name of ship?"

"The 'North Star'."

"Capacity?"

"800 tons."

"Oh! quite small," came the unwelcome repost.

"Big for a sailing ship." Mr Penaluna countered.

"A sailing ship – I thought it was a steamer."

Mr Penaluna just about kept cool – he was looking for a cargo and could take a little patronising in his stride.

"No mine is a sailing ship. We made the trip here from South Africa in just about the time a steam ship would take."

"Well we need some more details – your name is…?"

"Penaluna."

"It can't be – surely?" The official was really starting to annoy Mr Penaluna now.

"It is an old Cornish name," Mr Penaluna answered him.

"Really," came the supercilious response. The next question was too much for Mr Penaluna.

"Have your ever been convicted of any serious crime?"

"I hadn't realised it was still a condition of entry," Mr Penaluna said. "Come on Mr Baguly we have important business elsewhere."

They stamped out of the Government building. Mr Penaluna said "Let's go back to the George and sample some Australian beer."

The day produced little in the way of real progress but this did not reduce Mr Penaluna's determination to secure a cargo for his ship. The next morning was spent talking to other ship's masters, and at last he did receive a tip which was going to be useful: the Captain of a 4000 ton steamer had been offered the job of taking 300 tons of salt to New Zealand but he had turned it down.

"I don't expect to make money on that sort of trip," Mr Penaluna told the steamer Captain, "But it is better than travelling all that way in ballast – I am grateful to you Sir, and if you are free later on, do join me for an evening meal. I have an excellent cook, you will not eat better anywhere in Australia than on my ship."

"That is uncommonly civil of you – where is your ship?"

Mr Penaluna pointed proudly to the 'North Star'.

"Ah yes I was trained in a ship just like that one: the 'Cutty Sark'."

"Not under Captain Moodie?"

"The very same – I was a boy in the 'Cutty Sark' when she battled against the 'Thermopylae'."

"'Cutty Sark' lost the rudder didn't she?"

"She did, and we still made good time with a makeshift rudder. But Kemball – he skippered

'Thermopylae', was hard on his crew and even harder on his ships – he usually won any races."

"Well then Mr – err – I didn't catch your name," Mr Penaluna said.

"Edmondson – Philip Edmondson."

"Very well Mr Edmondson I look forward to your company this evening, shall we say about six o'clock?"

Mr Penaluna went back to his ship, and because he was aware that his guest that evening had sailed in 'Cutty Sark', he attempted to look at the 'North Star' objectively. Try as he would he could find no fault. During the long trip across the Pacific Ocean he had had cradles out all round the ship, so her cream paint was new. The masts had been freshly tarred and the yards painted white. There were no 'Irish Pennants', the decks had been holy stoned and the brass work to the wheel and compass housing shone like gold, as did the brass handrails. Hazel was entitled to full credit for a lot of the improvements, as he entered his own quarters his heart filled with joy and pride as the lovely colours in the wood welcomed him. He rang the bell for Steward, but it was George who came into see what was wanted.

"Ask Mr Strange to step this way please Mr Eefamy and I have a guest for dinner tonight – can you arrange to do one of your specials for about six o'clock? – there will just be three of us."

"I have just bought some very large chickens Sir, would roast chicken be alright with sausages, bacon and a chestnut stuffing? George asked.

"Capital Mr Eefamy – just like Christmas in England, I can't think of anything I would prefer, and for pudding?" Mr Penaluna continued eagerly.

"Would you like apple dumplings Sir?"

The expression on Mr Penaluna's face gave George an unequivocal affirmative.

"Very well Sir – I'll find Mr Strange now and ask him to come to see you Sir."

"Thank you Mr Eefamy – and have your written home lately?"

"Yes Sir I am writing one just now."

"Good – remember me to your Mama, and say I am looking forward to our next meeting."

"When do you think that may be Sir?"

"We have to go back to South Africa from New Zealand, and from Cape Town we might be sent to England, so I suppose we could be back home in four or five months, but it is by no means certain – why do you ask? – are you homesick?"

"No Sir. Not homesick – I now think of the 'North Star' as home, but I know they all worry about me and like me to be at No 18 some of the time."

"You are very lucky to have so many ladies eager for your company," a smiling Mr Penaluna said. "Don't forget to ask Mr Strange to come and see me."

"No, I won't Sir, and I'll have dinner for three ready at six o'clock."

Mr Strange received the message and made his way to Mr Penaluna's saloon. Mr Penaluna gave him a piece of paper with an address on it. "Please go to see those people tomorrow Mr Strange. They have 300 tons of salt bound for New Zealand. I think £1 a ton sounds reasonable – it is probably all we will be offered, but the salt will act as our ballast and we'll be paid for it – do your best." Mr Strange thanked Mr Penaluna for the assignment, he liked to think that he was more than merely a ship's clerk.

Mr Penaluna sat back in his comfortable chair, surveyed his beautiful quarters for a few minutes and fell asleep. He was wakened by Steward noisily setting the table – the clatter of plates and cutlery was just slightly noisier than it needed to have been.

"I understand you have having dinner for three tonight."

"Yes that's correct Steward – just Mr Baguly, the Captain of another ship and I will dine at 6 o'clock."

The aggrieved Steward continued "Yes I heard it from the Cook." Plainly the chain of command was not to Steward's liking. "It would help if I got told FIRST."

"You were not around at the time, Mr Eefamy came to see me, when I rang for you, and so I told him – anything wrong with that?" Mr Penaluna tried hard not to smile – he knew his grumpy Steward and saw the funny side of this ridiculous situation, but he kept a straight face. Steward continued to lay out cutlery, his imagined martyrdom made evident by his demeanour. Mr Penaluna thought "whose ship is it anyway?" But said nothing apart from "the table looks lovely Steward – a well set out table is a vital part of any meal."

"Will it be best claret?" Steward asked, somewhat mollified.

"Yes please – there are only three of us, so five or six bottle will be enough."

"I'd better bring seven," Steward said, determined to have the last word. Steward continued to mutter to himself about five or six bottles between three people and no doubt they would want sherry to start and port to follow – it would end up with at least twenty glasses to be washed and packed away – and so on.

George prided himself on his menu cards, and soon presented Steward with his plans for the evening.

Fresh Fruit
Roast Chicken with
Sausage, Bacon and Chestnut Stuffing
A Selection of Fresh Vegetables
Potatoes and Onion baked together with butter
Apple Dumplings with egg custard

"Why give it to me?" was Steward's response.

"Then you will know what cutlery will be needed of course." George answered pertly. Steward grunted and went off to check the cutlery.

The fresh fruit disappeared in seconds. To the three gentlemen around the table fresh fruit was a duty, nothing more. The chicken, stuffing, bacon and sausages, ah! that was a different matter altogether. The apple dumpling and custard went down nicely and soon the unused bottles of wine went down too. Steward had attended to everyone's needs, and was as always, efficient and officious at the same time. Mr Penaluna asked Steward to bring George to the saloon. George and Radford were just finishing off one of the chickens. He put on a clean white apron (courtesy of Hazel) and went to Mr Penaluna's saloon. There he was greeted with their rubicund faces and loud acclamation.

"Capital Mr Eefamy!" Mr Penaluna said, as George entered. "I agree" Mr Edmondson said. Mr Baguly rose with less than decorous stability to put his arm around George's shoulders. "Well done George, never had better," he said.

"Don't forget Steward" George said. "If he did not serve meals so elegantly they would not be same." Steward waited eagerly for similar praise to be heaped upon him by the satisfied diners, but he had to be content with Mr Penaluna saying "Steward knows his work well enough." Mr Penaluna continued "You may leave the bottles now, we will attend to them."

Once out of earshot Steward said "Attend to 'em – guzzle 'em more like – I don't know where they put it all."

"Let's try the port Mr Baguly" Mr Penaluna suggested.

"Very good Sir – I usually like to finish with port."

"Who said anything about finishing Mr Baguly – we have only just started."

"I believe you were trained in clippers Sir," Mr Baguly said to Mr Edmondson.

"That's right. I joined the 'Cutty Sark' in 1870 with Captain Moodie. He had quite a job tuning her. New rigging is always the devil, and it took Moodie six or eight weeks to get everything right. We made it out to Shanghai in one hundred and four days. We got a charter to load tea, and we hoped to make it back to London as quickly as the steamers did. They did it in sixty days – am I boring you – with all this nostalgia?"

"Not at all," Mr Penaluna said. "Mr Baguly and I are sailing ship men and 'Cutty Sark' to us is a legend."

Mr Edmondson continued, as Mr Penaluna charged his glass. "We thought the Red Sea would be the death of the stokers, and that would help us to regain all the tea shipping but the stokers survived, even thrived on the work, and the Suez Canal didn't cave in as we all thought it would, so steamers pinched the tea trade."

"Wasn't there some talk about tea being contaminated by being carried in steamers, so the flavour was spoiled?" Mr Baguly asked.

"Yes there was that rumour, but I think it was circulated by clipper owners, so they could keep the work. It didn't have any effect though, and by 1880 most of the tea was being taken to England by steamers."

Then Mr Penaluna said to Mr Edmondon "Tell Mr Baguly about the race with the 'Thermopylae'." Mr Baguly leaned forward eagerly. Mr Edmondon, aware that he had an appreciative audience, asked for his glass to be recharged and began. "Captain John Willis had 'Cutty Sark' built to beat all-comers in the tea trade. Willis was known as 'Old White Hat' because he always wore a white top hat. He had made his money out of clippers and he was a sailing ship man, through and through. He commissioned Scott and Linton to build 'Cutty Sark' for him at £21 a ton – they produced the ship and went out of business – the specification was too high, but they kept their word and created perfection. No expense was spared by 'Old White Hat' and he had a figure head carved by Hellyer of Blackwell, she was like a Greek Goddess, also there was a group of naked wantons dancing along either side of her bows. There was a man on a grey mare and wonderful scroll work. She was painted black and her sheer was picked out in gold leaf. She was brought down from Scotland to London for her first trip of general cargo going to Shanghai."

Mr Edmondson could not have found a more rapt audience. They broke off occasionally to recharge their glasses (or to do the opposite), but were quickly back to their chairs – ready for the next episode.

"'Cutty Sark' broke no records on the trip to Shanghai, but it was not the outward journey which really mattered. What was important was how quickly we could return with the new season's crop of tea. The sooner we were home, the higher the price on the market. 'Cutty Sark' came back to London in one hundred and ten days." (Mr Penaluna and Mr Baguly looked at each other – they knew this was an amazingly low figure) "But" continued Mr Edmondson, "'Thermopylae came back from Fouchow in one hundred and five days."

"That is about eight hundred miles shorter journey though," Mr Penaluna said.

"True enough, but Willis didn't like it – he wanted his ship to win. He wanted circumstances to be that both ships set off from the same port and the same time. Then they would see which was the fastest clipper: If Willis had been more realistic he would have seen that the days for clippers were numbered – begging your pardon for saying that."

Mr Penaluna nodded and said "Granted – I'm sure."

"They were offered £3 for fifty cubic feet of cargo, whereas five years before the price was £5 or even £6. It was ruinous. But steamers could make two or even three trips a year to the Far East, clippers could only make one."

"What trips did 'Thermopylae' make at this time?" Mr Baguly asked.

"She usually went to Australia with general cargo. No one not even steamers could beat her."

"Because of the westerleys – once you are past Tristan da Cunha it's ten knots minimum all the way" Mr Penaluna said. "I've heard of clippers doing over four hundred miles in twenty four hours." Mr Baguly expressed amazement and then said "All this reminiscing makes me a bit peckish – how about you Sir?"

"You are right Mr Baguly – ring for Steward."

Steward came in expecting to be asked to remove the plates and tureens. Mr Penaluna said "Fresh coffee would be welcome Steward and a plate of chicken sandwiches each would go down nicely. Ask Mr Eefamy to put some of that stuffing on the sandwiches too – thank you Steward."

Steward went to find George. "Them lot wants sandwiches now and coffee – after what they have shifted, t'aint natural." George just smiled and began to slice the chicken – he liked people to enjoy themselves – Steward didn't. Even so he did his work well, and laid the sandwiches out neatly on trays, and heated up milk for the coffee. He begrudged doing the job but still did it with a fair amount of flair. There were too many trays for one and George went with him to help out.

"Please continue Mr Edmondson" Mr Penaluna said. – his articulation just slightly obfuscated by his chicken sandwich.

"In 1872 'Thermopylae' went out to Melbourne, and then ran up to Shanghai and ended up next to us on the loading berth – I was only a lad then but I knew this was an important event. Captain Moodie had us up the masts, checking the ropes, buntlines and rigging. He unreefed some of the sails to check for tears and holes. He made sure the studding sails were lying handy."

"Never had a lot of time for studding sails," Mr Baguly said. "They look lovely but they don't really help you to crack on and they are such a fiddle."

"Captain Moodie just wanted to be sure you see, because this was going to be a race. We spoke to some of the crew of the 'Thermopylae' and it nearly came to blows. Both crews were determined to win."

"More coffee?" Mr Baguly said, and he refilled all the cups and topped up their wine glasses at the same time.

Mr Edmondson continued "Both ships left Shanghai on the same tide but then we met three days of fog, once this lifted we matched them through the China Seas, but a storm hit us in the Indian Ocean and we lost our rudder, but our luck changed. We had two stowaways on board and they turned out to be a blacksmith and a ship builder. They worked with our ship's carpenter and made a new rudder. Captain Moodie's son was on board as an apprentice and he was working with the blacksmith when a monster wave came at the ship and upset the forge. Moodie's son was covered in red hot coals, and was scarred for life. They rigged up block and tackle to lift the rudder, which weighted over a ton, and they got it fixed. But they had lost valuable time and to Willis' disgust they came second. Willis studied the log book and was amazed to learn about the loss of the rudder."

"I should think so – it was a great example of seamanship" Mr Penaluna interjected.

"But it was all too much for Moodie, he found himself a job as master of a steamer, and I lost touch with him."

"Did you stay with the 'Cutty Sark?" Mr Baguly asked.

"Oh! I had to – I was a tied apprentice – my parents had paid to have me trained. But I would have stayed anyway – I loved it all." "Next we got Captain Moore – he was a 'play it safe' kind of skipper. No risks were taken. He didn't mind if we lost a week or two, just so long as we arrived with all the tackle in good order. We went to Melbourne with general cargo and then with coal to Shanghai."

"How did she sail with coal – that's a heavy cargo?" Mr Penaluna asked.

"It made her a bit low in the water and she has a big stern, so it dragged her back a bit," Mr Edmondson replied.

"Captain Penaluna likes a big stern on his ship" Mr Baguly said.

"And his lady friends" Mr Penaluna put in, laughing.

"You get a good lift with a following sea, instead of it dividing and coming over the poop" Mr Baguly added.

"Well she was quick on our next journey and we did the trip to Shanghai in forty one days and that was two days quicker than the 'Thermopylae'." "The 'Cutty Sark' was able to show us on that journey another aspect of her skills – she could ghost along on almost no wind at all."

"Just like the 'North Star' – she does that as well," Mr Penaluna put in.

"Then we loaded with tea and came home in one hundred and seventeen days. Captain Moore did just one trip – then we had Captain Tiptaft." And so the stories went on, glasses were refilled and bottles emptied. It was nearly midnight and they were still drinking, laughing and reminiscing when the stern, disapproving Steward came in to tidy up.

"Is that all for tonight?" he enquired.

"Perhaps Mr Edmondson would like to stay the night with us" Mr Penaluna suggested. Mr Edmondson was not able to answer because he had just fallen asleep.

"These steamer fellow can't take their drink like us." Mr Baguly said.

"No one can" Steward said.

"Let's just take his shoes off and ease his collar and trousers – then we'll get him into my cot for the night" Mr Penaluna suggested. The three of them handled him like a baby and soon he was nice and comfortable. Mr Baguly and Steward went off to their beds. Mr Penaluna clambered somewhat uncertainly into his swinging cot, remembered he had still got his boots on, but was asleep before he could do anything about it.

Mr Baguly staggered and cursed his way back to his own cabin where he slept like a babe in arms. Next morning George and Radford were in the galley very early as was their habit. Hazel was close by waiting for breakfast. The smell of frying steak drifted all around the ship, a tiny zephyr must have blown a hint of it into Mr Penaluna's saloon, and he was up immediately, ringing for Steward.

"Let's have breakfast eh, Steward?"

"Steak and eggs is it Sir?"

"Yes I think so and a small brandy just to perk me up." Suddenly he noticed that his other bed was occupied, "Who is that in my bed Steward?"

"It's that Skipper who you were drinking with last night."

Mr Penaluna moved over to his bed – he squinted at its occupant, but though he was awake, his eyes were not.

"Yes I think I recall now – he drank a lot if I remember correctly – well bring him some breakfast too Steward, and then we'll get the day started properly."

An hour or so later, washed and fed Mr Edmondson was ready to leave. Mr Baguly escorted him on to the deck and saw him safely ashore. Mr Strange was just returning from his errand to the Agents where he had arranged for the salt to be loaded that same day.

"Fifteen shillings per ton was all they would agree to, but I did ask for a little more tonnage, and they say now the cargo will be 380 tons instead of 300, and all at fifteen shillings a ton."

"Well it will suffice Mr Strange – thank you. At least we are not travelling in ballast. Loading today you say?"

"Yes Sir. It will begin to arrive this afternoon."

"Very well Mr Strange – I'll see 'Chips' and we'll open up the hatches. See Mr Eefamy, he'll do you a good steak and make coffee for you."

Two days later they were loaded and ready to go to New Zealand. The orders were to make for Lyttelton just south of Christchurch on South Island, New Zealand. Mr Penaluna and Mr Baguly had spent some time over their charts and they decided to go due south from Adelaide in search of the Forties. These prevailing winds were powerful and easterly. It is roughly 2000 miles from Adelaide to Lyttelton and a good stiff wind would be needed to bring them in within two weeks. Mr Penaluna knew he had in the 'North Star' a ship which liked a challenge and one which would respond. He could have taken an easier route north of Tasmania, through the Bass Straits, around the top of South Island and use the Cook Strait to come south to his destination, but having weighed up the options they decided the Forties would serve them best.

The Agent came to shake hands with Mr Penaluna. The tug was in place.

"Stations," roared Mr Penaluna. Humpage was at the wheel. Mr Penaluna was in full regalia, on the poop deck, hands behind him. The pilot gave the nod to the tug to move the ship away from the wharf. "Let go for'ard." The head ropes were hauled in.

"Let go." The last ropes were cast off, and they were on their way to New Zealand. Many people were on the wharf and they waved and cheered as the beautiful ship was towed out of the harbour. She met the swell of the sea and bobbed a curtsey. Her lift spars swung and portrayed wide arcs in the sky. Sea birds were still perched aloft and they murmured slight objections as their vantage point and resting place was no longer assured.

Mr Penaluna moved from the poop to look at the hatches – just in case. But he need not have moved: 'Chips' had done them up beautifully, many wedges were driven into place – all was safely tucked away. The wind came at them out of the west.

"Topsails," Mr Baguly shouted. The tug skipper came alongside to wave his goodbye and collect his fee. The masthead men were aloft awaiting orders. Mr Baguly looked back to the poop, Mr Penaluna had returned and was getting the feel of the wind – he nodded to Mr Baguly.

"Main top sail" Mr Baguly shouted. Down it came and the 'North Star' noticeably increased speed.

"Lee fore brace." was the next call.

"Sheet home for New Zealand."

"Belay weather sheet."

"Haul in the tow-rope."

The orders came one after another punctuated by the cries of the sea birds as they at last realised that their perches were being removed. It was all music to George. He leaned on the taff rail watching the wake grow longer and luxuriating in the sound of the orders, the creaking of the rudder on its pintles, and the groaning of the shrouds and ropes. Suddenly there was a crack as another sail opened, gathering in the power which made the 'North Star' leap forward.

"Keep her full and by Mr Baguly" Mr Penaluna called.

"Full and by" Mr Baguly called to Humpage.

"Full and by," came the reply.

"Spanker Sir?" asked Mr Baguly. Mr Penaluna nodded.

"Spanker it is lads, lively now," Mr Baguly called.

Humpage was in his element – he believed completely that God had destined him to steer large sailing ships – that is why he was over six feet tall with long powerful legs, hands the size of shovels and the eyesight of an eagle. From the moment the wind hit the sails and took the ship forward, he was in control and Mr Penaluna knew there was no better helmsman anywhere.

"Main sail if you please Mr Baguly," Mr Penaluna called.

"Main sail lads, easy now, let her down gently." The mainsail was released slowly from her gaskets but such was the wind that she cracked open and shook the ship fore and aft. Gradually the noise subsided as the sheet became tighter and flatter. The men began to sing 'Sally Brown, I love your daughter' and then 'Away, haul away to Dover'. It took fifteen minutes to set the mainsail correctly and then 450 yards of best canvas was driving the ship forward. The lee rails were under water and the seas were leaping at the sheer-poles. Mr Penaluna stood on the now heavily sloped poop. "That'll do now Mr Baguly, call the men for dinner."

George was well prepared for Mr Penaluna's last order: huge beef stews and fresh bread were ready for the men. Roast leg of lamb for Mr Penaluna and chicken for the two ladies on board, Hazel and Tiana. George glanced back at the silvery wake as he walked to his galley. He had left a very long letter with the Agents in Adelaide and he wondered how long it would be before it dropped through the letterbox of No 18. It would certainly take at least three months, but a previous letter, one sent from South Africa did arrive and it was eagerly carried into the kitchen by Rose.

"It's from George" Rose cried. All George's devoted admirers assembled in the kitchen as Clarissa opened the letter. "From South Africa – he says he hopes we are all well, he is thinking about us and he is quite safe. The fighting is all taking place many miles away, and the harbour at Simon's Town is just like any harbour in England, except that there are prison ships nearby." Clarissa read the whole letter out loud, but that didn't stop all the girls from wanting to read the letter for themselves. Eager as Clarissa always was to start the day's business, she took the pressure off and decided they would all start work half an hour later than usual. Life at No 18 was humdrum compared with George's, but they would not have chosen to alter that. The routine suited them all, and it was now a happy home, a prosperous one too, but the main feature was that everyone was leading a happy fulfilling life. Clarissa had made a tremendous difference in the previous year and everyone at No 18 benefited from her assiduous but kindly regime. Her pottery company was thriving, the haulage business was growing, the Bank Manager treated her with the utmost respect and her Haulage Manager and love, Bert Tremblett continued to enjoy her favours. He had proposed to her on many occasions, but she always said "Let's not tamper with it Bert. It works beautifully as it is, and marriage might spoil it." If business took Clarissa to London or Bristol on urgent matters she and Bert would go together and stay in a nice hotel, but she paid the bill and Bert knew who wore the pants in their relationship. He was happy with that situation, mainly because she was so beautiful and so keen on bed. Clarissa was quite content to go away for a few days and leave the paperwork, and indeed the running of her affairs to Thurza, who was proving to be a real asset in the office.

Letters back to George were started by the six ladies and during the next two weeks they were completed. All six were made up into a packet. Clarissa usually included some money in her letter, and Tom then delivered the packets to Fothergill and Jones' offices. They were in touch by telegraph with Mr Penaluna, and knew where he was likely to be and when. Mail was always treated almost as a sacred trust and the Skipper took this responsibility very seriously. In this case the packet was going on to a ship connected with the Boer War and it ended in an Agent's office in Cape Town. Mr Penaluna however was in deep discussion with officials in New Zealand: they had orders to transport three hundred medical staff to England, where they were to undergo training. At Aldershot to be precise.

"Are you sure – let me see the papers. The trouble is in South Africa," Mr Penaluna said.

"Yes we know where the fighting is, but we have our instructions, and they are exact. The destination is Aldershot where they will be trained to English methods." This was straight from a top English Civil Servant in the Colonial office.

"Right then, let me have the necessary documents, and I will take them to Poole – that is about fifty or sixty miles from Aldershot."

"Is that as near as you can get?"

"Well it is 13,000 miles nearer than here, so it's not too bad is it?" Mr Penaluna said – trying to extract some humour from the situation.

"What about London or Southampton?" the official persisted.

"Too busy. Last time I was in London, ships were tied up three and four deep, and it'll be the same in Southampton. After three or four months on board my ship, or any ship, the three hundred people will want to be off and on to dry land. Poole is the best chance." Mr Penaluna won the day.

"Can you leave in two weeks time?"

"I can Sir – my ship will be ready – I promise, and I am a man of my word."

That gave Mr Penaluna two weeks to arrange some trading, he knew that there would be capacity for about 100 tons of cargo as well as the three hundred medical staff and their gear. Nothing appealed to Mr Penaluna more than being paid twice for the same trip. He went round the Agents and secured 100 tons of wool to go to England, what a splendid day he was having! He went back to his ship and told Mr Strange to go to the Agent's office and arrange the paperwork. He rang for Steward and asked for some devilled kidneys, coffee and a bottle of his best. He had his meal, slept for an hour, and decided to walk around the harbour at Lyttleton and look at the other ships, perhaps he would be able to find a skipper who regularly did the trip to London, it was over 13,000 miles and Mr Penaluna was not worried about pocketing his pride and asking for advice. The New Zealand shipping company used this harbour frequently and two of its square rigged ships were in. The 'Wairoa' and 'Rangitiki'.

Mr Penaluna walked by and saw they were not all that different from his own, then he noticed another person was equally interested and was examining the two ships from all angles, it was George.

"Good afternoon Mr Eefamy – are you going to buy one of these?"

"No – I prefer an all timber ship – these are made of iron plates."

"Fine ships though – both of them. I had heard about this New Zealand line and they really do know how to look after their ships. Let's go on board and see if we can find anyone to speak to."

Mr Penaluna and George went up the gang plank of the 'Wairoa' and were met by the Mate who brought the Skipper to meet them.

"Fine ship" was Mr Penaluna's greeting. The Skipper welcomed the two Englishmen on to his ship and introduced himself as Captain Bungard. Mr Penaluna then introduced himself and George – "He's my cook" Mr Penaluna said. "I've thirty years at sea and I have never met a cook like him, so I never let him out of my sight."

"Well my cook is nothing special, but he makes a decent cup of coffee." Then Mr Bungard said to George "Please find cook and ask him for coffee, we'll be on the poop," and he led Mr Penaluna aft to his private area. "She was built in Glasgow five years ago, I've had her ever since. She can carry 880 tons, and I do the trip to London regularly, carrying wool and bringing back general cargo, and sometimes thirty or forty passengers, people who want to make a new life here in New Zealand – where are you bound for?"

"We are taking doctors and nurses to the Boer War in South Africa, but we have to take them to England first." Mr Penaluna answered.

"Nasty business war, but it's what politicians go in for. Are you going to London?"

"No – I've told them it's too busy with all the ships going to South Africa, so I'm going to Poole – near Southampton."

"I have been to Southampton – good harbour, good facilities. What's Poole like?"

"A small harbour, but safe and it's always easy to unload."

Ah! Good here's the coffee, put it on that table."

George became a little uneasy he didn't know whether he should stay or not. Mr Bungard put him at his ease. "There's a cup for you lad, help yourself." "Do you want to look at some charts Mr Penaluna? I have done the trip to London eight times and I'll show you the pitfalls." Mr Penaluna eagerly accepted.

"There are differing opinions" Mr Bungard began, "But I think the Cape Horn route is best – the first 5000 miles are hard, but fast. Cape Horn can be difficult, usually is, but the winds do help. I have done it once the other way as second mate. We went to the Cape of Good Hope and up through the Atlantics, but we nearly wore the tackle out, tacking and tacking, and the men left us in droves as soon as we docked." Mr Penaluna nodded acceptance that it would be the Cape Horn route.

"I'll have about three hundred people on board, and that can be a problem – especially if it takes two weeks to round the Horn."

"You'll just have to regard them as cargo – there is no easy way – it is cold, rough, and dangerous, but there is no reason why a well run ship should not make it safely."

"How many days from here to the Horn?" Mr Penaluna asked.

"Twenty four is good, I have done it in twenty one, but ships don't last long if you drive 'em like that, twenty four to thirty is alright. Once you are round, keep well away from Staten Island, and then go right up North passing Argentina and Brazil and into the Sargasso Sea, there you'll pick up westerlies that'll take you home, it is about 4,000 miles from there. I've heard of it being done in two weeks."

"That was Baines – I think – they used to drive their ships very hard. They are in the emigration business and time is money," Mr Penaluna said.

Mr Penaluna thanked Captain Bungard for his hospitality, then he and George went back to the 'North Star', where things were beginning to happen. Eight doctors had arrived, they were the senior medical staff in charge of the group of the three hundred or so nurses, orderlies, stretcher bearers etc. They wanted a discussion with Mr Penaluna about what to do next. Mr Penaluna was able to assure them that he had acted as a troop carrier before and was aware of the pitfalls.

"I think I can provide you gentlemen with privacy, provided you sleep two or three to a cabin" Mr Penaluna began – thus making them feel easier. "How many women and how many men are there? – they will have to sleep separately" They were not absolutely sure but it was about one hundred and forty of each sex. "If you could be certain of that – I can get my ship's carpenter to put up screens to ensure that they are kept quite separate – please let me know numbers as soon as you can." Mr Penaluna then continued "Now as to catering – feeding three hundred people for up to three months, maybe four can be a problem."

"Four months – not as long as that surely?" one of the doctors said.

"It's easy to reckon up Sir" Mr Penaluna said. "The circumference of the World is 26,000 miles, we have to go half that distance. But, and it is a big but, we can't sail in a straight line because someone stuck South America in the way. If we have a good run we can do 800 or 1,000 miles each week, and I hasten to add that steamers can't do it any quicker as they often have to call in at a coaling station and that delay can last a week. So it is a long slow job, but I believe doctors do recommend fresh air and there will be plenty of that."

The doctors were perhaps wavering about having volunteered to help Queen and Country to retain South Africa. Mr Penaluna sensed a hesitancy but is was only momentary and the leading doctor – Dr McKinnon assumed control of the situation. "Our people will be arriving today and tomorrow, within three days they will all be here."

"And your equipment? Is there much of that to stow on board?" Mr Penaluna asked.

"I'm not very good at calculating weights," the doctor admitted. "But I imagine it to be about two or three hundred weights per person."

"Well that's about forty or fifty tons so that is not a problem for us – but we have to provision the ship so three hundred people can be fed for four months, and being fed means being cooked for, so we will need your people to provide six field kitchens, enough food for three hundred hungry people and finally enough fuel to keep the field kitchens alight for four months."

The doctors had not considered these points at all and had no experience to help them to plan for such an undertaking. They referred Mr Penaluna to the Colonial Office in Christchurch where Mr Penaluna went with Mr Strange to try to press events forward, so they could get underway. They found the officials there to be completely out of their depth, but happy to listen to Mr Penaluna's requests. He produced the papers given to him in South Africa which made it clear that he was hired to provide transport. There was no mention that he should feed the volunteers. The officials were satisfied on this point and asked him what he would need and then gave him the necessary authority in the form of Government Purchasing Orders to requisition field kitchens, supplies of food and enough fuel from the chandlers at Lyttleton port. Mr Penaluna felt he had made real progress, it worried him slightly that Mr Strange suggested on the way back to the port that they could use the Government orders to purchase enough food for the crew as well. "Who would know the difference?" Mr Strange asked.

"I don't do business that way Mr Strange – never have, and I do not recommend it to you either." Mr Strange took this rebuke somewhat sulkily, he had moved in business circles where his kind of behaviour was standard – Mr Penaluna was an unusual person – a man of honour. He had once been told by another sea captain 'If you want to succeed in business – keep your conscience firmly under control', but he had never subscribed to this theory, perhaps he could have made more money had he been less scrupulous, but doing it his way gave him peace of mind.

When he returned to the 'North Star' the majority of his passengers had arrived. Mr Penaluna despatched Mr Baguly, Bo'sun and George to the Ship's chandlers to obtain the field kitchens, food and fuel. He then went over the ship with Dr McKinnon and 'Chips' to agree where the partitions should be erected for the segregation of the sexes. Mr Penaluna was a realist – he knew it would not be entirely successful, not with three hundred young people aboard and nothing much to do........

CHAPTER 6

Cape Horn

Two days later and they were ready to leave. Mr Penaluna had been through this procedure before, when he left the docks at Tilbury with the soldiers. The three hundred volunteers were all on deck waving 'goodbye' to thousands of people on the docks. Government officials came on board at the last minute to wish the doctors well, and then finally the gang planks could be removed and Mr Baguly roared "Stations". Humpage was at the wheel. The pilot signalled to the tug to pull the ship's head away from the wharf. The waving became more fast and furious – they were definitely 'off' now. The tow rope tightened. "Let go for'ard". The ropes were pulled aboard.

"Slack away" called the pilot. The people on the wharf raised a cheer, and the 'North Star' was slowly towed out to sea.

"Barometer's falling" the pilot said.

"The winds should give us a good start – we'll get most of this lot below now – my men will need all the decks to get her underway" Mr Penaluna said. This had been discussed with the doctors and they shepherded their staff below.

"Topsails if you please Mr Baguly" Mr Penaluna called.

"Topsails it is Sir" Mr Baguly answered. The ship jolted as the winds filled the sails.

"Foresails and spanker men – easy now – it's blowing – go easy," Mr Baguly cried. Again the ship gained pace. Mr Penaluna looked across at Humpage. "She's away now Sir – she's flying," Humpage shouted.

"Leefore brace – look out aloft. Haul steady lads," Mr Baguly roared.

"Sheet home main topsail."

"Sheet home for England."

The main top sails bellied out and the ship became a great white bird.

"Was you ever in Dundee?

Donkey riding, donkey riding.

Where the girls they are all so free etc."

The men sang as they hauled away. Mr Penaluna assumed his Napoleonic stance on the poop. He wore his plum coloured coat and his Nelson hat, his hands behind his back, his feet firm but pliant, upon the deck. He swayed gently as the 'North Star' tossed and bucked its way across the South Pacific Ocean. All Mr Penaluna'a crew from Mr Baguly downwards were fully engaged in various operations all over the ship. Mr Penaluna looked aloft and saw the mast teams adjusting buntlines, and moving about over one hundred feet up, others were standing ready to release more sail. Sweeting was stood near the log with two able seamen, awaiting the order to heave the log and check the speed.

"Loose the main sail," Mr Penaluna called.

"Mainsail now men" Mr Baguly shouted.

Four men raced into the rigging, released the giant sail from its gaskets. Great sounds, like explosions shook the ship from bow to stern as the four hundred square yards of canvas bellied out. Gradually the noise subsided as the sheet was flattened.

"Away, haul away from Calais to Dover,"

"Away, haul away, haul away Joe."

It was good that the men were singing as they worked. Mr Penaluna knew the value of a happy crew. Over she went as the great sail took effect, the lee rail was under water, and the sea was leaping up the shrouds and sheer poles. Mr Penaluna waited until his ship had gathered speed, then he nodded to Sweeting, who called "Heave the log." The leather cup disappeared over the side at great speed. "Thirteen knots" called Sweeting. "That's fast enough Mr Baguly – we don't want to tear the sticks out of her."

"Dinner now Sir?" asked Mr Baguly, hopefully.

"Splendid idea Mr Baguly – splendid idea – ask Steward and Mr Eefamy to step inside my saloon – I must invite at least some of the doctors to celebrate the start of this journey." "Perhaps you would join us too Mr Baguly?"

"Delighted Sir" Mr Baguly answered, then he bustled off at great speed to find Steward and George. One or two of the doctors were not feeling too rosy, so they declined the invitation but four accepted and were amazed at the splendour of Mr Penaluna's private quarters and agreeably surprised by the meal supplied, apparently by a very young boy. Mr Penaluna loved these occasions and looked benignly on as his guests devoured his offering. Mr Penaluna's long term vision also ensured that good relations were formed early in the trip, he alone on board the 'North Star' had done this journey before. Rounding the Horn was no fun and rounding it with three hundred people on board was going to present problems of all sorts. He wanted to be sure that he had made friends with all those who carried authority among the volunteers. They were in for a hard time and during such occasions you need all the friends you can get.

Later that evening Mr Penaluna went all around his ship, to gather information: he wanted to be sure that everyone was comfortable, and so far as was possible, their needs were catered for, Mr Strange was in attendance, making notes.

"We had cold food, we couldn't light the fire for the ovens," one group reported.

"Make a note Mr Strange and ask Mr Eefamy and Radford to come tomorrow and show these good people how to do it properly."

"Some of our party are very sick and everywhere is in a mess," another man said.

"Ask Bo'sun and Hazel to attend to this as soon as possible," was Mr Penaluna's response, and so the inspection continued until Mr Penaluna was sure he had received all the complaints, and Mr Strange had listed them all. "Show the list to those named on it and put it to them gently that I want it done. Thank you Mr Strange that will be all." With that Mr Penaluna retired to his swinging cot, he did not expect to have a full night's sleep, but two hours would come in handy before the South Pacific began to register disapproval of the fact that yet another intruder thought it could approach the Horn and get away safely.

It was dark when Mr Penaluna went on deck, the two hours of sleep had revived him and he was ready to take on any ocean. The winds howled, and tons of water swept over the rails. He ordered the foresheets to be loosened off, so that the wind tended to lift the bows out of the sea, instead of forcing ever downwards.

"Haul out to starboard" Mr Penaluna shouted, and the huge main course was dragged round, it took about fifteen to do it. "Make fast."

"Make fast" came the acknowledgement. The song, as they hauled, was interrupted as seas came rushing over the oilskin clad men, but they did not give up their song, they merely allowed the seas to divide it up. The gale continued to shriek through the rigging. Heavy seas crashed on to the deck, filling the main decks from rail to rail and adding scores of tons to the total weight. The scuppers worked full time, as the unwelcome water rushed back into the sea, only to be hurled back over the rail in the form of flying spray and curling waves. It was possible to imagine that the curved waves were claws and the sea was trying to drag the 'North Star' downwards into its greedy maw.

"Thirteen knots" Sweeting cried.

"Take in the main sail please Mr Baguly" Mr Penaluna shouted. Forty minutes of hard wrestling with cold, wet canvas, and it was reefed up.

"We've hardly any sails out" Mr Baguly said.

"Enough Mr Baguly. Enough. If we can keep to eight knots through the night, we'll see what the morning brings."

"Are you going below Sir?" Mr Baguly asked, what he really meant was 'can I have some sleep now?'

"No, I'll be here now for the next four or five hours Mr Baguly – get some rest."

"Thank'ee Sir – I'm most obliged. Goodnight Sir."

"Goodnight Mr Baguly – sleep well."

Mr Baguly did sleep well, but he had spent most of his forty years at sea. The three hundred or so passengers did not sleep so well: water was finding its way into their accommodation and 'Chips' was up half the night trying to devise ways of keeping the below decks area dry. Next morning was fine, cloudless but blowing a gale. Most of the nurses, orderlies etc came on deck and of course had never seen anything like it: the waves were twenty feet high and flecked with white and cream, it was very cold. They were, at this part of the journey, only just north of the Antarctic Circle and in order to go through Drake Passage (South of Cape Horn) they had to creep even further south. But given this good sailing weather Mr Penaluna knew they would be challenging Cape Horn in about twenty days time.

George and Radford had a very busy morning: they were on the list written out by Mr Strange. It was their job to see that the field kitchens for the passengers were all working properly. Also to ensure that the people using the kitchens knew how to light them, and how long to allow to make sure they could cook porridge for fifty or so people by 7 o'clock in the morning. George would have preferred to do this work amongst good humoured banter, but that was a scarce commodity: many felt sea sick, the others were all cold and hungry. But George could not possibly cook for three hundred, so it was a case of visiting each group in turn and showing them how to coax the recalcitrant field kitchens into life. George and Radford spent two hours on this job and finally made their way on to the deck, for George to enjoy and Radford to endure, an hour or so before it was time to prepare the mid-day meal. George took two mugs of hot coffee with him as he went aft: one for Mr Penaluna and one for Humpage. He stood next to Humpage, who was at the wheel. He was due to be relieved at the wheel, and despite the cold he was perspiring heavily! The 'North Star' had a double wheel lifted off the Danish ship at the time Mr Penaluna refitted her. Humpage always manned the wheel alone, but Mr Penaluna knew it would take two men, one on each wheel to replace him. Mr Penaluna knew also that the timing of the change over was crucial. The wind was shrieking all around them, the rigging was rattling like a hundred drums, and the twenty-foot waves were a constant threat. Mr Penaluna had two men standing by to take over the wheel at his signal, but this was delayed, until there was a brief 'steady' between the ship's mad rushes off her course. Mr Penaluna nodded and two seamen took over the wheels. Suddenly the ship was going headlong down a steep incline. They were surrounded by sea in a great turbulent bowl of threshing water. Mr Penaluna shouted 'Nothing to starboard." The two new helmsmen gripped their wheels. Mr Penaluna looked behind him and saw a black tower of water on top of which was a white frill of flying spray. Somehow it went under the ship instead of on top of it and Mr Penaluna smiled a little frozen smile and thought of his ship's wide aft regions; the width had saved them, and the 'North Star' was lifted out of that trough, only to tackle another.

Mr Penaluna stood next to his men on the wheels, offering encouragement and occasionally glancing aloft, reckoning up if he had too much sail. It is a fine balance and only Mr Penaluna's seamanship was between them and broaching to. Mr Penaluna decided. "Clew up mizzen topsail" was the order. With fifteen minutes hard work the sail is hauled up and the watch goes up the shrouds to furl it. Forty minutes later the sail is safely tied in place. The wind becomes more fierce, the men clutch desperately on to the rigging as they descend, it takes minutes to make the descent, every move has to be done carefully, one slight lack of attention to detail and a man could be overboard and lost. No one would ever be plucked to safety from seas like this, and at the speed they were travelling he would be one hundred yards behind before a rope could be thrown. Mr Penaluna had been told about the southern ocean with its westerly gales and constantly high westerly swells. Then a south east gale could spring up, meeting the westerly swells and while they fight it out Mr Penaluna was told, you are in the middle of it. They managed to come through the resulting turmoil and enjoyed a spell of light, but useful breezes, good progress was made and the 'passengers' became used, and positively enjoyed exercising on deck forty or fifty at a time. One morning they woke up and came on deck to find it had gently snowed in the night and the whole of the rigging and the yardarms were four inches thick in snow. George was learning against the rail with a hot coffee in his father's decorated cup. He was entranced by the spectacle of the 'North Star' completely snow covered. Mr Baguly came on deck "Where's Bo'sun? come on Bo'sun, we can't have it like this, get it all swept overboard."

"Please Mr Baguly, please let everyone see it first." George pleaded. "It is so beautiful!"

Mr Baguly stopped for a minute and looked aloft. "You're right lad it is – go and get everybody on deck who wants to see it – you've half an hour."

George told Radford first but he was half way through a bowl of porridge. "I hates snow" was his response. But George did meet with enthusiasm among the medical staff and they all trooped on deck, craning their necks upwards to enjoy the best view. George went up to the cross trees of the main mast and looked down: all the decks were painted white with snow and the sea was cradling the ship so gently that the ship rails were six inches high with nature's icing.

Mr Baguly suddenly noticed George – hard to see in his 'whites' "Come down George - it's dangerous. Come down nice and easy." he shouted. George obeyed – Mr Baguly was never ignored by anyone – least of all George.

Bo'sun and his men cleared the snow from aloft first and then swept it off the decks via the scuppers, holystones were next, and the immaculate teak decks shone with their accustomed glow. The week of light breezes had enabled the 'North Star' to move about one thousand miles near to Cape Horn, but the respite was over: the westerly gales came again and brought with them lazy rolling hills of sea, a mile long and thirty feet high. As the wind grew in force, the hill became more menacing, some were over fifty feet high and travelling faster than the ship. As the monstrous ridge of water arches over and crashes down, the leaping crest reaches speeds of up to sixty miles an hour, bringing tons of water crashing into the 'North Star'. Sometimes she stopped momentarily like a boxer who has received an uppercut, then she goes forward hesitantly for a second or two, her giant sails flapping uselessly, then the sails refill and she is off – her consciousness regained, she sweeps on triumphantly, lurching, rolling, but yard by yard she is making progress.

The skipper and all the watch are straining their eyes ahead, the darkness is intense, so that even when they glance aloft there are apparently no masts, no spars. The only light is an occasional phosphorescent flash from the sea. Suddenly the heavy cloud covering breaks open and sinister stars look down and the tracery of the riggings and the spread of the sails are silhouetted against the sky. It is like being on a ghost ship. But they have come through another night, another unique experience, and the ship is still safe. George came on deck and handed out mugs of coffee, just a nod sufficed as a token of gratitude, hands, hardly able to function because of the cold, gripped the mugs and frozen lips inexpertly tried to cope with the life saving beverage. It was the end of their watch – they were now due for three hours sleep. Mr Penaluna would see what the dawn brought before he could decide to leave the poop. Skippers of sailing ships sometimes stay for two days on watch – the responsibility is theirs' and it gives them the determination to stay alert and stay awake. Sometimes skippers are led away by a caring crew, more or less comatose, but still erect. Mr Penaluna greeted Mr Baguly "Nothing much to report Mr Baguly" he said. Homer never coined a better example of litotes.

"Did you sleep alright?"

"I always do Sir – never fail – see if you can do the same."

"I'll just see what Mr Eefamy has in mind for my breakfast – do you know the hens are still laying? Brave little beggars aren't they?"

"Two or three fried eggs would go down nicely now Sir?"

"I was just thinking along those lines Mr Baguly – I'll ask Steward to bring them to me. Oh Mr Baguly rouse me if things get any worse."

"I will Sir, I will."

Mr Penaluna had his fried eggs, slipped off his sea boots, and rolled onto his cot. He was asleep even before he had closed his eyes.

Next day was fine not raining, not snowing, visibility was good. Mr Penaluna had spent some time over his charts, he rang for Steward.

"Ask Mr Baguly and Mr Sweeting to step this way please Steward and we'll have coffee if you please. Perhaps some scones too – ask Mr Eefamy to rustle up some butter, or if not cheese scones would be nice."

"Scones indeed" Steward said under his breath. "Where does he think he is, on the river at Henley." He barged into the galley and shouted at George, "Scones, they wants scones."

"How many?"

"Enough for three."

"Right" said George. "I'll make enough for six, then we can have one or two as well." Steward grunted, he liked George's scones, but lacked the generosity of spirit to ever display gratitude.

Next day the heavy westerly swells continued, and lookouts were posted. They were near to the Diego Ramirez Islands, sixty miles south west of Cape Horn.

"Land oh!" came the shout.

"Where away?"

"Three points on the port bow Sir."

It was the first sight of land in twenty four days, it was difficult to actually see land because the constant swell was crashing onto its shores and hurling spray and foam fifty feet in the air, but it was land alright and an excellent landfall. They now knew exactly where they were. Although the ship was still in rough water George took his breakfast most mornings up to the cross trees, he loved the views and the fresh air. This morning he had company: two white birds came and perched near where he was sitting. He broke off some bits of crust and gave them to the two visitors. They were pleased and edged a little nearer. They were two exhausted sheathbills, a long way from land. George used up most of his breakfast trying to ensure they had enough energy to make it back to Tierra del Fuego.

George stayed aloft for about half an hour and exulted in the way this great white bird, which was his home, was charging through the seas at a good thirteen knots. He looked down to see that scores of the passengers were also enjoying the first sight of land for four weeks, and they were renewing their faith in Mr Penaluna and his crew – they now knew that they were in good hands. They moved into Drake Strait, named after Sir Francis, who had sailed this way in his tiny ship four hundred years before. This is the great passage, five hundred miles wide which leads form the South Pacific to the South Atlantic. The first part of the journey was over. The hazards of great gales, unpredictable seas, swells fifty feet high, gave way to new and more terrible dangers: icebergs. But first there was the obstacle of Burdwood Bank. In most places in this area the seas are about two miles deep but suddenly, at this spot, the sea is only two hundred feet deep. There is a huge submerged island here, and because of the constant and powerful winds the sea is on the move even one thousand feet down. As this great weight of water meets the sides of the submerged island, it rears upwards and causes wildly unforeseeable tumult at the surface. The 'North Star' began to roll heavily, the mast heads were describing great arcs as she shifted first to port and then to starboard. The great timbers groaned and creaked because of the strain, but they held firm. As she rolled the rigging slackened on one side and tightened on the other. It was thanks to Mr Baguly's excellent judgement that the lanyards were just set correctly – not too tight nor too slack. Had they been wrongly tightened they could have lost their masts overboard. The swells became bigger and they broke all around the ship, one especially huge swell lifted the 'North Star' and there it hovered for a few seconds until it was dropped into a seething bowl of foam. From this momentary vantage point Mr Penaluna could see the horizon in all directions and nowhere was anything to be seen but hoards of swells all rushing to smash this small and fragile intruder. Progress was made and the fifty miles across this Bank was accomplished in about ten hours. They were clear at sunrise and the sea's colour changed from green and cream to deep blue. George looked back from his one hundred foot high vantage point and saw the green seas and tossed foam being left behind. Another battle won. A faint blue line appeared along the horizon – the Falkland Islands were about thirty miles to the north. A good strong wind came up and Mr Penaluna decided to 'crack on' and ordered sails to be unfurled. He moved next to the wheel "North east by east if you please Humpage" was Mr Penaluna's instruction. Humpage smiled and moved the wheel to comply. "Spanker and all I think Sir"

"And foresails too?" Mr Baguly surmised. "It helps to keep her on course and adds a bit to her speed."

"Yes I think you are right – Mr Baguly – foresails if you please."

With the additional sails, she went up to thirteen knots, this was soon confirmed by heaving the log. They were moving quickly now into the Atlantic. The 'North Star' went over as all the sails filled out. The men were singing and the tackle and blocks rattled aloft as she slammed her way through the heavy seas. The great swells were back with them, but there was an air of optimism and confidence on board the ship. Any sailor and any passenger who has rounded the Horn, has conquered the worst that can be thrown at them. No threat is as real as Cape Horn and they had beaten it.

Many sailing ships, having rounded the Horn, used to call in at the Falkland Isles for repairs to the masts and spars. They usually reported that the inhabitants: penguins, sea lions and Scots were all equally uncommunicative. They certainly had a reputation for very expensive repairs and some skippers, though badly battered after weeks of fighting to come into the Atlantic, would struggle on to Montevideo, and have their repairs done more cheaply there.

The light was fading on their first day in the Atlantic, they were going at a good ten knots. Mr Penaluna called Mr Baguly, Sweeting and Bo'sun for a little meeting. "I want extreme vigilance tonight gentlemen, and for the next few days. We are among icebergs and at this speed we could have the bottom ripped off her in seconds – I've seen it happen."

"Fewer sails then?" Mr Baguly suggested.

"Exactly Mr Baguly, fewer sails – cut down our speed at night and put good men on watch. Tell young Eefamy

I want coffee and food taken to the watch every hour, to keep 'em awake – Radford and Hazel will have to help."

Nothing was reported during the first night and the morning brought a foggy haze, with little to be seen in any direction. Mr Penaluna urged caution "Just let her have steering way, and soon the sun will clear the visibility for us." Two hours later the sun did it's work.

"Skipper" Sweeting cried loudly, panicking "Look."

There in front of them just a mile or two away was a three hundred foot cliff of ice. It stretched for miles each way, and had pale blue fissures in it, into which the sea crashed, sometimes cracking off huge chunks of ice, weighing hundreds of tons. The main iceberg was the General and he was sending out raiding parties against all who dared to invade his territories.

"Ice on the starboard bow" Mr Baguly roared. "Down with your helm – hard down" "Lee fore braces."

"Hard down it is Sir," replied the helmsman.

The passengers crowded on deck to see this beautiful but terrible sight. "How big is it?" one of the doctors asked.

"I've seen them fifty miles long and in some cases eight hundred or one thousand feet high" Mr Penaluna replied.

"Do they just drift?"

"They do, sometimes for hundreds of miles out as far as Tristan de Cunha to the east. One famous one was in the shape of a hook – sixty miles one way and forty miles the other. It was drifting at a point in the Atlantic where many ships could be expected everyday, and this particular morning in 1854 three ships were in the vicinity, and all three awoke to find themselves surrounded, because the gaping bay was facing the oncoming ships. One of them carried one hundred and sixty emigrants and she was in a position where there was little room to tack and slowly but certainly the doomed ship drifted to leeward. She crashed into the ice cliff and turned turtle. Two hundred people died. The other two ships were in a better position – they managed to find a little breeze and they were brought to safety. I am sorry to paint such a gloomy scene." Mr Penaluna said as he concluded his story.

"Well at least we know the worst," the doctor said. "And I have no doubt that you know all there is to know about keeping us safe."

Mr Penaluna made some suitably self deprecating comment and invited the doctor and some of his colleagues to his saloon for coffee. "Mr Baguly will keep watch while we enjoy our drink and then I'll be back on duty until we are clear of these killers."

All that day the 'North Star' stayed fairly close to the Argentinian coast where fewer icebergs were to be found. But Mr Penaluna posted a treble lookout day and night just in case. He, himself, stared ahead as well. He ordered all sidelights, normally lit on every ship at night, to be doused. He wanted no distractions at all, the risks were too great. Then the moon rose and helped, visibility was good enough. The gale blew for another day, giving them two hundred miles of northing. They were moving into warmer areas, the decks were filled with pale nervous faces. Everybody came on deck, it was the first warm day for seven weeks, and the nervous faces gradually learned how to smile again. It was a Sunday and one of their number was a Methodist Preacher, he had a small pedal harmonium, and it was brought up on deck. Three hundred voices sang heartily until their repertoire of hymns was exhausted. Sunday lunch was a roasting: Bo'sun, Steward and three of the orderlies, had killed seven of the sheep and a real Sunday dinner was promised. The 'North Star' was on an even keel – ideal for cooking and the field kitchens were all filled with joints of mutton. George decided he ought to visit the six other cooks, just to give them a little extra help and advice, if it was needed. The welcomes varied from the enthusiastic to the resentful, but he had considered it his duty. He was glad to return to his own galley to supervise the preparation of potatoes and onions for roasting. Radford wasn't too particular about washing vegetables once he had peeled them, and George was just the opposite.

Once the meal was over the three hundred people on board were treated to an afternoon of really fine warm weather. Some of the sailors brought their mattresses onto the deck and slept in a shady corner. The medical staff took the opportunity to have a Sunday afternoon stroll, take the air and enjoy the warmth. It all interfered considerably with what Mr Baguly and Bo'sun wanted to do but Mr Penaluna was in a different mood, "Let them be, they have had a hard seven weeks. Everyone needs fresh air, so we'll leave the holy stoning for a day or two, and we'll all enjoy the tropics." Bo'sun wasn't happy, he shook his head in disbelief when he heard Mr Penaluna's charitable little speech, and he went away muttering. George spent the afternoon going around the field kitchens advising the cooks how to use up the left over mutton to make stews. Again his advice was not totally accepted, so he made a thick mutton sandwich and went right to the top of the main mast to eat it. He gave some thought to the cooperation he had received from the cooks who looked after the three hundred passengers – it was very little. The six cooks who did the work had never been to sea before and did not know about scurvy. Large quantities of oranges and lemons had been bought for the three month trip, and now after seven weeks all the fresh vegetables were used up, it was vital to include oranges or lemons in everyone's diet. Mr Penaluna's men did not welcome citrus fruit as part of their daily fare but they did know that scurvy was a terrible disease and one which was easily avoided. Captain Cook was one of the first sea captains to insist upon lemons for his crew. The Royal Navy was as usual embedded in paperwork systems and was slow to respond. It is probably true to say the scurvy killed as many sailors as the enemy did, until about 1810 when Naval authorities began to see that the cure was so simple. The symptoms of scurvy such as sunken eyes, loose teeth, bad breath were incipient in some of the passengers and George decided to take his thoughts to Mr Penaluna who could always be relied upon to listen. Mr Penaluna sat quietly and listened to this handsome, refined, well mannered boy extolling the advantages of oranges and lemons. When George had finished outlining his worries Mr Penaluna said "Have you read up books about scurvy – how is it that you know all the details?"

"My teacher was interested in sailing ships and Naval history and he used to tell us about it."

"But these are medical men. How can I broach the subject? They could be very touchy about this."

George was not sufficiently grown up or sophisticated to be able to help, but he did suggest that possibly Radford could help.

"Radford?" Mr Penaluna exclaimed. "He is the last person to trust with information about a sensitive subject."

"Exactly Sir. He would just say to someone – your breath stinks – see your doctor. Then it would be out in open." "There might be a row, even a fight but wouldn't it cause everyone to discuss it?"

"Well it is all for the best" Mr Penaluna said "So try it."

George spoke to Radford about it and he in turn mentioned it to the formidable Hazel. "Leave it to me" she said. "No one will fight me." And of course she was right – no one would.

Two days later one of the doctors asked to see Mr Penaluna on an urgent matter. No, Mr Penaluna had to confess he had not been made aware of certain signs and symptoms. But then he was not a trained man. The young doctor continued "They need to be on anti-scorbutics, as soon as possible."

"Anti-scorbutics Eh?" Mr Penaluna said, inviting further details.

"Orange and lemons are best if there are no fresh vegetables," the doctor continued airing his knowledge.

"Right then – I'll see my cook and Steward, and I'll put my crew on to it from today – much obliged to you I'm sure."

"We do our best," the doctor said with mock modesty. Mr Penaluna thought, but did not say, will you do your best when you arrive in South Africa? And will your 'best' be of any use?

The journey northwards was painfully slow on some of the days. The winds were almost exactly opposite to what was required and even with Mr Penaluna's detailed knowledge of how to coax extra mileage out of the 'North Star', some days he barely managed fifty miles of northing. His thoughts on how to accomplish more progress were put to young Oliver and Mathew, the two apprentices. If they were ever to get their 'ticket' to promotion they would have to know how to sail against a wind.

"It is all a matter of mathematics" Mr Penaluna began. "The wind is coming from the north and that is precisely where we wish to go. So I put the ship on the port tack, east north east." "You will notice the wake does not go straight away from the stern, but slightly to windward, so she is losing about 7°. This added to the course of 65° means she is progressing 72° from the direction of the wind. Can you follow how I arrived at the figure of 72°."

Matthew and Oliver looked at each other – seeking inspiration.

"Well I did say it's all a matter of mathematics – 7° and 65° make 72°, your parents did pay me £50 to accept you as apprentices and to train you to be ships officers.

You have to master the calculations. I shall now adjust the lee backstays, come with me on deck and I'll show you how it is done. You see it braces the yards just a little differently and still the sails are not empty and shaking about." Matthew and Oliver nodded.

"Right" said Mr Penaluna. "We'll have all hands on deck and we'll go about on the other tack, and then well go through some more procedures."

The helmsman kept her clean full, all the sails were snow white now they were completely dried out, and they were making eight knots.

"Stations about ship"

George moved out of his galley to watch, he loved this particular manoeuvre. The men were ready at the main sail and more at the spanker. Mr Penaluna indicated a slight adjustment was needed and the wheel was eased down. Mr Penaluna was watching carefully – timing was vital. He nodded to Mr Baguly.

"Ready about" Mr Baguly cried.

"Lee oh" came the response. The sheets were let go.

"Helm's a lee," shouted the helmsman. The rudder and the new positions of the sails brought the ships bows towards the wind. All the sails, yard arms, blocks etc all started to object to the new direction.

"Raise tacks and sheets" Mr Baguly roared. The crew ran to their respective places and hauled the appropriate ropes. The sails on the main and mizzen masts hung loosely behind the foremast sails.

"Main sail haul." sang Mr Baguly.

And the great sail came from port to starboard tack. The men frantically hauled on the main braces. The ship had momentarily lost her forward speed and the sails were flapping uselessly. Mr Penaluna watched and waited for the precise moment. "Midships" he shouted.

"Midships it is Sir." came the reply. The after sails began to fill. The men hauled on the port fore braces and the yards came round. The sails filled. The 'North Star' went ahead and leaned over on the starboard tack.

"Thank you Mr Baguly" Mr Penaluna said. "That was well done." He then turned to Matthew and Oliver. "Did you follow that lads?"

"Yes we did Sir."

"Good, it is just as well that you did – because I want you to go to my saloon now. You will find writing paper and pencils on my desk. I would like you to write out the whole procedure for me." Mr Penaluna spotted George, who was by the taffrail taking the air. "Do you think it is coffee time Mr Eefamy?"

"It is always coffee time and two of the sheep have lambed, so there is milk too."

"Very well – bring some for Mr Baguly too, if you please Mr Eefamy."

The two hundred and eighty or so passengers on the ship now had a routine worked out by Bo'sun. About fifty or sixty at a time would come on deck and walk about, take the air, and find somewhere comfortable to sit. The doctors and some of the senior medical staff organised training periods when splints were applied and 'wounds' were bandaged up. Stretchers were carried about with 'patients' on them, and at least some of the time was usefully spent. The best time was in the evenings: some of the crew and quite a good number of the passengers were musical, so concerts were organised. The organ which played hymns on Sunday was used to accompany the solos, duets, choruses etc. 'Tom Bowling' was heard, also the 'Anchor's Weighed': this was followed by 'My Pretty Jane' and the 'Last Rose of Summer'. It was discovered by the organist that among the chorus was a fine bass voice. At home in New Zealand he had trained his local choir, so he was used to homing in on a good voice. It belonged to one of the doctors and he was dragged out of the chorus and made to sing solos. He soon mastered 'The Diver' and 'Asleep in the Deep' and began to learn the 'Messiah' bass solos. 'The Trumpets shall Sound' was soon heard to great effect. One of the nurses sang 'Home Sweet Home' with disastrous results: George had to retreat to his galley to wipe his eyes. Bo'sun was obviously affected – he must have been thinking about the plump prosperous lady he left behind all those weeks, months ago. No one would previously have suspected that Bo'sun had an emotional side to his character. Prolonged absence from home plays tricks, and even the toughest people are prone to tears at the mention of 'home'.

The 'North Star' was now off the coast of Brazil, still travelling north, she would not head east again until she reached the Sargasso Sea, but that was at least four weeks sailing away. One morning Bo'sun saw dust on the ships decks and rails. Bo'sun hated dust. He wiped it with his hand and asked Mr Baguly if it was foretelling of a pampero. "It is the season – but we are far out from Brazil, so it might have spent itself by the time it gets out here." Pamperos are winds which blow straight off the Pampas and sometimes go roaring for a 1000 miles into the South Atlantic. They arrive with little warning in the form of tornados, and are often accompanied by thunder, lightning and very heavy rain. Mr Baguly thoughtfully wiped some of the dust off the rail, and move aft right to the taffrail and looked back at the ship's wake. Suddenly he roared "Haul up the mainsail." "Get the passengers below NOW".

Sails parted and ropes went flying in all directions. The lightning flashed and the claps of thunder coincided exactly with the lightning – they were in the middle of it. The bangs from the sails bursting rivalled the sound of thunder. The passengers were panic stricken and soaking wet. Mr Baguly ordered Bo'sun and Sweeting to supervise their safe withdrawal to below decks. It was as well that their sails gave way and tore, had they been new ones, the winds would have carried the sails and masts clean away. The exultant pampero screamed through the rigging and reduced more of the sails to rags. The men were up aloft, still trying to reef up some sails and reduce the pressure on the masts. There were hardly any sails out and still they were doing fourteen knots. The ship was rolling and plunging, and all around were high tempestuous seas and black clouds rushing by at four times the ship's speed. The havoc continued all day. The men were exhausted. Mr Penaluna shouted for rum and everyone had a tot or two. The moon gave the impression that the sea was silver and black and that it was in huge silver topped mountains and black valleys. The pampero left the 'North Star' just as quickly as it had arrived, it hurtled off into the South Atlantic, searching for more victims and left Mr Penaluna's ship a sorry sight and one member of his crew fewer. Usually in the storm Mr Penaluna would ask for ropes to be rigged up as lifelines, but the speed at which the pampero arrived precluded that measure. He was worried. "Mr Baguly – I want every member of the crew on deck – I want to count heads." Some had to be dragged out of bed, many were cursing, but no one ever argued with Mr Baguly. Five minutes later Mr Penaluna's fears were confirmed, Matthew, one of the apprentices was missing. "Search the ship" Mr Penaluna ordered. Ten minutes later a very sad group of seamen gathered in the waist. Mr Penaluna did not need to ask, and didn't need to say anything, Matthew was gone.

"Let's have some decent sails aloft – set a jury watch, and then get some sleep. Mr Penaluna then asked Steward and young George to come to his saloon. Some members of the crew hovered on deck wanting to speak to Mr Baguly. "Couldn't we go back and have a look around?" "We might just find him," another said. Mr Baguly was not dismissive nor unsympathetic, indeed he liked Matthew. "If anyone goes overboard in a storm like we had, it's ten to one he was hit by something and he was unconscious when he went into the sea. A conscious man wouldn't last five minutes in seas fifty feet high, someone unconscious would be gone in thirty seconds. Mr Baguly put his arms on the seamen's shoulders "We've all lost a good friend and a nice young lad – but it would take at least an hour to go about and we wouldn't find him, not in these seas."

Mr Baguly went to Mr Penaluna's saloon and arrived just as George and Steward were leaving. He could tell from Steward's face that he had not enjoyed the interview. George always looked happy, so Mr Baguly had to ask Mr Penaluna what has transpired. "I told them I wanted the men to have a very special breakfast and to see to it."

"Quite right too Mr Penaluna – let Steward sulk all he wants – he won't have to go aloft and sort out all the ragged sails and rope."

"Exactly Mr Baguly, exactly. But leave the cosmetic work until they are all well fed and rested."

"It is a great pity about young Matthew Sir, I suppose you'll have to contact his parents when we gets in."

"I am not looking forward to that interview I can tell you. It is the first time I have ever lost a member of my crew, but that piece of information will not make it any easier for his parents." Mr Baguly turned to leave and just as he had his hand on the door knob Mr Penaluna said "Why do we do this work Mr Baguly – no one makes us, so why do we do it?"

"I don't know Sir – I really don't know – I suppose it must be that we are just drawn to it." Mr Penaluna nodded acceptance and said "Goodnight Mr Baguly and thank you for all you did today – you get some sleep now, I'll go on deck."

Mr Penaluna found Humpage at the wheel. He looked at the compass and as usual found that Humpage was as precise as ever. He stood there for a few minutes, all around was calm, he looked aloft, all the sails were out, some were torn, loose ropes dangled and flapped about, some of the blocks were hanging loose and banging against the masts. The decks were covered with bits of wreckage left by the storm. It would be three days before the 'North Star' was shipshape again.

"But I just love it" Mr Penaluna said aloud.

"What was that Sir?" Humpage asked.

"Oh! nothing, I was just talking to myself."

The next day work began to get the ship to rights. 'Chips' and 'Sails' did it by working. Bo'sun got results by shouting. Mr Baguly's contribution was experience and example, and gradually the 'North Star' became an efficient and beautiful ship once again. The winds were still not cooperating fully with Mr Penaluna's ambitions to go due north, but he was confident that within days he would pick up the Trade Winds – they had carried traders on swift journeys for centuries and since they are fuelled by the constant heat of the tropics, they too are constant. Around the Equator the hot air rises, and colder winds rush in from North and South, this fact combined with the Earth's constant revolving motion presents sailors, who are experienced enough to take advantage of it, with an almost constant power source.

Land was sighted, a very small piece of land to be sure, but a sight sufficiently welcome to bring all the passengers and crew to look at Trinidada. More accurately, Trinidad, and it served to remind George to continue with his letter to the residents at No 18.

Land has been sighted – not by me first, though I was one hundred feet up at the time, but by the lookout who was even higher up than I was. We are six hundred miles off the coast of Brazil and the Island we saw is Trinidad, but it is always called Trinidada to make sure no one mixes it up and thinks they are at the real Trinidad which is part of the West Indies and many hundred of miles north of here. We were going quite slowly (about three or four knots) so I did have time to have a good look through my brass telescope (did I tell you that I bought a telescope in Australia with the profit on the cameos – Mr Baguly came with me to buy it – he says it is very good quality and it is times twenty, that means it brings things twenty times nearer, so a ship twenty miles away looks as if it is only one mile away.) Where was I? Trinidada is a tiny island only three miles by one mile, but it has a column 850 feet high which looks as if it is going to fall over – it is just made of rock, the sea carved it out hundreds of years ago. There is also another rock 800 feet high which Mr Baguly says is exactly like the Sugar Loaf at Rio de Janiero. (Mr Baguly has been everywhere). There is also a giant archway carved out by the sea, big enough to sail a small ship through and it is occupied by giant land crabs! Horrible! I asked Mr Penaluna about Trinidada and he told me that Dr Halley (the astronomer Royal) found it in 1700 and decided to make it part of the British Empire, but people could not easily settle there and sometime later

Brazilian people tried to live there, but they had to be taken off too – probably because of the giant land crabs which do attack people.

They moved further up north and began to enjoy really warm days, lovely skies, brisk breezes and the kind of experience which a sensitive person would never forget. George Eefamy was just such a person. He spent certain times of the day up the main mast, he always had his breakfast up there, one hundred feet above the decks. The sun rose differently each day: sometimes it was red. It must have been on just such a morning that Homer coined the phrase 'the wine dark sea' 3000 years ago. For it was true that just for a few fleeting moments before the sun was fully clear of the horizon the sea took on the appearance of millions of gallons of Burgundy wine. George looked forward to magical experiences such as this and continued with his letters:

This morning was very special: I got up very early but nearly had to fight my way to the main mast. There are three hundred on our ship and because it was so warm and bright they had all decided to rise early and the decks were crowded with people all eating porridge or toast and trying to hold a mug of coffee at the same time. It was a lovely morning, all the sails were out including the studding sails and the sun has bleached them white – they look like a white cloud. After the storm (yes – we had another one) Mr Penaluna made the crew repaint the masts from top to bottom with black tar and all the yard arms white. The sails were all repaired – though they now carry many patches – they still look good to me. Cradles have been put over the sides so that men can repaint the ship (she is cream coloured) and the figure head was badly knocked about in the rough weather and so she has been repainted too. Mr Penaluna wants our ship to look splendid when we arrive back in England. I am writing this letter in case there is any change of plans, but if there are no changes I will probably deliver the letter myself I have forgotten where I was up to – Oh yes – I was describing breakfast for three hundred. The ship was making good speed – I heard Mr Sweeting shouting 'Nine knots', so the decks were leaning over to the lee side at quite an angle, but our passengers have mastered this, and many of them told me they would not miss this 'fresh air breakfast' for anything. Tiana (she is the girl who escaped from the prison ship with her brother – I think I wrote to tell you about this, in the letter I sent from Australia), she often comes up the mast with me for breakfast, there is just room for two in the cross trees. She is very good at climbing but I think she will leave us when we arrive in England – I heard her talking to one of the New Zealand doctors, and I think she would like to be trained as a nurse. When the sun came up this morning it was red and just for a few minutes it made the sea red, at first the red was just near the horizon and the rest of the sea was a deep blue flecked with cream, but as the sun rose it spread the deeper colour far and wide, it was just like some one unrolling a rich red carpet, until, just for a minute or two, all the sea was this wonderful dark colour.

Once the sun was fully up the carpet was gone and the sea was blue again. I asked the people on deck if they had seen it too, they said it was just for a second or two, but one hundred feet up in the air changes the angles at which the light falls, so I am going up there as often as I can.

Mr Penaluna came on deck amid the three hundred passengers, and checked with Humpage, who was at the wheel and with Sweeting, whose watch it was, if everything was alright. The answer was in the affirmative. Sailors love these conditions: fine weather, a good wind on the quarter, a lively speed and the finest fresh air obtainable. True, the food wasn't too good after three months at sea - it was salt pork or salt horse, but George did a good duff, the hens were still laying and once or twice a week fried eggs on toast went down nicely. It was beginning to creep into Mr Penaluna's mind that he objected to quite so much company on his ship, he discussed it with Mr Baguly one day on the privacy of the poop deck.

"It does make a change Sir and it pays the wages" was Mr Baguly's philosophy.

"True Mr Baguly, quite true – I suppose I am just selfish and crotchety."

"Not you Sir, no not at all – perhaps we could look for a different line of work when we gets back – the wool trade is brisk, and now we knows we can round the Horn…"

"No – I don't want that as a regular trip – I liked the Mediterranean, and I like Denmark too."

"You like England Sir, and both you and me has been away from it too long."

"You are quite a philosopher Mr Baguly."

"Oh I don't know about that Sir" Mr Baguly said truthfully as he wrinkled his brow pondering on exactly what a philosopher did.

"Well these trips have certainly given us the chance to get to know our ship – and I am not sorry I bought her – though somehow I do miss the 'Bulldog'. If she can be bought when we return would you like her Mr Baguly – it's time you had your own ship, as Master?"

"No thank you Sir - I'm not sure as I could handle the paperwork and reckoning. Humpage has his 'ticket', I expect he would jump at the chance."

"I'd hate to loose Humpage at the wheel but people do have to move on – I'll think about that."

"Young Sweeting is good on the wheel Sir – he's come on a lot in the last few months."

"But skippering is not for you Mr Baguly?"

"No thank you Sir – I'm happy working with you Sir – if it's all the same with you."

A week later the 'North Star' arrived in the Sargasso Sea, and they began to sail through patches of gulf weed. It is an area approximately a million square miles and surrounded by currents and eddys, so the weed is held within this area. But for Mr Penaluna the arrival at the Sargasso Sea meant a change of direction. This was the point where he must head across the Atlantic – the world's roughest ocean, and make for home.

George was still enjoying his breakfasts one hundred feet above the decks and most days found time to convey his sense of wonder and discovery to the occupants of No 18 Wellington Terrace.

Today is Sunday, but I am not sure what the date is and up here there are not many people I can ask (joke!). The sunrise was very beautiful this morning, just as the sun's tip came over the horizon I saw a bright green flash of light – and I saw exactly the same light as the sun set in the evening. It looks to me as though it is caused by the sunlight coming through a swell. I asked Mr Penaluna and he says the weather experts do know about it and they call it the Green Flash. Yesterday was very busy: Mr Penaluna decided the light weight sails would suffer crossing the Atlantic, so he told Mr Baguly to take the heavy sails out of the sail locker, to dry them out, check them over and to spend the next two days on changing all the sails over from light ones to heavy weights. The further we sail into the Atlantic the colder it will get, so this might be my last one hundred foot high breakfast for a while.

Changing the sails took two days: a lot of energy and bad language were expended during the process: the lighter sails are relatively easy to handle but the heavier ones, especially when they have been folded away for weeks, are very difficult to bend. They were all up in time for a fresh south west gale to come at them. They were running before it with just topgallants and still doing thirteen knots. Mr Penaluna, Mr Baguly and all the crew were in oilskins and sea boots.

Mr Baguly read the aneroid barometer and called to Mr Penaluna "Twenty nine and falling Sir." Mr Penaluna climbed into the rigging to obtain a good view all around him.

"It'll change to the North West any minute now."

George was stood by and he asked Sweeting how the Old Man knew that. "In the southern hemisphere the wind generally shifts North West to South West, but in the northern hemisphere is shifts the opposite way. It is South West now but it will more North West just about the time the rain hits us."

"Stand by the lee forebraces" came Mr Baguly's order.

"Nothing to windward" Mr Penaluna said to Humpage. It was all just in time as the rain and the wind hit the 'North Star'. Mr Penaluna's watchfulness had been timed to perfection – the few sails he had allowed were trimmed to the wind and she was off triumphantly racing for home at fourteen knots. The men were on duty and at the ready for hours, as squall after squall of snow and rain battered the ship homewards. As each gust of wind gained strength some of the sails were lowered to ease the strain on the masts, and hoisted immediately the squall passed. It was hard work for the men and required constant vigilance by the Skipper and his First Mate.

Excitement began to spread among the three hundred passengers: they had shown great patience on the three month long journey, but they had had enough of the sea and they wanted to see what 'home' was like. This is how England was still regarded by New Zealanders of that period: England was 'home'. They had heard all their lives about just how beautiful it was, and now at last they were going to see for themselves. A definite sign that they were over the majority of their long journey came from 'Chips' the carpenter: he asked Mr Baguly for help to 'shackle on the cables'. This all meant he was preparing the anchors for use, they had lain idle for three months, as had the capstan, and now it all had to be oiled and freed ready to do its job.

Mr Penaluna spied a really big trawler up ahead and he had a word with Dr McKinnon, the man in change of the three hundred volunteer nurses. Mr Penaluna's suggestion was that they should attract the trawler skipper's attention and buy enough fish to everyone on board.

"We all need and would welcome a change of diet," the doctor agreed. So Mr Penaluna sent a boat across to the trawler and they returned with 500lbs of cod. Everyone on the 'North Star' benefited – the passengers had fried cod for tea, admittedly it had to be fried in the 'slush' which rises to the surface as the cooks prepare salt pork, but no one grumbled. The chickens got all the fish gut and bits. The seagulls feasted on the fish heads thrown into the sea and the crew had George's fish pie – he topped it off with some stale cheese which he grated up finely and mixed with milk and mustard. This was received by everyone as a masterpiece. Mr Penaluna sent for George and proclaimed "Mr Eefamy, I must announce that Mr Baguly and I are for ever in your debt. That fish pie was among your finest efforts."

"Thank you Sir I'm glad you both liked it." George turned to go and had his hand on the door handle when Mr Penaluna asked plaintively "And now, what's for pudding?"

"Stewed apple and custard Sir."

"Is that egg custard by any chance Mr Eefamy?"

"It is Sir – yes, the chickens are laying regularly."

Mr Penaluna rubbed his hands together and grinned. "Think of that Mr Baguly: ninety days at sea and we are having apples and egg custard." "Steward" Mr Penaluna called out suddenly. "Rouse out three or four bottles of that La Rochelle claret – Mr Baguly and I feel a thirst coming on."

Steward went away to the pantry "Three or four bottles between two! I'll take five and I bet that won't be enough – thirst is one thing, greed is another."

A trawler skipper drew his ship within hailing distance of the 'North Star' the following day, and Mr Penaluna was able to ask for the exact position. It had been overcast for a few days and Mr Penaluna had not been able to do his usual painstaking checks and cross checks. He heard exactly what he wanted and got Humpage to hurl two pounds of good tobacco to the trawler – they came even nearer in response to this generosity and threw a sack of fish across. The two ships were desperately close but they never touched and Mr Penaluna had an enormous plaice for his tea.

They were surrounded by ships now – some leaving the western end of the English Channel, some entering it. The deck of Mr Penaluna's ship was crowded everyday by the excited volunteers – they knew it was now just a matter of a few days and they would be 'home'.

George still found time to go aloft and one morning he counted three barques, one four masted ship, two brigantines, two fore and aft schooners, two ketches, and three snows. He did not deign to count the steamships which were far more numerous. He saw the Bishop Lighthouse on the Isles of Scilly where Sir Cloudesley Shovel had crashed his fleet and lost fifteen hundred men – that was before the days of Harrison's chronometer, when longitude was a matter of guess work or dead reckoning, two methods not entirely unalike.

There was fog in the Channel. "Get the fog horn ready – and someone go to the look out position" Mr Baguly shouted. Their fog-horn was a huge pair of bellows with a brass trumpet fitted at the outlet. If conditions were right the mournful sound carried for three miles. But there was no guarantee that a powerful steamer would hear it at all because of the noise its engines made, and some steamer skippers were so keen to pass through the fog that they gave little thought to the damage they could do as they rattled along at fifteen knots. The air was raw and damp. Moisture ran down the riggings and the sails, white when dried by wind and sun, they were now brown and stretched flat and taut. Mr Baguly told the men to check the halyards and to slacken off any that were too tight. The dampness causes the ropes to shrink and therefore to tighten up and if too stretched they will part. Mr Baguly wanted all the gear to be just right. Everyone realised the seriousness of the situation and spoke in whispers. Mr Penaluna went forward himself as an extra lookout, staring and listening was all they could do. With the night, the fog thickened, Mr Baguly ordered extra lights, and one small light shone from the binnacle so the helmsman could see his compass. A sailing ship in the Channel, in a thick fog is in danger, when the watch was finished the men went below to their cabins, but did not undress: they were waiting for an emergency call. Mr Penaluna stayed on deck all night, peering forward, looking for some slight sign which would tell him that the worst was over. Suddenly Mr Penaluna ran from bows to aft. "Steward, bring my gun and cartridges" he shouted, and he went to the taffrail. He fired twice and indicated to Sweeting to work his bellows. They could all hear the mechanical thud of the giant propeller and the hectic wash of a bow wave. Somewhere, just behind, a steam ship was catching up with them at speed. The next moment, Mr Penaluna could see lights overhead – a huge ship was bearing down on them and was no more than forty yards away.

"Hard a port – hard – hard" Mr Penaluna bellowed. He had ordered the helmsman to swing directly **towards** instead of **away** from the danger. But Mr Penaluna's seamanship saved the day because his orders carried the stern of the 'North Star' in the opposite direction, and the steamer swept by without touching Mr Penaluna's ship but it missed by a few feet only. The skipper was furious

– this was not only selfishness taken to an extraordinary degree – it was bad seamanship and Mr Penaluna took the responsibility of being a skipper very seriously indeed. This avoiding action had thrown the ship off course, but there was a steady breeze, and with a few adjustments to the sails they soon regained their correct direction. There was still a good wind but it was blowing the fog along with them. They came level with Salcombe, and the sun rescued them; the fog lifted, parted, disappeared and it was a fine bright day. The crew and all the passengers crowded to see the Devonshire countryside. Mr Penaluna signalled to Lloyd's Station – 'Ninety six days out of New Zealand, report to Fothergill and Jones.'

By sun up next morning they were passing the Bill of Portland and Weymouth Bay. The crew were busy anticipating the arrival of the pilot who would take them into Poole Harbour. The anchors were made ready for dropping, so they could knock out the pin that held the cat-stopper, allowing the cable to run out and the anchor to fall to the seabed. 'Chips' had checked that all the gear was in good order and then he left matters to Mr Baguly and Bo'sun. The mainsail was furled and out of the way. The pilot's cutter came to them, and he climbed athletically aboard and immediately took charge. He is the person who makes all the decisions about how to achieve a safe entry into harbour, BUT if it goes wrong it is the Captain who gets it in the neck. The ship is STILL the Captain's responsibility.

Mr Penaluna asked Dr McKinnon to take all his staff below. "My men will need the decks now, if you please, setting out is a tricky manoeuvre but docking is three times as bad." Dr McKinnon of course agreed and ushered all his people below.

"All hands on deck NOW" Mr Baguly shouted. George, Radford and Steward handed out coffee to everyone and waited to collect up the mugs and cups. A tug came alongside and its captain shouted "Want a tow Skipper?" Mr Penaluna looked across at the pilot, who went to the side and looked over. He approved, because he knew this tug and its Captain. The pilot nodded to Mr Penaluna who shouted "How much?"

"Fifty."

"Forty" Mr Penaluna said.

"I've got a wife and kids," pleaded the tug owner

"How many kids?" Mr Penaluna asked jokingly.

"Fifteen" lied the tug skipper.

"Then I'll give you three pounds for each."

"Done. Forty Five it is."

"Pass the tow rope to the tug" was the next order. The hands had been listening to the banter and were ready with the line and made it fast round the bitts.

"All hands shorten sail," Mr Baguly shouted. The crew jumped to it with a will, the trip was nearly over and this was a very important step in the right direction. The whole ship was in a state of complete confusion. The jib, all seventy feet of it, needed to be pulled back on deck, all the sails had to be furled and gasketed. Neatly too, Mr Baguly would not allow any untidy work. He wanted the 'North Star' to enter Poole Harbour looking at its best. Bo'sun grabbed three of the seamen and "Sweep her up –

stem to stern – no bits anywhere – sweep it through the scuppers." The men dashed off with their brushes ready to do anything, pay day was near and they had just developed gigantic thirsts.

They were surrounded by ships of every type now, entering and leaving Poole. Flags of every nation were fluttering, George recognised a lot of them he had seen before in London and Copenhagen. The placing of the 'North Star' depended upon the combined skills of the pilot and the skipper of the tug: they judged it to perfection and they put her to rest as delicately as could be imagined.

Mr Strange had been busy too: reckoning everyone's pay and writing out small packets for the money. The agent, Fothergill and Jones, would be on board soon with cash and Mr Strange would make up the pay packets.

On deck Mr Penaluna was arrayed in his plum coloured coat and Lord Nelson hat – sometimes he wore it fore and aft, but today it was sideways. He looked very happy and he did allow himself the luxury of thinking if he came to see George at No 18, would Clarissa be there – he hoped so.

"Coil up the ropes men" Bo'sun shouted – that was the last order, after one hundred days of sailing. Mr Fothergill came bustling up the gangplank – the men looked eagerly on appraising the weight of the canvas bag he was carrying.

"There'll be some drinkin' tonight lads" one said.

"Keep your drink – it's a woman I'll be lookin' for."

"There's plenty of them in Poole – but watch your money."

"Don't worry – most of it stays in mi box – here he is now, with the packets."

The packets were all given to Mr Penaluna by Mr Strange, and the men came forward one by one. Mr Penaluna gave him a packet and in every case thanked the man for his work. "Give Mr Strange your address, we will need you again in about two or three weeks time." It all took about ten minutes. George's was the last packet to be given out. "I would like to visit you and your Mama – please let me know if it is convenient – you can get a message to me here – I'll be staying on board."

"Yes – we would like you to come to visit us Sir. Polly is a wonderful cook – she'll do you something special Sir."

Mr Penaluna smiled and tousled George's black curly hair. "Off you go Mr Eefamy and I look forward to visiting you at No 18 is it?"

"Yes Sir No 18 Wellington Terrace."

Most of the crew left the 'North Star' with their pay and some hand luggage. Their dunnage, ie, the main body of their possessions they left on board, because they intended to return for the next voyage. This was not usual: many sailors ended a long tour of duty swearing that they had finished with the sea and that they were looking for a permanent job ashore. Mr Penaluna's crew were a happy lot who knew a good billet, and would return when summoned. Mr Strange had all their addresses and in two or three weeks time they would reassemble. Dr McKinnon's first job upon arriving in Poole was to arrange transport for all his people up to Aldershot, he did this by contacting the Station Master who laid on a special train for the day after docking. Mr Penaluna let his crew go but hired four local labourers to tidy out the hold where the three hundred volunteers had lived for three months – they made an extra days wage by selling to second hand shops all the clothes, books, shoes etc accidentally left behind. Mr Penaluna surveyed his ship four days after docking and decided they were more or less ready for the next journey. He called at Fothergill and Jones to let them know of his availability and to ask them to seek for work for his ship. "I don't want to take horses to South Africa, nor ammunition, nor men either if I can get away with it."

Mr Fothergill smiled knowingly at Mr Penaluna's precise requirement. They had worked together for twenty years and he was well acquainted with Mr Penaluna's ways. "I'll look for a load of medical supplies, food, saddles, bridles, bedding, tents, building materials." Mr Penaluna stopped him there. "Building materials? – why would they want building materials?" Mr Penaluna asked.

"It is only what I have read in the Times, but I understand they are going to build small bullet proof huts in certain strategic places, and because so many of the Boer's houses have been destroyed they are setting up camp for the women and children."

"There is plenty of scope there but bear in mind what I don't want to carry. I have told the men to be ready in two or three weeks – I am ready to sail now, but they deserve a rest and will come back the fresher for it."

"Will they all come back?"

"Most will – I pay a copper or two more than most and the food is good."

"Of course – I remember now you have that boy who cooked for us."

"Young Eefamy."

"That's him – you will be lucky to keep him – he might leave you at any time: his mother now runs two of the best businesses in town and is very prosperous."

"Yes I have met Mrs Eefamy – quite a lady."

"There are a good few bachelors in town who are keen to hang their hat up there, but she is not having any – she is in love with her bank account."

Mr Fothergill then changed the subject. "How is your ship's clerk going on with your 'reckoning'?"

"I think he is doing alright – he was a ship's clerk before and he does write a good clear hand – why do you ask?"

"I am hoping to have a good reckon up with you before you leave – you took leather to Australia?"

"Yes that 's right."

"And salt to New Zealand?"

"Right again."

"And now you have some wool from New Zealand?"

"Yes – I am due a lot of money: I took soldiers out to Cape Town, leather to Adelaide, salt to Lyttleton, and now volunteers back to here."

"Well the good new is I have been paid for the trip to Cape Town and that is now in your bank."

"And the others?"

"I'll let you know as soon as I can."

"Good. I would now like to get my feet under a table, so join me and we will sample some lamb chops and some English beer."

"Gladly Mr Penaluna, gladly."

George half ran, half walked to No 18. He ran-tanned on the front door and was greeted by Polly who almost carried him into the kitchen. He was soundly kissed by all the ladies, it was dinner time so Clarissa, Ann, Caroline, Polly, Marie and Rose were all there, smothering him in a mass of eager female arms, lips, soft bosoms and luxurious hair. Embarrassed but joyful, shy but happy, George kissed his way through the next few minutes and collapsed exhausted onto a kitchen chair. The ladies stood and looked at this beautiful boy – his black shiny hair, tanned complexion, fresh frank smile, his yard-long eyelashes. Clarissa stepped forward gathered him up, held him very close and said "It is lovely to have you at No 18 again – for a week? – two weeks? – three weeks?"

"I think it will be two at the least but it could be three or four – Mr Penaluna will come to tell me."

"Good – that's settled. Now Polly how can we feed this young man?"

"I done enough sausage and mash for six, so I reckon it'll stretch a bit and do for seven."

George's letters had arrived – that is, those he had posted had arrived, some he actually delivered by hand. They had been written during the three month journey from New Zealand to home, a journey which offered no opportunity to post the letters. So after the evening meal everyone gathered round the kitchen table and George read his letters to the six ladies. The letters were long and the interruptions frequent, even heated, as the ladies competed to question George about the different aspects of his journeys. Ann and Caroline wanted to know how many nurses were on board during the trip from New Zealand – what did they wear? How did they keep up with their need for clean clothes? Polly was keen to know how they managed for food, three hundred people take a lot of feeding. Was there much variety? How did they take a bath? Rose was just so happy to see George looking so well and happy, at ease with life, that she couldn't think of any questions and kept saying "Well I never." Clarissa's main contribution was to keep gathering George into her arms and saying how delighted she was to have such a beautiful son. Tom came round after tea to see Rose, and he too joined in the merry evening, until Clarissa (always in charge) announced that it was bedtime. George willingly went up to his old room, Rose spent five minutes at the front door giving good night kisses to Tom and by half past ten No 18 Wellington Terrace was home to seven happy sleeping occupants.

George spent the next few days with Tom doing local deliveries around Poole. Once or twice they did go near the docks, and eventually George just could not restrain himself any longer: he just HAD to go on the 'North Star'. He took Tom with him and introduced him to Mr Penaluna. Mr Penaluna saw that Tom was a sturdy fit lad of about twenty. "Come with us to sea Tom" Mr Penaluna said. "It's a man's life and you'll learn to be a seaman."

"No thank you Sir – I know George here loves it, and thinks of you as a hero – but it's not for me, I want to marry Rosie and settle in a little cottage of my own."

"I own a cottage in Poole" Mr Penaluna said. "I'm never there to live in it – see my Agents – Fothergill and Jones – George will show you where their offices are, and I am sure we can come to some arrangements. You can pay the rent to them and keep a bedroom spare for me, just in case I do need it, so don't fill the house full of kids," Mr Penaluna said laughing.

"Well I do know Rosie loves children but I don't know how many we'll have," Tom stammered, blushing furiously. "But your offer is very kind Sir, and it will give us the chance we have been looking for."

"Right. Take Tom to the office now George and do you think I could take a meal with you this evening at your house?"

"Yes of course Sir, you will be very welcome, they all come home from work at about six o'clock."

"Good. I'll arrive at about six thirty."

Tom couldn't leave the ship quickly enough. "Come on George, let's go to the Agent's office now," he said, bustling George down the gangway.

It was the main topic of conversation all around the table that evening. Rose was overcome with embarrassment, and contributed little in the way of conversation but much in the way of unalloyed enthusiasm and tenderness. It was taken for granted that Tom and Rose would wed. It is doubtful if there was ever a proposal, such a formality was superfluous in view of this unabashed devotion. As everyone said "They were made for each other." And Tom and Rose gladly nodded acceptance of the delicious inevitability of it. Clarissa made a mental note to up Tom's wages by five bob a week. Ann and Caroline said they would provide the wedding dress. Polly and Marie were joined in earnest conversation "Would it be a roast beef dinner afterwards or would it be mutton?"

Mr Penaluna had never experienced much of family life, and he sat drinking his coffee, a spectator, whilst all these young eager people, chatted, laughed and gave of themselves so generously. Clarissa suddenly got up from the table and said "Come Mr Penaluna – we'll go in the parlour for a glass of port and leave these young people to their plans."

In the kitchen decisions were made about likely dates for the wedding, the best colour for the dress and whom to invite. In the parlour Clarissa and Mr Penaluna planned a clandestine meeting in London: Mr Penaluna would have to go there to secure another visit to South Africa. Clarissa would go to see some of the bigger shops and take some samples of the latest designs of pottery. She did employ representatives to do this, and they would be credited with any resultant orders, but it gave her an excellent excuse to visit London and that was what she wanted.

The wedding was fixed for two weeks hence, and the dress was to be pale grey. Rose walked from her mother's home in the country just outside Poole – a walk of perhaps three quarters of a mile and her two bridesmaids dressed in pale green walked with her. Clarissa offered a carriage, but no, Rose insisted that this was the custom in this part of the world and she was quite happy to walk to her wedding through the fields. Tom was bought a new suit by Clarissa and Mr Penaluna paid for a week in a good hotel in Torquay.

Mr Penaluna and Clarissa had their 'honeymoon' too in a small private hotel in Belgravia. Clarissa made some good contacts in Oxford Street and Bond Street and Mr Penaluna secured a contract to take tents, building materials and food to Cape Town. He had spent some of the time in London with Clarissa looking for a little extra cargo to take on his own behalf and he secured a contract to take about eighty tons of cotton in the form of bales of cloth. He contacted Mr Strange and asked him to come to London to attend to the paperwork and to arrange to have the cloth lying handy, so it could be loaded at the same time as the cargo for the Government.

CHAPTER 7

Off to South Africa with Emily Hobhouse

George had enjoyed his stay at No 18, but he was ready now to renew his love with the sea. Tom dropped off his dunnage at the docks, and Clarissa came to say 'farewell' with Ann, Caroline, Polly and Marie with her in the carriage. The crew was assembling: Humpage arrived with his wife and now three children. Sweeting came back too and his brother. Bo'sun turned up with his rich and gorgeous lady friend. Mr Baguly was already on board, as were 'Chips' and 'Sails'. Mr Penaluna in full regalia greeted everyone expansively. He had advertised his projected trip to South Africa, by having a big notice printed, which said there was room on his ship for passengers and it made clear that he had work for extra 'hands' provided they were qualified seamen. Two experienced sailors applied for work and were accepted by Mr Baguly. Only one passenger resulted from the advertising: a Miss Emily Hobhouse who insisted in paying in advance for the journey. She told Mr Penaluna she was interested in the plight of the women and children of South Africa, many of whom, or so she had heard, had been made homeless as a result of the war.

Mr Penaluna decided he would sail the 250 miles to Tilbury, it would be a good way of getting the men to work together as a team again and save him a lot in towing fees.

Everyone who arrived at the 'North Star' on the day of her departure was welcomed aboard by Mr Penaluna. He had arranged that one of the hotels on the sea front would bring suitable refreshments and these were laid out: some, for the more select guests in his saloon and the rest in the men's dining room. Steward was his usual ungracious self; he protested that he was the only person on the ship who was working while everyone else was having a party. "And I'll have all the mess to clean up and the fancy pots to wash." He need not have said anything really because his facial expression was far more eloquent than his tongue could ever be. Clarissa's management skills came to the rescue, when she took him on one side and told him that the success which the entertainment undoubtedly was, could only be attributed to his skills as a host and to his flair and expertise. For once Steward was speechless but later said "Perhaps others on board could learn a few manners too."

Miss Hobhouse took the opportunity to tell Clarissa, and anyone willing to listen, that this was her second journey to South Africa and that she was on a fact finding mission supported by the South African Women and Children's Distress Fund. She had heard of camps where women and children were kept, and having already put into official hands a report, via her uncle Lord Hobhouse, she was now returning to see if conditions had improved. She was a small dumpy lady of about forty, insignificant in appearance but incandescent with zeal and moral indignation. Mr Penaluna concluded correctly that she would not be an asset as far as the next six or eights weeks were concerned. But she had paid in full, and he was a patient man when good payers were on his ship.

The 'North Star' was fully loaded with 600 tons of supplies and 80 tons of cotton material. Mr Strange had successfully arranged to have the bales of cotton suitably stowed near to the main cargo. The 680 tons was not quite a full load, and during the last weeks before sailing Mr Penaluna and Mr Strange between them arranged for 2000 cases of good wine to be brought on board. Mr Penaluna reckoned the Army had a number of aristocratic young officers and some rather discerning senior ones who would welcome a good wine. Steward's summing up of the situation was quite different. As he and members of the crew were stowing this valuable part of the cargo he was heard to say "I'll be opening these crates before we are clear of the English Channel – there's no profit if they drink it in Mr Penaluna's saloon."

As was frequently the case Fothergill and Jones had left the finalisation of the paperwork to the very last minute! "Let go forrard" had already been shouted by Mr Baguly, and the gangplanks had been withdrawn when a young man came dashing onto the quayside. Luckily all the papers were in a strong canvas bag which he hurled onto the poop deck. Mr Penaluna picked it up, gave it to Mr Strange and said "Put this on my table please." He then carried on watching the towing procedure. He was accompanied by Miss Hobhouse, who wanted to ask various questions.

"Not just now Ma'am please" Mr Penaluna said. "This is an operation fraught with danger and we must get it right." The language used by Mr Penaluna and Mr Baguly was almost silent. It had been honed over the years and consisted mainly of glances and nods, but it worked and the 'North Star' was safely towed out the twenty miles or so to Sheerness. Here Mr Penluna paid off the tug owner and the last connection between the 'North Star' and England was severed.

"Royals and t'gallants Sir?" Mr Baguly enquired.

"And spanker I think Mr Baguly – for Humpage's benefit." Humpage was at the wheel – he loved this moment when he felt the response from the rudder. With his feet firmly on the deck – he usually manned the wheel without shoes, he was responsive to the slightest movement or quiver as the great ship gathered speed. His eye was on the compass, his powerful hands were on his beloved wheel and his heart was singing with the almost orgiastic joy of his union and closeness with this beautiful ship.

"Two of the stay sails, I think Sir, would bring her closer to the wind," Humpage called out. Mr Baguly resented an able seaman making suggestions of this type while at the same time both he and Mr Penaluna did respect this sensitive helmsman's judgement. Mr Penaluna nodded. Mr Baguly barked out the order. The younger Sweeting and two other men were at the running rigging, and the sails were in place and tightened within seconds. The two smallest sails on the ships added almost imperceptibly to the 'North Star's' performance but it meant a lot to Humpage. Mr Penaluna smiled knowingly, he knew the difference was minute, but he also knew that a happy man on the helm was vital to the journey which lay ahead.

Miss Hobhouse, a lady of great tenacity had waited three hours – agreeably punctuated by hot coffee brought to the poop by George and Steward, and now Mr Penaluna was free at last to be questioned by his inquisitive passenger.

"How long do you think it will take to arrive in Cape Town Mr Penaluna?"

"Well Ma'am we did it last year in about six weeks – that was a good run," Mr Penaluna replied, deliberately keeping his estimate a little on the pessimistic side. "It has taken eight or even ten weeks."

"My business there is urgent you see, people are suffering and I need to expose the incompetence of many of the doctors and the officials out there."

"Well then, we will all hope for a quick journey," Mr Penaluna countered. "Our journey is urgent too, much of my cargo is intended to help the people you are interested in, so we all have worthy priorities."

"But I understand you are carrying strong drink, in large quantities. Could not that space have been used to carry medical supplies or tents?"

"Had the Government filled my ship with the items you have mentioned, I would have been quite pleased. But I was allocated about 600 tons only and that left me with space to fill. I have to make every journey profitable and wine does being joy to those who like it."

"Six weeks you say and we will be there?"

"The seas and the winds are unpredictable Ma'am, that is what makes my work so fascinating. Last time we did it in six, this time could take eight or even ten. But you may be sure that we will do the trip just as quickly as we can – in the meantime is your cabin comfortable?"

"Yes it is quite adequate – I do not look for luxury not when I am making this journey to help people who are living in appalling conditions – it would not be right."

Mr Penaluna could not see how Miss Hobhouse's comfort or lack of it could possibly help people in South Africa, but he let it pass. He then went to his saloon and rang for Steward. "Please make sure that Miss Hobhouse knows that she can take her meals in her cabin if she wants to." Steward was not pleased at all. "It means I'll have to take her meals to her."

"Correct Steward – that is what Stewards do – but think of the benefit it will be to me if she does decide to have some of her meals there instead of with me."

Mr Penaluna then turned his attention to the canvas bag full of papers thrown on to the ship just as she left Tilbury. Most of the contents were Bills of Lading and copies of Army documents, giving entirely useless instructions about how their equipment should be stowed. One large white envelope intrigued Mr Penaluna. It was marked 'Private – for Mr Penaluna ONLY'. It was a long letter giving conclusive evidence of what Mr Strange had been up to ever since he joined Mr Penaluna's service. He had been passing himself off as Mr Penaluna's partner and taking a share of every contract he had been involved in. He did this by asking for some of the fees to be paid in advance, and not be shown in the paperwork. So in fact the agreed sum for taking leather to Australia from South Africa had been £1 per ton but the paperwork showed fifteen shillings per ton. Mr Strange had made £200 on that journey – more than Mr Penaluna, the ship owner had made. The salt to New Zealand was a similar case, as was the hundred tons of wool which they had carried from New Zealand to England. The paperwork systems operated by all Shipping Companies and their Agents were of necessity very slow – a letter could take four or five months from New Zealand to England. But the documentation was always thorough, painstaking and accurate. Mr Penaluna went through the list of transgressions a second time and put the papers in a drawer and rang for Steward.

Steward's grumpy face appeared at the door, but at heart he was a coward, and like all cowards he knew instinctively if there was a situation which required a different approach. Mr Penaluna's face told him every thing he needed to know. He had been with Mr Penaluna for about twenty years and somebody was 'in for it'.

"Can I help Sir?"

"Yes you can Steward – please ask Mr Baguly to step this way and please bring in a large tray of coffee."

Steward was off in a flash – Baguly was in trouble – that was the word and it was round the ship in minutes.

Mr Baguly came into Mr Penaluna's saloon and shortly after Steward appeared with the tray of coffee, he gave Mr Penaluna and Mr Baguly a knowing look, which because it was so ill founded, quite mystified both recipients.

Mr Penaluna waited until Steward had left and then said to Mr Baguly, "Kindly turn the key in the lock Mr Baguly. I have something I wish to discuss with you." He carefully calculated the details of every transaction entrusted to Mr Strange, making a list of Mr Strange's gains (and his losses) as he went. Mr Baguly was no expert at 'reckoning' but it was obvious that Mr Penaluna was a few hundred pounds short.

"I never heard of nothing like it Sir – it's robbery."

"It is worse than that Mr Baguly, it is an insult to my intelligence – now what do we do about it? He arranged for this cloth we are taking to South Africa, and helped to fix the deal over the wine. He could be making fifty pounds or so on this very trip – I rescued him from an unhappy marriage and a shaky financial situation and this is how I am treated. So what do we do about it?"

"Is it a matter for the Police Sir, and the Courts?"

"If it ended up in Court, I would look a fool."

"Call in at a French port Sir and just drop him off – let him get back the best way he can. Then we are shut of him."

"Yes there is some justice in that Mr Baguly – it will make life very inconvenient for him at least for a few weeks – we'll call at La Rochelle as you suggest. Do you recall that claret we bought there, on the way to Italy? Yes that's a capital idea, I wonder how many cases of wine I could stow away – check on that Mr Baguly, and let me know. This is just between us two Mr Baguly. We'll land him at La Rochelle."

Mr Penaluna's optimism returned quickly, he went on deck and looked at the trim of the sails, all but the main courses were out. The lee rails were hissing and the bow wave was creamy and wide. Men were at the halyards and up the rigging, adjusting the clew and buntlines, half expecting an order to put out more sail. They were doing about eight knots. He looked at the chalkboard kept near the wheel and compass and did some mental arithmetic. "Could we heave the log please Mr Baguly."

"Aye Aye Sir – heave the log" Mr Baguly called.

"Eight knots" came the response, a few seconds later.

"That'll do for now – it's fast enough" Mr Penaluna said.

They made their stop at La Rochelle and to Miss Hobhouse's undisguised disgust took on 600 cases of best claret. She bustled up to Mr Penaluna who was stood on the poop deck with Mr Baguly and Humpage. They had done this journey before, but previously they had gone through the Straits of Gibraltar, now they were choosing a route due south towards Cape Town.

"I fear this diversion is costing me valuable time Mr Penaluna, when do we leave?"

"Shortly Ma'am, shortly. The cook and two or three of my men are out in the markets looking for fresh meat and vegetables. So once these cases of wine are safely aboard and the men are back we will leave."

"I really must protest, I need to be in South Africa urgently and I have paid you to take me there," Miss Hobhouse insisted. Mr Penaluna took her on one side, out of earshot of the crew and made it quite clear to her exactly who ran the 'North Star'. "You only booked a cabin Ma'am, not the whole ship – I will be in Cape Town just as soon as I can be. In the meantime enjoy the trip and I am sure you will enjoy the meal tonight, I see my men are returning now with fresh fruit and vegetables."

Mr Penaluna then went over to Mr Baguly and enquired of him very quietly "Has Bo'sun got Strange's dunnage together?" Mr Baguly nodded. "Right I'll send him ashore now on a bogus errand, once he is off the ship, put his parcels on the quay." Mr Baguly nodded again. Strange was sent for and told to go to the Harbour Master's office, which was about half a mile off. As soon as he was out of sight his dunnage was laid on the quayside. On the top of it was, the white envelope addressed to Mr Penaluna, marked 'Private', in it was all the damming evidence.

"Make ready to cast off please Mr Baguly but do not wave to the tug skipper until I give the word. Kindly draw back the gang plank."

With the slackening of the ropes to the quay the ship drifted a few feet away. Mr Penaluna saw Mr Strange hurrying back. The gap widened. Mr Strange saw his dunnage on the quay. Mr Penaluna shouted to him "Open the envelope – all you need to know is in there."

All the crew were on deck and they saw what had happened. "Why have we left 'im behind" one asked.

"He thought he could diddle the skipper and the Old Man caught 'im at it," Mr Baguly said. "Serve 'im right then," one said. "'Ow will he manage?" said another. "Best way 'ee can" Mr Baguly said. Mr Penaluna knew he would manage, never a vengeful man he had put five sovereigns in the white envelope.

Mr Penaluna's course was now toward La Coruna on the north west coast of Spain which meant he had to proceed diagonally across the Bay of Biscay. This area has always been feared by sailors: the Atlantic is the most storm tossed of all the great oceans and possibly its most irascible part is the Bay of Biscay, but this time it was wonderfully well behaved. With a favourable wind on her quarter the 'North Star' was making a good nine knots hour after hour. It was warm and dry. Over a three day period Mr Penaluna was able to change from heavy weight sails to the lighter ones. Miss Hobhouse needed to know why they were taking sails off, when they were obviously essential to her progress south, but she accepted, grudgingly, Mr Baguly's explanation that the heavy sails were very hard on the men and the lighter ones much easier to handle.

Because the weather was so gentle, George was able to take his breakfast aloft and one morning called down to the deck "Whales – eight or ten of them." He pointed directly ahead. They were lying on the surface clearly visible and attracting attention to themselves by spouting and crashing their enormous tails into the sea. The whole crew came to look. Young Sweeting had worked on a whaler and he recognised them as sperm whales. Fifty or sixty feet long, weighing many tons, they eyed the 'North Star' as she glided by and very slowly moved out of the way to let the ship go right through the school. Three or four smashed their tails on the surface of the water and then spouted again. George's view from aloft was etched into his mind and he hurried down the shrouds to capture it all on paper, so he could try to give all at No 18 as vivid a picture as possible of his sightings.

Two weeks later they were off the coast of Africa and still making remarkable progress. Miss Hobhouse attributed it to the divine intervention of the Lord whose assistance she had pleaded for. He was aware (as was everyone on board) that her's was indeed a worthy mission. Mr Penaluna made straight for Cape Town. Twenty miles out he was intercepted by a tug looking for work. The main harbours were not now so cluttered up with ships, as they had been on Mr Penaluna's previous visit, so they did not need to make for Simon's Town as they had done before. He quickly took to this tug skipper, he knew what he was about and by the afternoon he had the 'North Star' safety tied up in Cape Town Harbour.

Miss Hobhouse wanted to be first off and Mr Penaluna was so glad to accede to this request that he loaned her a member of his crew for the day to see that her luggage was safely delivered to her hotel. Mr Penaluna's sense of humour was never far away, though it could be mordant, as in this case, when he instructed Steward to be Miss Hobhouse's ammenuensis.

Two weeks later Mr Penaluna had secured work with the Army authorities and he was ready to leave for London with one hundred and twenty wounded soldiers, twelve nurses and three doctors. It was not of his choosing, but it was the only work on offer and it was promised that he would have at least one further trip to South Africa bringing building materials for Kitchener's schemes. Three or four more engagements of this sort and the 'North Star' would be paid for. Once this was accomplished Mr Penaluna planned to have a major refit, and to occupy his time moving fruit and vegetables from the Azores and Madeira. He had also retained happy memories of his visit to Italy – would he be able to coax Clarissa into joining him on a trip to the Mediterranean, as his wife? Mr Penaluna was really smitten and Clarissa was never far from his thoughts.

Mr Baguly was always privy to Mr Penaluna's plans, so he told the men the shore leave would be in short supply later in the week. If they wanted a night out on the town, it was now or never. The casualties would be arriving, new compartments would have to be put up below deck. Field kitchens would need to be hoisted aboard and made firm. It would be a very busy time. The men needed no second invitation and twenty-five of them left together, all intent on having a good time. George had spent a lot of his spare moments in Cape Town writing home, and as soon as he heard they were due to put to sea he brought his letter to a close and decided to entrust it to a steamer. They were making it home in about three weeks, so the letter would be delivered in half the time taken by the 'North Star'. He left with the men and walked towards the offices of the Blue Funnel Shipping Company. Jan overtook him and asked where he was going. "Just to post this home," George said holding the envelope up. "I'll come with you and then we can decide what to do next," Jan said.

"I'll just be going back to the ship – I have some tidying up to do."

"Radford'll do it – come into town with me and have some fun."

George was fifteen, and he didn't really know what the men meant by fun, but he was keen to find out whilst at the same time he was still young enough to be very unsure about what lay ahead. Jan took him into one or two bars, but they were too rowdy even for Jan and finally they found a place which offered home cooked food and lots of it. The only drink they served was beer and George did not wish to appear unfamiliar with this beverage so he drank deeply for a fifteen year old, and after a pint and a half was in truth drunk. Jan realised the position and suggested a slow stroll back to the ship. "The fresh air will clear your head." "Take deep breaths – that usually works." All sorts of advice came George's way but none of it was any use. He was light headed and very unsteady on his feet. They tried to make their way through a busy part of town; it was full of bustling crowds all in a hurry and horse drawn vehicles everywhere. George was pushed by a burly man who wanted to pass, and he went headlong into the wheel of a truck and fell awkwardly. Jan heard the bone go. George fainted with the pain and the burly man moved away. Jan asked for help and after a few minutes four English soldiers came to ask if they could do anything. George looked very pale and his leg was a peculiar shape. Half an hour later George was in an English bed being looked after by an English nurse. He came round and asked where he was. Jan who was still with him answered "You 're in an English Army Hospital."

"Did I get shot?"

"No. You fell."

"I've fallen before but I've never ended up in hospital."

The doctor who had set George's leg was passing and he said. "No, that's because you have not broken your leg before, but now you have and you'll be with us for the next four weeks."

"My ship sails this week – I must be on it – I'm the cook."

"Well they will have to learn to cook for themselves, you will not be cooking for a few weeks yet – tho' once you are up and about you might just go into our kitchens and find out what they do wrong."

Jan was still standing next to George's bed. He was looking very worried and with some justification, everyone on board the 'North Star' knew that Mr Penaluna was very fond of George and he, Jan, would have to tell Mr Penaluna exactly what had happened.

When the doctor had left them George signalled to Jan to come closer.

"Don't mention the drink to Mr Penlauna – I promise I won't tell him, we'll just say I was pushed in a crowd and I fell against the cart."

"Thanks George – that would make it easier – though I do think I should have insisted on your having fruit juice or coffee."

"Don't worry – I enjoyed the beer – it was fun."

"Right. I'll leave you now and go and tell the Skipper."

"Keep the story simple – like we said."

"I will," said Jan. "I will."

Mr Penaluna and Mr Baguly and Radford came to see George the next day, by which time he looked very perky and full of life.

"What do we do now eh?" Mr Penaluna began. "With the most important member of my crew laid up."

"I can cook too," Radford volunteered. Mr Penaluna did not look convinced.

"It's true" George said. "He does very well and with Hazel to help, I expect you'll manage, until you come back – you are coming back aren't you Sir." It had suddenly hit George that perhaps Mr Penaluna's next journey was somewhere other than South Africa.

"Yes – I am chartered for more work this way, so if we leave this week – ah, just a minute here is the doctor, he'll tell me what I need to know." The doctor confirmed that George would be in bed for ten to fourteen days and a further two weeks convalescing.

"Right well that settles that – by the time you are up and about, I will be battling with the Bay of Biscay, and in say ten further weeks I will be back, so can you manage for fourteen weeks – let's say four months on your own?"

"Yes I am sure I can Sir – I have some money saved up – so could you ask Jan to bring my dunnage into here, and I'll be alright. Once I'm walking again I expect I'll be able to get a job in one of the hotels or cooking for the Army – I'll be alright – I'm sure."

"Right, that sounds convincing, but if you are in trouble, Forthergill and Jones have a temporary office here now, go and see them – they will help you – lend you money and soon, they will be able to tell you when we will be back here." "I think that has covered everything – do you agree Mr Baguly?"

"Yes Sir, except that I would like to say to young George here that we'll miss his lovely cookin'."

"Yes I agree with you there Mr Baguly."

They solemnly shook hands with George and left. Radford returned for last minute instruction about omelettes and scrambled eggs, Mr Penaluna was fond of both for his breakfast.

"It's simple: if you do an omelette, whisk up three eggs in a bowl and add a little water. If he wants scrambled eggs whisk them up with a little milk, and cook them slowly, so they don't go dry."

"I think I've got it," Radford said. George smiled at his helper reassuringly. "You'll be alright – look out for Steward though – he'll drop you in it if he can."

On leaving, Radford said "I'm sorry to see you stranded here". Now he really was alone, thousands of miles from home, with people he hardly knew, unable to move, no prospect of climbing aboard his beloved ship for at least four months. George turned over, buried his head in the pillow and cried himself to sleep, with the word 'stranded' uppermost in his mind.

CHAPTER 8

George is left behind - Stranded

Mr Penaluna's cottage became home to Tom and Rose, it was only half a mile out of Poole, so the young couple could easily walk to work, which they did everyday – hand in hand. The routine which they had established was for them to walk to the stables, where Tom put a horse to the little trap, he then drove Rose to No 18, where she still worked for Mrs Eefamy, and having safely delivered his wife, he then picked up his employer and drove her to work. All this took place at half past seven each morning. This routine was disturbed one morning in June: Mrs Eefamy wasn't ready and the occupants of No 18 were in a turmoil: Mrs Eefamy's daughters, Caroline and Anne were in tears as were the two servants Marie and Polly. News had arrived via Fothergill and Jones, the Shipping Agents, that George was in hospital in South Africa with a broken leg and he would not be home again for at least six months. The message also asked them not to worry and offered assurance that Mr Penaluna would be back in Cape Town just as soon as possible and he would ensure George's safe return. But assurances are no use in these circumstances: George was in trouble, probably in pain and they were all powerless to help.

"Why did he want to go to sea anyway?" Clarissa asked. "He had everything anyone could want right here, and we could have looked after him."

"He put his trust into Mr Penaluna," Polly said.

"Lot of good that's done him – ten thousand miles from home and a broken leg."

"The message does say it was an accident in the city, nothing to do with the ship," Caroline offered.

"Yes, well, they would say that wouldn't they," rejoined Clarissa, determined to not to be mollified. She still felt guilty about the way George had been beaten by her mother and Rooney and the guilt now expressed itself in her desire to be protective. Tom was out of his depth with this flood of female emotion all around him. He coughed nervously and said. "Excuse me Mrs Eefamy but I have a lot of orders to deliver today, had I better leave now and ......

"No, no. We're alright. Work will do us all good and we can't do anything now, but once George is back here I shall try to get Mr Penaluna to join me in persuading George to stay with us."

Clarissa and her two daughters climbed into the trap and Tom drove into Poole to the girls' shop and then to Mrs Eefamy's factory. The constant topic of conversation was George's plight and estimates as to where Mr Penaluna's ship was.

In fact the 'North Star' was making very good progress, but she was not a happy ship: the crew, and of course Mr Penaluna and Mr Baguly, had grown used to George's tasty inventive cooking and now it was quite different. The cook Mr Penaluna had hired was one Robert Bridgetower, a huge coloured man, part Negro, who had come to them with good recommendations but he was decidedly not a good cook. His sole claim to any sort of ability was his skill with the violin. Quiet evenings on deck were wonderful, because he had a wide repertoire of dances and reels which he played with great aplomb and the men danced and sang the evening away, quite forgetting the mediocre meals and concentrating instead on the musical and rhythmic accuracy of Mr Bridgetower's playing. He was a man of about fifty and he claimed to be the grandson of George Bridgetower who had been a friend of Beethoven. In certain circles this piece of information did bring forth gasps of admiration or incredulity, but not on the 'North Star' since no one apart from Mr Penaluna had ever heard of Beethoven and even Mr Penaluna wasn't sure if he was a composer or a writer. As a violinist, the cook was first rate and he had what he claimed was his grandfather's fiddle, a Grancino, but his cooking was limited. Food on board sailing ships, or indeed any kind of ship was usually good for the first two or three weeks. During this period all the fresh food was used up and then it was back to salt pork, salt beef and peas. Having firmly established in the first two or three weeks of a journey that the cook really could cook, all the recipients of his offerings would be more tolerant of salt pork once the fresh food was used up. But Mr Bridgetower's repertoire did not extend to expert use of fresh meat and vegetables and it was salt pork from day one. Radford and Hazel did try to emulate some of George's meals for Mr Penaluna and Mr Baguly and they met with some success, but Mr Penaluna had been quite spoiled by George's expertise and he quickly realised that he must forget his palate and superannuate his taste buds until his favourite cook returned. He still had some cases of La Rochelle claret and he could seek comfort in a bottle or two of that if life became too hard. Meanwhile he was making steady progress up the west coast of Africa with one hundred wounded soldiers and their attendant doctors and nurses. There were no grumbles from that direction as regards food – after bully beef and hard biscuits in the trenches for weeks, Mr Bridgetower's cooking was very welcome and apart from the wounds and the occasional passing away of the seriously injured, the time passed comparatively pleasantly for all on board.

Mr Penaluna was not looking forward to his meeting with Clarissa however. Hitherto their relationship had suited both parties to a tee: plenty of pleasure, indeed joy, but no real permanent emotional involvement. It worried Mr Penaluna that George's predicament might just cancel out Clarissa's sexual appetite. "Funny creatures women," Mr Penluna ruminated as he walked around his poop deck. "Funny but wonderful too." His thoughts concluded as he saw Steward passing by. He was not bearing a tray – Mr Penaluna thought –" Steward not carrying a tray – what are Stewards for?"

"Ho, there Steward – how about some coffee, is there any milk? Mr Baguly and I would welcome a drink – there's a good chap."

Steward's expression, never sweet and welcoming, turned to one usually seen on old woodcuts of martyrs burning at the stake. Without any indication of his intentions, he changed direction and walked towards the galley.

"Coffee for the bosses with milk," Steward shouted as he came within hailing distance of the cooks.

"You'll have to milk one of the goats, Radford," Mr Bridgetower said.

"Let's look at the colour of your hands before you milk any goats," demanded Steward.

"Goats don't care what colour my hands are, so long as I don't pull too hard."

"No, but I care," Steward retorted. "Dirty 'ands means dirty milk and I'll get it in the neck."

Radford rubbed his hands on a piece of cloth, thereby probably making his hands dirtier than ever, he finished this cleaning exercise by wiping his hands on his shirt and trousers which were both as far away from Saville Row as one could imagine, but he seemed satisfied with the result. Steward presented the two mugs of coffee – one was George's flowered mug taken from No 18 on the day he left home. Mr Penaluna surveyed the mug with satisfaction and tasted the contents with disbelief. "Can this really be coffee, Mr Baguly – is it possible to maltreat the noble beverage to this extent?" Steward shifted uneasily from one leg to another. "I've had better Sir – but then I've had worse as well."

"If you have had worse coffee than this and survived, it says much for your constitution. Your guts must be hewn out of granite."

"I can digest most things Sir and in my time I have had to."

Mr Penaluna watched with admiration as his first lieutenant finished off the offending liquid. "I would say the best place for this coffee would be with the medical people, where it could be used as an emetic." He dismissed Steward with a wave of his hand. "We are going to get this trip and the return voyage to South Africa over and done with as soon as possible," Mr Penaluna announced. "I want Mr Eefamy back on this ship and in that galley. Come on Mr Baguly, let's crack on – hoist the studding sails, increase our speed. It's our only way to save our digestive systems."

On the deck it was fine and warm, many of the wounded were taking the air and enjoying the experience of being on board a sailing ship. Like most of the 200,000 men now engaged in the Boer War, they had sailed to South Africa in a steam ship. This was a new and thrilling experience for all of them. Mr Penaluna's crew was engaged in rigging up the studding sails – small additional sails used high up to gain just that little bit extra. 'Sails' was grumbling as usual. "They looks good but they does nothing," was his assessment. "All this work, sorting out the sails and using the correct poles to hang 'em from and what do we get?"

"Beauty," came the answer from Humpage, the helmsman. "Don't you ever think how lucky we are to be sailing the oceans in something as beautiful as the 'North Star'?"

"What's beauty got to do with it?" 'Sails' snapped. Humpage knew he was not going to get through to 'Sails', so he dropped the subject, but continued to look up at the white clouds of canvas up above and all around him.

"Fine sight isn't it, Humpage?" Mr Penaluna said as he approached the wheel.

"It is indeed Sir, I was just saying exactly that to 'Sails' five minutes ago."

"Did it register?"

"No, I don't think it did – he has no eye for beauty."

"Ah well, that's his loss. Did the studding sails pull her forward do you think?"

"Mr Baguly will know, Sir, he heaved the log just before they went up."

"Right. I'll check with him." With that Mr Penaluna went aft to the taffrail and there saw a rather pale and wan looking Mr Baguly.

"You don't look too rosy – anything I can do?"

"I'm alright now Sir – got rid of that coffee over the side – you were right – it's poison."

"Pity the poor fish. Come on I've got some really fine brandy, a nip of that'll set us up."

"Yes that would be welcome, Sir – but you are right, we need young George back with us."

'Young George' had by this time had three weeks of lying in bed in an Army Hospital in Cape Town and he was just about to rise and try crutches for the first time. The stay in bed had weakened him and that coupled with his lack of expertise with crutches meant that his first short journey up and down the ward was a very erratic affair. But he had managed it. The nurse told him to try it four or five times a day and to gradually become used to the procedure. George's determination helped him and he deliberately lost count of how many attempts he made: it was nearer ten or twelve and within a week he was fully mobile and regaining his strength. The medical staff were surprised at his progress and he was allowed to try his weight just for small periods of time. Yes it was healing and George was able to be useful in the ward, helping those who were more badly injured than he was. He inevitably became involved in the kitchen and helped to prepare the meals for the doctors and nurses. They had soon assessed the situation and it was obvious to them that their best chance of a decent meal was if George prepared it.

After about ten weeks in the hospital George was sure he was fit to leave, but the medical staff convinced him that another week would be advisable. During this last week a Miss Emily Hobhouse arrived at the hospital and George noticed how everyone treated her with great respect. Miss Hobhouse was a dumpy little lady of about 40, she had 'connections' and inside her was a zeal which few could match. Her uncle was Lord Hobhouse, an influential and busy politician. He had access to Campbell-Bannerman and Lloyd George and knew Joseph Chamberlain very well. All these people were very involved with the Boer War either as advocates or opponents of it, and Miss Hobhouse was determined to find out all the facts, and then hurry back to England, using the six or eight weeks of the trip to compile what she hoped would be a damning report. She asked why George was in a ward which, apart from him, consisted entirely of soldiers. Her suspicious mind had decided that the English were now using under age soldiers and she failed to recognise him as the cook on the 'North Star'. She seemed to draw no comfort from the fact that she was quite wrong in her assumption. She was not looking for information which cleared the English Government's name, quite the contrary. A week later she returned to the hospital to ask if George was now well enough to travel. The doctors agreed that he was, and with that information Miss Hobhouse approached George with the proposition that he should travel with her, out to the concentration camps to help prepare food, and where necessary, teach the inmates of the camps how to make the best possible use of their meagre rations. George's first reaction was that of a cook who usually is paid for his services.

"Will I be paid for this work and can I leave as soon as my ship returns?" he asked his prospective employer.

Miss Hobhouse answered "yes" to both questions. "I have been helped to come here by a very worthy charity, and I am not without funds, what is considered to be a fair wage for a boy of your age?"

"I am a boy – I agree, but I am also a ship's cook and Mr Penaluna paid me three pounds a month."

"Very well – then I will pay you the same."

"In English money?" queried George.

"Yes in English gold – now collect up all your things, - say 'goodbye' to the staff here and join me outside in ten minutes. We have journeys to make."

The concentration camps in the first place were set up to 'concentrate' the women and children in confined areas where they would be safe from marauding blacks who had realised that if the white men were away at war, the homesteads would be easy to rob. So the women and children were taken into 'protection' and the motive, if not the handling, was praiseworthy. But the numbers got out of hand as General Roberts began a systematic burning of all farmhouses when the war hardened. The original estimates of how many people would have to be re-housed doubled and trebled without the facilities being extended to accommodate the extra thousands who were pouring in every week. The good intentions were not matched by efficiency and the chronic overcrowding led to dysentery and many other diseases connected with poor hygiene. George and Miss Hobhouse arrived at just such a camp and were met by the Camp Commandant Lt. Colonel Scott-Ridley whose intentions were to stop the unlikely couple from entering. Miss Hobhouse however came well equipped with the kind of key which in South Africa, would open any door: letters from Sir Alfred Milner, High Commissioner for South Africa and Governor of Cape Colony – in all but name, Viceroy of South Africa. The Colonel offered Miss Hobhouse and George tea and then asked "What exactly is the purpose of your visit, are you a doctor or a nurse – what are you going to do now you are here?"

Miss Hobhouse's answer was precisely what Scott-Ridley did not want to hear. "I would like to inspect the whole camp, especially the sickbays and I would like to talk to the people in the camp to see how they arrived here." Scott-Ridley tried to interrupt but once the good lady was in full flow there was no stopping her. "Did they came here voluntarily, was transport provided? – I have heard of open railway wagons being used even in the winter." (She did not stop for breath, she was aglow with zeal). "Are there facilities for the children's education to continue? Are pregnant women well catered for? There are so many questions I need to ask." At this point she fluttered her letters of authority in the Colonel's face and he knew he was in trouble. He sought to change the subject by drawing George into the conversation.

"And what part is this young man to play in all this, is he a relative of yours?"

"No, he is no relation. I found him in hospital in Cape Town and decided to rescue him from there." She deliberately phrased her answer in such a way as to further illumine the imaginary halo that she always wore. George's reply was more down to earth.

"I am really a ship's cook and I might be useful – not so much in actually cooking – because I cannot cook for 2000 people but perhaps I can show some people how to cook."

"That would be very useful – you see many of the women in this camp had 'house boys' – slaves really - and they cannot cook."

"Well, they will have to learn – slavery was abolished sixty years ago in England and so far as the Government is concerned South Africa is part of England." Miss Hobhouse ended this little speech by snapping her handbag shut and standing up. "May we walk round the camp now and meet some of the people?"

"Certainly, I will call my Sergeant Major, and he will escort you round." Colonel Scott-Ridley went off to have a word with this formidable N.C.O., he wanted to ensure that, so far as was possible this very unwelcome guest was shown as little as they could get away with, and that she was escorted off the premises, with transport provided, as quickly as this could be arranged. The Sergeant Major was a tartar with his men, but he had little or no experience of ladies like the one he was now expected to dictate to. He was defeated within seconds.

"Take me to the hospital first and show George where the food is stored." He knew that neither visit would result in credit for the authorities, but he humbly complied with Miss Hobhouse's peremptory requests. George went off in one direction towards a large wooden building where the food was stored and the Sergeant Major with his busy bustling companion walked towards the 'hospital'. It was actually six large tents which had been joined or tacked together. Every bed was occupied and there was barely space to walk between each bed.

"May I see the medical supplies?" The tireless invigilator asked. Miss Hobhouse was shown the meagre supply of bandages, lint, splints, and crutches. "What use are these?" she demanded of the medical staff. "The people here are not injured, they have illnesses and need medicines – and where are the clean sheets, so the beds can be changed?" One or two of the nurses held up their hands and shrugged their shoulders in gestures of helplessness. Miss Hobhouse sat down by a table and took out her paper and pencil – the report had begun!

George wandering into the food store was met by two English soldiers. He told them why he was visiting the camp. "The lady I am with has an uncle who is part of the Government and she is going to report back to London if she thinks things are not being run properly."

"It'll be a bloody long report then," one soldier said. "Nothing is right here – this camp is in the wrong place, the land is too rocky, so we can't lay proper drains. The sewage is lying everywhere. It is not near a forest, so it is almost impossible to collect up firewood. Little arrives by train – they must think we like raw meat." He was in full flow and obviously he could have gone on. But George broke in and asked if he could look at the food supplies, adding that he was really a ship's cook. He was shown barrels of salt pork and beef, exactly like he was used to on board the 'North Star'. "You soak this overnight – do you have hard peas as well?"

"Yes, we do" came the answer. "But how do you soak it when you have no water?"

"Have you any spare tents?" George asked.

"Yes, there are a few."

"At this time of the year doesn't it rain fairly regularly?"

"Yes, it does – how does that help?"

"Well," said George, now drawing upon his experiences at sea, "You cut up the tent to make a giant basin and you catch the rain as it comes down and run it off into barrels." The two soldiers looked at each other and one said, "First sensible thing I've heard said for weeks – come on Bert we'll rig up something now, it usually rains in the afternoon." George felt quite pleased with his first contribution and he want off in search of Miss Hobhouse to see how she was progressing. He found the Sergeant Major who directed him to a tent which had been set up as H.Q. for the good lady. She was busy with her notes and hardly noticed George's arrival. George looked round the tent and saw that it was equipped with two camp beds – they were obviously expected to share a tent – perhaps it was part of Colonel Scott-Ridley's plan to get rid of them as soon as possible. George didn't mind he could sleep anywhere and by the time her notes were finished Miss Hobhouse was too tired to care.

The next morning the Sergeant Major arrived and it is to his credit that he did look embarrassed by the inadequate facilities he had been able to provide. "The Colonel says you will be welcome in the officers' tent for breakfast – it'll be ready in about fifteen minutes.

"Very well Sergeant Major" came the reply from beneath the blankets. "But tomorrow morning we will eat with the men."

This was bad news on two counts: one – she would see the contrast in what was on offer and two – she meant to stay for at least another day. The poor man went off to find the Colonel and to impart the kind of news which does little to improve one's appetite.

After breakfast Miss Hobhouse and George went to speak to some of the families who had been brought into the camp for protection. They confirmed that they had been transported many miles in open railway trucks and that their homes had been burnt down and now they were overcrowded and many were ill – this was what Miss Hobhouse had expected to hear and she bustled off back to the hospital tents to inspect the records there of how many people were ill, how many had died and what proportion of the deaths were due to cholera and similar diseases. She left George with instructions to stay with the women and help with the mid-day meals.

Many of the women were poor cooks: they had had 'house-boys' who saw to that side of running a home and they did not take kindly to having to cook. But George's easy manner and obvious skills gradually won over four or five of them and some sort of rapport was established. Later in the day it obligingly rained and some tents had been cut up to make rain catching equipment. Everyone agreed that this was a real step forward and George could show some of the women how to soak the pork and peas overnight and make quite an acceptable meal the day after. He found that though few clean sheets were to be seen in the hospital, in fact large quantities were available in the stores. George obtained some of these and proceeded to cut them up – he was going to show the ladies and the Army cooks how to make duff! George was happy doing this sort of work and he returned to the shared tent each evening ready to sleep and to continue his now very long letter to No 18 Wellington Terrace.

Miss Hobhouse and I are now in a camp where the Boers' wives and children were brought. Many farms and houses have been destroyed in the fighting and the black men are wandering about all over the area causing trouble. It is not all their fault: they were employed on the farms (many were actually unpaid, but they were housed and fed) and now, because of the war, the farms are not working they have nothing to do and nowhere to live. The trouble is the South African women were not used to cooking and they do not take kindly to the kind of food they are being told to cook. Miss Hobhouse says everything is wrong with this camp: it is overcrowded, with too many people trying to live in small tents, too few proper ovens, poor water supply – though we are near to a river. Another trouble is, the river has dead horses in it (there are rotting carcases everywhere) and the water is not fit to use. I feel just as sorry for the horses as I do for the people – most are English horses and they cannot digest the tough dry grass which grows here. Tom would be very upset if he saw what happens to horses here, because I know he loves Mum's horses and knows them all by name. Oh! I do hope Captain Penaluna comes back soon and I can get away to sea, and smell some fresh air again. Everything here smells horrid. The people can't wash properly, their clothes aren't clean, there is no proper system for anything, but I expect Miss Hobhouse will want to move on in a day or two and perhaps we will have an exciting train journey. I have made friends with some of the soldiers on this camp and they say I can post my letter with theirs' and it should arrive in about six weeks. So I will finish now, give my love to Polly, Marie, Rose, Ann, Caroline and Tom, and of course to you Mama

– I am alright now. My leg is quite healed, and I am quite
safe with Miss Hobhouse (who is a funny little woman,
she reminds me of the drawing of rabbits which were in
the books I had when I was little) – I think she is an
important person – even the Colonel in charge of the camp
is frightened of her. So I will not end by putting "I'll see
you soon" – but I will be home just as soon as I can. If
Captain Penaluna comes to see you – just tell him I am
safe.

Love to all

George.

George's letter did not make much progress for the
first two weeks, but then it was put on a steam ship with
thousands of other letters going back to England, and
within six weeks of leaving George's hand, it was being
put through the letterbox of No 18. It was addressed to
Mrs Eefamy (Clarissa) and Polly knew from the writing
who had written it, but it had to wait until midday, when
all the ladies assembled for a meal, before its contents
could be revealed. It brought forth the usual number of
gasps and expressions of surprise, horror and delight and
was finally put down by Clarissa with the question "Now
Polly, what are we having today?"

"Liver Ma'am" came the ever welcome answer.

"Good – let's be having it then – I have a lot to do
this afternoon."

The midday meal was usually a substantial one course
affair, followed by a cup of tea. Clarissa liked to be away

201

from work no more than an hour and she encouraged Ann and Caroline to be equally abstemious with their lunch break. "We can't keep the customers waiting – no customers means no money in our purses." This was Clarissa's way of running her business and it worked. She knew it was a source of entertainment for Ann and Caroline and to a lesser extent for her three servants – she didn't mind that – she knew that her fixation about work and success was really in danger of becoming too much and the fact that the girls occasionally made fun of her helped to keep everything in proportion.

The writer of the letter, meanwhile, was travelling by train with his now constant companion, Miss Hobhouse. They were on a supplies train heading for Bloemfontein in what became the Orange Free State. The Army had rigged up a covered-in wagon, so as to make it just a little more comfortable than an open wagon would have been, and two beds were placed in it. The journey was about 600 miles and they were told that it would take three or four days to complete it. In fact it took over a week. Marauding Boers gave them a lot of trouble and though the train was heavily guarded with English soldiers, the Boers found ways of delaying trains and often de-railed them. This did not happen in this case and after seven days they arrived in Bloemfontein. Miss Hobhouse lost no time in asking to see the camp Commandant, and she went through her usual procedure of waving her papers of authorization in order secure compliance with her demands. Like many zealots, she lacked charm, and made few friends, but she had a cause and that was all that concerned her. She was shown to the 'hospital' facilities and asked to see the records.

"What records do you mean?" the Army doctor asked.

"Why, the papers which are prepared when anyone goes into hospital – name, age, symptoms and so on."

"They are confidential – no doctor would divulge that sort of information to a casual visitor."

"Casual visitor," Miss Hobhouse spluttered, "I am no casual visitor – read this." She produced her now much travelled and somewhat crumpled letters, some signed by Sir Alfred Milner. The doctor read the papers and handed them back to their custodian. "Are you trained as a doctor or as an administrator for hospitals?"

"I have no qualifications, but what I have in abundance are standards, and I see no reason why a hospital in South Africa should be less efficient then one in London, Birmingham or Edinburgh."

"But we simply do not have the necessary equipment."

"What have you done about it?"

"We send in requisitions for what we need but only a quarter of it arrives."

"Then ask for ten times as much as you need and perhaps you will receive enough for what you want."

"The Commissariat vet all our requests for supplies and amend them to make savings."

"And where are they?"

"In Cape Town."

"And what do they know pray, about the circumstances out here?"

The poor dejected doctor was cornered. He was a very worried and no doubt a caring and sensitive man, but he was hemmed in by a system. "I only know that this war is costing over one million pounds a week to run, and the people in their comfortable offices are trying to save money." If Miss Hobhouse's make up had contained an ounce of pity she would have seen that her poor victim was already at the limit of his endurance, but she continued her questioning with relentless and chilling enthusiasm.

"I would like to see the patients record sheets please – I believe there is typhoid here and I need to see how many are dying and how many are cured." The appalling facts were that ten died every day during this period. The town of Bloemfontein in peacetime had been home to four thousand souls and over ten times that number were now within its boundaries. There was not enough water and the soldiers drank out of streams – further up the stream, it was probably being used as a repository for waste and sewage. Also decayed carcasses of mules, horses, oxen, sheep and indeed humans were quite likely to be found in every lake, river and stream. Field Marshall Roberts (Little Bobs) had ordered 'half rations' of food and water, and some of his men desperate for a drink in the long sunny days did drink out of streams with disastrous results. Milk was in short supply for the hospitals because 'Little Bobs had put cattle on half rations too and his men were dying in huge numbers. For forty years he (and his father before him) had been 'political army officers' in India, and he was hardened to the fact that soldiers do die in large numbers. He seemed to accept it as though to die was the inevitable lot of the common soldier. Like many Generals before and since, he forgot that they had family and friends too.

George was not with Miss Hobhouse during her long discussions with the doctors: he spent his time among the families trying to improve their cooking skills, but he found it all very wearing. The women did not want to learn to cook – their spirits were broken by the loss of their homes and their possessions. The main topic of conversation was about who had died and who was about to. The death rate went up to twenty-five each day and all pretence of formality or ceremony was forgotten. The bodies were sewn up in sacks and carted away for rough burial. It was all too much for George, he realised that his input was negligible. The problem was more than all the officers, doctors, nurses and even Miss Hobhouse could deal with and he made his mind up to leave Bloemfontein, and trek back to Cape Town. He knew it was hundreds of miles and he would not be allowed to go by train. He spoke to Miss Hobhouse about his plans and explained to her that he had tried to be of use, but now felt that he was resented and regarded as a young English upstart.

"Well, how do you propose to return to Cape Town – you will not be given permission to travel on the train."

"No, I know I won't, but if you could bring my pay up to date, I would buy a pony and small cart, stock it with food and make my own way back. Captain Penaluna will be back in Cape Town soon, and then I can join my ship and enjoy the fresh air again."

"How much do I owe you?"

"I have been with you for seven weeks, so that is just short of six pounds – if you reckon it at three pounds a month. Five will be fine with me, if you agree."

"Very well, I will pay you five pounds, and I do thank you for what you have done. I agree that the problems here are too much for boy to solve, but you have helped me and I will help you – here are ten pounds – buy a good strong pony and when you return to England, tell them just how dreadful the situation is in South Africa."

CHAPTER 9

George plans his return to Cape Town

George said his farewells to Miss Hobhouse and went off to look at some ponies he had seen over the last few days. He knew where there was a small two wheel cart which did not seem to belong to anyone, so he pulled it to a position near his tent and took a wheel off it so it was not such an attractive proposition to any other would-be owner. The man who owned the ponies could not believe his luck when a genuine customer arrived to buy a pony for ready cash. He had lived in fear for weeks in case they were requisitioned by the authorities, in which case he would have to wait for his money. Or worse still, he often wondered whether they might be driven off in the night by the Boers who needed them for their forays. George knew something about horses, thanks to his days out with Tom doing deliveries around the Poole area. Teeth were the real clue, and the evidence led George to a coal black mare standing only about twelve hands, but sturdy, and as he walked around to the other side of her, he saw she had only one eye. She was quiet and biddable.

"How did she loose one eye?" George asked.

"Bullet wounds." The owner answered. "She was on raiding parties for over a year and a bullet just grazed her eye, but the vet took it out – said it would never heal if he didn't." George moved a little closer and patted her, the pony turned its head and nuzzled George. She was an affectionate creature, he looked at her teeth and guessed she was about five or six years old.

"She's three years old" the owner lied. George kept his council and said "I'll give you two gold sovereigns for her – that's my limit." The horse dealer winced as if in pain and held out his hand. "Are you going to ride her – you'll need a saddle?"

"No – I have a small cart, so I need long reins and tackle to put her between the shafts."

"Come this way and take what you want – I have a shed full of the stuff. Just before you go, I'd like to give you a tip – always approach her from her good side. She must have been ill treated by some previous owner and if she is not just sure about who is coming near her she can kick, and a kick from her can break a man's leg."

George made his selection and put the chains and other items into a sack. He slung them over the pony's back and walked her back to his tent which was three miles away, right at the far side of Bloemfontein. He passed some English soldiers who were sat by the roadside. He hardly recognised them as members of the Army, their clothes were torn to ribbons and some of them had no boots, their feet were wrapped up in dirty rags. They had rifles but little else to identify them as soldiers. George stopped and asked why they had no proper clothes. "We have been here for a year now," one said, "and we have fought battles all over the place. We waded through deep rivers too." Another said, "We've climbed up hills, even mountains, and this is how we have ended up – like tramps. Anyway what are you doing here – you're English too aren't you?"

"Yes – I came here to teach the people in the camps how to cook."

"You should come back with us and show our cooks how to make a decent meal – our grub is lousy and not much of it."

"Well to be honest, I didn't have much success: the Boer women did not want to learn and those who did, had little to cook with, so I am going to find my own way back to Cape Town."

"Phew – that's about six or seven hundred miles – that's a long way for a young shaver."

"Yes, it is. My ship will be due back in about eight or ten weeks and if I can make it in that time I can get my job back as ship's cook and go to sea again."

"Back to England?"

"Yes."

"Where are you from then?"

"Poole in Dorset."

"I bet it nice there – near the sea is it?"

"Yes – Poole has a big harbour – we bought our ship there – it isn't my ship, you understand – I just work on it."

"Well – young man, we wish you well – do you think your horse is good for seven hundred miles?"

Another soldier broke in and said – "Keep to the railway track, go South and it will take you all the way to Cape Town."

George had been worrying about exactly how to navigate the huge journey and this piece of advice solved the problem for him. He let is sink in for a minute and said, "Thank you for that – yes you are right, I shall do and since they have built a railway it must be fairly flat land for my horse and cart."

"That's right mate – well get on your way and think of us when you're back in dear old England – give our love to the Queen."

George waved goodbye and led his pony away. Female she may be, but she was already named by George. In view of her optical inadequacy he named her Nelson. He put his arms around her neck and cuddled up to her as they walked along. They both knew, in spite of the brevity of the relationship, they could rely upon each other.

They continued the walk and as they went on George leaned closer and tighter – it was his way of shielding himself from the horrors that were on all sides: starving naked children, black and white looked out with huge pleading eyes - their parents squatted outside tents, mostly exhibiting vacant expressions and a body language which asked the question – what's the use? Some approached him and asked if he had any food or water to spare, and at the same time eyed George's plump pony: horse meat is always welcome when you haven't sampled any good food for days. George and Nelson hurried on. At last they reached the part of the town where his tent was – it was midday and a meal was ready. Miss Hobhouse asked George to join her and suddenly became very practical. "Put your pony in our tent and tie the flap so it is shut."

"Why? What's the point?" George asked.

"She looks like a desirable pony – someone could steal her to ride away on or indeed to eat – she would feed many families for a week."

"Yes – you are right – I hadn't thought of that – not here in the camp. I'll just get something from the canteen and I'll come back here and eat it."

George popped Nelson into the tent and went in search of something he could carry back. Once in the queue he noticed fruit was on offer, so he stuffed his pockets and his hat with apples and went back to share three or four of them with his new friend. He backed Nelson between the shafts of his little cart, collected up his 'bedding', which was really sacking, said his 'farewells' to Miss Hobhouse and went back to the Army stores. He had an idea that the two men who ran the stores might just be persuaded to part with a few useful items, and he knew they had been in South Africa for over a year, so they could prove to be a source of very useful information.

George had built up a nice relationship with the two storemen/soldiers, and they asked about his plans.

"All the way to Cape Town? – never," Bert said.

"It's true – that is my plan."

"Plan – I wouldn't call it a plan – more like a damn-fool thing to do."

"Well – it's horrible here and I want to try to meet up with my ship – they will not take me by train – so I'll go my own way – I crossed Denmark last year, on horseback, so now I'll try Africa."

"Well full marks for trying – what do you say Alf?"

"Yes. I agree – the Sergeant Major is away all day with the Colonel – so it is help yourself time – you are English aren't you?"

"Yes," George said, - not really understanding why the question was asked.

"Well – all this stuff in the stores is paid for by English taxpayers and you are one of 'em. So it's not stealing really you are just claiming what is rightly yours." Army storemen had always had a very hazy idea about storekeeping. If it can be sold or swopped, then it is usually alright by them. They understand the paperwork system so well that what ever goes missing they made out a requisition to cover it with an indecipherable signature at the bottom. Bert and Alf had taken to George and their largesse knew no bounds. The shed they 'looked after' was huge, so they invited George, Nelson and the cart inside and then they shut the big corrugated iron doors. "That'll keep all the nosey parkers out until we have finished all our business," Alf announced.

"Bully beef – one pound tins – best quality, officers for the use of. Thirty tins be alright for you Sir?"

George was speechless – he hadn't really thought out the practicalities of undertaking a journey which could take eight weeks. Bert and Alf had – they were experienced soldiers – they had been Sergeants but had been reduced to the ranks for stealing and could not believe their luck when they were made storemen. In Civvy Street they had been professional criminals, and this new job offered them unprecedented opportunities to ply their trade.

Bert put the tins onto the cart. "Tools, Sir – how are you off for tools?"

"What will I need do you think?"

"A spade, a 'ammer – a good axe and some cooking pots – they're all over there Sir – help yourself – they're all cheap today and matches, Sir?"

"Matches?" George asked.

"What you lights a fire wiv – to make your supper." It was all too much for George, he really didn't know whether to laugh or cry.

"Colonels and above – you know the ones with red tabs – their horses get oats – yes oats – now your horse is called Nelson, and he was an Admiral – so oats it is." Bert and Alf were now beside themselves with laughing, George too was helpless. "Oh you two. You'll be drummed out of the Army and all on my account."

"Don't worry son, we haven't had so much fun for weeks. You'll need a big piece of canvas to make a kind of tent for you to sleep under and an eight foot pole – if you gets bogged down you can lever the wheel out of the mud. Do you recall Alf when we had to use poles to lever those guns out of the mud?"

"Yes I do, Colonel Long ordered the guns forward and they came under heavy fire, most of the crews were hit and General Buller wanted the guns brought back. Long was hit and so was Hunt, and by then the guns were bogged down, we had to drag 'em out. We got them loose, but finally we just had to leave 'em, 'cos the Boers shot all the horses, and so we had no means of dragging 'em back." George was hearing it straight from the best

213

possible source – these men had been among it all and faced the enemy.

"Right now. Two or three Army blankets I think would come in handy. Oh! yes. We have some small tins of vegetables, everybody doesn't like 'em, but they are alright, stewed up with a bit of bully beef." Twenty or so tins went on to the cart.

"Keep the blankets off the cart, just for now," Alf called. "We'll put 'em on when we've finished – it'll cover up all the mischief." Alf gave a wink and a nod to George. "We don't want everybody knowing our business, do we George? Now what have we got? Food, tools, blankets, a good strong pole, matches, how about a good knife?"

"It's alright." George said. "I've got all my kitchen tools and they do include some good knives."

"Well then. That's got you fixed up I think, is there anything else you can think of Alf?"

"No, I reckon that's about it Bert."

"Would you mind if I delayed just for ten minutes? I would like to write home to tell them what I am doing. I can post the letter with you and it will be with them in a few weeks time?"

"Good lad – you write and tell your Mum all about it – we'll see it gets posted wiv ours – not that I ever write to anybody, but there's a lot that does."

As George was about to start on this great adventure, very strong feelings about his home at No 18 Wellington Terrace arose in him. True he had suffered there, but he had had more good times than bad, and because he was an optimistic person by nature, the worst experience had by this time faded right to the back of his mind, and although he was thousands of miles away from his home and because he was about to undertake a journey of many hundreds of miles alone, he felt the need to reach out mentally to No 18 to sustain him. Not that his strength of purpose was wavering but he was only fifteen and had comparatively speaking been 'gently bred'. He wrote the short letter and did not notice the two or three tears which fell upon it – some weeks later, Clarissa noticed, she didn't mention it but she held the letter to her bosom and subliminally tried to connect to George via a powerful loving upsurge and to wish him well, with all her emotionally charged heart and soul.

George handed the envelope to Bert and made a small speech. "I really don't know how to thank you." Bert and Alf looked sheepish. "We don't get much of a chance to help anybody here, so if our little gifts from the Government help you out, then we are happy, aren't we Bert?"

"Yes we are, my son, glad to help."

"Well I would like to give you a present – if I may?" George said.

Bert and Alf liked the sound of the word 'present', and moved a little closer. George took two gold sovereigns out of his purse and gave them one each. Bert made a move to try it with his teeth, in the time honoured way – Alf nudged him and made disapproving gesture. George explained "I have been well paid by Miss Hobhouse for coming out here, so I would be glad if you would accept these as a 'thank you' for all your help and kindness."

"Well I wish I was just landin' at Tilbury Docks with one of these in my pocket" Bert said. "Elsie would be in for a bit of a shock."

"And for a bit of something else too – if I know you" Alf added. "We accept gladly George and here's a little present for you." Alf gave George a large bottle of rum. Bert said. "'Ere Alf that's a bit risky, that's the Colonel's."

"Bugger the Colonel," Alf said. "It's George's now – just for those very cold nights between 'ere and Cape Town. In fact three would be better."

George's two friends carefully tucked the blankets over the little cart's contents. George took up his position on the cart and made the sounds with his tongue, just as Tom did as he started his day around Poole doing his deliveries. Then he stopped, jumped off the cart and ran into the arms of the amazed Bert and Alf – they both patted him and made the right sounds. George resumed his place on the cart, bravely waved and he was off.

"Follow the railway lines," Alf shouted.

"Poor little sod – he'll never get there," Bert said quietly.

"Do you know Bert – I wish we was going with 'im – there's bugger all for us 'ere," Alf replied.

CHAPTER 10

Trouble and Matrimony at Number 18

Back in Poole, at about the same time George broke his leg, Bert, Clarissa's full time Haulage and Stables Manager and part time lover, was spending the night on duty in the stables: one of the mares was about to foal and Bert wanted to be there. The mare was called 'Dasher', so called, sarcastically, because she liked nothing better than being left in her stall with some hay and half a bucket of oats. She was used in the haulage business as well, but because of her dilatory ways all the drivers complained about her, and if she was one of a pair on a bigger cart she didn't pull her weight and that made it difficult to keep the pair going in a direct line. But what she was good at was producing foals. This was to be her fourth, and it was no trouble at all to her. Bert moved into the stall with her and sat in a corner – he knew that Dasher would wake him up when she was ready. About five o'clock in the morning Bert was awakened by a large wet tongue being draped over his face – Dasher was ready. In fact the foal was half way out. Bert patted the mum-to-be and whispered gentle words in her ear (rather like he did to Clarissa), he continued petting her and moved to her rear where all the action was. He took hold of the baby and gently drew it out – she was beautiful, and Bert preferred mares, they were easier to train. Dasher looked round to examine the fruit of her labours, her eyes twice the normal size, enlarged by fear, pain and concern. Bert brought the foal to Dasher, who greeted the new member of Clarissa's haulage business with gentle licks and motherly murmurings. Bert opened the stall door, so he could drag the after birth out when it became tangled in his feet and he crashed onto the hard tiled floor. His head made violent contact with the open stall door and he lay unconscious until Tom arrived at half past seven. Dasher meanwhile had tidied up her beautiful daughter and shown her how she could obtain breakfast. Tom weighed up the situation in a second and began to gently splash water onto Bert's face. Bert came to and said. "Is she alright?"

"Yes she's fine – but how are you? – not drunk I hope – Mrs Eefamy will be here any minute to look at Dasher."

Clarissa came into the stables and saw Dasher and her foal and then saw Tom cradling Bert who was still on the floor.

"I found him like this," Tom said. "He must have slipped – there's blood everywhere – I thought it was from the birth but it is not – most of it is from Bert's head. Look at that cut – his head's split open."

"You stay with him – I'll go for Dr Montrose, that'll need stitching up." With that Clarissa went back into the yard and set off to the doctor's house at a good steady trot. They were back in half an hour and quickly went into the stable. Bert was still being cradled by Tom and was obviously in a bad way. Dr Montrose did all the checks such as pulse, regularity or otherwise of breathing, then set about cleaning up Bert's wound and stitching it up.

"This will hurt me more than it will hurt you," he said to Bert, comfortingly. "Or the other way round." Bert wryly answered with an attempted smile. Clarissa and Tom looked on as Dr Montrose put about fifteen stitches into Bert's skull.

"Let's get him to bed now," Clarissa said, and together they saw him safely to his bedroom.

"He can't go to bed like that," Tom said, indicating the blood stained clothes.

"You're right Tom. Leave him to me – I'll sort him out and get him into bed. You take Dr Montrose home."

Clarissa sat Bert on the bed and gradually peeled all his clothes off. She joked with him. "No. It's not what you think – it will be, as soon as you re fit, but just for now, you'll have to be a good boy and do as Mama tells you." She gave him a big kiss and in seconds he was fast asleep. Clarissa went back to the stables, told one of the men what had happened – that Bert would be 'off work' for a week or so, and then she asked him to clear up the mess which had been the cause of the accident. Next she went in search of the apple-bucket which was always kept in the stables to give the horses a little treat. She picked an especially rosy one and gave it to Dasher. "Well done Dasher," she said. "You and your baby have saved me about eight pounds."

George's accident took place about the same time as Bert's. George received first class help in the Army

Hospital in Cape Town, and Bert received tender care from Clarissa and a few fee enhancing visits from Dr Montrose. Bert commented upon this to Clarissa but although she would end up paying the doctor's bill, she was quite philosophical about it. "We all have to make a living somehow Bert," she said. This all took place in the Spring of 1901. By June Miss Hobouse was back in England distributing her findings to Lloyd George, Campbell Bannerman, Sir John Brodrick and to anyone else who was interested. Sir Alfred Milner returned to England to find that he was now Baron Milner of St James, and his dreams of renewing his delicious relationship with his Cécile would have to be put at one side. No more six day bicycling trips over the South Downs. One cannot keep a mistress and be such a prominent member of the Establishment – or so he thought. At least half of the members of that group of worthies could have told him exactly how it could be done. But he had suffered disappointments before – Margot Asquith had rejected the proposal of marriage which he had made nine years before in the shadows cast by the pyramids. He was of that metal, and he further stiffened his already taut upper lip.

Others who returned to England about this time, were Dr Conan Doyle (of 'Sherlock Holmes' fame). Rudyard Kipling and the young Winston Churchill. They were all eager to tell their stories. Perhaps the most cogent information would come from Sir Frederick Treves, an eminent surgeon whose opinions on medical matters could hardly be contested. His sympathies were always attached to those less fortunate than himself – witness his kindness to 'The Elephant Man' whom he had rescued from being an exhibit in a travelling show. His experiences in South Africa were heartbreaking and no doubt his opinions would be sought by Government and Opposition alike. Ghandi also saw the killing and the callous way people were treated. He said, "This is a white man's war."

But to return from world renowned individuals to lesser mortals: in the Spring of 1901, Bert – for the first time in his vigorous forty years – was in bed – not to sleep – not to make love – but to recuperate. He tried to supervise the yard, the loading bays and the haulage business from bed, but after a day or so, he realised it was impossible. The doctor had been very specific in his instructions, which were to rest properly otherwise the shock to the system caused by a bad fall would have lasting affects. Dr Montrose said to Bert and to Clarissa, "At least a week in bed, with a light diet and plenty of sleep and he'll be ready for two or three days of work a week, and then, see how it goes."

So the regime started whereby Polly walked from No 18 at about half past eight to Mrs Eefamy's yard where Bert had some rooms. She brought him his first cup of tea of the day, filled up his jug and bowl, so he could freshen up and as part of the light diet, prepared his ham and eggs for his breakfast. Mid-morning Clarissa brought him a mug of tea and at midday Polly was back with hot-pot or sausage and mash. Bert soon had his strength back and within ten days was back in charge of the yard and fully recovered.

Polly and Rose were busy in the kitchen at No 18 a few weeks after Bert's accident when Rose said, "You look a bit off colour today, did you not enjoy your breakfast?"

"It came up again – I don't feel well at all."

"Just you sit down Polly, I'll make a fresh cup of tea, you'll feel better after that."

"I don't think I will – I've been very silly, and I've got myself into trouble."

"What kind of trouble Polly?" Rose asked casually as she refilled the kettle.

"The worst kind."

"You don't mean ….. ?"

"Yes – I think so – I've missed twice now – Oh! Rose what will Mrs Eefamy say?"

"Are you sure, Polly – are you really sure?"

"Yes, I think so, but what do I do?"

"We'll tell Mrs Eefmay today, when she comes home for her dinner – there'll only be us three 'cos the shop's busy with a special sale today."

"What will she say to me – she'll put me out – I know she will."

"If she does – I'll go with you – I'll leave and you can come and live with me and Tom."

"Oh! Rose, I think I've gone and spoiled everything."

"Of course you 'avn't – anyway who was it – we'll 'ave to talk to 'im."

"It was 'im, at the yard."

"'Im" Rose said. "'Im? – and you were walking all that way to and fro to look after 'im."

"It's as much my fault as 'is – I should 'ave said 'No'. But I didn't – I suppose I thought he would know a thing or two – it seems he didn't."

Rose took Polly into her arms. Polly shook with violent sobs and it was just at this moment when Clarissa came home for her dinner.

"Now what's the matter, have you hurt yourself?" she asked. Polly couldn't answer for herself. Rose spoke up for her. "She's in a bit of woman trouble Ma'am – you know what I mean."

"Not ….?"

"Yes – that's it – a baby," Rose said.

"Who with?" demanded Clarissa.

"Tremblett."

"At my yard?"

"Yes Ma'am – 'im."

"Right – he'll have to wed her then."

Polly had never thought of that – neither had Rose – they looked at each other – was this the solution?

"Would you like him as a husband Polly? Well you must have liked him."

"Yes – I'm all confused now – I don't know what to say."

Clarissa was always wonderful in such fraught situations: It was just back to basics. "Let's have a cup of tea first, then we can talk about it over our meal – I think we can solve all these problems, it just takes a little time. You sit there Polly. Rose and I will serve the meal and then we will see what is best to do next."

Polly and Bert were married two weeks later with a special marriage licence and they settled down very nicely in Bert's room at the yard. Clarissa took on a young girl, Ruby, to help Rose, and everything calmed down nicely except for Clarissa's libido which now had no way of expressing itself. Bert was wise enough never to try any 'moves', realising that he was really lucky to have kept his job. Clarissa kept him in his place by invariably referring to him by his surname, although she used Christian names always for all her other employees. He never looked his boss in the eye again – it was just as well – he would not have liked the contempt that was there. He had lost a mistress but gained a wife.

Clarissa's thoughts began to turn towards Mr Penaluna more and more. The object of these (kind) thoughts was battling through the Bay of Biscay, after a very difficult passage up the west coast of Africa, Mr Penaluna made for Gibraltar for repairs. He had always carried what he considered to be a good supply of spars and upper masts, but the South Atlantic had been especially capricious and the damage led to his not being able to handle his ship as he would wish. He also discussed the plight of his one hundred wounded passengers with the Army doctors on board and they all agreed that a two week stop during the refitting would be beneficial and so the trip from Cape Town to England took longer than Mr Penaluna would have bargained for. At the back of Mr Penaluna's mind however there were advantages being considered. He had called at Gibraltar once before, whilst en route from Italy to Madeira and there were really good inns there. Geographically it was not part of England and never could be, but culturally it was. So good beer was available, as was steak and kidney pie, lamb chops, roast goose etc. Mr Bridgetower, his new cook, was fairly efficient but totally without imagination and Mr Penaluna did enjoy good tasty food with real gravy. Yes, he thought, two weeks or so in Gibraltar will put my stomach right. He was just a little bit afraid of what Clarissa's reception of him might be: she was very fond of George and it was natural for her to attach at least some of the blame to his skipper. Mr Penaluna's mind dwelt for some time upon the variety of dishes which George cooked so well – fish pie, chops, roast mutton. Mr Penaluna wandered round the taffrail and allowed his hand to feel the smoothness and quality of the teak, he looked back at the wake, at last there was one; after weeks of tacking, going about, searching for a good blow, there was a wake, they were making perhaps eight knots. He looked up at the sails, all was correct aloft and alow, Mr Baguly saw to that, they were missing one top-gallant mast, and that led to an irregular look to the mass of canvas, but the spares were all gone and 'Chips' could not fashion one of those. There had been talk of cutting up one of the sweeps, but Mr Penaluna decided against that. It would have ended up one hundred feet above the decks and well out of sight, but, no, that would not do at all, not for the 'North Star'.

CHAPTER 11

The Trek Begins

The cook who was so sadly missed by the skipper and crew of the 'North Star' left Bloemfontein by leading Nelson and his little cart out of town and towards the railway station. He had looked at some maps and if he was going to stick to the railways as his main guide, he reckoned Kimberley would be a good place to make for. It was about one hundred miles due West from Bloemfontein, he really needed to be heading South, but the main North/South line ran through Kimberley and if he could link up with that, there should be no navigational problems. He was reckoning four or five days of trouble free trekking and he would be at his first goal.

He walked steadily with Nelson for an hour or so talking to her some of the time, then he decided to try his hand with the reins. He kept the same type of conversation going and his transport system worked well. She liked George's voice and she pulled nicely at a good walking pace. After about fifteen miles George came to a Railway Depot, where locomotives stopped for coal and water. He drew up and tied the reins to a post, then he walked around to see if there was anyone around, he had two good sized carboys on his cart, they had contained disinfectant but now they were empty, and it would be handy to have them full of clean water. Two black men suddenly came round a corner and at first they were aggressive then they realised he was just a boy and they were very helpful. They smelled the carboys and advised George to give his containers a really good rinse out. Once they were full George could not lift them, and they laughed when they saw his futile efforts to lift the big glass containers.

"Bring de horse and cart here and we will put 'dem on for you."

George eagerly complied and the two ten gallon carboys roughly doubled the weight of Nelson's burden, but the total, including George was probably under three hundred pounds and George knew from his delivery trips around Poole with Tom that this was not unduly heavy for a sturdy pony like Nelson. As George drove away he shouted his 'thank you' and tossed his two helpers a one pound tin of corned beef. The smiles of the recipients seemed to be a yard wide.

George carried on for another hour and then he found a disused shed, only three sides were standing and it had no roof but this was a windy season and it offered some protection. He saw to Nelson first, by taking off her collar and tack, looking carefully at her hooves, and then tying her to a post with a thirty foot rope, so she had plenty of grazing. He laid out a ground sheet, ate an apple and was fast asleep in minutes. Millions of stars looked down on him, Nelson also came to look at him, but George was really tired and he did not wake up until dawn, which was about six o'clock. He looked around – Nelson was still grazing, she came over to him, he gave her an apple and a few good handfuls of oats – the kind which according to George's two friends in the army stores was for horses belonging to Colonels and above. Then a good drink of water and some gentle stroking and George could prepare his own breakfast: about half a tin of corned beef and an apple. He carefully wrapped up the remains of the corned beef – he didn't want any big flies, and there were plenty of them, getting interested in his meat. He wrapped up his blankets and ground sheet – decided that sleeping out was not so bad after all, and he was ready to be on his way. Nelson was wonderfully biddable, she took to pulling a cart very well. George looked around to check he hadn't left anything behind, saw the thirty foot rope, and was glad he had taken the trouble to be sure of his vital possessions, and they were off.

George sat on his cart and looked around. Everything was unfamiliar, and he tried to take it all in. He had become used to distant horizons on board ship. The horizons here were equally distant but the scenery was in every respect foreign to anything he had ever experienced: there were stunted, gnarled trees with few leaves and little sign of actual life. The grass was thin and tough, some of it stood up like handfuls of knitting needles, the colour was more or less the same wherever he looked. The grass, the trees, the bushes and the earth were all a dull faded brown and nothing moved. There were no animals, very few birds and no wind, so the trees and bushes were still and silent. At sea, movement was constant, the ship, the flap of the sails, the sea was never, or very rarely, without motion of some sort and the colours. George dwelt upon these colours, deep blue and every shade of green, and if you were lucky enough to be at the top of a mast as the sun rose (and George often took his breakfast up there) then there was purple and a dark wine red, just for a few seconds. The dullness of the scenery reinforced in George his desire to get back to sea, and he clicked his tongue to urge a few more knots out of Nelson.

The day became hotter and hotter and by midday it was too much. Nelson was a tough little lady, born and bred in South Africa but George knew it was too much for her, so he sought shelter under some trees, gave Nelson some water and decided to light a fire and try out his cooking skills. He soon found the kindling, and using the pots he had been given by Alf and Bert, he mixed up some corned beef, two biscuits, a little water and made himself some broth. He made sure Nelson was securely tied, took a roll of blankets from the cart and had a siesta for two hours. He arose from his sleep quite refreshed, gave Nelson half an apple, munched the other half himself and they were on their way again. They pressed on until sunset, George reckoned they were about thirty miles from Bloemfontein, and he was quite pleased with the progress they had made, but there were about seven hundred miles still to do.

George settled down for the night with his hands behind his head looking upwards at the sky. At least the sky was the same. He had often adopted just this position on the deck of the 'North Star', as she proceeded through warmer climes he had often slept on deck. He fondly remembered the sounds he loved: the creaking of the ropes, the bells at the correct intervals, the words that passed between Mr Baguly, who often stood watch at night, and Humpage who would have liked to man the wheel twenty four hours a day.

"Watch your bearings Humpage."

"I'm watchin."

"Hmmm"

"She won't go no nearer than that."

"Maybe two or three points?"

"No. Not with the sails as they are – I'd take up the main-course just a little."

"Mr Penaluna says not to alter sail without his say-so."

"Then she'll have to stay as she is, if we go over, the sails will empty, start a-flapping and Mr Penaluna will be up here in a flash and we'll both cop it."

"Right." said Mr Baguly.

George could remember these conversations in detail. They happened so often and Humpage always won. Mr Baguly used to get annoyed, probably still did. George smiled, he liked Mr Baguly and Humpage very much and with that he fell asleep.

Day three began much as day two had, except that everything happened more quickly: George now handled Nelson's tack with more expertise and he realised that he could save time by having his breakfast once he was underway, by controlling his pony with one hand as they went along, and eating with the other. Nelson also got to know the routine and would back between the shafts of the cart, ready to do her duty. It would have made an incongruous sight, had anyone been there to see: George looking typically English with his immaculate boyish complexion, still dressed like an English middle class boy of fifteen, driving a small plump pony and a decidedly ram-shackle cart piled with what looked at first glance like a collection of junk, but of course there was no one there to see it, there were just wide open spaces, a few birds wheeling overhead, but no people at all and apparently no animal life either. George had no watch, so he could not say what time of day it was, nor could he accurately calculate how many miles he was covering per day, but he reckoned he was on the move for about eight hours, at what was a brisk walking pace, so he was thinking in terms of twenty-five or thirty miles done when he decided to stop at the end of day three. He knew from his days out with Tom, doing deliveries, that a fit well fed horse could pull a cart for eight hours a day because that was a normal working day. He was comforted by the thought that he was not asking too much of his faithful and affectionate companion. He spent time each day walking with an arm around Nelson's neck, and he spoke to her a lot: he told her about Mr Penaluna, Radford, Hazel and how they kept chickens on board ship. He was always at her 'good' side as he walked along and occasionally she would wink at him, as if to say, "I know what you are talking about." As he drew up, at what he decided was a nice place to stop, he realised that his cart was very untidy. He had always hated his galley aboard the 'North Star' being disorderly. The only real rows he had ever had with Radford were about tidiness. George used to say to his helper 'If we know where everything is then, in the long run, it saves time'. So this evening he decided he would take his possessions off his cart, lay them all out on his ground sheet and then put them away tidily.

His first priority upon stopping was of course Nelson: he looked at her hooves, tied her onto the thirty foot rope, gave her a good long drink of water, and decided his evening meal would digest better if he had put his mind at ease vis-à-vis his possessions. He laid out his ground sheet and on it put his spare clothes and boots. The telescope he had bought in Australia with the profit of the cameos. His package of letters from home was next. Then he found quite a heavy parcel wrapped in canvas which he did not recognise. He unfolded the canvas and revealed an Army revolver and four packs of twenty bullets, with it was a little note which read "From your two mates Alf and Bert – just in case you need it." George picked up the weapon – it was quite heavy and saw that underneath it was an instruction book, which he read very carefully. Then, following the guidelines, he broke open the revolver, saw the six barrels were empty. Checked carefully how to load it and saw that it recommended that five bullets only should be put in position and the sixth chamber should be lined up with the gun barrel but left empty, so that if the trigger were pressed accidentally there would not be any disaster. He looked again to see exactly which was the 'safe' position for the safety catch and put the gun down on the groundsheet. He then read the instructions right through again, so he would know how to hold the revolver, how to aim it, and what sort of a 'kick' it would give. George then carried on sprucing up his cart, when he was quite happy about the state of his things he put them all back, except the telescope and the gun. He made up what was to be his bed for the night and popped the gun under his pillow. He then walked off fifty yards or so to a small hill so he could have a good look round with his telescope and see what sort of land lay ahead for tomorrow's journey. As he walked away Nelson whinnied, and George realised that she valued his closeness, and did not feel happy about his walking away, so he untied her, whispered some words of comfort and took her up the little hill with him. He put the rope on the ground and put a big stone on the end of it and Nelson carried on grazing whilst keeping her one good eye on George.

George found he could not keep the telescope steady enough for really good viewing so he walked around, watched with interest by his faithful steed, until he found a 'y' shaped branch of wood which he could use as his tripod. With this he obtained excellent views of his surroundings and using his slight knowledge of navigation and the position of the setting sun, he could see that tomorrow's twenty or thirty miles should be fairly flat, but there was a river or wide stream to be crossed. If he was lucky there would be a bridge, if not perhaps a ford would come to his help. It was suppertime, he was hungry now and tired and he was well equipped to satisfy both these needs.

Day four started all bright and clear. He carefully loaded his bed in such a way as to make a comfortable seat for himself on the cart, he tucked his revolver under part of the seat, checked that he had left nothing behind and as was now his custom he began the day with a brisk walk holding on to Nelson's bridle and talking to her. They reached the river George had spotted through his telescope and saw that there had been a good bridge but it had been blown up, and was now completely wrecked. It contained some useful wood however, and George cut up enough for four or five good fires and loaded it onto the cart. Cooking for the next few days would not now be any problem. George tied Nelson to one of the few wooden posts which had remained standing and he went to the side of the river to see if it could be crossed. The river was about sixty feet across but not more than two feet deep so there were no problems there but the most consistently level place for crossing was impeded by four large stones, each weighting two or three hundred pounds. George remembered Bert and Alf telling him how they had used poles to lever out guns. So he took off his socks and boots, picked up his pole and tried to lever the offending rocks away from his chosen fording place. He obtained some movement but not enough, so he put his pole back onto the cart, took his axe and decided to further dismantle the wrecked bridge. He selected a length of wood which measured about twenty feet long and was about four inches square. He sharpened one end of his lever to a wedge shape so he could slide it under the rocks and within an hour the job was done. He had spent a very pleasant hour in the water, and decided to undress, have a bath and to freshen up. This completed, he brought Nelson in with him so she would know it was not deep, and she drank her fill. Using his cooking pan he re-charged his carboys with fresh water, hitched up and crossed the river. He pressed on until sundown covering about thirty miles in the day and bedded down for the night.

Day five began early with the sound of gunfire. George had been in South Africa for about four months, and had travelled extensively with Miss Hobhouse, but he had not seen any actual fighting – only the terrible results. He took out his telescope and walked toward some acacia trees. Using a branch of the tree to steady himself, he looked carefully at what was happening. Men were entrenched about four hundred yards apart and were firing at each other. George had no way of knowing which were which, but an expert observer would have been able to distinguish between the two sides, because the Boers were using very modern Mauser rifles and special bullets which gave off no smoke when fired. So in fact the British soldiers were on the left and the Boers on the right. George kept moving his telescope from one area of action to the other. On the far right behind a big clump of trees, he could see about forty ponies were being held by four or five boys of about his own age. An officer in the British half of the conflict suddenly rose, pistol in hand, and signalled to his men to break cover and charge. He was immediately shot and dropped to the ground, but his men obeyed his last words, and with bayonets glinting in the early morning sun, they ran forward shouting. Some were picked off but about fifty of them managed to get within one hundred yards of the Boer position. The Boers rose out of their trenches. George thought they were going to run forward and fight their enemy, but no – they ran to where their horses were tethered, and galloped away. This was typical of how the Boers conducted their part of the war: they worked on the basis of doing as much damage as possible. When things were too hot, they dashed away, to live and fight again another day. George realised that the group who had suffered the most in the way of casualties were English and he hitched up Nelson and drove towards them at a steady trot. As he came near them he shouted, "Can I help?"

"What do you mean can I help," a Sergeant shouted back at him.

"I thought you could put one or two of the wounded men on my cart and I could take them to your hospital."

"Hospital! What hospital? We've got a tent and no proper doctors – but yes, it would help. Fred," the Sergeant shouted, "See if his Lordship can be moved and we'll get him on first." The Sergeant was referring to the young officer who had given the command to charge.

"No he's gone," Fred called. "Dead as mutton."

"Poor little bugger, he's only been out here two weeks – more or less straight from school. Put him on the cart and one other with a big wound."

So the weary procession made its way back to the camp with George in front. Seven other soldiers were wounded besides the one on the cart, but they did not seem to be unduly upset about being wounded. What they were really angry about was the fact that all their training and the various army exercises they had been involved in were of no use when confronted by an enemy who leapt onto swift ponies as soon as they had had enough.

"Why don't they stand and fight? – we'd show 'em if they did," one soldier asked.

"That is exactly why they don't stay," their Sergeant said. "This is a new kind of fightin' and our officers are going to have to sort out a way to beat them."

"Fat chance of that," another soldier contributed. "Our Generals have only fought fuzzy-wuzzies and Indians, and they were armed with spears and out of date muskets."

"Aye, well never mind. Now you are wounded you'll be sent back to Cape Town, and then shipped home. The war is over for you – lucky bugger."

George went into the camp and quickly decided that some people regarded him as an intruder and others were displaying a quite unusual interest in his noble steed. So he decided not to stay in the camp and he jumped onto his cart and encouraged Nelson to adopt a swift but not unseemly trot. After six or eight miles he linked up with the railway line and saw that it ran more or less due south. He turned in this direction and made his camp for the night - he was now approximately six hundred miles from Cape Town.

Day six began quietly and with no creature, human or animal anywhere near him, George had a creepy feeling he was being watched – it was too quiet and his suspicions were aroused. He went about his early morning routine rather like birds do when they are feeding: he was constantly stopping and checking halfway through each little chore, taking out his telescope and examining the immediate area and then right out to the horizon. Nothing to be seen, but his normal confidence was disturbed. He looked at his pistol, put it back under his cart seat, and used his telescope again. This time he did see something, some slight traces of smoke about two miles away. It was in the direction he was intending to take. He stood on the cart to gain a vantage point and saw the smoke more clearly. He also saw that all the terrain in the vicinity was devoid of cover and very flat. So the only sensible thing to do was to head in the direction of the smoke and hope for a friendly meeting. As he drew nearer two men stood up and looked in his direction. George withdrew his pistol from underneath his cushions and pushed it into his belt, at the same time concealing it with his coat. The two men walked towards him, one he noticed was carrying a very large ominous looking stick.

"What are you doing around here?" one of the men shouted.

"I am trying to make my way to Cape Town."

"Cape Town – that's five or six hundred miles from here, do you know your way?" The two men came nearer with every question.

"How about food – how will you manage for grub – can you feed yourself for weeks?" They came nearer. George halted Nelson, by now they were only a few feet away. George didn't like the look of them at all – they looked capable of anything.

"This is the railway line – it goes right back – it's run by the English Army, you could go to Cape Town that way, and give us your horse and cart," the other man added.

"No – the Army won't let me travel on their trains. I did ask at Bloemfontein," George replied, ignoring the suggestion about the horse and cart. Suddenly one of the men made a dart for Nelson – on her (literally) blindside. She lashed out with a rear leg and caught him in the stomach. His companion came forward at George wielding his stick, and noticed a .38 pistol being pointed right at him. His stick was raised above his head ready to strike and there it stayed – frozen whilst he weighed up the situation. The man on the ground was busy parting with his breakfast, so he was no use and the man with the heavy stick thought, 'if this stick moves even an inch he could fire at me'. He tried charm but nature left him ill-equipped for this method, he only came across as a rogue and a liar.

"Right. You got us beat – be on your way."

"You just stay where you are – don't move. Drop your stick and pick your friend up and walk slowly back to your camp."

"Yes. Alright – we'll let you go – but don't shoot."

George did not say anything, but he used the gun to wave them away. He looked carefully which way to make an exit, chose a route, jumped on to his cart and was away, at a fast trot. He looked over his shoulder and saw the victim of Nelson's hoof leaning on his companion. It could have been so different, George thought. If they had been welcoming, they could have opened a tin of corned beef together and had a pleasant breakfast, exchanged a few words, gained information. If that is how it is going to be, I must be on my guard, and I must if emergencies do arise in the next four or five weeks – I must make sure I steer Nelson around so that unwelcome intruders make for her blind side. He leaned forward and patted Nelson on her considerable rump. "Oats for you tonight my Darling," George shouted – "Oats – only for Colonels and above – but you'll have some." Nelson pricked up her ears and increased her pace a little. He kept going a little longer on Day six than he usually did, he would never have admitted it, but he did need to put some distance between him and the morning's activities.

George knew the seven hundred miles journey would take about thirty days to complete, and after about five days of travelling he realised that he was not really sure if he had been en-route for five days or six. It was vital to him to know accurately how many days he had been on the road, because he guessed he was doing twenty five or thirty miles each day. This way he would have a rough idea of what was to come. He did not want to arrive at a conclusion by way of two guesses. So he started to make a small mark with a knife in one of the side rails to his cart. He did this every morning and then multiplied it by twenty five, and then he would say to Nelson, "When we stop for tea tonight we should be six times twenty five, that's one hundred and fifty miles on our way towards home."

Day seven began very early, at 4 am to be precise: it was raining. George had become used to sleeping outdoors and not putting up any overhead protection. He regretted that as he roused himself and looked around, water was lying everywhere and the surface was bubbling as it often does when a lot of water is trying to soak its way into very parched earth. George's clothes and bedclothes were drenched. One of the cart wheels was axle deep in mud, causing the cart to tip many of George's possessions into the mud. Nelson looked on and came over to offer sympathy. George played with her ears and stroked her nose – she liked the rain. George hitched her up between the shafts and encouraged her to pull the sinking wheel out of the mud, which she duly did. Then George picked up his dripping wet bed and spare clothes and dumped them on the cart. He made sure the pistol was dry and wrapped his parcel of letters from home in the waterproof canvas with the pistol. Then he went to Nelson and made the right noises to indicate that they were off – it was still only about 5am, the sun was not up but it seemed like a good idea to leave this dismal, wet, dank place behind and to try to do a few miles. The rain continued, making progress slow because the hard ground of previous days was now replaced with clinging mud. George walked much of the day in order to reduce the weight on the cart. They had perhaps covered twelve or fifteen miles when they came to a river which was in flood. Swollen by the torrents of rain it looked quite terrifying and quite impossible to cross. George noticed the remnants of a bridge, and saw that part of the structure had been erected to adjust levels as well as to bridge the river, so he put the cart beneath it, tied Nelson to one of the posts and set about trying to make his first meal of the day.

The days travelling had been hard on Nelson because of the mud under hoof and wheel, so George decided to spend the rest of the day drying out his goods, and with luck the river would drop overnight and then he could see about a fording. He was aware of the fact that twelve or fifteen miles was not enough but they had averaged twenty five or thirty for the previous week, so he was not unduly concerned. Nelson was happy and doing what she did best – she was turning the dry crunchy hard South African grass into energy for the next day's pull. George spent part of the time examining what was left of the bridge and thinking of ways to repair it and get his equipage across.

Day eight began early: the sun was up and steam was rising from the ground. The river had dropped a little but it was still too dangerous to even investigate the possibility of fording it. George decided he would do his domestic chores first and then see how the day went, so using some broken spars from the damaged bridge, he rigged up a kind of clothes maiden and began to dry out his clothes and his bedding. He then climbed on to the bridge, all the time closely watched by Nelson, who by this time had come to rely upon him. Once he was on the bridge he quickly realised that the damage was not complete – not by any means: the gap blown in the middle of the bridge was no more than four feet, and as a result of the explosion many long lengths of timber had been blown loose. George walked back and soon found the track which led to the bridge and it would be perfectly possible to manoeuvre his horse and cart round to the track and to go over the bridge, provided that he could repair the four foot gap. He decided to have breakfast and then make a start on trying to contrive a method of bridging the gap. Having had his first meal of the day and seen to Nelson, George began to work underneath the bridge with his axe, and his pole. With a combination of cutting and levering he obtained about ten good lengths of timber and one by one he took them on to the bridge and laid them over the gap, beneath which the river raged and splashed. He walked over his repairs to the other side and saw that if he could traverse the mended part of the bridge, he was away. He knew from his many conversations with Tom that horses are blessed with something called 'horse-sense'; on occasions it can be very useful as it sometimes foretells disaster, and if heeded will avert unwelcome situations. He decided he would lead Nelson on to the bridge, without the cart, just to show her how well he had done and see if she accepted it, then he could collect his things together, get hitched up, and try to make up for lost time. She walked out on to the bridge with George but stopped six feet short of the repairs, looked at the bridge and then looked at George as if to say, "Well you are not Brunel or Telford are you?"

George said, "Alright, you wait there and watch me walk over it." He began, and kept turning round to Nelson.

"You see it is safe," he called. Nelson whinnied quietly and backed away. George walked back over his 'masterpiece' and took hold of Nelson's bridle and whispering to her all the time, led her forward. She stopped just before the repair and would not budge.

"Well what's wrong with it – you tell me," George said. He looked at his morning's work, and could find no fault with it, but he decided he would have a drink, gather his possessions together (his clothing was now dry). He would load up the cart and then try again. But no, Nelson did not fancy it and would not put a hoof on it. George stood there holding on to Nelson's bridle and looking at his work – it was the way to Cape Town, where he hoped eventually to meet up with his ship and all his colleagues, but how could he cross the bridge?

It suddenly occurred to him as he looked down at the timbers that he had laid them lengthways, that is, in the same direction as the length of the bridge, and he wondered if he re-laid his repairs sideways would his 'Clerk of Works' find that more acceptable? In half an hour, the new method was in place and he led Nelson over it without a murmur. "You funny old girl," George said gently patting his lovely companion. Soon she was hitched up, George checked the surrounding area to make sure that he had left nothing behind, and he took Nelson onto the bridge complete with cart. He proceeded gently but firmly and they were over safe and sound. "Come on beauty," George shouted. "You can make up for lost time now, we have a long way to go."

The going was good and flat and as one could expect right next to railway lines, and they made a nice steady six or even eight miles an hour until well into the afternoon, when George saw a train approaching. First he heard it, then a few minutes later it came round a bend and into view. It was drawing twenty or so wagons, all piled up with army supplies and an English soldier sat on top of every wagon with a rifle across his knees.

"Are you English?" George shouted.

"Yes, are you?"

"Yes, where are you from?"

"Manchester – best place in the world." Came the answer – there was no time for any more conversation – the train was gone. George waved and the soldiers waved back. No doubt the soldiers were curious as to how a young English boy could be here, thousands of miles from home, driving a little horse and cart across a deserted plain. Somehow these thoughts transferred to George himself and just for once he did allow his thoughts to go over the events of the last few months. His mind wandered over the beatings he had suffered at the hands of Mrs Collins and Rooney and how he had walked to Southampton and stowed away on the 'Bulldog'. George's mood brightened as he went over in his mind the wonderful stay he had had in Denmark, and how jubilant he had felt when he saw the 'Bulldog' moored in Copenhagen harbour. He then pictured himself sat on the jib of the 'Bulldog' looking back at that one hundred foot of canvas as she creamed her way in the wondrously blue Mediterranean sea. He gave a shout as this last picture went through his mind. "Giddy up Nelson, we are going to Cape Town, to re-join our ship and sail back to England – and you are coming with me. Tom will look after you – come on Nelson – let's get going." They covered over thirty miles on the eighth day of the epic journey and George gave Nelson a well deserved half bucket of oats and an apple as a 'thank you' for a hard day's work.

Day nine began later than usual: George had slept well and Nelson had good grazing, so she was quite content. Blue sky was what George noticed mostly, and the heat, it really was building up. By mid morning he began to wonder just how long they could keep it up. He cut up a sort of monk's hat for himself out of tarpaulin, and he found it so useful in protecting his head from the worst of the sun, that he made one for his faithful companion. She accepted this mild eccentricity with a resigned air, but George was sure that it was for the best. At about midday when the sun was at its hottest and was beating down mercilessly on the two travellers, a small clump of trees came into view and there was a stream nearby – heaven sent! George guided his rig into position and obtained the best of the shade. He uncoupled Nelson and led her to the stream, she walked into it gratefully, George removed his boots and socks and did the same. He then tied his thirty foot length of rope to Nelson's bridle and fastened the other end to a tree, so she could both graze and take advantage of the shade. He then took out his telescope and climbed one of the trees until he was about forty feet up. He knew from what little mathematics he had learned as an apprentice seaman (before he was 'promoted' to ship's cook), that his horizon from such a height would be twice what it was at ground level. He used a convenient branch of the tree to rest his telescope and survey his surroundings: about ten miles to the east there was a really large cloud of dust it seemed to cover acres of land. The cloud was so dense as to preclude any opportunity of deducing the actual source of the dust. George moved the telescope round but saw nothing else which would interest him or cause him concern. He moved his instrument back to the dust cloud, when a sudden sharp breeze blew the dust cloud away and revealed about two thousand oxen – they were harnessed up in fours and were pulling huge carts. It was part of the British Army's transport system. They were on the move – very slowly, grumblingly and erratically but they were moving – just. George decided that when they were nearer he would go and talk to the drivers. These few days of being alone and fending for himself had engendered in him an ability to plan ahead. He knew his journey was barely a quarter done and he must make provision for the rest of it. He wondered – could they spare him some hay? Had they any bread, apples? - a hat would come in handy. All sorts of things came into George's mind and perhaps they could spare him a little of what they had. He hitched up Nelson and decided to go in the direction of the dust cloud and try his luck. As he neared them, he saw six outriders, scouts, who were looking ahead and checking the lie of the land. One of their number spotted

George and rode over to him, few could resist George's winning smile and the soldier immediately asked, "Are you English?"

"Yes – how did you know?"

"You look English – hey Fred, Sarge – look what I've found, miles from anywhere."

"Are you English?" The Sergeant asked.

"Yes, I am Sir – from Poole in Dorset."

"What the hell are you doing out here then?"

"If you'll take me back to where you are camping for the night and if you'll let me have a cup of tea, I'll tell you all about it."

"Right come with us, we were looking for a place to stop. The oxen are just about buggered, great clumsy things, so we will be stopping soon and you are welcome to a cup of tea – can't promise you'll enjoy it mind."

The group of six scouts and George with his little wagon arrived back at the English camp and were greeted by an officer. "Is this a prisoner?" he called to the Sergeant.

"No. He's English, Sir. Found him wandering about out there." The Officer addressed George with the obvious. "What are you doing wandering about – there are Boers all over the place – you could get shot." The Sergeant interrupted by saying, "If it's all the same to you Sir, we'll take him for some grub and a cup of tea, and then I'll bring him round to your tent."

The Sergeant saw that George was a little uneasy and guessed the cause. "I see," he said. "Feed the horse first and then look after yourself. Is that it?"

George nodded shyly.

"Quite right too. Here you" the Sergeant shouted to one of his men. "See to this young fella's horse, give her some hay and a bucket of water. She'll be alright now – we have enough hay for a herd of elephants." George advised the soldier to stay on Nelson's 'good side', and pointed out why, and then followed his new friend to enjoy a cup of tea and some army stew.

George gathered from the evening's conversation that the oxen were to be rested for a day and he decided to accept the invitation to rest with them. He saw to it that Nelson was nicely settled and spent most of the time round a camp fire exchanging stories with the soldiers. They were surprised that this very young, very English looking boy had so many tales to tell. The men he was with were all from around Bury near Manchester and had never been anywhere prior to this war. The story they liked best was of George's brush with the pirates in the Mediterranean.

"Pirates?" one shouted. "Who are you kidding?"

"No. It is true." George's honest face and broad smile want a long way towards convincing them. "My Skipper shot their Captain, and we had a lot of muskets and we shot holes in their sails so they could not chase us. It's true – honestly it is."

"Where else have you been – tell us that?" another asked.

"Italy, Australia, New Zealand, and then back to here."

George then told them about the Concentration Camps and the horrors he had seen there.

"Are we fighting women and children too?" a soldier asked his colleagues.

Another one said, "What's it all about anyway? If the truth came out, none of us knows why we are here."

At this point the Sergeant came back and joined the little group. "'Ere Sarge, do you really know why we are here?"

"Cos that is what we gets paid for – I'm a soldier, not a bloody philosopher – I just do what I'm told and you had better get used to doing the same. Come on its time we all got some shut-eye. General Warren is coming tomorrow and everything will have to be in order." He then turned to George and said, "You go and see your pony and then turn in for the night."

Just as George was settling down for the night one of the soldiers came to talk to him. He was a strongly monarchist young man who had volunteered to come out and fight for the Empire. He was by this time more than a little disillusioned by what he had experienced, but it was greatly to George's advantage that he had been a Geography teacher at a Public School and he had a detailed knowledge of South Africa. He spent an hour or two with George and drew a good map of the route he thought would best suit George's ambitions. George carefully rolled up the map and promised to make frequent references to it. The young teacher/soldier was also interested in plants of all kinds and as the conversation veered in this direction, George was hoping for some tips about what he might find to eat, and just as importantly what to avoid. But this was not the young man's area of interest at all, he was a plants man. "Do you know that many of the most beautiful gardens and parks in England are planted up in beds during summer with flowers which grow naturally in this part of the world?"

No, George didn't know that, in fact he knew nothing about gardens, and if the full truth were known, he had never even noticed flowers at all. Although many parks and open spaces around Poole were beautifully planted out in the summer months, he along with ninety-five percent of boys of his age had never noticed them. But he listened politely to the young soldier's eulogy about flowers and the value of colour. He always responded to genuine enthusiasm and he promised the young soldier that he would look out for flowers as his journey progressed.

George wandered off and found Nelson with about twenty other horses, all contentedly munching hay. George laid his hand on Nelson's neck and wished her a good night. Next morning George awoke early and immediately went in search of his faithful steed. She was exactly where he had seen her the previous evening, still eating Government hay and looking very contented. George's experience with the two army storeskeepers at Blomfontein led him to believe that strict regulations were not adhered to this far from Aldershot. So he wandered about until he found some soldiers who appeared to be in charge of the drovers who tended the oxen. He made himself known, told them his plans for a trek to Cape Town, and asked if he could beg, borrow or steal a few things which might help.

"As it 'appens," came the reply, we 'ave about four hundred tons of hay, and yes, we 'ave apples and we are not short of bread. Now what 'ave you got?"

George opened his hand, wherein lay a half sovereign.

"For that you can have the bloody lot." The soldier pocketed the coin and said "Bring yer cart round and take it over there, where it'll be surrounded by oxen – Wilf, stir 'em up a bit – raise some dust, so nobody can't see what's goin' on. Now come with me and we'll load you up."

The men loaded George's cart with enough hay to last Nelson a week, a forty pound box of apples and three large loaves of fresh bread. This was all not very cunningly concealed under blankets – it did look suspiciously bulky.

"Right – on yer way now – no goodbyes – or they'll cotton on – off you go. Wilf, cause a little diversion over the other side, rouse a few oxen up and made some dust – Good luck young 'un – I hope you arrive alright."

George turned to wave but it was pointless: the dust storm had begun. Idle, discontented oxen were being stirred into activity – they knew not why. But they created a screen under which George could make his exit. He felt guilty about not saying 'thank you' to the Sergeant and his men who had gone to a lot of trouble on his behalf, but his cart did look conspicuously well loaded and so he carried on. Day eleven had now begun and he was well provided for, certainly for the next few days. George decided that, since he had 'lost' a day resting up at the army camp he would carry on until Nelson decided she had had enough. Well fed and watered as she was, she kept going and a good thirty miles were covered before she finally came to a halt. Her body language spoke with great clarity – this was enough. George agreed, made camp for the night, gave Nelson an apple and a 'goodnight' hug, and was soon asleep. Day eleven was over and everything was going according to George's plan.

It rained during the night and this caught George unawares: he had not put up his makeshift tent and he was very wet. The sun rose early to dry him and all his goods out, and he was soon on his way munching some army bread and an apple. A few birds wheeled overhead, occasionally he heard a scurrying in the bushes and scrub as soon little animals ran into hiding at his approach. He descended from his perch to stretch his legs and walked for a few miles, talking to his companion and offering her some words of encouragement. Nelson enjoyed their one- way conversations and seemed to up her pace a little as a result. It was not as hot as some days they had experienced, clouds shielded them from the sun for the whole of the afternoon and they made very good progress. Around teatime, a time fixed in George's mind because of his English upbringing, he came upon a burnt out farm. So far as he could see there was no one around, but he popped his pistol into his belt, told Nelson to stay and went forward on tiptoe to investigate.

The farm was one of many which Lord Roberts, the top English General had decided to destroy because they were harbouring Boer soldiers, and no doubt its original owners were now in the Concentration Camp, or at any rate, the women and children would be. George could see that some of the timbers of the farmhouse roof were still smouldering, so the house must have been a recent victim in the purge. George heard a scuttling noise in one of the burnt out buildings, and pistol in hand went closer. The noise had been caused by chickens, left behind when the farm was destroyed, there were six or eight of them, and though George had never killed anything in his life (Bo'sun and Steward did the killing on board Mr Penaluna's ships) he decided that, if he could catch two, he would do the necessary. He went back to his cart to fetch a crust of bread and the axe given to him by the army storemen back at Blomfontein. The bread acted as bait and two chickens were soon put on to his cart ready to be plucked and cooked. George wandered about looking for eggs and found about ten. This was proving to be a very profitable stop. He then looked around what had been the kitchen and found the kitchen chairs, these he broke up (except for one) and he threw these onto his car, they would act as his cooking fuel for the next few days. And the undamaged chair would come in handy if he fancied somewhere comfortable to sit as he had his tea, George was very English and a chair at teatime became a nightly routine. Further investigations in the burnt out kitchen revealed quite a nice drinking mug and a frying pan, these he added to his booty. He then went inside the remains of the house again and looked around. This time his thoughts were deflected from what he might salvage to what someone else had lost, as he picked up some scorched photographs and some children's toys, it came upon him very suddenly: this had been a home just two days ago, with children running around, probably a dog or two. The chickens would have been more like pets, and no doubt the children would have taken delight, every morning, going around the barns looking for newly laid eggs. He remembered Mr Penaluna saying once, "In war there are no winners, only losers." He had stayed there long enough, he had a journey to complete. He checked that he had put all his acquisitions onto the cart and he led Nelson out into the wide open country again. So that was Day twelve finished – he counted the notches on the rail, and realised that he had forgotten to make a notch in the morning. He did it straightaway and decided that, in future, he would do his notches at teatime. "That makes twelve," he said to Nelson, "And twelve times twenty-five, as we all know is three hundred and that is about one third of what we will have to do. So to celebrate – are you listening Nelson? I am going to have an English tea of two boiled eggs and bread and butter – well bread anyway." He put his pan of water carefully on his fire and cut Nelson a thick piece of crust. "You wouldn't like a boiled egg, but here is some bread for you – sorry there's no butter."

Day thirteen began extra early, the sun was up, no clouds to be seen and the morning was very bright, extra bright in fact because George was surrounded by flowers. They had not been there the day before tho' George had noticed that some of the vegetation was a new fresh green but he had thought of it only in terms of nice grazing for his pony. Mother Nature had to find ways of speeding things up, and just as frogs in the Arizona deserts have hastened up their metamorphosis to take advantage of the very occasional rain, so the flowers of South Africa have learnt to speed up their cycle: they rush into flower to attract insects, they become pollinated and produce seed when the conditions are warm and damp and by the time the flowers have cast their seed, the burning hot dry conditions have returned, possibly for a year or even longer. But the seeds are there waiting for the ideal combination of dampness and warmth, to begin the cycle again and perpetuate their own species.

George dismounted from his cart and walked with Nelson. She had tried the vegetation but it was not to her taste. George looked around and felt his spirits lift at being surrounded by colour as far as the eye could see. He was reminded of the local sweet shop near his home in Poole; the colours were so bright and cheerful, just like the rows of bottles of sweets on the shop shelves – bright yellow, red, orange, purple and some flowers were striped – like humbugs, George especially liked humbugs. This reminder of home helped George to smarten up his step and he whispered words of encouragement into his companion's ears. She trusted George and matched his pace and his enthusiasm with real eagerness. Day thirteen was a good one: the weather was ideal for their purpose: warm, even hot, but cloudy too, and they ended with Nelson tucking into the Government hay, and George roasting chicken over an open fire, exactly as shown by the tramp, who had cooked a rabbit for breakfast on the morning after George had made his escape from Number

18. When they had both eaten their fill, George decided to do another hour or two on the road, it was still light and with luck they could knock off another six or eight miles. An army train came along, loaded with horses. Nelson greeted them as they passed, eight or ten in every wagon. The sight of Nelson and George caused them to be restive, no doubt they were envious of Nelson's comparative freedom. Perhaps by way of horse sense they knew that they were to be part of that appalling statistic which showed that 400,000 horses and mules died during the Boer war – more than Napoleon lost in his retreat from Moscow. The train was guarded by soldiers, some of them waved to George, some, perhaps horse lovers, sat there glumly with a rifle across their knees thinking their own thoughts.

George completed his extra hour of journeying, Nelson did not seem to be any the worse for it, and he resolved to do this on future days if it was possible. He found a small but very active and clean stream to camp near, and led Nelson in for a paddle. After five minutes in the stream he waded out, undressed and went in again for a bath. He decided he would bath Nelson too and she patiently stood there, as George using his shirt as a sponge, gave his companion a real good cooling bath. He spoke to her as he way doing it – remembering how he was bathed as a little boy. "Good girl, you'll feel better after this, then you can have some supper and it is off to bye-byes, for a good sleep and tomorrow, if you are a good girl, I'll show you some more pretty flowers." When Nelson had had enough chatter and enough water, she thought, "I have indulged him enough, I want some hay," and she left him there laughing as she rooted under the blanket on the cart for her supper.

Day fourteen began early with giant ants everywhere. George had been tired by his long day the day before and he had tumbled into bed naked. He awoke before sunrise covered in ants – big ones, and they bit. His first thought was for Nelson – yes, she too was covered. He led her into the stream and rinsed them all off her, and then attended to himself. He returned to his little camp and saw all his possessions were crawling with the little invaders. He decided he could not cope with the huge numbers, so he put all his goods and chattels on the cart, hitched up Nelson, and, still naked, moved off for half a mile up stream, then one by one he took his boots, clothes, blankets, telescope etc into the stream and washed the ants away. The whole procedure took over two hours, until he was sure that he was rid of all his unwelcome guests and then he had breakfast. He looked back in the direction of the ants' nest and he thought had seen a dog or some similar sized animal in the area. He used his telescope and trained it on the place where he had camped. He recognised from books on animals that he had always had in his bedroom at No 18, that a giant anteater had moved in. George was not a vindictive person but he was quite happy to think of his tormentors being eaten. He was still itching all over and since it was a warm but cloudy day, he decided he would have another bathe in the stream, don his socks and boots, and spend the day naked, to give the all-over itchy feeling a breath of fresh air. Certainly there were no neighbours to complain, he did not see anything that moved all day, and by teatime another thirty miles had been completed.

Day fifteen began wet and stayed wet all day. George had never seen rain like this, it thundered down. George decided after half an hour of it, that there would be no point in even trying to stay dry. He used his tarpaulin to keep his goods dry and just let it all happen. He was soaked and so was Nelson. She kept looking back towards George as if to say "Can't you do anything to stop all this rain." Some of the time George did walk with her but his boots were full of water and his feet began to rub raw. The cloud cover did appear to be complete and the rain came down mercilessly. The lovely flowers which only the day before were so bright and cheerful were now closed up tightly in an attempt to save the precious pollen from being rinsed out prematurely.

The rain continued for hour after hour, until George realised that his cart was consistently rolling through six to eight inches of clinging mud and this was placing a real burden upon Nelson. The cart was becoming harder to pull, he really did not want to reduce Nelson's work by walking, because his feet were rubbed raw already. He knew that if they stopped, shelter of any kind was out of the question, and to add to his worries, it could become very cold overnight. If he and his trusty friend were soaking wet, it would be quite possible that they could catch pneumonia or some such fatal illness – and these thoughts were passing through George's head. He heard himself say, "If it carries on as bad as this, I could wake up dead." His sense of humour came to his rescue, "Come on Nelson, or you'll wake up dead as well," and he began to laugh – he laughed with his mouth wide open so the rain ran down his throat. "You'll wake up dead," he shouted. Then he got down from the cart, picked up his axe and smashed the fuller of his two carboys. He then lifted the broken glass off the cart and arranged the tarpaulin so it would catch fresh water. By this action he had lightened the burden on the cart by over one hundred pounds and ensured that his water supply was fresh. He did not climb back on the cart, he stood next to Nelson, naked as the day he was born, slung his boots on to the vehicle, and said to Nelson, "How do you fancy a stroll my little sweet heart – come on we'll go towards the park and perhaps find a little teashop and have tea and buttered crumpets. Come on my dear, follow me," and she did.

By mid afternoon George could see that up ahead, perhaps another ten miles on, the cloud cover was thinner, and as he got closer he saw that the cloud actually ended, and beyond that was blue sky. "Come on old girl," George whispered. "I think another hour, and we'll be out of this and into warm sunshine." It was the hardest day so far; day fifteen had provided no more than ten or twelve miles and it had been a real hard slog. Nelson was breathing heavily and hanging her head. She had given all she had got and George knew this. The sun must have known it as well, because mid afternoon, there he was in all his glory, making steam rise from the soaking wet land. There was no stream handy, so George used his newly collected water to refresh Nelson and to wash his muddy feet.

"What would Polly have said? he thought as he removed the mud from between his toes. Most of his few possessions remained dry beneath his tarpaulin – he offered thanks yet again to the two soldiers who had kitted him out at the beginning of his trek. He saw to Nelson's needs, gave her two very juicy apples and finished off yesterday's chicken. Then he removed all Nelson's tack and laid it out to dry in the sun, with his boots and all his clothes. There would be no little extra effort after tea to extend the day and add a few more miles to the tally; they had both had enough.

Day sixteen began early, a good night's sleep had worked wonders for both of them and they were ready for off. George's boots were not dry enough to wear, but he had spare pairs of socks, so he donned two pairs and decided to walk thus shod. A welcome breeze tempered the heat of the sun, there was a vast horizon all around and apart form the railway line, the whole area was exactly as it had always been for hundreds of years. George felt good. He slapped Nelson on her splendid backside and asked how she was. She looked at him as if to say, "it's alright for you." So George gave her an apple, she nodded her appreciation and slavered copiously. George thought he could see some movement up ahead, perhaps a mile in front. He got out his telescope and saw it was six or seven men, and they were coming his way. As they walked nearer to George and his vehicle he stopped, and they spread out into a line. He did not like the look of this at all. He thought of reaching for his gun, but decided not to – he couldn't shoot all seven of them. He just waited until they approached him. He soon realised they were English soldiers.

"Good morning – I'm English, are you?" he called.

"Yes, we are – what are you supposed to be doing out here – are you alone?"

George thought quickly "No I'm not alone, my father and my elder brothers are a mile or two back, they have been shooting hyenas."

"So why aren't you with them?"

"I'm not such a good shot as they are so I'm looking for water, and a place to make a meal."

"That's what we could do with – a good meal – what have you got?"

"Very little actually – some bread about two or three days old and some corned beef."

"That'll do for us," their spokesman said. George reached into his cart and uncovered the corned beef and the bread. Unfortunately one of the three bottles of rum given to him by Alf and Bert sixteen days ago also came into view. One of the soldiers reached in and then held it up triumphantly, "Look at this lads, we're in luck." They had the cap off in seconds and started to take swigs of it and it was quickly emptied.

"It's alright," one of them shouted. "Look I've found another," and they emptied that one just as quickly. One or two of them fell over straightaway and most of them sat down suddenly. The quietest one of the seven came over to George and said, "You've nothing to fear from me – I don't drink and I deserted for different reasons from all these men – I left because I was sickened by the incompetence of the officers – they left because that's the way they have always run their lives."

"What happens to deserters?" George asked.

"We would try to prove that we got detached from our comrades on a sortie – but if that failed we would be shot."

"Trains go past here every day, why not jump on one – at least you would get something eat – you are one hundred miles from anywhere – I know, I've walked it from Kimberley."

"There is an Army camp about thirty miles south of there, we dare not go there, but you could – you look as if you've been out here for months." George had never considered his appearance, but upon receiving this appraisal he looked down at himself and laughed. "You're right – I don't look as though I'm dressed for Sunday School, do I?"

The young man smiled and said, "Sunday School – that does sound like something a million miles away." They then surveyed the six other men: they were very drunk. They had guzzled the rum on empty stomachs and were no use to anyone for the next few hours, but George took comfort from the fact that they were not a threat either. George reached under his tarpaulin and gave the quiet man two tins of corned beef and seven apples. "These will keep you going to today, sorry I can't spare more, but I've a long way to go."

"You are very generous, and it's lucky for you that they found the rum, these are desperate men – I think they would have stolen everything you have and possibly even have killed you. Now go as quickly as you can, before they wake up."

"Why don't you come with me?" George volunteered, " I could say I found you out on the veld, delirious through lack of food and I've brought you back." The young man thought about it and then said, "Yes, I will. Thank you. When this lot wake up, if they saw I had let you go they would kill me anyway – so I will try to rejoin and we'll see what happens."

"Tell the officers you were taken prisoner by the Boers and you managed to escape."

The young man looked at George and said, " You've got an old head on young shoulders."

"As you can see, I have not had an easy life, I learned to lie when I was about eight because cruel people came into our family and it was a way of keeping out of trouble." Then as a complete change of subject asked, "Where are you from?"

"From London – I was at University, and I got this crazy idea about wanting to save the Empire. They said I should return after the war and resume my studies, so I thought I would see the world at the army's expense."

"And are you glad you did?"

"No, not at all – I wish I was at home – this war is all about money, and we are finding it very difficult to win."

It was too complicated for George, his aims in life and his pleasures were straight- forward things – he was not and never would be a philosopher. He said. "Grab an apple, we'll carry on for a couple of hours and then decide what to do next."

The day was an ideal one for travelling and they covered quite a few miles in the next two hours. When suddenly Nelson stopped. "Come on old girl" George called to her. No. She was adamant – it was teatime and she was ready for it. "Come on then, we'll stop for a meal here. How far do you think it is to the camp?" he asked the young man, whose name was Robert.

"We left there the day before yesterday and walked a long way the first and second days – I would say about fifteen miles from where we are now – at a guess."

"So if we have an hour's rest here and something to eat, do you think we could find it tonight?"

"But it will be dark soon – won't we get lost?"

"Not if one of us goes ahead and keeps us near the railway lines – is the camp near the railway?"

"Yes, it is" replied Robert. "But what's all the hurry?"

"This cart leaves a track that is easily followed – when the drunks wake up they might decide to come after us, and I don't fancy being wakened up at three o'clock in the morning with a knife at my throat."

"Yes, you are right, it is safer to carry on – so that is what we'll do."

They reached the army camp at about two o'clock in the morning. The guards were a bit jumpy but Robert and George managed to convince them that they were harmless and the duty Sergeant Major allowed them to sleep in the guard room which was just a wooden hut. Nelson was put into a big fenced off area with scores of other horses, but was soon enjoying a bag of hay. George rose very early next morning but was soon reassured that his little friend was quite content. When he returned to the guard room, Robert had gone, so George assumed that he mingled with the thousands of soldiers in the camp and probably no one in authority was any the wiser. George's nose led him towards the canteen and he queued up with all the men for his breakfast. They all wanted to know why he wore no uniform and why someone so young was wandering about in war torn South Africa. He told them his story – they listened and offered help. George knew the ropes by now and asked if any of them were storemen. They introduced him to the officer in charge of the stores – he didn't look much older than George – and he generously provided bread, corned beef, fruit and water, also a complete change of clothes – George's were in rags. George asked for a hat to ward off the sun, and was found one of the 'officers only' variety but was asked not to wear it until he was well clear of the camp. He put his 'stores' into a wheelbarrow and wheeled it back to his cart. When he returned to the cart it was surrounded by young soldiers who were all inquisitive as to how it got there – who he was – where he was going etc. He told them a very much shortened version of his story, wished them farewell and made a start to day seventeen.

The day was bright and clear, the flowers soon responded to the temperature and lifted up their many coloured faces towards the sun. Way over to his left George saw some dust being raised and by using his telescope saw that the six rum-swiggers of yesterday had given up their ideas of deserting and were heading back to the camp. George could not help feeling sorry for them and hoping that their undoubted mastery of mendacity would see them safely through. George looked down at his new self – the army had very kindly kitted him out with tropical clothes: cotton trousers and shirt and a broad brimmed hat. Since George was fairly big for his years and because the army did cater for its smallest soldiers, they were not a bad fit. George felt quite pleased with himself and he whistled as he went along. Nelson too seemed pleased with life, and so, she stepped out with real enthusiasm. He confided in Nelson, and told her of his main ambitions, they were (a) to arrive safely in Cape Town. "Are you listening? George asked. Nelson gave him a quizzical look, and he continued. "Then we have to find somewhere to stay – some place with a nice stable for you." He patted her at this point to emphasise his thinking, "and a bed for me – then we will have to wait for Mr Penaluna to come for us in the 'North Star' and when he is ready to leave, why then, we will sail back to England – you've never been on a ship before, but you will like it – I promise." He had started out this speech intending to go through it systematically or seriatim as Latin students would say, but his enthusiasm made him forget the 'b' and 'c' and 'd', as the speech became more and more detailed. "Then when we arrive in England," he continued, "You will go to the stables where Tom and Mr Tremblett will look after you, you'll have to work of course, Mama will see to that, everybody has to work if you are connected with the Eefamys, but you will like it and when you have finished your day's work, you will go back to a nice yard and meet all your friends, they will all be back after their day's work and then you will get tucked in to some really nice oats and hay – how does that sound?"

Nelson by now was used to George's conversation – it happened everyday. It helped Nelson a lot and it kept George sane. She seemed to recognise when a question was asked and this time she realised a response was due and she nodded her head. "Good Girl – I knew you would be happy with the arrangements." George reached in the box for an apple and gave it to his 'audience'. They carried on in silence. Silent except for the crunching and splashing sounds Nelson made as she excitedly ate her apple.

George climbed on his cart, arranged the sacks so they offered the maximum possible comfort, held the reins loosely in his hands and whistled the morning away. By mid afternoon he was looking ahead at a small town. It was Hutchinson, though George did not know that until two hours later when he rode into town. The first few people he spoke to did not speak English, but eventually he found someone who did and he was able to ask about the location and more importantly to George, how far it was to Cape Town – the man reckoned it was about four hundred miles.

"Well in that case – I have done most of my journey," George said.

"Most of the journey – where the hell have you come from then?" the man asked.

"Bloemfontein," George said nonchalantly.

"What! Bloemfontein – in that cart?"

"Yes, on this cart – with this pony," George said playing with Nelson's ears.

"Phew! You deserve a bloody medal. Come back to my place, my old woman will make you some hotpot, and you can take a rest with us for a day or two."

The man sensed that George was hesitating. "It's alright your horse can come too, I've got a big place – no horses myself, what I didn't sell got stolen, so I've plenty of room."

"Will mine get stolen too, do you think?"

"No. You'll be alright – we haven't seen any Boers here for weeks, all the fighting is hundreds of miles from here."

They drew up at a small tumble down house with a lot of out buildings. Nelson was led into one of them which had a proper stable door. She quickly turned round as the half door was closed and she began to kick it.

"She has never been inside anywhere before – I think she would prefer it if we didn't close the door," George said. The man nodded – he obviously understood animals.

"Come on let's see what my missus has got for us. Hello where are you?" he called, "we got a visitor."

A woman of about forty came out of the kitchen and was from the start glad to see George, he had that way of arousing a motherly instinct. He was soon sitting at the table with his hosts and learning all about them. They were Jim and Helen Starling from Yorkshire, they had come to South Africa originally to work on farms but Jim had gone to work with Barny Barnato for a couple of years and had made enough money out of diamonds to buy his own place. He and his wife had bred native South African ponies but were now out of stock, partly due to theft, but mainly due to excessive demand by the Boers and the English army.

"I wanted to keep my best stallion and say twenty of the brood mares but they insisted that I should sell the lot. So now we have money but no real way to making a living for the future. They did promise that I would be able to buy back the ponies after the war, but when will that be and will they survive?"

George had seen hundreds of dead horses in the Bloemfontein and Kimberly areas and knew they were being treated very poorly by both sides, but he had sensed that they were horse lovers, so he kept his information to himself. He changed the subject and asked "Would you mind if I just stayed one night? I know you did suggest I should rest for a couple of days here, and it is very kind of you, but I have a long way to go……."

George's sentence tailed off. Helen looked at her husband and hoped for some inspired reason why George should stay. The recipient of this warm sympathetic treatment was reminded of his stay with the doctor in Denmark, when Mrs Schymberg, the doctor's wife desperately wanted him to stay with them. George was not ungrateful, far from it, but he had been away from the sea for many weeks now and he had a great longing, which was to be with him all his life, and only at sea was he really fulfilled. So just as he had to be firm in Denmark, now he had to put his point gently but firmly. "The sea is very important to me – did you come out here in a sailing ship?" he suddenly asked.

"No. We came in a steamship."

"Ah well. There's the difference."

George's facial expression changed, it lit up as he began to think of the 'North Star' and that great cloud of canvas, and blue water sailing – as sailors call it when they are completely out of sight of land. "I don't know why it is so magical for me," George continued, "but it is and out at sea I am completely happy." And just as Clarissa had come to realise that she could not influence George, so Helen too, knew they would not persuade him to stay longer than he wanted to.

After the evening meal George and Jim went into the yard to make sure Nelson was comfortable. She was quite happy to be in the stable, just so long as the door was open. Jim looked at George's cart and said, "Look at the axles, they are very worn, a few more jolts and your wheels are going to fall off – come and look at this one." He led George over to a big shed in which a variety of vehicles were kept. He showed George one which was about the same size as his and said, "I'll swop you yours for this."

"That doesn't seem fair – mine is worn out."

"No. Your's is fine, it's only the axle that's worn. I can remove the old one and replace it. I've nothing else to do. Come on, we'll put your things onto this and get you tackled up, then you can be on your way."

An hour later Nelson was between the shafts of her new cart. George held the reins and was off. Waving goodbye to his friends in Hutchinson he began day eighteen of his journey. Suddenly he stopped and jumped off and began to cut notches on the side of the cart. He explained, "This way I keep track of how many days I've done, and it allows me to roughly calculate how much of the journey I still have to do." He made the right number of notches, day eighteen had really begun now, and he was on his way. The new cart was almost the same as his old one but it went along more easily. Jim had smeared thick grease onto the axle and he gave George a small tin of it, to use later on. "It'll make it easier for the horse." Jim had explained, and that was good enough for George. George had become used to all the squeaks and groans from the wheels but now they were silent.

Hutchinson was a little town very much on its own and so George was soon out into the remote and quiet areas many miles from any town or settlement and moving more or less towards the west. The sun was with him and in his eyes all day as he covered his twenty five or thirty miles and settled down for the night. Mrs Starling had given him a beef pie, big enough to last for two days. Jim had given him a bag of oats for Nelson, so they both fed well and day eighteen drew to a peaceful close.

Next day they were up early. George had a breakfast of bread and some corned beef. He ate it perched on the cart, and after an hour or so got down and walked with Nelson. They discussed the weather, their rate of progress and how much they were looking forward to finding Mr Penaluna's agents, asking when the ship was due in, when it was due to sail back to England. Nelson nodded agreement to the matters that George raised and seemed to be well suited with all the arrangements. Progress this morning was rapid, the freshly greased axles made all the difference and the cart glided along with little effort by Nelson. They stopped at midday as they usually did, this time they found a watering hole and Nelson took full advantage of it, threatening to empty it completely so enthusiastic was her imbibing. They entered an area, after their midday break, which was full of acacia tress and various kinds of bushes. George became suspicious of scuffling noises, and reached for his pistol. He could see nothing, but was aware that the branches on some of the bushes were being disturbed, but as yet he did not know the cause. He then came into a clearing where six hyenas were moving around menacingly. They ran quickly, but in no particular pattern, they yelped and screamed and showed their less than attractive teeth. Nelson was terrified. George descended from the cart and cocked his pistol. He had had it in his possession since Kimberly but had never actually fired it. One of the hyenas came a bit closer and taking a firm grip on Nelson's bridle, he fired. The bullet missed but the ravenous hyenas re-grouped, hesitated and came forward again, all the time making blood curdling sounds which could hardly have been more threatening. They had decided that Nelson was their prey and they were now as fearless as they were determined. One of them leapt at Nelson's neck and another at her haunches. The one that chose her rear came off worst because it received a hoof powered by six hundred pounds of bone and muscle – that one went yelping away, but the one at Nelson's neck did inflict a severe bite, before it was shaken off. The remaining four moved in quickly, George fired again, but the smell of Nelson's blood, charged the predators with something beyond courage; they were now quite deranged. They ran in together and all tried to leap onto Nelson or onto the cart. George jumped on to the cart, and still standing up, whipped up Nelson into a quick start, this threw off some of their opponents but one suddenly arrived on the cart, George pushed the pistol into its mouth and fired. The other hyenas stayed back for a second, and this was all George and Nelson needed, they put a few yards between themselves and their assailants and this gave George time to push the dead hyena off the cart. The group rushed forward and began to devour their erstwhile colleague. The scene of carnage was frightful, but just minutes later they turned their blood smeared faces away from the few bones that were left and yelped and screeched their angry message to the world. George could see that Nelson had sustained a nasty wound to her neck but he kept her going for another hour or so. She was more than willing to put some miles between her and the events of the afternoon, so she kept up a steady trot for many miles – sometimes trying to look behind as she went. Just making sure that their dreadful assailants were not following on. She and her master were safe, hyenas do not wander very far from their territory and the travellers had put at least twenty miles on to the distance between them. George put some of their success so far as mileage was concerned down to the new cart and the well greased axles. He reassured himself as to the exact location on the cart of the precious tin of grease – it was there alright. George began to whistle, Nelson liked the sound, pricked up her ears and quite spontaneously changed to a brisk trot. Perhaps this was something she had learned from a previous owner, but George made a mental note of it: the whole purpose of the past nineteen days had been to make it back to Cape Town. Any little additional skill which could be learned to expedite this end was not to be overlooked. Nelson's rhythm was greatly improved by the whistle and the grease, and the miles were ticking away.

Day nineteen ended in a railway marshalling yard, the men who worked there were all English, freshly arrived and eager to learn just what it was like further up north where the fighting was taking place.

Before George settled down for the night and after Nelson had had a good tuck in at the hay, he took a close look at the bite on her neck – there was quite a large loose fold of flesh and skin, so he washed the wound gently and wrapped it back into place with a large clean cloth which one of the engine drivers had given him.

George spent a wonderful evening round a camp fire exchanging stories with the engine drivers and firemen. There were in fact two varieties of each type – there were engine drivers and firemen (stokers) who worked on locomotives, and there were men who drove steam traction engines. George had never seen one before and next morning he had the wonderful experience of seeing them loaded on the flat railway wagon by means of long sloping ramps and their own power. They could do the work of twenty oxen and provided the land was fairly even and flat, they could travel up to one hundred miles in a day. George awoke next morning to witness the loading up procedure, he waved goodbye to his 'steam driven' friends and then coupled up his own outmoded form of transport and began day twenty with the strong but attractive smell of hot-coals, steam, oil and grease combining to make that aroma which, to steam enthusiasts, is so irresistible. He saw as he continued alongside the railway lines that many locomotives were waiting their turns to move into the marshalling yards. They carried horses and men as well as provisions and George was reminded of the chaos at London Docks when he left for South Africa for the first time. The skipper didn't know what to do next because too many ships had arrived at the same time, and again, when they arrived at Cape Town and then left for Simon's Town because there was no room to tie up at Cape Town. Confusion everywhere, and there did not seem to be anyone capable of solving the problem. The same lack of planning seemed to have spread inland to the railway yards.

The land rose a little and from the top of a small hill George could see his next twenty miles laid out before him. The railway line described a large loop but George could see the direct route through his telescope and so he decided to take the shorter road. At the far end of it was a water tower used by the engine drivers to fill up their water tanks, so he had a prominent datum point which he could keep an eye on, and three hours later he arrived there. He had expected it to be manned but it wasn't –

there were no workmen or guards to be seen anywhere. George could see that the water was guided into the engine's water containers via a tarpaulin tube. He decided he would like to avail himself of these first class shower facilities. He climbed up a ladder which led to a big valve, he turned the wheel and water gushed out of the tarpaulin tube. He tightened the wheel down a little to control the flow and when it was just right, he undressed and stood underneath. It was lovely! Still naked he loosened Nelson's tackle and drew her under. She was a biddable animal and obligingly stood there whilst George rinsed her off, she drank some of the water which had fallen into a trough. And so this scrupulously clean pair had their 'tea' and decided to make camp there for the night.

Next morning they were awakened by the arrival of a train, it stopped to take on water and coal. George had noticed that there were bays full of coal and the stoker was soon hard at it hurling shovels full of coal onto his tender. He saw George and shouted "Good morning" to him. They soon began exchanging information; he too was from England.

"Came out here for a change – it's a change alright – we have mechanical loaders at home – designed by Brunel – but here we have to shovel it on."

"Some of it misses," George said with a broad smile.

"You're right it does, but who cares? And once I've shovelled it on – then I have to shovel it into the fire."

"So how much do you shovel every day?"

"I don't really know, but I suppose it must add up to a couple of tons."

"Hard work," said the sympathetic George.

"Yes – but you get used to it and of course when you have stood on the foot-plate of one of these monsters, you really would not want any other job."

"I know what you mean," George said. "I feel exactly the same about sailing ships."

"But will you ever be skipper?"

"No – I think I will always be a cook."

"Well, there's the difference – one day I will be trained up, and I will be the driver, and someone else will be my stoker."

The engine driver had been following the conversations and broke in, "If you're a stoker, get stoking – we want to move out of here."

"He's alright really," the stoker reassured George. "He's a bit jumpy this morning because he thinks we might start to come across Boers as we go north, and they might fire at us."

"I've travelled all the way from Kimberly and seen very little action, so you can tell him that."

The stoker carried on with his back- breaking work and the driver descended to have a word with George. "There was supposed to be two blacks stationed here to help with the shovelling," he confided.

"I've been here since yesterday and I haven't seen anybody until you came."

"Ah! well. Never mind we're loaded now, so we'll move off – good luck with your journey.

Just as the stoker had completed his task and the driver had shouted, "That'll do now Jim," the two elusive incumbents came forward and gallantly offered every assistance. They had hidden behind a particularly hospitable pile of coal as the train arrived, and now made their entry upon the scene with consummate timing. A routine they had honed to perfection over the previous two years. They had compunction enough to offer very wordy apologies, and then burst into helpless laughter as soon as the train drew away. As it left the area, it revealed George and his vehicle on the other side of the railway. They looked guilty, then realising he was only a boy went across to him.

"What you want here?"

"I slept here last night, but now I am on my way south." George saw they were approaching very slowly.

"You got any food on dat cart?"

"Yes, I have," George said, and he put his hands under the tarpaulin to bring out a tin of corned beef and at the same time he slid his revolver into his jacket pocket.

"Only one – I tink you could let us have a few more."

George took out his pistol and clicked the safety catch.

"No, you don't need dat – we are not thieves and robbers."

"Very well," George said. "Just stay well back, it is loaded and I will use it."

The two men held their hands aloft and backed away. George suddenly realised that they were focusing beyond him and he turned round to see another black man coming towards him with a shovel, which he wielded like a weapon. George deliberately fired at the business end of the shovel, his aim was good, and at such short range the power of the bullet knocked the shovel out of his assailant's hands and the stuffing out of all three of them. They ran off into the bushes and George urged Nelson forward, Day twenty of George's and Nelson's journey had begun.

The flowers were still in full bloom. Tamarisk and worm-wood bushes were on each side. Sometimes the wheels ran over the worm-wood and this gave off a strong and decidedly pleasant scent. So with the attractive colours, the scent, and the sunshine, the morning passed exactly as George would have wished. He spent his usual hour walking next to his faithful companion, whispering words of comfort and whistling for her. This morning he decided to tell her in detail about all the people at No 18 who would be so pleased to meet her, and how she would be expected to work hard for Mama's business, but there would be days off and holidays, unlike the journey she was doing now. Nelson nodded and blinked her one good eye and put her weight against the collar. George's conversations always enthused her and she upped the pace a notch or two.

"Not long to go now old girl – well just between me and you – I think it is about three hundred and fifty miles to go, but that's not far – not compared with what we have already done – thanks to you – thanks to you my little friend." George carried on whistling and Nelson continued pulling. Thirty miles or so were covered in the day and it was corned beef stew for tea. George had helped himself to about thirty pounds of coal, so he was able to make a really lasting camp fire. Mr Starling had given

George a small sack of potatoes just before he left Hutchinson, and he placed three of them in the hot glowing embers of his coal fire. Half an hour later they were ready. George impaled one with his knife and tossing it from hand to hand, gradually cooled it off so it became edible. It was delicious, as were the other two. George gave Nelson an apple – and a good patting and tweaking of ears and settled down for the night. George looked around before he put his head on the pillow. There was Nelson grazing as usual, the daylight and the fire were dying out. Everything was alright. He closed his eyes and knew nothing for the next eight hours.

Day twenty one began the, by now routine, way of seeing to Nelson first, making some sort of breakfast, and eating on the cart so as to save time. This time he decided he would cook extra potatoes at teatime and save half of them for his breakfast the next day, he had always liked cold cooked potatoes. So with that important decision made he slid down from the cart, so he could walk and talk right next to Nelson's left ear. The land around gradually changed and they left behind the trees and the flowers and were among grass about two feet high. Nelson wanted to stop – this was the time honoured fodder for South African ponies, so George made an extra stop so she could fill up her considerable stomach. George stood up on his cart and using his telescope looked all around, it was grassland for miles except that about five miles away, where the breezes were coming from was a Boer farmhouse that was still smoking from its recent ravagings. George kept his eye on it and saw the grass nearest to the farmhouse catch fire, the flames leapt up and within seconds the wind brought the smoking fumes to Nelson's nostrils. She knew the signs, the information was in her genes – this was danger. She went forward at a smart trot. George was still surveying the smoke when the cart sprang into life. He just managed to hang on and eventually he got hold of the reins. Within half a minute the area to their right was all in flames and the more smoke came their way, the more Nelson increased her pace. The land ahead as far as George could see was quite flat, ideal for the present circumstances, but the flames and the heat were gaining on them, George tipped the remaining carboy full of water off the cart. Lightening the load by about one hundred pounds, next he threw off the box of coal and all his firewood. His glance lingered on the tins of bully-beef, but only for a second, and thirty or so one pound tins were thrown off, no doubt to be examined by some incredulous natives the day after, who would not be able to believe their luck. Nelson, wild eyed, nostrils flared, carried on mile after mile. George sitting in the driver's position imagining that he was actually in charge, but he wasn't. There are moments when training in obedience is subservient to dire necessity and Nelson knew what she had to do. The crackle of the flames grew louder, and the heat intensified. Dense smoke was now around them and George could not see the way ahead properly. He need not have worried; Nelson knew exactly where to go, she was looking at the road in front with her one good eye. The worst of the flames she could not see, and this was a blessing; if she had been able to see properly what was to the right of them, she might have panicked completely. As it was, she still gave all she had got, but in a controlled way. The flames sometimes licked against the cart and George tried to pull the tarpaulin around him to ward off the heat. He felt his hair and realised it was on fire, as was part of Nelson's main. George stood up on his hurtling cart like Ben Hur and thrashed at Nelson's burning main with his coat. Eventually he put out the flames only to find his own hair was again on fire. He put a coat over his head and damped the flames down. His scalp felt very tender and he looked at Nelson's neck, still sore from hyena bites, and saw that she too was scorched. Some of the time the flames arched right over them and they were going through a tunnel of flames and hot smoke. The fire and the terror it caused was not just experienced by George and Nelson: impalas were running ahead of them as were buffalo and wildebeest. George also saw his first lion, a female with two half grown cubs, they joined in the mad dash alongside animals which would under normal circumstances have been their prey. But there was no thought of killing now, only of surviving. The lioness, usually thought of as fearless, was just as terrified as the delicate impala. Their number grew, so that in front of George and his high speed cart were now scores of animals all trumpeting, howling or groaning their way out of this potentially lethal predicament. Nelson just followed them. Instinctively she knew that they knew where they were heading. Scores of animals were unified in their desire to escape the fire, all thoughts of supremacy were shelved, lions and impala ran together, desperate to escape their mutual enemy. None of them was more intent than George and Nelson. "Go for it girl" he kept shouting. "We are nearly out of it now – keep going Nelson, keep going."

Nelson's ears were flat to her head and her muzzle was flecked with foam. Like all of the herd of escapees, she was by any estimate giving way beyond what could reasonably be expected, but reason does not enter into it – fire is a spectacular source of adrenaline – and this largely un-researched attribute was being manufactured in huge quantities, and especially by the redoubtable Nelson. In spite of having a cart to pull she held her own for pace and stamina with all the other fleeing animals. George saw something up ahead which flashed. Now in the middle of one disaster, he imagined that the flash presaged yet another misfortune, but it was in fact the saviour of the whole situation: it was a wide shallow river, and all the animals splashed into it. The flames seemed to grow more angry at not being able to finally catch their victims, but the animals once in the water were safe and the fire, raging impotently, now remained on the bank. Having reached the imagined security of the river, many of the impala and wildebeest were set upon by crocodiles. The river changed colour as the crocodiles carried on their frenzied attack upon the defenceless animals. The more the river filled with blood the more crocodiles appeared. Some impala and wildebeest tried to turn towards the shore they had just left, and were immediately turned back by the flames and smoke. The monsters were ready for them, some of them were over twenty feet long and displayed amazing agility and flexibility as they dragged their prey under water and concussed others with their prehensile tails. Many half dead and limbless creatures floated away in a river swollen with their own blood. They would die a slow death and their rotting carcases would be the crocodiles' larder for the next few days.

Presumably they decided that a cart was inedible and allowed safe passage across to Nelson and her vehicle. The lioness and her cubs safely reached the other side, looked back over the river, saw the flames and continued to run at high speed. George noted the direction they had taken and went off at a tangent so as not to presume upon a hitherto trouble free acquaintance. A small stream now crossed their path, George, with his pistol in his hand checked it for crocodiles, seeing none, he alighted from the cart and led Nelson into the stream. He had heard Tom say that horses should not be allowed to drink excessive amounts of water after a hard run. So he brought Nelson out after two or three minutes and set her to grazing.

The frenzied attack by the crocodiles had left many crippled animals. George saw two impala wrecked beyond any help, and having seen Bo'sun and Steward on the 'North Star' finish off goats and sheep he decided to put an end to the misery of the two crocodile victims and at the same time furnish his table for the next week with fresh meat. He still had just a few good pieces of coal, which must have bounced out of the box just before he threw it off the cart. He had a few sticks of firewood, and his matches, so he made a small fire and started to go in search of more firewood when he noticed that Nelson had run off. She had enough fire and smoke for one day and even this small campfire was too much for her. George eventually caught her and led her back so she could, with her one good eye, see that this was a very small inoffensive fire. Nevertheless, she decided to keep well away from it, so George tied her up about thirty yards away from his overnight camping area and carried on looking for firewood. His dinner took about an hour to cook, it was haunch of impala and it was quite delicious. George then carefully piled sand, soil and stones onto his fire to put it out. He peed on it to make quite certain and then brought Nelson closer for the night. He didn't like the idea of sleeping thirty yards away from the love of his life. He notched the cart to indicate day twenty one and settled down for the night.

Day twenty two began early, the sun was up and Nelson was having breakfast. George decided he would delay his own meal until they were on their way but first he wanted to check on his possessions, he knew he had lost a lot of them during yesterday's mad dash, what he did not know was that he had gained nearly fifty miles. He still had his long pole and the tarpaulin. His telescope was there and his bundle of letters, also the pistol and some ammunition, and his small collection of cook's knives. He had started off with various cooking pots and pans, thanks to Alf and Bert in the Army Stores at Bloemfontein, but now he had just one metal cooking pot, the rest must have bounced off the cart during yesterday's mad dash. He still had one bottle of rum (thanks to Alf and Bert again) and some potatoes and apples were rolling about loose in the cart. His thirty foot rope was tied to Nelson and he found his tin of grease given to him by Mr Starling. He liberally applied this to the axles and noted how scorched, they looked. They owed their appearance to friction as much as to actual fire but they were still sound, and newly lubricated the wheels rotated silently as Nelson set off for the next part of the journey. George had his breakfast on the cart, it was cold impala meat and a not very bruised apple. Having finished he tossed the bone and the apple core into the scrub which was all around him and slid off the cart to have another one sided conversation with Nelson. Today he decided to tell his friend about 'Bulldog', his first ship, and how by an accident he became ship's cook. Nelson cocked an ear indulgently in George's direction perhaps hoping he would fondle it, and she plodded on. George regaled her with infinite details as to Mr Penaluna's likes and dislikes. He also told her about how awkward Steward could be, he then recalled that he didn't actually know what Steward's real name was, he had never heard it used. He mulled this over for a while, it gave him something to think about. George had a name; although he was 'Cook', he was never called that, all the crew called him George, though Mr Penaluna usually referred to him as Mr Eefamy. George realised that the skipper was gently pulling his leg by giving him this formal nomenclature. But George liked it, in fact he liked everything about Mr Penaluna and he told Nelson so, with great emphasis. And so the morning passed very pleasantly. At one point George did look back via his telescope at the scorched area behind him. It was still smouldering but the flames had died down, and he felt quite safe with the river between him and any possible further outbreaks of fire.

It was wide open country all day for George and Nelson: the land was dotted with tamarisk, marula, and leadwood and buffalo thorn. Dazzling Malachite kingfishers added streaks of colour. As with British kingfishers, they are not strictly speaking seen, they are merely experienced as they flash by at speeds too fast for the eye to really focus upon. The flowers were out enjoying the hot sun. George felt like indulging himself so he climbed back on to his little cart, drew out a good sized piece of meat, pushing his 'officers only' hat to the back of his head and had a mid morning meal. Feeling slightly guilty after this indulgence, he looked among the surviving apples, chose one with fewest bruises and offered it to Nelson. She nodded her thanks and approval, as she dribbled and scrunched her way through it. George stayed by her side and whistled the rest of the morning away disturbed only by his lack of knowledge: he kept seeing some birds slightly bigger than blackbirds, which were bright yellow but with black faces, he did not know what they were called and he decided there and then, that once united with his ship, he would buy books about bird life and then add to his knowledge as he went around the world. He confided this decision to Nelson, who nodded and winked at him. George took this as a mark of approval and putting his arm around her neck, he twiddled with her ears and they contentedly progressed towards the end of day twenty two and Cape Town.

Day twenty three began in a leisurely fashion; George decided to build a good fire and cook enough potatoes to last two days, he also cooked a good sized joint of impala meat. He was really keen to make Cape Town now, and since the weather was ideal for travelling, he thought he would take advantage and press ahead. He knew that the exercise of the last three weeks had made Nelson and him fit. He thought of Nelson's inspired and heroic dash through the flames and smoke, so he knew he was not going to ask too much – this was a very fit hardy pony but the sooner they were in Cape Town the better for both of them. George put all his cooked food into his cooking pot and put it on the cart. Then he carefully put out the fire by the now traditional if ill-smelling method, harnessed up his equipage and was away. He alternated between walking and riding and stopped only when Nelson spotted an area of really good grazing. This new system added impetus to the two travellers. At first George was not sure if he could really make it and, as much as anything, had started out to escape from Miss Hobhouse and the terrible Concentration Camps, but now he was confident he would arrive in Cape Town.

"Do you realise," he said to Nelson, "That this is the twenty third day of our journey and twenty three times thirty is six hundred and ninety, and even if we have only averaged twenty five miles a day it is (George got lost in his mental arithmetic) hundreds of miles we have covered and in a few days time we will be able to smell the sea." He was delivering this lesson in mathematics and optimism as he walked along – he leaned a little nearer to Nelson. "You have never smelled the sea have you? It is a wonderful clean smell and you will love it – I know you will." Nelson continued pulling, winking and nodding. All indications, so far as George was concerned, of approval and happy anticipation. At the end of day twenty three George and Nelson had covered nearly forty miles and for once they were uneventful miles. He started off the next day with renewed energy and a long day before them: George kept to his system and had a roasted (burnt?) potato for his breakfast with a little impala meat – that was the end of that source of supply as the rest was becoming a little 'high'. There were still a few potatoes left and a few lightly bruised apples but this did not really concern George any longer. He had gone without food before during storms at sea and he had survived. What had really become uppermost in all his thoughts was their arrival at the docks in Cape Town. Ahead of him lay about one hundred and fifty miles and the terrain was altering: he would have to surmount or negotiate very high mountains, but what made him optimistic about his chances of success was the fact that the railway ran, somehow, from where he was to Cape Town and though George did not regard himself as an expert on railways he was sure that the people who built the line had found valleys which, though not necessarily offering the shortest route, would in fact find a way through the mountains. He was about to find out because as the day wore on, the gentle hills became steeper until they kept him in shade, but the valley, sometimes the ravine, was wide enough for the railway line and for his cart. He had travelled through hundreds of miles of flat land, and now he was tackling the mountains, which he had previously seen from the 'North Star', when he first arrived in South Africa. Fortunately the supply of grazing for George's noble steed was undiminished and as long as she was well fed, George's motive power was assured. He decided that for the last few days he would manage some way or another. He was no expert with the pistol, but if he was presented with a chance to shoot some goat, deer, or sheep he would do his best. He slept next to a little stream which offered pure drinking and bathing water. Nelson had a good drink to start the day, and an apple. George had a scorched potato and day twenty five began, it was by no means epicurean but the weather was good, and so far as he could see with his telescope, the land ahead was predictable. A railway engine went by and the driver tooted George enthusiastically. George waved in response, each wagon had a least one English soldier perched on it with his rifle at the ready. George must have looked very peculiar to them; his cart was now virtually empty, he was almost bald because his hair had been scorched off in the fire, his cart was a ramshackle affair and Nelson didn't look too convincing because her mane was so badly burned as to bring to mind equine alopecia. Perhaps George realised his appearance was less than attractive, so he hurriedly put his 'officers only' hat on to cover up his bald patches, and he began whistling in order to exude some degree of insouciance. He drew some comfort from the fact that the soldiers were heading towards trouble and he was doing the opposite. Progress was good on day twenty five because the engineers who had laid the track had been instructed to level out a double width, just in case another line needed to be laid, and so George and Nelson were proceeding on a comparatively level road. The next morning because they were in a valley, the grazing was almost pasture, and George left Nelson for half an hour longer than he would have liked, so she could take on this excellent fuel. George's breakfast was one smallish pre-cooked potato, but they were off on day twenty-six.

Two longish trains went north in the morning. George managed to shout to one of the soldiers who threw him a partly eaten corn beef sandwich. George expertly caught it and consumed it slowly and with great relish. No luck with the second train which was devoted entirely to open trucks carrying horses, they were very restive when they saw Nelson – free, and they were couped up. Nelson stopped, a thing she rarely did unbidden, as though out of respect for her fellow creatures almost certainly going to their death. No more trains that day and no more corned beef sandwiches, so it was a very full Nelson and a very empty George who went to sleep at the end of day twenty-six.

The next morning George arose very early, awakened by his gnawing gut. He searched the cart. Nothing. Just the bottle of rum. He was tempted, but wisely decided against it. He made sure Nelson was securely tied on to her rope because if he found some suitable prey and fired his pistol it might just 'spook' her and she would be hard to catch. He stalked for about an hour, but saw nothing and decided to give up and restart his journey. He sat on the cart feeling just a bit fragile and off they went. After an hour or so Nelson began to look round, as best she could. Then it dawned on George that she wanted her early morning cuddle and chat.

"You old softy," George called. "You just want to be loved and to have your ears tickled." So he got off the cart and began his usual routine but found that after twenty minutes or so his legs were giving way. He had not had a proper meal for two days and it was beginning to have its inevitable effect. He made his excuses to his friend and climbed somewhat uncertainly back on to the cart. He held the reins and made the right noises and promptly fell asleep. Nelson was so used to the routine that she just kept going and it was two hours later that George woke up with a start.

"Look where you're going, you bloody fool, you're wrecking our camp." These words were shouted by an especially hirsute gentleman of enormous girth but little sophistication. George looked around and he was in fact in the middle of a camp – though even that lowly word was elevating the shambles that Nelson had stumbled into.

"Sorry, Sir – I was asleep."

"I could see that – how do you hope to control a horse if you spend your time sleeping?"

"I don't usually sleep as we travel, but I haven't eaten for two days and I must have nodded off."

"Well we've got food, but it's hard come by out here, what have you got?

George pointed to the back of his cart where some sacks lay. "In there," George said.

The man reached in and produced the bottle of rum. He held it high. "Rum, lads it's rum and a good make too – well done lad. Get down off your cart and join us."

George again offered thanks to Alf and Bert for provisioning his cart and in a very gingerly fashion, he descended from his perch to see what they had by way of food. He was not disappointed – they were roasting a sheep. There were four men in the camp and George didn't like the look of any of them. They came forward eagerly to sample the rum and began to rummage through George's possessions to see what else he had. They found the pistol, the telescope and George's packet of letters. They shook the parcel to see if it contained coins, and then threw it back on to the cart. They examined Nelson and commented upon her being one eye short.

"We'll get nothing for that old nag," one said, and Nelson was dismissed as useless. George realised he was in with a rough lot, but the smell of the roasting meat kept him there, as did his exhaustion.

"What else you got?"

"Nothing Sir – nothing – I assure you – look in the cart – I can't, I feel faint from lack of food – but do look, whatever there is you can have it."

"I've found something," the hairy one said. "What about these?"

"They are my knives – I am a cook and they are kitchen knives."

"A cook eh?"

"Yes, Sir – I was a ship's cook and I am going back to Cape Town now to rejoin my ship."

"So if you are a cook you'll know when this is ready," he said pointing to the fire and the carcass.

"It will need a bigger fire than that and some system of turning it, so it is cooked right through."

"Right. You do it- then you can eat and so can we."

"We need wood," George said.

"You," the hairy man shouted, pointing to one of his gang, "Smash up that bloody cart and let's have a proper fire."

George, even when fit, would not have been able to stop them, so he just let it happen. Nelson happily started to graze and ignored the behaviour of the uncouth humans she was now forced to associate with. The fire improved in size and intensity and after half an hour one of the men said to George, "Is it ready now?"

"Let me have a knife and I'll see."

The man gave him a knife and he plunged it into the thickest part of the rear leg – it ran pink."

"No, not yet it must run clear – if it runs pink it is not done."

"It'll do for me," the big man said. He grabbed a piece of cloth and using it to protect his hand he tore a leg off only to find it red inside – he looked at George with something akin to respect and said, "Alright, you clever bugger, speed it up or I'll throw you on the fire."

"There is no quick way, Sir, I promise you if we build a bigger fire we won't cook it, we'll just burn it."

The big man was desperate to have the last word as it was beginning to look as if his authority was being undermined by a boy. "Well think of something – we're not cooks, so think of something – NOW!

George went to his smashed up cart and retrieved his one cooking pot – this he placed in the fire in a strategic spot where the fat and juices were dripping. He asked if he could have a big spoon from his collection of cook's implements, and once the juices had reached the required depth he began to baste the carcase. The men were impressed and left him to get on with his work. An hour later they all had an excellent meal. Table manners, there were none, but enthusiasm, even a kind of awkward gratitude, there was, as the men wiped their hands on their shirts and lit their pipes. The mood changed, they were all friends round the campfire now, friendlier still when they recalled that there was half of the rum left. They did, to do them justice, offer George a swig of his own rum. He declined, and they finished it off.

George, feeling much better after his meal of roast mutton, wandered over to where Nelson was grazing, he held her head and said, "Never mind what those horrible men say, you're not an old nag, and I don't care even if you have only one eye, you are my favourite pony and somehow I'll get you away from here as soon as I can." George still had a kitchen knife in his belt and with it he cut away the long trailing reins which had been needed when there was a cart to pull. He left a short rein, long enough to ride with and looped it back over Nelson's neck. George was a good early riser, he guessed that the four toughs would not be and he planned to wake early, help himself to a leg of mutton and be off before the others were up, and this was exactly how it worked out.

The twenty eighth day of George's trek began very differently from the first day: now he had a leg of mutton tucked inside his shirt, on day one he had a cart well provisioned, and equipped. From now on it was just Nelson and George and they would have to take each day as it came and see how their luck ran. He gently approached Nelson at about five o'clock in the morning, before sun up. He put his hands to her muzzle to stop any little whinny of greeting, took hold of the bridle and together they walked away from the little camp and the four men. When they were about two hundred yards distant from the camp George jumped gently on to Nelson's back – this was her metier – she had, before George came along, always been a riding pony and she loved the contact and the interaction between herself and her rider. She adopted a steady trot, and George was now faced with the problem of learning how to ride bare back. Compared with what he had learned to do in the past month this was easy and within an hour he had the knack and felt confident enough to ease Nelson into a canter. They covered vast distances and by the end of the day were over forty miles nearer to their destination. George had so much confidence in the idea of following the railway that he kept to it even though he no longer had to consider the clumsy cart. He could have sorted out a direct route but using the railway as a guide precluded the possibility of becoming lost and occasionally, it did offer some fleeting contact as indeed occurred that evening. George stopped at a depot where the engine drivers took on water and coal, and sure enough a train drew up to take advantage of this facility. The driver and fireman were English and George had his first drink of tea since he didn't know when. He flourished his (partly gnawed) leg of mutton and the men had a good supply of fresh muffins. So with George's kitchen knife and his expertise, fairly presentable sandwiches were soon being enjoyed. The driver gave George two spare muffins, and thus tomorrow's food was certainly catered for.

"How far it is to Cape Town?" George asked.

"We were told we could expect water and coal one hundred and twenty miles out, so I reckon this is it."

"So with luck I could be there in three days," exclaimed George.

"You'll have a sore arse if you ride like that for three days."

"Well – I don't care, in the last month I've had a sore everything else," George said, ruefully indicating his singed hair and still rather sore looking scalp. He lay down in some deep tufts of grass quite near to the water and coal depot for the night and was soon asleep. Early next morning he treated himself to a shower, as he had done once before at just such a depot, saw that Nelson had a good drink and cheerfully munching the first of his two muffins he started off towards Cape Town. A few trains passed him, some going towards his destination, one driver did offer him a ride, assuring George that he would be in Cape Town by the next morning, but it would have meant leaving Nelson to look after herself and George did not contemplate that possibility not even for a minute. No. They would enter Cape Town together and wait for Mr Penaluna to arrive.

George had not given much consideration to the difficulties of actually managing his life once he and Nelson arrived in that big city, but, as he jogged along in the afternoon, he did begin to think just how it could be arranged. Money had not occupied his thoughts during the last four weeks, but now that the prospect of entering a city was a real possibility and practicalities like money do have to be considered, George began to think about Miss Hobhouse and the fact that she had generously paid him ten pounds in gold for his weeks of work in the camps. He had paid some money to Alf and Bert for helping him to provision his cart, and he remembered giving the two helpful soldiers some money when he had the overnight stop in the camp where the oxen were resting. So he should have some money left – then he remembered that he had pushed it into the tight hatband which went round his 'officers only' hat. He reigned Nelson in so that he could look properly and there cuddled tightly and safely were five full sovereigns and four half sovereigns. He confided this wonderful piece of information to Nelson and said, "Do you know what this means? It means that when we arrive in Cape Town we can find a little place where I can stay and sleep in a proper bed, and I'll make sure that they have a yard where you can be looked after properly, while I go into town to buy some new clothes and to enquire from Mr Penaluna's agents about the 'North Star' arriving back in Cape Town. It also means that during the last one hundred miles or so of our journey, if we see a nice farmhouse we can stop and buy food or perhaps ask for shelter and pay for what we have. Do you know what Nelson? I think we are going to make it – so come on let's do some more miles while it is still light and perhaps the day after tomorrow we will actually arrive in Cape Town." Day twenty nine ended quite peacefully, not in anyone's home but George could sleep anywhere, and the weather was kind to him, so sleeping outdoors was something he was now hardened to.

He rose early the next day and without anything to do but collect up Nelson and say a few words to her, he creakily climbed on to her back. He was not used to riding, and riding bare back meant he had to tighten his knees against Nelson's rotund body and the continuous use of relatively unused muscles left him very stiff. After twenty minutes or so of riding he slid off her back and decided to walk and then jog trot for a few miles to try to loosen up. He could not keep this up for long because he was short of food, so he found a suitable rock he could use as a mounting block and rode on at a walk for the rest of the morning, flexing his leg muscles as he rode to try to loosen up his locked and tired legs. About midday he arrived at a small farm and decided to enquire about food. They were an old couple who had lost their business because of the war and had little to spare but they did give George some bread and milk and George left half a sovereign on the table once he had finished eating. He suspected that they would have been too proud to take it from him, but perhaps, he hoped, they would be glad to find it. They gave him enough bread to last him for the day. George noticed by mid afternoon that the pain and discomfort had largely gone from his legs, the gentle pace of the day, and contact with Nelson's flanks had massaged the muscles, so he encouraged her into a canter and they kept this up for about two hours.

The next day was day thirty-one and George began it with real enthusiasm. True, he had nothing for breakfast, but his legs were easier and there was everything to look forward to. He called to Nelson who seemed to be just as eager to make a start as George was. He put his arm around her neck and they set off at a brisk walking pace. George was in grave danger of repetition as he listed all the advantages of a sea-going life. Nelson nodded appreciatively and seemed quite convinced that everything George said was true. Then after an hour or so he mounted and set off at a canter. By mid morning George was decidedly peckish, but no suitable stopping place offered itself, indeed this stretch of land just to the north of Paarl was quite underdeveloped with no properties of any kind, much less one which might offer food or help. Mid afternoon came and at last a very rickety farmhouse came into view. There were a few animals about the place and the front door was open. George dismounted, tied Nelson to a post and respectfully knocked and then called, but no one came. Suddenly an upstairs window opened and a large and menacing rifle was pushed forward.

"Get off my land, you have one minute, and if you are not off it by then, you'll get it." George looked up and saw a wild looking old man, just as rickety as his house. The rifle shook and trembled in his hands.

"I'm not a thief Sir, – I am just travelling through – I can pay for food, if you have any to spare."

"Moneys no good when there's a war on, and I need all the food I've got – so move off. Now."

"Right – I will, Sir. I am sorry I disturbed you – please don't shoot – I'll go now." George moved slowly towards Nelson, and led her away, he looked back and saw the old man making threatening gestures with his rifle. The man's hands trembled so much that George was afraid he would press the trigger by mistake. He jumped on to Nelson's back and trotted away from danger but into a seeming eternity of waste land and emptiness. He did see other houses, but they were deserted, and a thorough search did not reveal any food. Some of the places he saw had the odd chicken but they were too quick for him, as no doubt they had been for their legitimate owners, hence they had been left behind. Each successive hour raised and then dashed George's hopes and by nightfall he realised that he just wasn't going to find food or shelter. He found some fairly accommodating turrocks of grass, and dozed off into as good a sleep as a completely empty stomach will allow. In the night it grew very cold and it rained steadily. George woke up and decided they might as well make a start and try to gain a few miles, anything was better than sitting out on the veldt, miles from anywhere, cold, wet and hungry. He was at his lowest point now, so far as his spirits were concerned, and his stamina was also quite drained by the lack of real deep sleep. The dangers and uncertainties also inevitably played their part in dragging him down, and the hunger, cold and dampness of his clothes made it impossible for him to present any picture other than a bedraggled hopelessness. He was shivering, and feeling quite flaccid and beaten.

Cape Town was just a day's ride away as he approached Paarl, a small town which, when George rode in, was just ceasing work for the day. There were shops and stores but the shutters were up and one place, that looked as if it offered food was empty, giving the impression that it had ceased operations for the day. George took a half sovereign out of his hatband and held it in his hand. He had had no contact with any 'respectable' premises for over four weeks, and as he glanced down at his clothes he knew that he did not look like the kind of customer which any shopkeeper would welcome but he decided to try his luck. He knocked on the door and then walked in, a man and a women both well dressed and in aprons, stood there looking at him as he walked into their establishment.

"This is no place for you and we do not feed beggars," the man said. His wife stood beside him presenting a united and hostile combination.

"No. I am not begging I can pay, but I have been on the road for over four weeks – me and my pony, so I am sorry I am so untidy, but I need food and a bath and a bed and I can pay." George could not say anymore – tears of relief and exhaustion poured out of him – he stood in front of them shuddering from top to toe, slowly he opened his hand and revealed the half sovereign and slumped to the floor, the coin rolling away under the tables. The man and the woman picked George up and carried him to a bedroom, slid off his boots, put his hat on a chair, covered him up and gently closed the door. Nelson was watching through the shop windows, and somehow sensed that they would be safe here. The man came out and led her to a yard at the back of his place, then brought her a bucket of water and some stale crusts, a handful of carrots and some cabbage leaves, all new and very welcome flavour for a pony that has subsisted on dry tough grazing for weeks. Nelson made quite a few appreciative noises and decided that Paarl was a good place to be.

Inside the house the man said to his wife, "What are we going to do now?"

"I'm going to let him sleep for about two hours then I am going to wake him up."

"On purpose," interjected the man.

"Yes, on purpose, give him some food and then let him sleep until he feels right."

"I'll leave that to you then, I'll go and see if the pony is alright – then I'll lock up for the night."

It was just going dark, two hours later, when Mrs Woltjes went upstairs with a bowl of bread and milk with honey poured over the top. She woke George who responded eagerly to the proffered food and immediately went back to sleep. She then went downstairs and sat at a table opposite to her husband, looked across at him and burst into tears. Mr and Mr Woltjes were Dutch, they had come to South Africa to seek a new life, with their two small sons, that was ten years ago. Both the sons were now young men, they had ridden off months ago to fight the English and had not been heard of since. Now the chance had arisen for her to use her motherly instincts again and it was an English boy she was, completely by chance, going to look after. She did not bear any grudges against the English, she knew the war was about who could vote in the elections and who couldn't, it was also about money. Mrs Woltjes was not interested in politics or money, she wanted her boys back and in the meantime, even if it was only for a day or two she would look after the boy upstairs and do what she did best – make a home – a real home. She even allowed a tiny hope to creep into the back of her mind that this boy would stay. She thought this way because she had a dreadfully empty feeling in her gut that she would never see her two sons again.

The next morning began early as it always did for the Woltjes family. They ran a small business where anyone could call in at anytime and get something to eat and drink. It was a rough place, there was no choice, if you asked for food you got some. It might be a sandwich or soup or hotpot of some kind. Strong coffee was brewing all day. The customers were hard working men who were employed making roads, building houses or moving horses or cattle from one place to another, and so long as they could sit down for twenty minutes at one of the tables they didn't care what arrived on their plates. If the place was busy, then they would stand and eat, perhaps until a space at one of the many benches was made. It was an especially busy day when George opened his eyes, it was midday and the room downstairs was full of men, twenty or thirty of them, all asking for food. George had slept for about sixteen hours, he was now much refreshed but hungry. He found a bowl and washed his hands and face, thought about Nelson, looked out of his window into the backyard and saw her going merrily into a pile of hay. He raised the window and shouted. Nelson looked up and saw him, but immediately resumed her attack on the hay, she had more important things on her mind than idle conversation.

George went downstairs and arrived in the thick of it: midday was their busiest time and men were struggling to gain access to premises already bulging with hungry customers. Mr and Mrs Woltjes were busy making sandwiches – all the cooked food had been served. George weighed up the situation and decided that he could be most useful collecting up used plates, dishes and cutlery so he did this with some difficulty in such congested premises, then he started to wash up. He received smiles from the two owners and some help from one or two of the customers, who brought piles of dirty plates into the kitchen, and gradually the men's stomachs filled up, the dining room emptied and order was restored.

"I don't know any boy of your age who would have had the sense to help like you did there," Mrs Woltjes said.

"I'm a ship's cook, when I'm working, so I can usually see what needs to be done as far as food is concerned."

"Well, there's a job for you here – you stay here, my wife will look after you, and you'll have a roof over your head."

"That's a very good offer and I am very grateful for the way you helped me yesterday and let me sleep here, but I've been away from the sea for weeks now, and I do miss it. I would like to rest up for another night, if that is alright with you. Then I'll stay to help with the mid-day rush and be off to Cape Town.;"

Mrs Woltjes looked to her husband for help, she wanted to keep George with them. Her maternal feelings had been aroused, Mr Woltjes put his arms around his wife, who was missing her two boys terribly, he looked across at George whose expression said it all: he looked guilty and at the same time resolute. Mr Woltjes guided his wife out of the kitchen and called back to George, "Bring us a cup of coffee please – when you have a minute."

George carried on tidying up in the kitchen for about twenty minutes by which time, he guessed Mrs Woltjes would have regained her composure. He took in to the living room a tray of coffee for three, and a pile of thickly buttered toast.

"If my guess is right, you are just about ready for this – I know I am," George said. They all fell to, and a now resigned Mrs Woltjes said, "Your clothes look the worse for wear. I don't know why I kept them, but I have cupboards full of my boys clothes from when they were your age – I'll show you later and you can pick what you like."

"That would be very nice – I know I must have looked awful when I arrived yesterday – oh – that reminds me I must go and say hello to Nelson – is she alright?"

"Never seen a horse with such an appetite – she eats all day – so she must be alright," Mr Woltjes said. Together he and George went out in the yard and Nelson came to them to have her ears fondled.

"Are you sure you must leave – my Missus would give anything to have your say here with us?"

George's face again expressed guilt and shame at causing this very nice lady so much anguish. "I am what they call a 'sea going man' – I just love the blue sea, the fresh air, the great towers of white canvas and the adventure…….."

Mr Woltjes looked at George's face and realised, just as Clarissa had twelve months before, that argument and persuasion, logic etc were useless – he would not move.

"Come on, we'll go inside and you can sort out some of the boys' clothes. Oh. You mentioned that you would help out at mid day again tomorrow and then start for Cape Town – I wouldn't do that – I would advise you to spend the full day here, get up early the next morning and you should be able to make it in the day. But I would not advise you to be looking for somewhere to sleep between here and Cape Town. Wars throw up a lot of misfits, no good deserters, and they might hang about just outside a big city like Cape Town – you'd be better arriving there in day light." George thought about this advice for a minute and agreed to stay an extra night.

As George lay in bed that night looking at the ceiling, he thought this is the first proper roof I have had over my head for weeks – months in fact. He reviewed his present situation and regretted a few aspects of his journey: most of all he was sorry he had lost his bundle of letters and of course his lovely and very expensive telescope, but he still had Nelson and a very good chance of being reunited with his ship, Mr Penaluna, Mr Baguly, Radford and all his other shipmates. These thoughts raised his spirits considerably. Thinking about the bundle of letters reminded him that Rose, Polly, Marie, his sisters Caroline and Ann, and of course Mama would all be glad to see him and to make his welcome at No 18 Wellington Terrace. He reviewed his situation, decided that on the whole, he had a lot to look forward to. He turned over and fell into the kind of sleep known only to optimistic people.

The next day was again a very busy one with customers jostling for food in a good natured way. By two o'clock the worst was over and the hard working trio could settle to their own meal. When it was over Mr Woltjes took George into the yard and offered him any one of the many saddles he had. They tried one on Nelson's back, she seemed to approve, George sat on it and pronounced it ideal, so it was put at one side and would be very useful in ensuring that George had a comfortable forty miles ride the next day.

CHAPTER 12

George arrives in Cape Town

George rose early and went out to look at Nelson, and to tell her all the plans for the day. He put her saddle on and was tightening the girth when Mr Woltjes came out with saddle bags, which he laid over Nelsons ample flanks. He buckled them into place and explained that they were full of clothes on one side and cold pies and sandwiches on the other. "They'll keep you going – now come in and have some breakfast." The morning meal was a fairly sombre gathering. No one had anything to say, and when it was over Mr Woltjes said, "Make the best of this early start, forty miles is a pretty long trip in one day – so off you go and the best of luck." Mrs Woltjes got up from the table and went back into her bedroom, she had had enough of 'goodbyes'. George eased himself into the saddle and was off on the last leg of his journey. His host for the last two days went back into the house to comfort his weeping wife.

Once he was out of earshot, he leaned forward, played with Nelson's ears, patted her neck and with a loud shout cried, "Cape Town now, come on Nelson, we're off to Cape Town and to see the sea." His mount responded and they were covering the ground at a good canter. The saddle made it easier for both rider and horse, Nelson was tireless if she was allowed to choose her own pace, and by midday half the journey was done. George slid off Nelson's back and eagerly opened the saddle bag with the food in it. There was a big cheese and onion pasty for a start, and some big carrots too. They both munched their way through their treats. They were by a small river, one of many running through the area, and completely refreshed, they started the afternoon in very optimistic mood.

Properties of one sort or another were coming into view regularly but George had in mind Mr Woltjes' word of warning about misfits and deserters. Some people he saw George waved to, or raised his hat by way of greeting but he kept right on. They looked like people who were having a rough time and George knew that he looked comparatively prosperous. They were good clothes he was wearing and his pony was sleek and plump – jealousy can incite hatred, so feeling slightly less than secure, George kept going. Mid afternoon he met up with a man and a woman on a cart rather like the one which had served him so well. They looked very respectable and they greeted George very civilly.

"How far it is to Cape Town you ask?" the man said in response to George's opening remark. "Well I'd say on a good pony like yours, you could be there tonight – it is about eight or ten miles – look out for yourself in about two miles there is a little settlement there of blacks who are all out of work and there could be trouble."

"Could I find a way round them?"

"Not easily – some of the rivers are in flood, so it's best to stay on the main road."

"So what would you advise me to do – I would like to make Cape Town tonight?"

"Find yourself a good sized stick, wait until it is dusk and make a dash for it. If anyone comes after you, use the stick and go like hell."

"Did you get through alright?" George asked.

"Yes, some of them used to work for me before all this trouble started – my farm was burnt down because the Army thought it was being used by the Boers as a depot – it wasn't – in fact they stole all my horses."

"Will you be paid for them?" George asked.

"There is some talk of a compensation scheme, but we have to make do somehow until the war is over and the scheme gets started. Good luck to you – but find a heavy stick to increase your luck." George dismounted to look around for a suitable piece of wood to defend himself with. He found a piece of broken fence wood about two inches square and three foot long. Using his only surviving kitchen knife he pared away some of the wood so as to fashion a convenient handle. He tucked his weapon under one of the many saddle bag straps, and made his way towards the possible danger area. The light was beginning to fade and the frequency of shacks, tents and huts was increasing, so George knew he was in the shanty town area he had been warned about. He was going at a good canter when he saw three men, one of them on a horse about one hundred yards ahead, George moved slightly to his left to show them that he wanted to continue. They moved also, George withdrew his cosh from its straps – they too had sticks, nothing more lethal – George noted that – spears would have been another matter, but a clout with a stick he could put up with. The men began to shout – George was now within twenty yards of them – he raised his stick – Nelson raised her pace, and reared right at them. She decided the best form of defence was attack. The sudden shift of direction took the three men by surprise and Nelson's considerable shoulder knocked one of them spinning. Another aimed a blow at George which he countered with his own stick – it parried the blow but broke in two. George held on to his broken stick and urged Nelson to greater speed. The man on the horse urged his mount into the chase – his was a lightweight pony, faster than Nelson, and she might have the edge so far as stamina was concerned. The chase was soon lost, the man gained on George and he came alongside trying to grab the reins or the bridle to bring Nelson to a stop. George screamed at the man but he would not let go. The look on his opponent's face told George all he needed to know about his fate, if he lost this struggle. He rammed his broken jagged stick into the man's face. The man took both hands off his reins and held them next to his ruined face. George looked at his stick as he rode off. One of the assailant's eyes had been extracted and was impaled on the sharp splinters of George's stick. He hurled the stick away and vomited.

George drove Nelson on like he had never done in the five weeks of their friendship – he wanted to escape from the horrors of the fight and from the appalling injuries he had inflicted. Nelson responded as she had always done, by being the best little horse anyone could imagine. Up ahead George became aware of lights – he was on the outskirts of Cape Town. He rode along New Market Street towards the castle. To his right was Table Bay. "We are here Nelson – this is it – this is Cape Town – can you smell the sea?" No she couldn't as a matter of fact, but she could smell the carrots in the saddle bag. "You funny old thing – all you think about is food." George gave Nelson chunks of carrot, he found her mouth by putting his hand containing the precious vegetable in roughly the right place and waiting until she dribbled – this gave him a clue as to exactly where her mouth was – he could not spare even a glance to help with the feeding of his friend, he eyes were glued to the Bay – it was FULL OF SHIPS. There were barks, brigantines, snows, clippers, and many steam ships. George examined the sailing ships but 'his' was not there – "It could be at Simon's Town" he thought – but enough of conjecture – they were here – where they wanted to be and now the main job was to find a bed for the night and a yard to keep Nelson safe.

George decided that Nelson had done enough work for one day and he walked her into Darling Street. He asked a few people where they thought there was a place which could accommodate him and his mount. One man suggested Long Street, and he showed George where it was. He went into the first place he saw – it was quite an expensive establishment. The Manager told him it was five shillings a night for man and horse, fully expecting

George to turn away. George reached into his hat, produced a sovereign and said "there's four nights in advance." The Manager's attitude changed as if by magic, (it does in these situations) and he walked round the back of the hotel with George to show him where he could stable Nelson.

"Thank you," George said to the Manager. "I'll sleep here just for tonight, and I'll come in in the morning to get cleaned up, but I need to spend tonight with her." He began to fondle her ears and to whisper to her. Then just as the baffled Manager turned to go back into his hotel, George said, "Do you think I could have half a bucket of oats – or better still a full one?"

George found some spare horse blankets, and made himself a bed in Nelson's stable. He slept very well, and judging from the oats bucket and the supply of hay, Nelson must have spent the whole night eating. George woke up early, played with his friend's ears and went into the hotel carrying his saddle bags. The Manager showed him to his room, where he laid out the splendid clothes given to him by Mrs Woltjes and ran himself a bath. He luxuriated in the hot water for about twenty minutes then, selecting carefully, he dressed himself in what must have been a Boer family's idea of Sunday best. With the confidence that smart clothes do undoubtedly give, George went down to breakfast. The hotel's clients all ate at a large refectory type table and breakfast was concealed under large silver domes. George began at one end with his plate at the ready. Under the first dome was bacon, George took two rashers, then came sausages (two for George), eggs, tomatoes, kidneys and so on. George's face must have given evidence of unconcealed glee as he put his plate down. He offered a 'good morning' to his fellow breakfasters and fell to. Around the table were an English Colonel, a prosperous looking business man, two very prim looking ladies of uncertain age and two men who were sea captains. The sheer burden of George's plate and the gusto with which the design on the plate was gradually revealed brought forth a variety of responses. One of the sea captains said, "Well done – you must have been ready for that." The other captain applauded and started to laugh. One of the prim ladies who had breakfasted handsomely (for her) on a round of toast, was heard to whisper – not too quietly, that she did not approve of excess. The Colonel was very blunt and could not fathom out just how a young boy could afford such a good hotel and he said so.

"I can't actually afford to stay here for long, but I have some money and I have just ridden about eight hundred miles, so I thought I would treat myself and my pony to some luxury." George said this, but kept going, he still had a sausage and an egg to eat. His retort brought forth a variety of results: the spinsters received the information with incredulity. The Colonel said "Childish nonsense, who ever heard such blether? I know this country pretty well – tell us where you have been." He said this in such a way as to give the impression that he was laying a clever trap for George to fall into.

"We went by train to Bloemfontein," George began.

"Who is we?" the Colonel interposed.

"I was with Miss Hobhouse."

"Miss Hobhouse. What were you doing with her?"

"I went along to help teach the Boer women how to cook."

"This is preposterous nonsense – I've never heard such stuff."

"Well that is what I did – you can ask her yourself, she is coming back to Cape Town to catch a ship for London to make her report."

"Who will she report to – she has no real authority?" the Colonel said, determined to have the upper hand.

"To Lord Hobhouse, who is her uncle and he will take the report to Parliament."

"You seem to know a lot for a boy," the business man said. George was now able to give his undivided attention to the discussion because he had at last finished his huge breakfast. But before he could reply – the business man continued, "Who else did you come across?"

"We met Colonel Scott-Ridley who was in charge of the Concentration Camp at Bloemfontein."

"Did you stay long in the Camp?" one of the ladies asked timidly.

"Long enough to know I didn't want to stay any longer – it was awful."

"In what way awful?"

"Typhoid, cholera, not enough water, or food and people were dying every day."

The Colonel exploded, "I don't believe a word of this, it is organised and staffed by English soldiers – the finest in the World – they know how to run camps."

George said quietly, "There were thirty thousand people in a camp intended for four thousand – that is why I left."

One of the sea captains asked George how the Army managed to move its equipment over such vast distances.

"By railway Sir" George said. "I made use of the railway." The Colonel burst in at this point rather rudely, "I thought you said you rode the eight hundred miles."

"I did ride from Bloemfontein to here – what I was going to say was, I made use of the railway because of navigation problems which could arise on such a long journey, so I followed the railway lines, knowing it would end up in Cape Town." At this point George's eye alighted upon a rack of toast and a pot of butter which he thought warranted his attention. The Colonel was still determined to undermine George's story and he asked, "Did the British Army, in your experience, use any other form of transport for bulk materials."

George looked at his round of toast, noted with some pleasure that his teeth marks were already visible in the butter and replied. "Yes, mules, hundred of them, but General Warren favoured oxen as his preferred method."

"And how pray do you know about General Warren?" the Colonel asked.

"Because I spend one night on an Army Camp and they mentioned that he was at the camp supervising the methods by which the oxen were handled." George sensed that most of his fellow diners were impressed by his story and were tiring of the Colonel's blustering ways. Over a month spent looking after himself had imbued George with a quiet confidence, he had been there, he had seen action, death, and destruction and these things do equip a person to face up to life.

One of the sea captains then said to George "Are you staying here for a few days?"

"Yes – I have paid for four days in advance, but after that I will have to think about what to do. First of all I am going to see an Agent in town who works with Fothergill and Jones, they are my Skipper's Agents, and they will know when Captain Penaluna will be arriving."

"Penaluna." the Captain said. "I think I know him, sailed with him some years ago on the China tea run, must be the same one. Is he small, and always cheerful?"

"That's him," George said. "He's my boss. He owns the 'North Star' now, a clipper, and she IS beautiful."

"Owns his own ship does he? He always said he would, and he's done it."

"Yes, and I am the ship's cook."

"Cabin boy or some such I should think." The Colonel said – determined to make George look small.

"No – I assure you I am the ship's cook – we left the proper cook in Italy by accident last year, and I stepped in. I was made to cook when I was at home, and I learned the hard way – but I am a cook not a cabin boy."

The gathering around the table broke up and George went into Cape Town to enquire of the various agents, just who was connected with Fothergill and Jones and without much difficulty, he located Statham and Pomfret, an English firm and they confirmed that they were indeed associates of Fothergill and Jones. They were awaiting the arrival of Mr Penaluna's ship and concluded with the question "And who might you be?"

"I am George Eefamy – Mr Penaluna's cook."

"In that case I have good news for you – wait there a minute."

Mr Statham came out from an office at the back and presented George with five gold coins. These are with your Mama's best wishes – she is on the ship with Mr Penaluna, and they hope to be here in the next two or three weeks."

George was delighted, he still had some of the money paid to him by Miss Hobouse, but now he was rich, or at any rate, handsomely provided for. He thanked Mr Statham and told him he would be back in ten days or so to check on the 'North Stars' progress.

"If you need more money do call back – I was instructed to give you five pounds only, but there is more if you need it – so do not go short. Where are you staying?"

"At the Ram's Head Sir."

"Not a cheap place."

"No Sir. But we arrived late at night and they were good enough to take us in – so we stopped."

"Who is WE?"

"My pony Nelson, and I. I have to find accommodation for us both."

"But you don't need a pony now – sell it – horses are scarce, you would get a good price."

"No, I can't sell her now, she saved my life. She is going back to England. Mama has a small haulage business, Nelson will be very happy just doing local deliveries around Poole, and I'll ride her when I can. But she's mine, and not for sale."

With more expressions of gratitude, George left the Agent's office and went for a walk around the harbour. It was full of ships, mainly steamers, but there was a fair scattering of sailing ships too. He spent an hour or more looking at the ships, some of which were tied up at the wharves. He could see that they were unloading mules, horses, ammunition, food etc, all the things which were needed to run a war. He had had enough of war, he turned his back on the harbour and went back to the Ram's Head for his midday meal. On the way back he went into a little shop and bought all that was necessary to write a letter. Ships were leaving for England everyday and he wanted to form a link, however tenuous, between himself and all the people he loved so much at No 18 Wellington Terrace.

CHAPTER 13

Mr Penaluna's Interview

Some weeks before George's arrival back in Cape Town, Mr Penaluna had safely arrived in England and had discussed at length with Mr Baguly how he could tackle the daunting task of going to see Mrs Eefamy, to explain how it came about that George had to be left behind.

"I'll come with you, if you think it would help," Mr Baguly bravely volunteered. "There wasn't nothing you could do about it – you couldn't leave two hundred injured and wounded soldiers on the docks at Cape Town waiting for George's leg to mend."

"No. But I could have turned the work down."

"You might have been crossed off the list for good – and from what you say, his mother is a business woman – she wouldn't expect you to take such a risk."

"Do you think he will have been well looked after in hospital?"

"I'm sure of it – it was an Army hospital and a broken leg would be routine for them."

"Well thank you Mr Baguly for your support, as always. I'll call on Mrs Eefamy, no doubt there will be a storm, but with luck it will blow itself out."

"Ladies has to put on a show in circumstances like this, but you'll talk her round – take an expensive present – a nice piece of jewellery or a roll of beautiful cloth she can have some dresses made of."

"You're a crafty one I must say – I think I'll go for both – jewellery and cloth – no expense spared."

As soon as he had finished all the formalities of arriving back in port, Mr Penaluna made his way to Poole armed with a pearl necklace and as much silk, shantung, bombazine and satin as he could carry. He had asked Steward to make a special effort to bring out the best so far as his plum coloured coat was concerned, and standing at the door at No 18 he felt trepidation, anticipation (he was dying to see Clarissa again) and what was also going through his mind was that, encumbered with the parcels, he probably looked ridiculous as well. He knocked with difficulty and then tried again, Rose opened the door but what she saw was a great array of parcels surmounted by an Admiral's hat, and her laughter added to Mr Penaluna's already considerable discomfort. Mr Penaluna heard a familiar (and to him) much loved voice say, "What are you laughing at Rose – what is so funny?" The magic voice came closer, "Oh, it is you hiding behind those parcels – you'd better come in."

It was not the warmest welcome Mr Penaluna had ever experienced but at least he was over the doorstep. He laid the big parcels on the kitchen table and then gave the smallest one to Clarissa. It was usually considered in the polite society of those times that to eagerly unwrap a parcel showed indelicate haste, but Clarissa had no such effete inhibitions: she tore open the parcel and expressed great delight as she surrounded the alabaster column which was her throat with the four rows of pearls.

"You darling man," she exclaimed as she showed off her very expensive present. "But you have a lot of explaining to do – you'd better start now and I advise you to ensure that you had a good reason to leave my George behind." All the other girls in the family began to unwrap the bales of cloth. Marie, Ann and Caroline knew about cloth, and they made very appreciative noises while Rose and Clarissa set about making tea. Mr Penaluna soon found that he was invited to a meal and his worst fears were in fact unfounded. He sat at the kitchen table with the five ladies and waded into hotpot served with roast potatoes and cabbage – Mr Penaluna's kind of food.

As soon as everyone had made a start into their dinner, and at a moment when Mr Penaluna had hopes that he was to be let off lightly, Clarissa said, "Now we want to hear about George's accident, and how you came to leave him in Africa – I warn you," she added with a twinkle in her eye, "your story had better be good."

"As good as this hotpot for instance?" Mr Penaluna retorted, catching that the mood was not nearly as severe as he expected.

"What I cannot understand," Clarissa stated, "Is why if you were bringing two hundred injured soldiers home, you did not include George amongst them – why leave him there?"

"Because most of the injured were severe flesh wounds, or worse still amputations. Those with fractures of any kind were left in Cape Town, because the doctors thought a rough sea passage – well just imagine a real storm at sea, and people with broken legs or arms being thrown out of their bunks."

Clarissa smiled in a reassuring way at Mr Penaluna and said, "What do you think ladies – do we ask him to leave now (Mr Penaluna quailed) or do we ask him to stay for treacle tart and custard?"

The girls cottoned on to the feelings of the moment, and Ann said, "We think he is not guilty and has earned a portion of treacle tart."

"Just a small one," Marie volunteered. Laughter is a very reassuring factor in family life and a much relieved Mr Penaluna looked forward to his pudding and more ………

He looked across at Clarissa and saw a smile so welcoming, warm and complete that he almost choked. "You are very good to me ladies, and I do intend to returned to South Africa just as soon as I am allocated a suitable consignment, and I will bring George back to you. Believe me, I miss him too – he is a very good cook – this chap we have now is alright, but he is not George's equal – not by a long way, and having sampled your food here tonight I can see exactly where he learned his trade."

"I think I shall come with you," Clarissa said, stunning all those around the table.

Mr Penaluna quickly recovered his composure – thought of the delights ahead, and stammered, "Of course, you must have my cabin."

"But why, Mama, and how will the business run?" Caroline asked.

"The business runs itself now. And with Thurza to look after the bookkeeping – why, it is no problem at all." Thurza looked pleased to know that Mrs Eefamy had so much confidence in her abilities. "They can manage without me for six months and I shall take out – on Mr Penaluna's boat – sorry, ship – crates of pots – they will have broken thousands – they always do in a war, and I will find agents over there to market our plates, cups, bowls, and so on, it will be a very profitable trip. And of course I – we (she nodded to Mr Penaluna) will bring George home, and a lot of business. Anybody for more pudding?"

"Well said," Mr Penaluna averred, clapping his hands. "Two birds with one stone – I like it – is there any more treacle tart for me, do you think?"

Clarissa took Mr Penaluna into the parlour for a glass of port and a kiss. Both were enjoyed and warmed the happy recipients. "Can you find room for perhaps one hundred crates of pottery? – I insist on paying the proper rate – I do like to pay my way."

"In that case I shall refuse to have them loaded aboard – no – you will not pay, and I look forward to you and your crates joining me as soon as it can be arranged." He kissed Clarissa again with a tenderness and sincerity from which she gained much reassurance and happiness. He returned for another but she gently put two fingers across her lips and said "That's enough excitement for one evening." As she said it, her eyes twinkled and were harbingers of greater pleasure to come. Mr Penaluna got both messages loud and clear. He was a good judge of a situation and he had enjoyed a wonderful re-union with a beautiful woman. What more could any sailor hope for?

Two days later Clarissa and Mr Penaluna left for London, separately, but with carefully arranged details as regards their destination. They had a wonderful time together in London and saw all the sights. The food during the impending journey to South Africa came up for discussion and Mr Penaluna was quite frank about the possibilities.

"If Mr Bridgetower is not really up to it, why not ask him to come to No 18 for as long as you are in port and let him learn?"

"Well I must say that is a splendid idea, George learned in your kitchen so why not Bridgetower?"

A few days later the giant Negro reported for duty. Polly (duly primed) let him in and his rigorous training began. He was by nature a happy man who exuded good humour. Clarissa often came home at midday to hear gales of laughter emanating from the kitchen. She asked covertly if 'anything was going on'.

"No." Polly assured her mistress, "Everything is fine and he is a willing pupil as well as a good helper." When he had been there for about a week, Polly asked if she could have a week off because her baby was not so well. The request came at lunchtime when all the girls were round the table. Clarissa said it would be in order and Marie, who usually helped at Ann and Caroline's shop, volunteered to stay at No 18 and help with the household chores. Ann and Caroline agreed. So Marie became a part-time cook and general housemaid again.

Rose, Marie and Bridgetower ran the house, did the shopping and attended to all the cooking. Mr Penaluna was a frequent visitor, sometimes Mr Baguly came as well and splendid meals were produced. The girls were generous in their praise. "Mr Bridgetower made the steak and kidney pie" or " Mr Bridgetower made the apple crumble." It was a very democratic household and at midday they all sat round the table together, Mr Penaluna, Bridgetower, Baguly and all. They were jolly meals and only Clarissa's work ethic broke them up. Everyone agreed Bridgetower was now a much better cook (even he admitted it) and as a bonus he was good fun to have around the house. The training carried on for three weeks, Polly was allowed to stay with her baby, but finally a date was set for the off. Mr Penaluna announced it one day, "Ten days from now we will set sail." Turning to Clarissa he said, "So if you are firmly set on South Africa – there are ten days only to put everything at your works in order."

Clarissa's ability to answer was somewhat impeded by a particularly succulent pork chop, but she nodded her assent. What no one noticed was the look of concern that spread across Bridgetower's face and Marie's ....

When Clarissa made a move to leave No 18 for her factory, Marie asked if she could have a word in private. Clarissa took her into the front parlour and closed the door. She was an observant and caring employer but what came next was a complete surprise to her. "Well what is it Marie, do you want to go back to the shop full time and give up cooking, is that it?"

"No Ma'am I likes cookin' but it's like this – you see, with 'im goin' away."

"Who is him? I am not with you yet – who do you mean?"

"Mr Bridgetower and me….." The sentence stumbled to a halt. Clarissa summoned up all her strength and self control to avoid laughing – it flashed through her mind that Mr Bridgetower was a fifty year old part Negro penniless cook, but she just hesitated for a moment and said, "Do you have to get married?" Clarissa was thinking about Polly and her little upset of a year ago.

"No. Nothin' like that – Mr Bridgetower is a real gentleman – there's been no funny business." Clarissa had heard it referred to as all sorts of things but this was new terminology to her.

"Well then, what are we to do next – do you want to marry him – his is about fifty you know?"

"Yes, but he acts young and he is full of fun – he makes me laugh…" Again Marie's reply petered out.

"I must say that a husband who can make you laugh is a great asset. We would need a special license to get married so quickly and people would talk."

"Let 'em talk – I don't care what people say, some people say." She was going to make a reference to Mr Penaluna, but quickly decided that it might be dangerous ground. Clarissa took the point - she was no fool and no prude either.

Marie then said, "I don't want to die wonderin'", and it don't look like anyone else is going to come along." Clarissa put her arms around Marie and cuddled her. "I'm sure he is a lovely man," she said gently. "I'll arrange the license, you'll be married this week – I'll see to it today – choose a dress from the shop and I'll pay for what ever you like best."

And so the wedding took place, they celebrated it at a dinner aboard the 'North Star', paid for by Mr Penaluna, then they were sent away with enough money to pay for a hotel in Bournemouth for a week and strict instructions to be back after seven days, so Mr Bridgetower could resume his duties as cook on Mr Penaluna's ship.

"Careful with those crates lads," Mr Baguly shouted. "Handsomely now, we don't want no accidents." Well over two hundred crates of pots had arrived on the docks at Poole, though Mr Penaluna'a ship was already well loaded with provisions, stretchers, saddles, uniforms, and roped (Mr Penaluna hoped, safely) on deck were four steam driven traction engines – if they ever got loose in a storm they would create havoc and probably go straight through the sides of the ship. Some of Clarissa's crates were stowed below but some had to stay on deck – roped into place and cuddled round with tarpaulins. The fact that the 'North Star' had had to call in at Poole had delayed matters and Mr Penaluna further delayed his sailing for South Africa for a week to allow Humpage to spend some time with his family, for Mr Baguly to see his sister, Bo'sun to renew acquaintance with his prosperous lady friend and last but not least for Mr Penaluna to pursue his affair with Clarissa. Mr Baguly had received exact instructions from Mr Penaluna as to how Mrs Eefamy was to be accommodated on board for the journey to South Africa. 'Chips' was told to divide up Mr Penaluna's dining area and cabin so as to make him a separate bedroom, the dividing area to include a bathroom to which both Mrs Eefamy and Mr Penaluna would have access.

Mr Penaluna showed Steward how he wanted things arranged so far as changes of sheets and towels were concerned and left him to think his own thoughts. Steward raised an eyebrow but no objections, sniffed and went about his business.

CHAPTER 14

Clarissa's First Big Sea Trip

Mr Penaluna arranged for a tug to give them a pull out into the English Channel, and the time came for the 'farewells'. Ann and Caroline were there to wave off their mother, as were Marie, Rose, Polly and baby, Tom had provided the transport, and he was there next to his beloved Rose. Thurza had also joined the party and she had her own thoughts as Mrs Eefamy's last words were going around in her head. "I know I can leave everything to you Thurza." Mrs Eefamy had said. Thurza waved "Goodbye" to her employer and allowed herself the luxury of thinking "Yes. You can leave everything to me."

Bo'sun's lady friend had bought a new hat, whether this was to celebrate her lover's departure or to remind him to return quickly was not quite certain. Mrs Humpage was surrounded by her beautiful children, and if sheer enthusiasm played any part in fertility then there was every chance that a fourth would appear after the allotted span of time.

The 'North Star' looked splendid – Mr Penaluna's pennants were flying from the main mast, she was newly painted cream and her red Plimsoll line was a foot above the water. So she was fully loaded but well within the law. Mr Penaluna had arranged for coloured flags to be acquired so she would leave Poole dressed overall, as Royal Navy ships are for special occasions. Clarissa had spent some time considering how to dress for this six or eight week sea trip and after visiting all the best shops in London had decided that the latest in riding outfits would give her greatest freedom to go up and down companion ways and enable her to climb some of the rigging. She decided however to wave goodbye to her family less shockingly dressed and stood on the poop deck in her Sunday best. She looked around her and could not help admiring all she saw, the rigging and shrouds were newly tarred as were the masts, not a rope was out of place.

The whole crew – or at any rate those who could be spared, crowded to the port side of the 'North Star' to wave 'goodbye' when Mr Penaluna's attention was drawn to twenty or more gentlemen in clerical garb who were also gathered there waving in a decorous and half hearted manner.

"Mr Baguly," cried Mr Penaluna. "A word in your ear – who are all this lot – may I enquire?"

"I forgot to tell you, Sir – what with getting two hundred crates of pots stowed and the traction engines."

"Yes, Yes. I know all that, but where did THEY come from?" said Mr Penaluna pointing to the parsons.

"While you was in London, Sir – they arrived with a letter from some Bishop or other to say that they had to be taken to Cape Town, housed respectably, fed well, and delivered safely at £40 per head. So I got 'Chips' to knock 'em up some cabins – two in a cabin, and they are here."

"Yes I can see they are here, but don't you see trouble ahead – what will they think about Radford and Hazel?" He was also thinking of a relationship even closer to his heart.

"Well Sir, I reckoned it up, twenty five of them at £40 quid each."

"You reckoned it up – well what did it come to?"

Mr Baguly looked dumbfounded and had to admit he couldn't reckon it. Mr Penaluna clapped Mr Baguly on his massive shoulders – "Never mind it's a lot of money but I have no doubt we shall have earned every penny by the time we get them to Cape Town."

Mr Penaluna took up his stance next to the wheel, he wore his Lord Nelson hat and his plum coloured coat, Clarissa stood next to him. Mr Baguly looked back at Mr Penaluna. Mr Penaluna nodded.

"Let go for'ard. Let go aft." The tug took the strain. The waving on shore and for the most part on board ship became more enthusiastic, Humpage was at the wheel, his feet a yard apart, his powerful hands locked onto the wheel. His wife was hoping for another wave, a smile, even a nod, but the first love of this helmsman's life was in his grasp and everything else was forgotten.

Clarissa was excited and kept jumping up and down to wave to her family. Mr Penaluna contented himself with a quiet smile as he thought of the delights which lay ahead for him. "Bugger the parsons – she'll be in my arms tonight," he thought.

"Keep her like that, Mr Baguly," he called out. "That's fine – call all hands ready to make sail as soon as we are out." Then he caught sight of Steward. "Steward," he called. "We need to discuss our passengers and how we are to feed them – please ask Mr Bridgetower to come to my cabin – you must come too." He was a touchy beggar this Steward and he did not wish to offend him – not just at the start of a long trip. He then invited Clarissa to go below with him to look at the cabin and bathroom arrangements. She approved.

Within an hour they were out into the English Channel with a good firm breeze coming from the east. The 'North Star' quickly acquired her full array of sails and looked a wonderful sight. Clarissa stood next to Mr Penaluna who was close to Humpage. Mr Baguly was up and down all over the decks shouting that he wanted all the ropes tidy and the towing hawser stowed properly. Some of them were new hands and were not yet used to his aggressive ways, but they would become accustomed to him, he was no different on the last day of a trip, nor on any of the intervening days. Mr Baguly wanted everything shipshape and Bristol fashion, and he was determined to have his way. He had been in the Royal Navy when Bo'suns used two foot long canes (known as starters) to emphasise their orders. It was not unknown on merchant vessels too, some years ago, but Mr Baguly needed no 'starter'. His voice, his size and general demeanour offered little escape for dilatory seamen and they knew it.

After two days at sea Mr Penaluna politely enquired as to how the men of the cloth were coping with the sea. They had all adjusted very well. So Mr Penaluna's enquiry was followed up with an invitation to join him and Mrs Eefamy for a meal that evening. He had warned Steward and Mr Bridgetower of the possibility and now he confirmed the plan. "Roast leg of pork, I think, Steward, with roast potatoes and vegetables, and then I think we'll go for a plum duff with custard – are you writing this down?"

"No need – I told Bridgetower what you would ask for two hours ago," and with that he walked away. Mr Penaluna called him back, determined to have the last word. "Make sure he scores the skin so we have plenty of crackling." Steward listened patiently and then said, "You can't have roast leg of pork WITHOUT crackling." Mr Penaluna always went away from their conversations with Steward just a little unsure as to who actually owned the ship they were sailing on.

Mr Penaluna invited the two new apprentices, sixteen year old twins, who were the sons of a local merchant, Mr Baguly, eight of the parsons and of course Clarissa. Mr Penaluna's original saloon would seat twenty but the revised lay out could just about manage the thirteen who turned up punctually and they were all eager to see what surprises awaited them. Steward was very good at these occasions, he donned a smart uniform, did the serving with style and flair and kept the egregious Radford well away and out of sight. Beef soup was first, everyone agreed that they had rarely had better. Steward let it drop casually that it was his own favourite and he had shown Mr Bridgetower how to make it.

Wine bottles (plural) were opened with ginger beer for the two boys. The two legs of pork were brought in ceremoniously and the domed lids removed in a theatrical manner – they were placed next to Mr Penaluna so he could carve and a kitchen size pair of tweezers was put nice and handy to distribute the crackling. The vegetables were in large silver tureens and were delivered hot, and with great cobs of butter on top, so it would melt down into them. Two ornate and matching gravy boats were strategically positioned and as Mr Penaluna handed round the plates with sliced pork on, everyone was invited to help themselves to the vegetables. Clarissa helped the two boys just in case they were a little shy or timid with all those learned gentlemen present. Mr Penaluna then checked just how many bottles of wine Steward had opened – there were enough and he said, "Very good Steward. Have your's now, and come back in half an hour."

Steward went back to the galley, to regale Mr Bridgetower, Radford and Hazel with precise details as to the animal greed of 'that lot' in the skipper's cabin and concluded his tirade with, "I don't suppose you kept anything for us poor buggers, did you?"

"Fear not, O Lord and Master – just look at this." The now experienced cook had taken a full two inch thick slice off each leg and roasted them separately crackling and all. There were vegetables, gravy and apple sauce. "I thought it would have been wasted on them," Mr Bridgetower said, bursting into gales of laughter. Hazel and Radford tucked in merrily. Steward tried to laugh but even smiling did not come easily to such a face – he was predestined to be a martyr and preferred misfortune, because it confirmed what he had always thought: that someone, everyone, was always against him.

He went back in half an hour and was greeted by Mr Penaluna's rubicund face. "What's to follow Steward – my guests are full of curiosity?"

"And of roast pork too," volunteered one of the parsons – trying his best to enter into the spirit of the evening.

"Well if you are all full, you might not have room for plum duff then," Steward answered, it was also meant to be a joke but somehow Steward just hadn't the knack for jokes and it came out somewhat contumaciously.   Mr Penaluna used to Steward, picked up the conversation by the scruff of its neck and said, "Yes if it's plum duff, we're all ready and willing."

"Right. I'll just clear away these things and I'll be back soon." Again the air was heavy with martyrdom, and Steward's gait became a laboured trudging, punctuated with sighs. He had the magical gift for making happy people feel guilty. He went back to the galley with the news. "Yes plum duff – whacking big ones."

"White wine with the dessert I think, Steward," Mr Penaluna called. "Perhaps six bottles would be nice – are they chilled?" Steward did not answer, instead he produced the bottles one at a time out of a barrel of broken up ice – he held each bottle up for inspection and then removed the corks. It was dumb insolence, but Mr Penaluna ignored it – in fact he no longer saw it. He and

Steward had been together now for fifteen years and he considered Steward's little ways to be the product of a very small mind. He did his job and that was all that concerned Mr Penaluna. He accepted that Steward was by nature a growler. Clarissa did ask Mr Penaluna about it, because she would certainly not have tolerated it, had Steward been one of her employees. Mr Penaluna said, "He did have a major disappointment when he was a young man, whether it was over a girl or perhaps a hoped for inheritance, I really don't know."

"Well it is about time he grew up, he can't go through life sulking all the time – I lost my husband when we had only just started a very happy marriage. I was upset of course and I was very sad but I did not sulk."

"Well my dear you can tease him, coax him, or order him to change, and if you succeed I for one would be very pleased."

Steward came back with two enormous plum duffs and plonked them on the table. By now he had become bored with stylish presentation and dumping them down satisfied him – he then went back to the galley for the brandy sauce. As he returned to the saloon he heard Mr Penaluna say that the duff looked well stuffed with plums. He immediately said, "I told the cook to double up on the plums." Wishing to garner as much praise as he could for himself. "Capital idea, Steward," Clarissa piped up – "I am sure we will all enjoy it the more because of your suggestion."

"Just as we shall enjoy the cheese too, if and when it arrives," Mr Penaluna said. Clarissa gave him a black look and when Steward had left the room she gave Mr Penaluna a good kick on the shins, and a smile to go with it.

The two sixteen year olds had said very little, but they had displayed their enthusiasm and gratitude by sweeping away anything and everything put before them.

"I dare say cheese and port wine are not exactly your favourites, are they boys?" Mr Penaluna said. The boys took the hint. Mr Penaluna pointed to the apples and nuts on the sideboard. It was always understood that if members of the crew were lucky enough to dine with the Skipper, they should try to beg or filch for their mates who had not been quite so fortunate. Mr Penaluna looked on benignly as they swiped as much as their pockets would hold, he then explained the obvious theft to his other guests once the boys had left the room.

"The wine is with you, Mr Baguly," Mr Penaluna said, in an attempt to hasten its arrival. "And we have a very ancient and therefore desirable Stilton here and some very strong Cheddar." The group of parsons had appetites which could not be satisfied and they waded manfully into the cheese. Mr Penaluna looked on the whole procedure with a business man's eye, at £40 per head, he couldn't lose, no matter how much they ate.

At last the party broke up and Mr Baguly said he would go on deck to see that Sweeting, his second mate was coping. "I think I would like to come too, if I may," Clarissa said.

"Certainly, my dear," Mr Penaluna agreed. "Do use a warm wrap, it can be quite chilly out there."

The night was perfectly clear and a million stars looked down out of the inky blackness of the sky. Enough lamps were lit on the ship so that the poop deck, the taffrail and some of the companion ways were safe to walk on. There was a steady breeze on her port quarter and the lee rails were under water as the 'North Star' cut through the Bay of Biscay at a regular eight knots. Mr Penaluna never liked to drive his ship overnight because if a real wind did blow up it is difficult to take big sails up quickly. So the main courses were reefed up, but with her Royals and topgallants she could still produce a good turn of speed.

Some of the parsons were taking the air after their sumptuous meal and one, who was in England an Archdeacon, approached Mr Penaluna with the suggestion that tomorrow being Sunday, would it be possible to arrange a service. Mr Penaluna readily agreed and asked Bo'sun to rig up an awning. Archdeacon Williams asked if Bo'sun could also bring the little harmonium on deck. Since Bo'sun could, with the help of ropes and pulleys, move almost anything to anywhere, the harmonium was no trouble at all. Mr Penaluna and Clarissa bid everyone 'goodnight' and they retired to their respective (if not respectable) quarters for the night.

The men were treated to bacon sandwiches for their Sunday breakfast and some were suspicious. "Something's afoot," Humpage said. "The Old Man (ie Mr Penaluna) told Bridgetower to be sure to give us a good breakfast, now what has he got in mind – bend all new sails on, I'll be bound."

"No," young Sweeting said. "He wouldn't do that to us, Sunday is still a Sunday after all." Their curiosity was soon satisfied when Mr Baguly arrived eating an enormous bacon sandwich with, "Right lads," he said, between bites, "Church Service at eleven o'clock – Mr Penaluna says clean and he means clean clothes and shaved too, so you look like human beings – do you know any hymns? I hope you do, and he says it's plum duff and honey today – so sing up."

"Honey would be better before the hymns," Radford advised. "Lubricates the throat you see."

"You've had enough bacon drippin' to oil ten throats this morning," Mr Baguly said. "So I'll be listening out for you specially."

They gathered under the awning, thirty five of a crew, minus one at the helm and one up the main mast as lookout. All of the clergy, Mr Penaluna and Clarissa, the latter in hat and veil.

"Why the veil – are you thinking of becoming a nun," Mr Penaluna gibed at her.

"They wouldn't have me – but I thought I would wear it in case I start to giggle."

Archdeacon Williams nodded in a dignified manner to the little Curate at the harmonium, his feet began treadling and they were off. "Rock of Ages," got them off to a good start, and Archdeacon Williams then intoned various prayers in a suitably sepulchral voice. Mr Penaluna surveyed the gathering and began to count heads to see if any of his lot had scived off. No, they were all there. Then he continued and counted the men of the cloth and found there were twenty-eight. Not twenty-five as the paperwork said and indeed as had been expressed to Mr Baguly when they first arrived. 'Chips' had been told to knock up cabins to accommodate them, two in a cabin. So they were all looked after alright, and thanks to this Morning Service Mr Penaluna was now £120 better off. He sang more loudly from then on and had not enjoyed a Church Service so much for years. The Archdeacon was not going to miss an opportunity such as this to deliver a sermon with as many maritime analogies as he could muster. His imagination was considerable and his stamina unimpeachable. The combination of these two attributes lead to a homily of thirty five minutes duration and it afforded boredom to the crew and self-satisfaction to the Archdeacon in equal proportions. The parsons had heard it all before, the analogies previously had been rural, industrial or medical according to where the Archdeacon found himself. In the main they spent the half hour wondering if the Sunday lunch could possibly equal last night's roast pork. The men began to move uneasily from one foot to another and were vastly relieved when the last maritime metaphor was coined and the Archdeacon compared their passage through life to a journey, partly rough and partly smooth. The opportunity to sing again was a welcome relief and the gentleman at the harmonium was now joined by Mr Bridgetower. Mr Penaluna had noticed that the cook had taken it upon himself to walk off part way through the sermon and he was envious. No doubt he needs to baste the roast beef Mr Penaluna thought. But no Bridgetower returned to the deck with a huge grin and his violin, and as they started up "For those in peril on the sea" he joined in with some choice and soaring harmonies.

Mr Penaluna shook hands with the Archdeacon once the service was over and said, "I'm sure we are all the better for that Vicar." Which was fulsome, which ever way you took it. The men told Bridgetower to stay on deck and play a few reels and the men began dancing and singing. It was a complete contrast to the previous hour and the Archdeacon's visage darkened noticeably. Mr Penaluna ever perspicuous looked on and just said, "To each his own Vicar – live and let live."

"Yes, indeed – my thoughts entirely," Archdeacon said – though his immutable expression did not concur.

CHAPTER 15

Storms and Salvage

Mr Penaluna and Clarissa wandered aft, and looked at the wake – it was surprisingly short and much disturbed. Clarissa commented upon this and such powers of observation brought forth praise from Mr Penaluna.

"You are correct, it is unusual and what is more it tells us a lot."

He looked at his turnip timepiece, "Mr Baguly will still be asleep – I won't wake him, he'll have a busy time ahead of him and he'll need all the sleep he can get." He saw one of the apprentices cleaning some brassware and asked him to bring Mr Sweeting aft.

"Look at that, Mr Sweeting."

"No wake to speak of Sir – bad sign is that."

"Just my thoughts exactly Mr Sweeting – call all hands to bring the t'gallants down on deck, masts and all, and main courses reefed up securely - doubled roped around. Same with the boats and those dammed traction engines – make 'em secure a thwart ships and tell 'Chips' to hammer chocks under the wheels. Have you got all that?"

"Yes Sir, I have."

"Good, I'll be on deck now until Mr Baguly is rested – we are in for a blow."

"It'll get us there faster Sir."

"Faster is the right word Mr Sweeting."

"Oh Mr Sweeting – I know it is Sunday and Sunday is a day off – but I'll make it up, tell the men."

Once Mr Sweeting had gone off to find Bo'sun and assemble the men, Clarissa asked for the full details. "The reason we have no wake is because the wind cannot make its mind up which way it wants to go and it is erasing the wake by dashing this way and then that."

"And that is a bad sign?"

"In an hour or so it will have made up its mind and it will throw everything at us, and we will have to be ready, so I think it would be best if you went below and left the decks clear – my men will need all the space there is."

Mr Penaluna then went to the galley where he saw Mr Bridgetower and Radford well ahead with Sunday lunch of roast beef. "Belay that," Mr Penaluna said. "Is the roast beef cooked through."

"Three quarters I'd say."

"Right – slice off the outer part that is cooked and make sandwiches – ah there you are Steward, you'd better hear this as well. Make sandwiches for everybody out of bread, muffins or duff and dowse the fires."

Radford looked sadly at the lovely glowing embers he had so carefully created.

"And then Steward, grog all round for them." Radford perked up at that. "But half strength ONLY – mark that Steward – I don't want the men drunk – not with what is ahead." Radford's enthusiasm subsided again – he didn't enjoy watery grog. As a parting shot Mr Penaluna said

"Steward tell all the Bishops what is for lunch and why."
Steward's face told its usual story.

Mr Penaluna caught hold of Bo'sun. "Life lines
anywhere you like but plenty of 'em – no tellin' which
way the wind will come at us." Then he saw 'Chips'
knocking chocks all around the traction engines and
shouted "You and 'Sails' put tarpaulins and battens for
the hatchways." 'Chips' nodded. 'Sails' did not like
orders from anyone except the Old Man. Things went
ominously quiet and still. The wind had made its mind
up and it came full at them over the bows, bringing with
it tons of water and creamy spray. The wind screamed at
the 'North Star', how dare it intrude into this private area.
Four men on the wheel could hardly hold it. Bo'sun hadn't
had time to remove the stun sails and they were carried
away, their poles and all, as the wind exulted in its own
strength. Ropes flew loose, some became entangled in
each other, some flogged the masts like Captain Bligh
had flogged his men. Mr Baguly appeared in his night
shirt – trying to drag a pair of breeches on. "What the
hell's goin' on?" he bellowed, as though the present
situation had been caused by some negligence.

"Windy ain't it?" Mr Penaluna said.

"The 'North Star' lifted clear of the water and crashed
down again as if to confirm Mr Penaluna's remark.
Suddenly she was 45° this way and then that, she was a
mere toy for the sea to play with, to dash to pieces or to
spare. This is how it would seem to the unpractised eye.
But the people who were running this ship knew a thing

or two about storms and had ridden a few out, including Cape Horn.

"Mr Baguly, some men will be hurt – so please ask among the parsons and the like, if any of 'em had any medical training – let's make 'em do something useful."

Mr Baguly knocked on the cabin doors, and found most of the clerics on their knees praying, but three of them had some knowledge and with Mr Baguly made an area in their dining room which could be used for cuts and bruises. Mr Baguly told them to attend to what they thought they could manage and to leave broken bones and stitching to Mr Penaluna.

The ship's boats were well seized around with one and a half inch rope, but two were wrenched free and brought together in such a way as to render then suitable only for firewood. Four men were taken below with splinter wounds of the type previously associated with battle on a man of war. One had a gash in his thigh a foot long, another's arm was deeply penetrated by a jagged splinter. Mr Penaluna saw them briefly and said, "Withdraw the wood and leave the wounds open – I will look for bits later." With that he went on deck again. "Mr Baguly," Mr Penaluna began, "We are the wrong way round – it's coming over our bows – I want it under her backside – dare we try to go about?"

"Risky Sir."

"How long will she stand for two hundred tons of water smashing on the fo'c'le

"We'll have to bend on a really thick top sail."

"I don't want any men up so high."

348

"Right it'll have to be the main course then."

"But use a smaller sail, and double and treble bunt lines and a yard arm perpendicular lashed to the mast with the sail between it and the mast."

"Could work, Sir."

"Right, bring Sweeting, Bo'sun and Humpage here and we'll tell 'em." Mr Penaluna looked round and saw Clarissa on deck looking triumphant, "It's wonderful," she cried. "I would not miss this for anything."

"Hold this life line – both hands, or with the next wave you'll be gone."

"This is nature as I have never seen it." And with that came a wall of solid green water four feet deep, it hurled Mr Penaluna and his favourite passenger thirty feet along the deck where they crashed into the resilient Mr Baguly. The water raced through the scuppers and over the rails, contrite about its capricious ways. Mr Baguly picked up Clarissa and Mr Penaluna, both battered and soaked but none the worse for being catapulted into him.

The team was gathered together and they all clung to a lifeline. At least two feet of water swirled about them. Clarissa held on tight, but Bo'sun put an extra rope around her waist and seized it to the rail.

"Now listen" Mr Penaluna began. "We are going to go about and this is how we will go it. We need the spanker for say twenty seconds and it must be roped up so when I say 'Up' – then up it goes and two men must be there at the mizzen to seize it up. The spanker is vital to taking us round 180°. When I shout 'Helm' – then it is hard a lee." This instruction was directed at Humpage who nodded.

"I want the fore stay sail on like the spanker, for say twenty seconds and I want two men with axes to cut it adrift when I say 'Cut'." Sweeting nodded. "Now Bo'sun I want you and 'Sails' to sort out a thick hard wearing sail – any size will do and bend it on for a main course, I want double or treble bunt lines and an extra yard arm perpendicular to clasp the sail between it and the mast. You will have men positioned to seize it to the mast. Now reckon up how many men you will all need and tell me NOW."

They reckoned up and even Radford and Bridgetower would be needed. "Right, now comes the difficult bit." And with split second timing, as if to emphasise Mr Penaluna's dilemma, a forty foot wave crashed into the 'North Star' and engulfed the meeting, they all survived and arose wiping their faces – only Clarissa was laughing, to her it was tremendously exciting, to the others it was a matter of planning how to remain alive.

"One more problem," Mr Baguly said. "Who is going to pull the main course around and sheet it on."

"I am just coming to that." Mr Penaluna did manage a wan smile as he expounded his last part of the grand solution. "You," he said – his smile extending slightly, "You Mr Baguly with your powers of persuasion, will recruit the Vicars to pull the sail round."

Smiles spread amongst the gathering; all except Mr Baguly registering amusement. "Christ Almighty," Mr Baguly said.

"No, he's not aboard, but his underlings are and they must pull." Mr Penaluna said concluding the meeting.

"I think you should go below now my dear, climb into some dry clothes and look after yourself."

"For once you are going to be disobeyed on your own ship, Penaluna – I am tied here by your Bo'sun – I am safe and I am staying right here." With that she gave the Skipper a salty kiss and he knew, for once, he was beaten.

The storm continued with the same tumultuous ferocity, as the various teams made ready to follow Mr Penaluna's plan. Mr Baguly's task, perhaps the most difficult of all, did bring about the desired result, and twenty-two clerics came on deck to be assigned to ropes and to be secured by them. The other six were either too old or too sick or two terrified to join in. Mr Penaluna surveyed the groups of men and received a favourable wave from each leader, the spanker and the foresail gang ever ready, as was the gang on the main-course.

Mr Penaluna waited until a really treacherous wave hit the bows and came over, once it had gone overboard – he knew he had a few seconds grace.

"Helms a lee," rang out.

Humpage, plus three did their work. She was coming around, she answered.

"Cut," Mr Penaluna shouted.

But before the men could wield their axes, the seas took hold of the jib from below and tore it from its capping, jib and sail went overboard – different method – desired effect.

"Up," rang out next.

The crew under Bo'sun had the spanker boom roped to the mast in seconds, and she continued to come round.

Now was the vital part of the sequence, Mr Penaluna needed the sail to fill immediately, so as to give steering way. He signalled to Mr Baguly who trumpeted "Pull," as only he could. The seas took fright and there was a ten second cessation of the battering, and the rigged up main-course (such as it was) was brought round, secured and she filled.

Humpage's face was a picture of triumph. Bo'sun ran as best he could to report. Mr Baguly thanked the Vicars. Sweeting was terrified – he had to report the loss of the jib complete. Mr Penaluna reassured him with an arm around his shoulder, "Never mind – no one could have foreseen that." Mr Baguly reported that his team had pulled to a man. "They did indeed," Mr Penaluna said. "Now they know what 'For those in peril on the sea' really means."

The 'North Star' was now taking the storm under her shapely but considerable behind and coping wonderfully. Mr Penaluna's face was a picture – it registered pride and contentment, pride in his wits and know-how and content that he has saved his crew and his ship. Clarissa looked on and thought 'what a man'.

The Archdeacon came along to Mr Penaluna and was immediately congratulated. "We'll make a seaman of you yet," Mr Penaluna said.

"I would rather not – but I am glad we were able to help."

"Invaluable help, Sir – we could not have done it without you."

"But aren't we going the wrong way now?"

"We are indeed, but only to ride out the storm, then we will take our bearings and resume the proper course. Now I must see to the injured, a few have cuts, please send any of your men who have strong stomachs and some knowledge of medicine, and I'll be in your dining room, patching a few of 'em up."

One called Rose had a gash on his left cheek and some damage to his left eye. Mr Penaluna looked and then told Radford to give Rose half a bottle of neat rum.

"Half a bottle won't have no effect on 'im, Sir."

"Right a full bottle then, and I'll stitch 'em up."

"Hold still, Rose, this will hurt." He signalled to two of the clerics to move in and hold Rose fast. The gash to his cheek was four inches long and the injury to his eye looked bad. When he had finished he awarded Rose a Lord Nelson patch.

"I'll look like a pirate or a smuggler now," Rose said.

Mr Penaluna replied, "From what I hear neither calling describes your crimes."

Rose laughed, "I daren't set foot ashore in England, Sir – I'd be scooped up for sure – but then I don't intend to."

Rose had worked as a Senior Clerk in a large firm of family solicitors in Falmouth. He realised that two at least of the Senior Partners were using clients' money for their own gain. He was in a trusted position and saw an opportunity to clear out the firm's client account at one swoop, and he took it. His philosophy was that it was not robbery to rob a robber. The law would have taken a different view, but he was successful. His wife was sent to the North of England with sacks of coins and there she awaited his arrival, having bought a small cottage near Berwick on Tweed. Mr Rose would one day find a ship bound for Newcastle, or a coasting collier bound for Seaham or Sunderland, and he would live his days out fishing and walking his dog. That was his dream.

All the injured attended to, Mr Penaluna called Steward and Mr Bridgetower for a little conference: "You have all the firewood you will ever need for the galley, as 'Chips' tells me two of the boats were smashed to pieces."

"And all the chickens is running loose," Steward added – ever eager to pass on gloomy news.

"Well no doubt 'Chips' will knock up a chicken coop when he has a minute."

"And they'll be layin' where they shouldn't, and the crew will not own up to what they've 'ad."

"No, No. Quite, Steward, but let us make progress – I want the fire lit and bacon sandwiches – large ones, handed out to everyone."

"All your bacon will be gone – don't blame me."

"No, I won't – I promise – coffee to them who wants it or grog – whichever – now is it quite clear, or do I ....."

"Ship, just one league off, starboard bow." The voice came from aloft, to interrupt Mr Penaluna mid sentence.

"One league – that is dangerous," Mr Penaluna said. "Sweeting take my glass aloft and have a squint at it."

Two minutes later Sweeting shouted down, "Schooner Sir, about five or six hundred tons, can't see no one on board. Sails, yards and ropes all ahoo."

Mr Penaluna went aloft – the storm though not abated was much quieter and Mr Penaluna smelled money – salvage money. He took his glass and concentrated on the wheel – it was this way and then that way. The rudder was in charge of the wheel, not vice-versa.

"Bo'sun have we a boat that'll swim?"

"Yes Sir."

"Right – you and four men take belaying pins – just in case, and row across – see what is happening. Wave three times if there is no one aboard." The wave soon came.

"Mr Humpage – lay us alongside that schooner if you please."

Within fifteen minutes Mr Penaluna, Mr Baguly, Radford (a known scrounger) and three or four more were on board the schooner.

"She's from Holland Sir – loaded with harness, saddles and hay – no one on board, over three foot of water in her." Bo'sun's report was just what Mr Penaluna wanted to hear. Mr Penaluna turned to Mr Baguly, "We can't tow her to Cape Town, she'll have to sail with a jury rig. Would you like to take her – pick eight men to work her? We will keep in touch all the way, and two hundred miles out we'll meet up and I'll tow you in. I'll send extra men over for the first day, to help get her pumped out, and 'Chips' will have to look her over for leaks."

Radford then came up from below looking pleased with himself. "Thirty good chickens and three fine fat pigs – never seen bigger pigs, than they lot."

"Very well done, Radford, you can see to it that twenty of the chickens and two of the pigs are transferred over, then you and Hazel stay with Mr Baguly. You can be cooks and general helpers."

That was all settled after suitable arrangements were made to rig up lights each night so they did not lose touch with each other.

Mr Penaluna arranged with Steward for a quiet cosy meal for himself and Clarissa for the evening. They would just be staying put for twenty-four hours while the schooner was checked over, pumped out and some sails were rigged. After all the excitement they all needed a quiet period.

"Who does the ship belong to?" Clarissa asked.

"That is a very good question – you see the rules regarding salvage are very complicated and they vary from one country to another, but my experience is that although ship owners and insurers hate to lose a ship, they are very slow to reward anyone who rescues one. They like to say – well it is common courtesy and we would be glad to do the same for you."

"Will the crew be lost, do you think?"

"I think they must have taken to their boats, in a moment of panic, and small boats would simply be swallowed up in the kind of seas we have just seen."

"Poor men and so many families without a bread winner – very sad."

"We might pick them up, of course, but I don't think so."

"So the ship is yours then – is she?"

"The laws governing salvage are difficult, we are English, the schooner is Dutch, it will be decided in South Africa – but I am going to let her sail with us until we are two hundred miles out, then I'll tow her in – that should make it convincing."

"And if she went in on her own?"

"The first thing the owners and insurers would think of would be piracy."

"Not of Mr Baguly, surely?"

"No. And of course, if we never had reason before to be glad of twenty parsons, we have now, because they saw it all happen."

Then, Clarissa, ever the business woman, asked the crunch question, "What is all this extra worry and work going to bring you?"

"Well I should say the ship is worth £5,000 and the cargo not much less. If I do not receive twenty-five percent, I shall have been short changed."

"Two and a half thousand then Penaluna – what kind of South African diamond ring could you buy for a loving lady friend with that kind of money?"

"I would never find one which would be able to express my gratitude for what I have in mind for the rest of the evening." Mr Penaluna slipped the bolt into place, Clarissa was already unfastening buttons..............

The 'North Star' and the Dutch schooner (looking very distressed) arrived in Cape Town two weeks later. Mr Penaluna reported the details to the Harbour Master. He had been informed that the ship was indeed regarded as lost, and that six members of her crew had been picked up and had reported their ship 'Marken' was wrecked and sunk at sea.

"Let us hope then that her insurers and owners will be grateful for her safe arrival," Mr Penaluna said.

"I am sure they will be, and where can you be found, when you are needed?"

"I will be on my own ship The 'North Star' – there she is anchored out in the bay – I expect to be here at least another two weeks, possibly even four."

"Thank you, Mr Penaluna. I am sure you will be kept in touch with all developments."

CHAPTER 16

Family Reunion

Mr Penaluna then met up with Clarissa who was anxious to make contact with George as soon as possible.

"He is a sensible lad he will have made contact with my agent or one of their associates – come on we will soon know exactly what has happened."

The agent put their minds at rest straight away. "Yes, young Mr Eefamy made contact, we gave him some money – he was staying at the Ram's Head. But I think he is now working there as a cook and by all accounts doing very well."

"Where is the Ram's Head, can we walk there?"

"Oh yes – come to the door and I can show you the street."

Clarissa set off at a cracking pace with Mr Penaluna trying to keep up. Clarissa walked in the hotel foyer, banged the bell and an attendant came hurrying in.

"Is George Eefamy working here?"

"Yes – he's cooking lunch just now – who shall I say is here Ma'am?"

"I'm his mother."

"Yes – he's told us about you, and are you Mr Penaluna Sir?"

"Yes, I am."

"I'll bring him now – he'll be absolutely jumping with excitement."

Two minutes later George came running into the foyer and clasped his two favourite people in his arms and gave way to floods of tears – Clarissa joined in and Mr Penaluna did his best to console them, pat them, talk to them, and in the end just gave in, and ordered himself a pint of their 'best'.

Five minutes later the Manager came into the foyer to see where his cook was. He was very understanding but said, "I do see your points of view but please try to see mine too."

Clarissa recovered her composure and took control of the situation. "We will stay for lunch. George can return to his work, and then we can talk afterwards."

The Manager was very grateful. "Thank you Ma'am – I really am very appreciative of this arrangement, and of course the meal and any drinks you would like are on the house."

"Now George, what is your recommendation?"

"Mixed grill – I know Mr Penaluna loves it and you will too – I will bring it to your table myself." Mr Penaluna's face glowed with anticipation. "And afterwards?" he said with a smile a yard wide.

"Syrup sponge, Sir."

"With custard, Mr Eefamy?"

"Gallons of it, Sir."

"I'm your man – come on Clarissa – we are ready for this."

Once the midday rush was over, George went off to his room – bathed and came down nicely dressed and ready for a very long conversation. This took place over a pot of tea – once the pot was empty, George said "Come and meet Nelson." They made their way out to the stables via the kitchen, where George picked up two large carrots – "What do you think of her Mama?"

"She is sturdy and a lovely colour…."

"Yes. I know what you are thinking – why have a horse with only one eye? But that is how I got her and I do want to keep her – can she be part of your haulage business?"

"Well – yes – I suppose so, if Mr Penaluna can take her back to England for you."

"Yes, I can do that – just make sure Radford doesn't arrange for her to be made into horsemeat."

"How are Radford and Hazel and Mr Baguly?"

"All the crew are fine – we have a few new ones, but all the old faces are still there and no doubt they'll be glad to see you and sample your cooking again."

"Did you find another cook – will my job still be open for me – or will I be putting someone out of work?"

Mr Penaluna thought for a minute and then said, "There will always be a job for you on my ship as my cook – always. Bridgetower – that is the name of the man who replaced you. He was alright, but I did tell him that the job was your's as soon as you were fit again, and that he must stay as a seaman with us, or look elsewhere for employment. He knows that, and he is a cheerful man, as your Mama can testify, he is not the sort of person to bear a grudge."

"Come back into the lounge – I'll order another pot of tea, and I'll tell you about my adventures, then you will see why I must find a nice home for Nelson."

It took more than one pot of tea to recount George's trek across Africa, and he had his two guests gasping with astonishment at his audacity and at the calm way he told his story. Later in the day Mr Penaluna suggested that they could perhaps stay in the hotel for the night or would they prefer to sleep on the 'North Star'.

"On the ship for me, Sir – please – I would love to see all my old friends and then perhaps sleep in my cabin and could Bo'sun row me ashore early tomorrow morning – they will need me here to cook breakfast."

Clarissa looked on admiringly – this work ethic – so important to her, was firmly part of George's character and she loved him for it.

The next day Bo'sun rowed George to the shore and was then George's guest for a sumptuous breakfast. Mr Penaluna went ashore to begin the quest for another consignment for the 'North Star' and Clarissa took samples of her wares and went in search of orders for her pottery. The next four weeks were very busy for them all, and at the conclusion, all three, in their different ways, were ready to make sail. George had worked his notice at the hotel, Mr Penaluna had secured work for his ship and Clarissa had cleared all her pots out to hotels and shops and at a good price. She was triumphant, especially so because she had made connections which she hoped would be long term.

CHAPTER 17

More Trouble at Number 18

Meanwhile, back at Number 18, everything was going just as Clarissa had hoped it would: the two girls were running the shop profitably, the household activities were in the capable hands of Marie, Rose and Polly, and perhaps most importantly, certainly so far as Clarissa was concerned, Thurza was looking after the paperwork at the factory and running the haulage business.

Thurza started each working day even earlier than Clarissa would have insisted upon. There was much to do and she did not wish to be found wanting. So she would be in the yard by half past seven to check that the haulage men had a full list of where to go and what to drop off. Once the rigs were on their way, she and Bert Trembelt would spend half an hour together, planning the next day's journeys, and then it was into the office to attend to the day's post. Thurza understood the bookkeeping and invoicing system, and had in fact, with Clarissa's approval, made many improvements to the systems originally devised by the late Mr Eefamy, many years before. The office routine was now simplified, and the cash flow was quicker. Many of the local customers were encouraged, by means of a small discount, to pay for goods or services in cash and this was Thurza's scheme. Now that Clarissa was absent, Thurza started to keep two sets of books. The family failings regarding money had been passed down to her, and she took the opportunity afforded by her employer's continued absence to see if she could syphon off some money for herself. She knew the business was increasing by a small percentage all the time. She reckoned if she found a system by which she could keep roughly that amount for herself, no absentee employer could grumble if after an absence of many months the firm was doing just as well as when she left. Thurza had no need to resort to a ploy such as this: she had been made welcome at Number 18, indeed she was treated like one of the family and received a wage for the help that she gave at the factory. Although she did not know it, Clarissa was planning to give her a handsome 'thank you' upon her return, such was her confidence and trust in her young deputy.

Thurza knew nothing of this nor did she care, she had a system and it involved keeping two sets of invoices and two sets of books. The cash which came in was carefully pared down to coincide with the lesser of the two invoices prepared for every cash transaction, and it was banked. Thurza balanced it up every week and ensured that, to the penny, the calculations were correct, and Mr Copeman, the Bank Manager, would pay Thurza a visit every four or six weeks (Mrs Eefamy's account was now a very important one) and would compliment Thurza upon the speeded up cash flow she had instituted. During the months of Clarissa's absence, Thurza's little nest grew, and the complexity of it sometimes meant she had to work late to keep on top of the paperwork. Tremblett would sometimes come into the office, just before he want home, initially to "try it on" with Thurza, he had a wandering eye, and would have had wandering hands, given the right signals. But having failed in that direction, he was conscientious enough to say,

"Don't forget, if you are here alone at night, Mrs Eefamy's gun is in the left hand drawer. This is a port, so you never know who is in Poole, or where they have come from. And don't forget to lock up."

Thurza sometimes took the little pistol out of the drawer and fondled it. Clarissa had told her how to use it. She knew its dangers and its possibilities.

A young policeman had been recruited into the Poole Constabulary, Edward Shorrock was his name. He was a tall upright observant young man who was determined to do well in his chosen employment. His beat included all the area where Mrs Eefamy had her factory and stables, and any lights in offices and gates not locked attracted his attention. This set of circumstances arose one evening, and he considered it his duty to investigate. Imagine his surprise when he opened an office door, to be confronted by a gorgeous twenty year old girl with a gun in her hand.

"You did frighten me," Thurza said. She had good reason to be frightened: she had just struck a balance for the week, and had in fact robbed her employer of seven pounds twelve and sixpence.

"Now, now, Miss, point that thing away, or better still, just put it down."

Thurza trembling all over, slipped the gun back into the drawer and began to rearrange the papers on her desk – the evidence was there, and right before her was a policeman. But this was long before the days of a Fraud Squad. Policemen were trained to keep good order, to stop fights, to quell drunks and arrest burglars. P. C. Shorrock knew nothing of embezzlement. But, observant as he was, he was very much aware that the young lady in front of him was the most beautiful creature he had ever seen.

"Well Miss," he said, "Do you often work her alone – I wouldn't advise it really."

"Usually on Thursday I do, I have to balance up you see, so I can bank it tomorrow."

"And do you take the money yourself to the Bank on a Friday?"

"Yes, I usually take it on Friday morning at about half past ten."

P.C. Shorrock took onto himself the air of an experienced policeman and said,

"It's best not to have a pattern Miss. If someone of doubtful reputation got to know that you regularly went to the bank on a Friday at half past ten. Why then Miss, he could form a plan to waylay you, between here and your rightful destination."

"Yes officer I do see what you mean, and sometimes it is a large sum of money – I don't suppose you could escort me there tomorrow morning could you – I would feel so much more secure if you could?"

P. C. Shorrock received this request with many things hurtling through his head. To gain time, and to extend as far as possible this delightful interview, he reached into his capacious pockets and produced a notebook. It contained not a single entry, this had been a singularly uneventful tour of duty. He thumbed over four or five pages, all equally innocent of inscriptions, then looked intently at two or three more equally empty pages and made the weighty decision. "Yes, I think I can arrange that Miss, shall we say ten o'clock?"

Thurza received this information with feigned relief and fluttered her eyelashes at the now intoxicated officer of the law.

"Right then Miss, I'll be here at ten o'clock tomorrow morning, on the dot."

"Yes, I'll be ready, and thank you officer."

"Goodnight Miss, don't forget to lock up."

P. C. Shorrock moved out of the office and yard, on a cloud. He was aware of nothing until he came to the glare of the main street, when he came back to earth. "Blimey", he thought. "I've never seen one like her – where have I been looking?" It occurred to P. C. Shorrock that ten a.m. was his 'brew time'. "Never mind about that Edward," he thought to himself. "This could be the most important twenty four hours of your life."

The protected convoy to the Bank, the day after, completed its hazard free journey and Clarissa's money was left nice and cosy in her Bank account, just as she would have wished. Not all of it, true enough, but a goodly sum and enough to leave Thurza's non too sensitive conscience in a state of repose.

"Right Miss", P. C. Shorrock said, as Thurza emerged from the Bank. "Well, I've got one or two things I have to see to now, so I'll be on my way."

"If you would care to walk me back to my office, we could have tea and toast. It is about half past ten." Said Thurza, consulting the lovely fob watch Clarissa had bought her.

"Well Miss" P. C. Shorrock coughed, and spluttered "P'raps"

Thurza took his arm and they set off. The young policeman was not too sure what the Sergeant would say if he saw one of his men gallivanting down the main street of Poole with a dazzling beauty on his arm. Right at that moment Edward didn't care if the Lord Chancellor saw him, he was the happiest Bobby in the land.

They had their tea and toast and just as Edward was leaving, Bert Tremblett came into the office with a bundle of papers concerned with the haulage side of the business.

"What's he want?" he said to Thurza, after Edward had gone.

"Oh, he came in last night, when I was working late and he escorted me to the Bank, also he gave me good advice about breaking up my routine, and taking different routes and different times."

"He'll be round here regularly if you ask me?" Bert said.

"I wouldn't be surprised," said Thurza, not lifting her head from her papers.

"I should watch him if I was you," Bert continued.

"Yes, I will Bert, and I'll watch you as well."

He knew who was in charge and his reputation had gone before him, so he took that as a dismissal and want back into the yard. Thurza carried on with her work at which she was very good. Ninety per cent of her time was devoted to making money for Mrs Eefamy, but ten percent of the week, Thurza was working for Thurza.

P. C. Shorrock was greatly smitten by the events of the last twenty four hours, and without making a note of it in his book, he reckoned he could work out reasons to call at Eefamy's yard once or twice each week, it was in the public interest to do so.

CHAPTER 18

St Helena

Mr Penaluna was not completely happy with the work which had been allocated to him: he was commanded to take one hundred and fifty influential Boers to St Helena, where they would remain as British prisoners until the war was settled. He knew the climate there was damp and unhealthy, it was not easy for ships to manoeuvre in harbour – the tides, currents and eddies were treacherous. But he was told – 'Refuse this work and it will go to someone else and so will the next job as well.' So he shrugged it off and began planning how to sail there, then to the Azores to pick up fruit and nuts and home to England. He reckoned it would take him four months and he got down to the reckoning as to what would be required to restock his ship, victual it, take on water etc. And he was still in a 'daggers-drawn' situation over the ship he had rescued. The owners and insurers had offered £200 for his help. Mr Penaluna regarded this as an insult and he told them that he was tempted to hire a tug, take the 'Marken' out to sea and scuttle it. The ship was still in his possession, because, just as the owners were playing games with Mr Penaluna as regards salvage money, HE was playing games with them, by saying he would need to see an original title of ownership before he would hand it over to them. He knew this was kept in Holland and would take weeks to arrive. So it was stalemate! They could not off-load the harness, saddles etc (a valuable cargo) and Mr Penaluna could not be rewarded for his efforts. Mr Penaluna was a man of long patience – the stakes were high and he could wait.

The man whom George was most worried about was Mr Bridgetower. He did not like to think that he was putting anyone out of work. He need not have worried: this cook was well able to look after himself: he went ashore as soon as the 'North Star' docked, he had drawn his pay and he was off. This was common practice for seamen in those days, they were bound only for the journey and if they did not wish to make the return, well, that was up to them. Most of Mr Penaluna's crew had good reasons for wanting to return to England and would do so, but our cook/violinist had pursued his own agenda all his life and would continue to please himself. He had a very good reason for going back to England: Marie, but he had also interests in Cape Town in the form of another 'wife' and a child and a nice little house he owned. He was careful with his money – never drank or gambled, and so he was able to go to this South African family with his pockets full of money and become again, for a short while, the devoted husband, father and house owner. He also had a 'wife' in New Zealand and one in Montevideo. He loved all his 'wives' and he was a very keen lover but he hated the idea of spending his hard earned money on harlots, so instead he kept his money and gave it all to the lady who he knew would be waiting for him. In this case it was in Cape Town. Here he would enjoy connubial bliss for five or six weeks. He always kept some money back as a final payment and as he left, he gave the lady, whether she be in South Africa or New Zealand or Montevideo every penny he owned. Once on board he had no need of money and his wages were accruing from the day they set sail, so that he had money to give to his next 'wife' – wherever he made a landfall. It must have been his own confidence in this system which ensured that Mr Bridgetower was always so happy. It never occurred to him that what he was doing was immoral, indeed cruel. But seafaring men have always had this attitude: Nelson himself said 'Once you have passed Gibraltar, every man is a bachelor.'

The 'North Star' was now ready for her next journey. Mr Penaluna had settled with the insurers and ship owners and was £1,000 better off. He had indeed bought a diamond ring for Clarissa, and by his reckoning, the gratitude tenderly offered by his lady – love, was beyond all price. So Mr Penaluna and Clarissa were about to begin the journey back to England in a very happy frame of mind. Bridgetower was now 'Chips' assistant and had proved to be a more than just a useful carpenter, and they had both had a very busy time of it: when Mr Penaluna was told he that he would have to transport one hundred and fifty Boers to St Helena, he insisted that he would have to have the time and the money to convert his hold into cabin space. This was granted and so 'Chips' and his new assistant had knocked up seventy cabins to accommodate the Boer officers, and in many cases their wives. Field kitchens were fixed on the deck again, as they had been for the 'North Star's' first trip to South Africa, the ship was victualled , after careful consideration between Mr Penaluna, George, some of the Boer wives and the Army Authorities, enough cooking equipment, food and fuel were brought on board to sustain the crew and the prisoners/passengers for the journey.

Good progress was made out into the South Atlantic, Given favourable conditions Mr Penaluna reckoned the two thousand miles would be completed in four or five weeks, and he made this known to eight or ten of the senior Boer officers. He also told them that they could have the run of the ship, except in really bad weather and he asked for their word that they would behave and not cause any trouble. He reminded them that they were prisoners, but so far as he was concerned if they conducted themselves like gentlemen, then they would be treated accordingly and everyone could look forward to an enjoyable four weeks at sea.

George and the ever adaptable Bridgetower taught the ladies how to cook for their menfolk and the first two weeks went very smoothly, but the Boer officers were not content and decided to hatch a plot, take the ship and return to South Africa to re-join the struggle.

The luggage they had brought aboard had not been thoroughly searched and some of the Boers had secreted pistols and ammunition among their wives' clothes. Mr Penaluna made a habit of inviting some of the Boers to his table and one evening four of them appeared, as invited. They were de Kok, Steyn and Reity, all were high ranking members of the Boer army but Mr Penaluna always referred to them as 'Mister'. He explained, "There is no point in carrying on with army titles: when you go back to South Africa the war will be over and you will be Mister again."

Even though they were Mr Penaluna's guests and were enjoying his not inconsiderable hospitality, they were becoming quite heated about Mr Penaluna's refusal to acknowledge their rank.

Clarissa offered her words of advice by asking for calm and saying, "You have always been treated like gentlemen and to me, that is far more important than being a Major or a Commander."

"I'll not take that from you," Steyn said bitterly. "What is your position on this ship anyway – the Captain's woman?"

"Steward," Mr Penaluna called loudly. "These gentlemen are just leaving – the meal is over." Steward came into Mr Penaluna's saloon just in time to see Reity draw a pistol from his tunic. Steward was carrying a large coffee pot and he smashed it down onto Reity's hand. Fortunately the safety catch was on, and the gun did not go off, but it gave time for Steyn and de Kok to also draw pistols and they told Mr Penaluna they were taking his ship.

"Taking it where exactly?" Mr Penaluna asked.

"Back to South Africa," Reity said.

"That is ridiculous – as soon as you arrive at Cape Town you will be arrested by English troops."

"We are not going to Cape Town, we are planning to beach the ship twenty miles to the west and escape back on to the veldt."

"You can't beach a ship of this size, it's too risky, there are nearly two hundred people on board, and you will put every ones life at risk, and more to the point how do you intend to navigate the ship back to precisely where you want to be? We are now over one thousand miles from Africa, can you read maps? Do you understand navigation?"

"You will have to navigate for us," do Kok said.

Mr Penaluna was quite adamant on this point "I will not – I work for only one master and that is the master who pays me."

"This is your master now," de Kok said, and he tapped his revolver. We have thirty more on board and we have worked out a routine where by we can keep your men at gun point night and day if necessary, and if we have to, we'll take hostages and shoot them too if you do not do exactly as we ask."

Mr Penaluna knew he was beaten, but was already, just minutes after his acceptance of defeat, working on how to reclaim his ship. His was not the kind of mind which wasted time on rancour, his thoughts were restricted to positive planning.

"Very well – you have my ship now – you will make the decisions. Steward – ask Mr Baguly and Mr Sweeting to come here please and we'll tell them what has happened."

So a system evolved over the next few days of Mr Penaluna's men, working at gun point, turned the ship around and headed back towards South Africa. Mr Penaluna and Clarissa continued to walk the deck and enjoy the fresh air as if nothing had happened. The South Atlantic can be a wonderful area to sail through: there is much to see in the form of whales, dolphins, porpoises, and bird life, as well as flying fish and Mr Penaluna was quite prepared to wait until his time came. He had told the mutinous Boers that only by using Humpage, and young Sweeting and Yardley as helmsmen did they have any chance of reaching their destination, and privately Mr Penaluna told these three to be most particular about their keeping records of the distance covered in their time of duty of the helm. He also emphasised to Mr Baguly, Sweeting (senior) and Bo'sun that they must heave the log on the hour and take particular note of the results. All the data to be brought to his cabin as the watch changed.

"What's all this about Sir – why so very careful?" Mr Baguly asked.

"Because," Mr Penaluna explained. "This lot know nothing of navigation, but they are giving all the orders. When we do retake the ship – and we will Mr Baguly – Oh yes we will retake her, I want to know exactly where I am, but I have allowed the chronometers to run down, and I have hidden them. These are not pleasant men to have on board and it occurred to me that if they did know a little about navigation they might be able to fathom out why we had two chronometers, but now the navigation will be by dead reckoning and I think I'll have the edge on 'em over that."

"But why hide the chronometers?" Clarissa asked.

"Because, if they found them they couldn't sort out how to calculate from them, they might be tempted to heave 'em overboard. As I say, these are not pleasant people. And my chronometers are a matching pair of Barrauds at £400 a pair. So we will wait our turn."

They were heading back roughly in the direction of Cape Town but at a slow speed. The decisions about how much sail to carry had to be left to Mr Baguly, and he just kept enough way on the ship to give them the ability to steer. A week had gone by and they had covered barely four hundred miles. But a week is a long time living under conditions where it is almost impossible to walk anywhere without seeing someone with a gun in their hand. Clarissa asked Mr Penaluna if there was anything which could be done to overturn the situation.

"The sea will give us the solution," Mr Penaluna replied enigmatically.

"How can the sea help? It hasn't helped up to now."

"I have been across the South Atlantic many times during the last thirty years and I have never known it to be as docile as this. Why – it is like crossing the Mediterranean it is so calm and warm, with clear skies. But there is a menace in the seas." He walked Clarissa to the taffrail and they looked back, it was indeed like the Mediterranean sea; deep blue, three and four foot waves gently moved along and tossed creamy white foam ahead of them. The sky was clear too, just a few clouds hovered.

"I have never seen this area so gentle, so well behaved – it will make up for it and then it will be proved just who this ship belongs to – they think sailing is like a tea-party – but it isn't and they will know it soon."

"But in the meantime?" Clarissa asked.

"We just wait, enjoy our stroll, contemplate what George is preparing for our evening meal, enjoy the view and wait, the sea will do the rest."

The Boers attitude changed radically when they took control of the 'North Star': the women folk took to walking on the deck more often and were condescending in their treatment of the sailors. The men started to use small but bullying ways of dealing with Mr Penaluna's men and there were one or two skirmishes, one in particular involved Hazel. She was no great beauty, that was beyond question, but she was by this time a valued member of the crew and quite vital to the health and hygiene on the ship. Beds were stripped every week, and the crew were now used to the (at that time) unusual idea that one had clean clothes to wear every week. One day when Hazel was pegging out the washing on the deck, unkind remarks were passed concerning her girth. The taunts were greeted with a smile, and because this was the opposite response to the ones the Boers soldiers had expected and indeed wanted, they tried again and the insults became more barbed and direct. Radford whose life had been completely changed by Hazel, was just arriving with a big basket full of wet clothes when he heard the remarks. He hurled the heavy basket at the Boer officer and set about him. He was a wiry little man and inflamed with a strong desire to right the insults, a very dangerous one. Hazel tried to separate the two, when de Kok came on the scene and fired his revolver in the air.

"Why are you both fighting my officer?" he demanded.

"I wasn't fighting - I was trying to separate them," Hazel said.

More Boers came running to the scene, and de Kok, said "Tie them to the rigging we'll flog the pair of them – I will not have my officers treated I this way."

Mr Penaluna and Mr Baguly arrived to find Hazel and Radford tied up, the clothes torn from their backs – all was ready for the punishment to begin.

Mr Penaluna was his usual calm, assured self. "This is not justice Mr de Kok, surely in a civilised society, people aren't just flogged without hearing them out, all the right is never on just one side – let's hear what they and your officer have to say."

"I saw two of them on to Mr von Rensberg and that is good enough for me."

"Not good enough for me though," Mr Penaluna insisted. "There are no two people less likely to fight on this ship than these two. Look at Radford – would he tackle Mr von Rensberg under normal circumstances – he weighs no more than seven stone?"

By this time all the crew and all the Boers had assembled and were listening to the arguments. In spite of the unusual circumstances of the crew working with the threat of guns every day they had come to very sensible and friendly arrangements existed with most of the Boers and they were able to talk about the proceedings and no one was getting heated in their discussions. Von Rensberg was not popular even with his own men.

De Kok however felt his authority was being undermined. He was used to obedience especially when he had a gun in his hand, and now he flourished his revolver and shouted "The flogging will go ahead now."

"No it will not." Came an even louder voice. Everyone looked round and on the higher deck were Bridgetower, George, Humpage, Sweeting AND Clarissa all holding muskets – the old ones Mr Penaluna had had on his first ship the 'Bulldog'. It was Bridgetower who had shouted. Many of the Boers had revolvers in their hands, but by this time all the Boer women were on deck too and it would have been very dangerous to open fire, bullets would have been flying everywhere.

Bridgetower shouted again, "Throw your pistols into the sea." Mr Penaluna started to move amongst the Boers, gently removing the guns from their hands and tossing them, one by one, overboard. Mr Penaluna then signalled to Bo'sun to release Radford and Hazel, and the whole incident was defused.

Mr Penaluna moved to Mr de Kok's side and said, "A near thing – as we would say in England – I think we need a glass of something rather special and we can then put the events of the last few days behind us. Come with me. Steward, Steward, where are you? Three or four bottles of our best Madeira if you please Steward – in my saloon, we'll sink today's events under a bottle or two of good wine."

Mr Baguly burst upon the scene, and grabbed Mr Penaluna by his coat, "Look Skipper, look at that." It was a tidal wave at least fifty feet high and it was no more than two miles away and heading straight for them. Mr Penaluna turned to de Kok and said, "Take all your people below now and we'll batten the hatches down – 'Chips' see to that now. Humpage, make sure that the wave comes at us from the rear – and not one degree out of ninety. Bo'sun, rig up life lines both ways and quickly. Mr Baguly shorten sail and bring down the t'gallants if there's time – if not cut 'em loose and throw 'em overboard."

He then took Clarissa's arm and guided her down to his cabin, and was up on deck again in seconds.

"Steward, Steward – tell George to dowse his fires – it'll be on us any second now." He added under his breath – "under us I hope, if it is ON us we are lost."

As soon as the order to put the fires out was received in the galley, George dashed to the furthest part of the hold where his precious Nelson had her quarters. She knew intuitively that things were not just as they should be, and she was not easily calmed down. But George knew how to talk to her and to take her mind off worries by whistling, and gradually she lost interest in the storm up above. Perhaps the apples George allowed her to steal from his voluminous apron pocket helped just a little……..

The wave was a vast wall of seething foam fifty feet

high and many miles wide. They are caused by the constant building up of ungovernable power which rules the seas in the South Atlantic. Often the waves are ten or fifteen feet high and they are not difficult to deal with. But very occasionally, and for no explainable reason, five or six of these waves join forces and rush headlong for many miles consuming everything in their path. Normally a look out would spot this phenomenon many miles away, but because of the fracas with Mr de Kok, look out was not at his post and so the wave was able to creep up unannounced.

Mr Penaluna had made what preparations he could in the short time available and he knew the testing time was only minutes away. It went through his mind that the 'North Star' was six or eight hundred tons lighter than usual because her 'cargo' was one hundred and fifty prisoners. He had taken on some extra ballast but she was still light, and he wondered if the relative lightness would be an asset or his undoing.

The roar was louder than anything Mr Penaluna had ever heard, it was of volcanic proportions. As it arrived, it lifted the 'North Star' like a toy and at the same time squeezed it down with the weight of water it put onto the decks. Masts, riggings and sails tumbled on to the deck and in seconds converted the area to a breaker's yard. The whole ship was lifted up again by an after-wave and again the decks took two hundred tons of water, and withstood it. The water poured over the rails and through the scuppers. Scores of men were hanging on to the life-lines Bo'sun had laid out, all were drenched but they were alive. Mr Penaluna just managed to make a grab for his Lord Nelson hat as it was on its way over the side. He clamped it on his head – looking quite ridiculous but it was safe there. In fact everything was safe. The freak wave had passed by and was miles away, looking for more victims, but the 'North Star' had come through another emergency, not unscathed but still intact and sadly denuded of ANY means of propulsion. The few surviving yardarms were all ahoo, ropes dangled uselessly and there was tackle, blocks and tarpaulin everywhere – all wrecked and torn.

"Well I had heard of these freak waves," Mr Baguly said. "But I always thought people was making it up, like sea monsters, giant squids and the like but now we've seen it with our own eyes."

"Yes, it is terrible Mr Baguly" Mr Penaluna averred. "But there is no longer any doubt who is in charge of this ship." At this point Clarissa came on deck and threw herself into Mr Penaluna's arms sobbing with relief. "As I said my dear – the sea will sort this out for us – and it did. Steward, ho there Steward, be so good as to ask Mr Eefamy to come forward, we have need of his skills."

Radford lit the fires and soon the ovens were hot enough for oven bottoms – a flat cake of bread, quickly baked and ideal for clapping bacon on. Trays full were distributed to crew and Boers alike and the mutiny seemed to be over.

Mr Penaluna and Clarissa spent some time arranging the furniture in his saloon, and when it was in order George presented himself to find out what was in Mr Penaluna's mind.

Mr Penaluna began, "We have had a troubled time Mr Eefamy, what with the mutiny and that freak water, we need a calming influence and I feel one of your special meals will help us all."

"Not least our Boer friends," Clarissa butted in.

"Quite so my dear – now what do you suggest from your vast repertoire of dishes?"

"Legs of pork Sir – done crispy and with apple sauce."

Mr Penaluna's face became incandescent with anticipation. "And to follow?"

"Figgy pudding with honey Sir."

"Bravo Mr Eefamy – now I must ask Steward to call forward some of our – how shall I put this – guests, and we shall eat and drink and plan how to live peaceably on this ship." "Go forth Mr Eefamy and proceed with your alchemy." Mr Penaluna smiled as he said this – then he called loudly, "Steward, Steward – come on man, step lightly, we are to have a feast." Steward came in positively exuding lethargy and curmudgeonly vibrations.

Three hours later Mr Penaluna, Clarissa, Mr Baguly and two apprentices gathered around the table with ten of the prominent Boers. The table looked quite splendid: Steward knew how to lay a table and at Mr Penaluna's request he positively excelled himself.

"Well, ladies and gentlemen," Mr Penaluna called. "Let us toast our safe arrival in St Helena – for now with my ship in this state it must indeed be St Helena. How have your rigged her Mr Baguly?"

The Boers stayed sullen and silent – their mutiny well and truly scuppered. "Only the way I could Sir, like an old Viking ship. Most of her tackle is gone and we'll be lucky if she makes four knots."

"Well we must all be thankful she didn't go under. With these Trade Winds fixed as they are in these waters, there is only one route for us gentlemen, and that is westward. Tacking, luffing, seaman-ship are all out of the question. She cannot manoeuvre without full tackle, so we have to follow the wind and pray that there will be no more waves like the last one. Now Steward – enough of our woes and discomfortings, what have you for us?"

"Fortified sherry from Madeira – ten years old."

"Capital! Steward, serve our guests first."

Mr Penaluna then rang a bell – a prearranged signal for George and Bridgetower to enter with two legs of pork. They were secreted under silver domes which were removed with theatrical elegance by Steward. Roast potatoes and apple sauce came in too, as did carrots and turnips mashed up with butter and cream. Mr Penaluna was a dab hand at carving – a job he greatly enjoyed. "Help yourselves to the crackling, show our friends how to use the tongs Steward – there's a good chap." Mr Penaluna had specially large tongs, like sugar tongs, but larger, for distributing the pork crackling. Clarissa glowed with happiness, this really was her sort of evening and she entered into conversation with the Boer ladies to try to lighten the atmosphere and ease the tension. Gradually, as the Madeira and the La Rochelle wines found their way into the veins of the diners, the meal took on an almost festive mood. Mr Penaluna kept repeating that they were all lucky to be alive, and since the Boers were religious people (which Mr Penaluna definitely was not) he emphasised how grateful to the ruler of the waves they should all be, and that they were still here and enjoying such a fine celebratory meal. He kept raising his glass and proposing more toasts.

The ship returned to normal – normal that is for a ship full of prisoners, but the storm and the way Mr Penaluna had handled it had convinced the Boers that any future mutiny would be pointless, and they made their slow trudging way towards St Helena. One day, as they leaned over the taffrail together, Mr Baguly asked Mr Penaluna why he just kept a jury rig on the ship when there were spare yardarms and masts aboard. "Oh it's true Mr Baguly. I could almost put the ship back to rights, but that would then give them ideas about steering back to South Africa, so I am quite content to go along at three or four knots and continue with the story – which they do believe - that we are using all the tackle we have got and the only way is westward. They are not seafaring people, and they also believe, because of the way we handled that freak wave, that their lives are in our hands. So it is just an uneasy truce. Give them the slightest idea that this ship could be fully manoeuvrable again and we would have another mutiny."

"The seas are being kind to us at the moment," Mr Baguly said.

"They are indeed – if we can make St Helena, with no more storms, we will be very fortunate, but the good fortune will have to last for another two weeks. Let's go and look at the board."

They went together to the wheel where the board was kept.

"Have your logged her, Mr Sweet?"

"Ay we have Sir, every hour on the hour, it's all wrote on the board. Three, three and a half, sometimes four knots, just once it was four and an onion."

"There it is Mr Baguly, seventy or eighty miles a day. But we'll arrive never fear, and we'll stay there for a month or so for a refit, and George can take his pony ashore and let her munch some fresh sweet grass."

The 'North Star' duly arrived in St Helena and there were problems as to how to get in. The ship, fully rigged, could perhaps have made it, but the jury rigging offered little in the way of precision and Mr Penaluna decided to stand off when he was two miles out and tow her in, using his own boats, since there was no tug boat on the island. It was hard work, but using the combined strength of their backs and Bo'sun's foul language they put her to rest. Mr Penaluna went ashore and made it known to the authorities what the precise nature of his 'cargo' was. They were used to having prisoners there, in fact, hundreds of Boers were already housed there, so they were disembarked, and in the main left the 'North Star' without a word, to serve a sentence of uncertain duration and certainly one which would offer little in the way of hospitality or comfort.

Colonel Price was the commanding officer on St Helena, and he was well surrounded by fully armed soldiers as the Boers left the ship. They would be in no doubt as to their position on St Helena: they were prisoners and there was no chance of any escape. Colonel Price came forward to greet the senior Boer officers but his approach was deliberately ignored by de Kok and his fellow officers. Mr Penaluna got the impression that it was all rehearsed or at any rate prearranged. Mr Penaluna shook the Colonel's hand and said he would like a few words in private. The Colonel moved towards his deputy and told him to take the prisoners to Deadwood camp and that those unable to walk that distance must be taken by horse and cart.

"Now Mr Penaluna, what did you want to tell me?" Colonel Price began.

"They are a mutinous lot. They tried to take the ship, and you can see the state of her – if we hadn't gone through freak conditions which wrecked her, we would have had to sail back to South Africa."

"Well, we can repair the ship here, we haven't much spare timber, but we have good carpenters and they will be your's to call upon – now tell me about the mutiny."

Mr Penaluna told the Colonel all the details and how the position was put back to rights by the mutineers' fear of being lost at sea after the freak wave.

"You could have had two or three platoons of soldiers put on board at Cape Town – they would have kept order for you."

"Yes, it is true, we were offered that protection but when I met de Kok and some of his officers and all their wives, they did appear to me to be in a mood to accept their fate. They were among those known to us as 'tame Boers', in other words the faction that was looking for a compromise type of settlement. They gave me their word as officers and gentlemen, and I accepted it. As it turned out I was wrong, so I am here to say don't trust 'em, if they can escape they will and if they can cause trouble, they will do that too."

"Well, they are here now and believe me there isn't a boat here capable of a hundred miles journey let alone the two thousand miles back to Cape Town. So it is just a case of helping them to settle in. We put them on really good food, our theory is if the food is good the bitterness ebbs away. We let them do some agricultural work, they keep chickens, as you see we have a thriving coffee shop, opened by one of the Boers. So I try to encourage them to indulge in as many diversions as possible. My position here is useless to my career but if anyone escapes, then my prospects are nil. It's a dreadful place, it's damp and windy and I think our Government have forgotten about us. It was no different when Napoleon was here and Lord Hudson Lowe – the then Commander of St Helena hated it too. Trouble was he became neurotic about Bonaparte escaping, and I don't intend to go down that road. There are no means of escape and I keep a rota of lookouts all around the island in case any ship creeps up on us – we knew you were coming as soon as your masts rose above the horizon."

"And you say there are no really seaworthy boats on the island?"

"That's right, what there were I forced the owners to sell to me and I destroyed them, but I have allowed them to makes small boats out of waste timber and canvas, and if the day is calm enough they do a little fishing."

"I had heard something of this story when I was in South Africa and because my ship was travelling light I bought two hundred tons of good timber to sell to prospective boat builders."

"Don't worry, we need wood; it rots at an alarming rate in this climate, so I'll get the Provisioning Officer to see you. Now. How long do you propose to stay here?"

"It will take three or four weeks to put my ship back into shape. So shall we say five weeks maximum."

"Very well – you see I will have to place ten or fifteen men to guard your ship night and day because it is a possible link to South Africa. Some of them might try to take your ship from you and the first duty of any worthwhile prisoner of war is to escape, so bearing that in mind – from tonight onwards I shall have a full platoon of armed soldiers guarding your ship."

"Well – that is a comfort. I just need your signature now Colonel Price to say the prisoners are safely delivered, and I'll be on my way to supervise the refit."

"Keep in touch Penaluna" the Colonel said. "There are plays put on regularly, also concerts, we have an excellent pianist amongst the Boers, so many evenings can be passed quite pleasantly – it is just the days that drag."

Mr Penaluna walked back towards his ship, and met George mounted on Nelson.

"Hello there Sir – we are going for a gentle walk to show Nelson the island and to let her have some fresh sweet grass."

"Very commendable Mr Eefamy – be back in time to cook something special for our evening meal – I hear the beef is very good here and try to locate a supplier of fresh vegetables while you are out and about."

Mr Penaluna then walked off towards the harbour, the serious business of refitting his ship was about to begin and he had one or two theories about the positioning of some of the sails which he wanted to try out. The 'North Star' was Mr Penaluna's toy and he was going to enjoy the next four weeks, playing with it.

George rode Nelson for half and hour or so and then dismounted and walked with her. He whistled for her and whispered in her ear. He recalled for her the long walk from Kimberley to Cape Town, remembering most clearly the best parts and in the main omitting the frightening episodes. She eyed him up as best she could in her optically disadvantaged condition, and took every opportunity to stop and graze the sweet grass which St Helena's damp climate produced so freely.

Back at the harbour Mr Penaluna and his men began to refit the 'North Star' much as they had done all those months ago when Mr Penaluna bought her from Mr Strange.

"Where do we start – that's what I want to know?" asked 'Chips' in his usual contumacious manner."

"We'll start by looking at everything we have and

seeing what's usable and what ain't – for instance a smashed up jib might be useful as a t'gallant mast. So throw nothing away – let's look at every item and use our brains to save too much work."

"And too much spending," 'Chips' added, somewhat crustily.

"Exactly, let's avoid too much spending as well – do you know why?"

No answer came forth.

"Well I'll tell you – because I am the ONLY one who does the spending – that is why." Mr Penaluna then continued addressing the crew - " 'Chips' here might be grumpy but he does know about timber ('Chips' managed a bleak smile – his face was out of practice) so take notice of him and we'll soon have her all ship shape again."

He walked over to Radford and Hazel who were not going to be used as part of the refit team. "How about bacon sandwiches and coffee can you manage that?"

Yes - they could, and were soon busy with their particular part of the refit – ensuring everyone was well fed and that 'Chips' had nothing to grumble about.

Mr Penaluna spent a lot of his time in the Government Stores and was quickly made aware that the storemen were just as corrupt as they were when Samual Pepys took over the paperwork system of the Royal Navy in Charles the Second's time. So far as they were concerned everything in the stores was for sale and their pockets were very ready and willing to receive coin of any description or origin. Mr Penaluna was quite willing to cooperate with them but only so far as tipping them. He was not prepared to 'buy' any stores. He didn't have to, because Colonel Price had told him that the spares for sailing ships were rarely called for now, because it was mainly steamers which arrived at St Helena and Mr Penaluna would be helping them to modernise the stores by taking out rope, masts, blocks and yards. Mr Penaluna therefore helped himself to the best that was on offer and used Nelson and a small cart with George at the reigns to move the spares back to the harbour.

Under these circumstances, Mr Penaluna did not know the word 'tired' even existed, and as George arrived with yet another load of booty, Mr Baguly pleaded for mercy. "The fellas is knocked up, Mr Penaluna, let's call it a day now."

Mr Penaluna was amazed, but when he looked at Mr Baguly and his band of honest hardworking assistants he knew Mr Baguly was right.

"Right you are. George, tell Steward from me to bring out some grog. We'll unload the cart, you get some bacon frying and we'll all have bacon and eggs, and open up some of those tins of plums – can you make some custard?"

George nodded. "Right then lads, just empty the cart and stow the stuff nice and tidy. Mr Eefamy will look after us." And so the work continued with Mr Penaluna a genial but a firm taskmaster.

The masts were replaced with new, and the young apprentices tarred them (and themselves) from top to bottom. New yards were painted up, and positioned. The blocks and ropes were cut away and scrapped if they were damaged, and beginning with the fore, main and mizzen trucks and down to the cross-trees the 'North Star' was made to look like new. The flying jib-boom, the bowsprit cap and the martingales were renewed and painted. Mr Baguly was especially careful to ensure that safety nets were hoisted out beneath the men replacing the timbers in this dangerous position. The men became used to the position and stopped for meals by deliberately dropping into the nets and scrambling out laughing and exulting in their own agility.

The back and fore stays, some experts argued worked well using wire rope, but Mr Penaluna was determined to use wire only when insufficient Manila rope was to be found. 'Cuts the men's hands and hard to grip when it is wet'. These were his reasons, but if they could be suitably spliced, so that the part of the stay his men handled was rope, then, grudgingly, some wire rope was allowed on board.

Gradually the work came down from the dizzy heights of the Royals and t'gallants and then to the cross-trees and of course the spanker, so beloved by Humpage, who usually manned the helm and felt every tiny response through his sensitive and loving hands. The crew whistled and sang more and more as the work progressed: they knew they were helping to create a thing of beauty, and they were proud of their work and of their ship. Gangs were over the side, slapping on coat after coat of cream paint, and Dredge – the artist among them, was titivating the figurehead to make her look as attractive and feminine as possible. Some of the ginger bread work was carefully painted in gold. It was actually orange paint but it was near enough to gold for the purpose.

Mr Penaluna had traded his two hundred tons of timber, and had laid in supplies of food for the trip to the Azores. Despite all his best efforts they would have to sail in ballast and Mr Penaluna hated any journey which did not pay him a wage, but this time he would have to make the best of it. He had telegraphed Forthergill and Jones, his Agents, and they had confirmed that a journey to the Azores would be worthwhile, so profit would be made eventually.

Mr Penaluna had two boats with eight men in each made ready to tow the 'North Star' out to sea. Colonel Price insisted on two of his officers conducting a minute search of the ship to see if any Boers were aboard as stowaways. Two English soldiers were found. They were hoping to escape the drudgery of a two year stay on St Helena. The two young officers were triumphant about their discovery and they promised the two culprits severe sentences and a flogging.

"Not flogging surely?" Mr Penaluna said.

"I wouldn't be surprised," one of the lieutenants said, "Colonel Price is a hard man – and here we are a long way from the War Ministry."

"I'll come with you and have a word with him."

An hour later Mr Penaluna returned with the two soldiers. Mr Baguly was waiting by the ship as Mr Penaluna approached. "Report to Bo'sun – he'll tell you what you have to do," Mr Penaluna said to the two (now) ex-soldiers.

"Colonel Price said they were sailors, who fancied being soldiers, and now they wanted to be sailors again, so they have sacrificed six months arrears of pay and bought themselves out."

"Yes, but are they any use to us?"

"Course they are – they are grateful to me for saving their hides and it's up to you and Bo'sun to sort 'em out."

CHAPTER 19

Fair Weather and Good Trading

The ship was now ready to leave. Little happened on the island of St Helena, so the leaving of a full sized sailing ship constituted a major event, and they were not disappointed – there was much to see. Clarissa was on deck in her finery, Mr Penaluna had donned his plum coloured coat, his Lord Nelson hat and his most authoritative demeanour. His men were poised, ready to release the sails, and the crew of the jolly and the long boat had their oars in position to pull the 'North Star' away from the wharf. When all was ready Mr Baguly looked round at Mr Penaluna, the latter nodded. Mr Baguly bellowed. "Leggo forrard" and then. "Leggo aft." Bo'sun yelled "Pull now" and the two crews bent their backs with immediate effect. A light wind came on the ship's quarter and with perfect timing, sails were dropped and sheeted home. They filled, and the 'North Star' – a wreck on her arrival at St Helena five weeks ago was a thing of beauty again, alive, vibrant and stately. Those on shore burst into spontaneous applause, and Humpage stood next to his beloved wheel. Mr Penaluna smiled, and sought Clarissa's hand. He found it beneath her cape and a small intimate squeeze welcomed his hand into her's. Clarissa was a sensitive as well as a passionate woman, and she knew just how much occasions of this sort meant to the man in her life. She did not try to compete with his 'other love', she was happy with the certainty that she might not be the sole love of his life but she was the only woman and she was determined to keep it so.

The journey from St Helena to the Azores took them from one thousand miles south of the equator to two thousand miles north of it. It was one of those journeys which sailors look back upon fondly because it was quite uneventful. The winds were favourable and steady, so the sails needed little in the way of adjustment. The only work they had to do was imposed upon them not by inclement weather, nor by Mr Baguly but by Hazel: she insisted upon the men changing their clothes and their bedding every week, as she put it, "I wants no bugs and no fleas on my ship." Mr Penaluna witnessed the use of the possessive pronoun but bowed to its impertinence, and his clothes and his cabin were also subjected to the same ruthless and vigorous treatment. Bed bugs were an almost constant hazard on board ship in those days but not so on the 'North Star'. Hazel saw to it that and the men slept easy in their beds, whereas the vast majority of sailors shared their beds with small creatures in search of blood for their nourishment.

They reached Azores in a little over three weeks and Mr Penaluna was very pleased with how his refitted ship had handled. He and Mr Baguly passed many happy hours during the journey discussing various combinations of sail but had actually ordered very few changes, and the men had spent the time sewing new suits of working clothes, inventing hats to keep off the worst of the sun, doing jigs in the evening to Bridgetower's violin and singing sea shanties. Some had brought their own drink on board and they got thoroughly drunk, but so long as they did their watch and were alert when Bo'sun went round shouting 'show a leg', then such misdemeanours were overlooked. Many of them could hold an astonishing amount of drink, the diminutive Radford among them, and they were none the worse the day after. What it did to their livers would no doubt be revealed in later life, but for now it didn't concern them. Their theory was 'we all have to die of something – we don't have much sex, so let's have a drink'.

They arrived in the Azores and quickly made contact with merchants who had fruit and nuts to sell. The Harbour Master was a stickler for detail and when he discovered that the 'North Star' was in ballast and was about to take on a cargo, he rowed out to tell Mr Penaluna about his new regulation regarding the disposal of ballast.

"Now I know it has been the custom to wait until it is dark and then tip two or three hundred tons of stinking rock and gravel into the harbour but I'll have none of that – let me see your hold and bilges." The Harbour Master and Mr Penaluna went below together and found to the Harbour Master's surprise just now clean and sweet smelling (for a ship) the 'North Star' was.

"I must say Mr Penaluna you do keep a clean ship – but I'll not have your ballast in my harbour just the same, so I'll ask you to go two or three miles out and tip it there,

I won't charge you for re-entry (Mr Penaluna smiled) and then you can load up and be on your way."

"Thank you Mr Lorenzo – I will of course do as you ask – will you keep a place for me at the wharf and I'll see to the ballast today."

Mr Penaluna then arranged with Mr Baguly and Bo'sun what had to be done. "We'll have her towed out – they have a little steam tug here, so the Harbour Master tells me."

Bo'sun offered to tip it over after dark. "They'll never see us if we use the starboard side."

"No. I want to come here regularly and I want to be welcome, so we'll do as they ask," Mr Penaluna said.

Seven days later they were fully loaded with six hundred tons of oranges and nuts. This was not freight in the ordinary sense of the word – this was an investment by Mr Penaluna and Clarissa, who were into this venture jointly, and it was a lot of money. What was of more interest to the two entrepreneurs was the fact that with luck they would make £200 each out of this transaction.

The timing of the loading worked out that it was complete by mid-morning but because so many ships were in the harbour they would not be able to leave until seven or eight o'clock in the evening. Mr Penaluna hated waiting and hated wasting time even more. It was a beautiful day so he sent for Bo'sun, Steward and George and announced that he was going to have a special meal and because it was so warm, it would take place on deck.

"Bo'sun – I want you to rig up an awning big enough to give shelter for all the men to eat under, and another one for say about ten or twelve to sit under." Bo'sun nodded. Steward piped up. "Don't put 'em together though."

"Why ever not?" George asked.

"Cos you don't see 'em eatin' – Mr Penlauna and his lady wouldn't want to see 'em neither."

"You have a point Steward – put the smaller one aft, near the taffrail, Bo'sun, probably the men will feel more relaxed that way. Now Mr Eefamy what had you in mind for this feast."

"Well Sir – I have looked around the markets here and goose seems to be a good idea."

"Goose eh – I like that suggestion – what do you think Steward?"

"Goose – pork – beef, it's all the same to me."

Mr Penaluna made a mental note not to ask Steward's opinion in future.

"Right, goose for say ten or twelve and what would the crew like, do you think?"

"Chicken Sir."

"Ah chicken. Why chicken?"

"Well I know they like chicken and sometimes they have bought one or two and I have cooked them."

"Very well then," Mr Penaluna readily agreed. "How many will you need?"

"One each Sir."

"One each – surely not?" Mr Penaluna said.

Steward said. "Oh! Yes! – One each, if that's enough. They are a greedy lot."

Mr Penaluna looked at Bo'sun for confirmation and got it by way of a nod.

"Right Mr Eefamy, better get thirty chickens to be on the safe side, and what's to go with them?"

"They have nice potatoes here and onions and I think it will have to be carrots and cabbage."

"Well why not indeed, carrots and cabbage are very good for you. And what is to follow?"

"Trifle Sir."

"Oh, trifle is it?"

"Yes – you can make a lovely orange trifle and here they brew a wine from oranges and then they distil it, so I'll soak the sponge cake in that."

Mr Penaluna's face was a picture of combined glee and anticipation. "You'll need some money for the market. How much do you think will cover it?"

"About five pounds Sir – I'll reckon it up carefully and bring you the change Sir."

"If any," Steward added in his crusty way.

Bo'sun piped up with a more useful addition to the conversation. "George, take Hazel, Radford and the three apprentices with you to carry all the stuff."

The little shopping party of six left the ship and walked to the market. They were so intent on their expedition that they failed to notice that two men were following them from stall to stall. George had not yet made any purchases, because he was weighing up quality and prices, but at last he found the ideal stall where they had plump chickens and four nice geese. He made a move for his leather purse and as he retrieved it from inside his shirt, a hand made a grab for it. Radford drew his knife and impaled the hand in a trice, he then brought his bony elbow back into the man's face with sickening force. The would-be robber fell to the cobbles, increasing the wound to his hand as he fell. His partner, who would no doubt have loved to share the money, did not wish to share the blame, and he ran off and disappeared amongst the shoppers. Three members of the Azores militia came onto the scene when they heard the screams and Radford was marched off to the local prison. George told Hazel and the three apprentices to return to the ship and ask Mr Penaluna and Mr Baguly to come to Radford's rescue. The wounded man was also taken by the militia and George, showing great presence of mind asked the stallholder to come with him to talk to the soldiers about the exact timing of the event. When Messrs Penaluna and Baguly arrived everyone was shouting, but the arrival of these two worthies, both dressed to impress, soon helped to regain order. The man was undoubtedly very badly injured, and the militia were right to arrest Radford, but the man who held the key to the situation was the stallholder, and in a quaint mixture of Portuguese and English he explained what had happened.

One of the soldiers kicked the injured man and took him to a cell. The officer asked everyone to leave except Mr Penaluna, so George and his little gang of shoppers waited outside until Mr Penaluna emerged – he did not look pleased: the officer demanded, and received, twenty gold sovereigns, Mr Penaluna had come well prepared, being a much travelled man, he had assumed that there would only be one way out of this situation.

"Well Mr Eefamy – are you now ready to resume your shopping?"

"No Sir – I'm afraid I can't – I had to give the stallholder all my – sorry, your money to get him to come and speak up for Radford."

"So now will you return to the same stallholder to buy chickens?" Mr Penaluna asked.

Somewhat sheepishly George admitted that it was his intention to do just that.

"Well this meal had better be good – bear that in mind." And Mr Penaluna and Mr Baguly went into a nearby inn to sample one or two quieteners for their nerves.

The day continued to be hot and the awnings Bo'sun had put up were very welcome. The big meal even more so. Because of George's absence, the men had had to resort to something very simple for their mid-day meal and had knocked together a hash of left over potatoes, smashed up ship's biscuit and corned beef, so the evening meal of chicken was eagerly anticipated. Each man had a roasted chicken and roasted potatoes. Just as Steward had forecast, etiquette vanished as soon as the meal appeared. Cutlery was not thought necessary by the majority of the crew and chicken bones were being thrown overboard at a rate likely to cause the house-proud Harbour Master some concern. The dessert was a handsome plum duff with hot syrup poured over it. Spoons were essential for this but a few had lost their spoon and they used knifes and forks or some other method best not described too graphically.

By contrast the meal served under the awning by the taffrail was stylish and genteel: Mr Penaluna's Karelia birch table had been brought up on deck and laid with an immaculate white linen tablecloth, his best silver cutlery had been cleaned up by the apprentices and carefully washed and rinsed, so to ensure that no taste of metal polish was discernable. Three geese were presented under domed lids (a fourth was held back in reserve!) and the potatoes and vegetables were served in large pot tureens. Those present were Mr Penaluna and Mr Baguly, Clarissa (looking quite lovely in a white lace sleeveless dress), three apprentices and Mr Sweeting, the second mate. There was a bottle of wine in front of every adult and a bottle of ginger beer each for the boys.

Bridgetower had his meal early and volunteered to play for Mr Penaluna's guests, his repertoire was wide and beautiful and his old Grancino violin caressed the ear, just as George's goose delighted the palette. The two legs from the fourth goose were in fact aloft in the crosstrees where George had taken himself off with a bowl of roast potatoes. Occasionally he would look down and wave to Clarissa, who was always nervous about his liking for meals sixty feet above deck. The sound of the violin floated gently all over the ship and Mr Penaluna offered up a silent prayer that the men would not ruin this blissful evening by brawling and swearing. When he was sure that the crew had finished eating, he signalled to Bridgetower that he wanted a quiet word.

"You have delighted us and we are grateful, but play a few reels for the men now, and perhaps 'Tom Bowling' – they always sing well in that."

"A good move Sir," Mr Baguly said. "Dancin' keeps their minds off fightin'."

Bo'sun rushed to Mr Penaluna and whispered something to him. "That's all right Bo'sun – let 'em come on, but keep 'em all at that end."

"What is that my dear? What is happening?" Clarissa enquired.

"Oh nothing to worry about – some ladies heard the music and have rowed out to join in the fun."

"I wouldn't exactly call 'em 'Ladies' Sir," Sweeting volunteered.

"Well it's a lovely evening Mr Sweeting, let's not spoil it by being too critical."

The music continued and the dancing and yahooing became slightly more indecorous, but it was well forrard and it did not unduly disturb the more sophisticated party who talked about this and that and sank bottle after bottle of wine. The apprentices were getting restive and obviously wanted to join in the rumpus at the other end of the ship. "How old are you?" Mr Penaluna asked the three boys. "Thirteen", came one answer. Mr Penaluna nodded to the next boy. "Fourteen", and the next "Fifteen."

"Right Steward, bring some more ginger beer and more pudding, the boys are staying with us."

After an hour or so the fiddling stopped, all was quiet. "That's funny," one of the boys said. "It is quiet now –

they've stopped dancing."

"They have settled down for the night," Mr Penaluna said. "Bring a blanket each and you three can sleep up here just for once. Bo'sun – make sure they keep their activities to their own cabins or well forrard and get 'em all off the ship first thing in the morning." And then to the boys, "Sleep here tonight – don't wander about and I'll get George to do you bacon and eggs for breakfast."

Mr Penaluna then gently took Clarissa's arm and let her back to the cabin. Forrard or aft, Captain or seaman – there was only one way to finish off such a wonderful evening.

Next morning Clarissa woke up in Mr Penaluna's bed naked as the day she was born. In the adjoining room Mr Penaluna was preparing her bath, she tripped lightly across the room, was kissed by Mr Penaluna as she went by and she sank languidly into the warm welcoming water, she smiled invitingly at Mr Penaluna, who took up his position by the bath and lovingly caressed her well covered back with a soft sponge.

Up on deck gratitude for a night of love was different. The girls woke up when Bo'sun's boot landed in their ribs. They put on anybody's clothes amid shouts and screams as one lady saw yesterday's dress on someone else's back. Those who were slow to respond to Bo'sun's persuasion were hosed down and the men helped to get last night's sweethearts over the side by the quickest possible route – the lucky ones landed in the rowing boat. The smell of bacon and coffee drifted about the ship and gradually, achingly, grumblingly the day's work began.

Mr Baguly went around the ship with Bo'sun and told the men to holystone the decks. "Nothing like a good hour of exercise to sober 'em up, eh Bo'sun, and tell the three boys to tidy up all the plates, cutlery and spare items of clothing and then in a couple of hours we'll be ready to get away and back to England.

"Skipper was sayin' we could do it in two weeks," Bo'sun said.

"Well it is about twelve hundred miles and at the time of year we are more or less sure of westerleys and the Old Man reckons she'll do twelve or fourteen knots no trouble, so it could be less."

"He'll make her go with all these oranges on board, nobody wants overripe fruit, so it'll be extra back stays and stun sails all the way."

"We'll feel the benefit if he makes a profit and we'll be back home all the sooner, and you can see your lady friend, Bo'sun."

"It'll be nice to be back at her place, she's a handy cook and a cosy bed full."

"Can't ask for more than that."

With that Mr Baguly concluded the conversation and went below to make sure that all of the 'ladies' had actually left the ship.

It was a beautiful morning, the sun was up and set about its business of slowly clearing the slight mist.

Mr Penaluna found Mr Baguly, "Is everyone who should be off, off?"

"Yes Sir. I have checked, all the girls 'ave gone, and I hope they haven't left our lads with a dose of the clap."

"No. Not out here – they should be alright. But are we ready?"

"Give me an hour Sir. The men don't work quite as quickly after a night like last night, but they are all up and I reckon if the tug is here in an hour, we'll be ready for then."

"Ho, there 'Chips' batten down now, we'll be ready shortly," Mr Penaluna called to the ship's carpenter, he then noted the grumpy look on his face. Mr Penaluna's next call was at the galley. "Good morning Mr Eefamy, are you happy about the thought of going back to England?"

"Oh yes Sir – I am."

"Good we should be there in two weeks or less. Take 'Chips' some coffee and a bacon sandwich, see if you can extract a smile from him. Ah, I see Radford is in there with you. Did you have a good night Radford?"

"Yes I did. Thankee Sir. Course I didn't 'ave nothing to do with all them whores what came on board."

"No. Quite right Radford, stick to the woman you've got."

"She's enough for me, right enough Sir."

'She's enough for anybody,' thought Mr Penaluna as he walked away. 'She must be sixteen stone – and I doubt if he is more than eight!' The thought kept him amused until he spotted Bo'sun.

"Send one of the apprentices to find the Tug Skipper, and tell him we'll need him in an hour."

"Aye Aye Sir."

Mr Penaluna then continued his walk around his ship, tugging a rope here and adjusting a halyard there. He went aft and looked over at the giant rudder, and noted there was plenty of grease on the pintles. He looked at the chains which hauled in the anchor and saw the rust had been chipped off and noted the fresh paint. So bows to taffrail, he had looked over his beloved ship, firstly to check that everything was shipshape, but also because he loved every inch of her.

Clarissa came on deck bearing Mr Penaluna's Nelson hat and his plum coloured coat, which she had carefully, indeed lovingly brushed. She slid his coat on and placed his hat on - fore and aft, then she stood next to him as the moving out procedure started. Bo'sun checked that the tow rope was correctly seized to one of the bitts. Mr Penaluna checked the wind direction and had men placed on the yards ready to release the fore and main topsails. The wind was brisk enough and once the 'North Star' was five miles out, two sails would be enough to give her steering way, and then Mr Penaluna intended to pack on all possible sail and make a quick passage.

Mr Baguly roared, "Stations", and then checked that everyone of the men was where he should be, he then moved to the bows where he could see, and be seen by, the tug skipper. Everything was as it should be. He looked towards Mr Penaluna and saw the Admiral's hat nod permission to proceed. "Let go forrard," was given and at the same time Mr Baguly waved to the tug to move away. Two or three hundred people were gathered on the wharf. There were always ships to be seen entering and leaving the Azores but a three master was always a big draw, and the crowd whistled, roared and clapped its approval, as the 'North Star' was brought to life. When the tug rope tightened, Mr Baguly shouted "Let go aft", and she was off. Humpage steadied the helm and she fell into line behind the smokey tug. A picture of grace and symmetry and also a biddable thing, but like all thoroughbreds capable of quite extra ordinary bursts of mettle and character. As she met the Atlantic, her forefoot lifted, in deference to the most turbulent of oceans. The flag was dipped three times to say 'Goodbye' to the Azores and to the helpful tug, and Mr Baguly yelled, "Fore and main." The sails fell as if by magic and were sheeted home in seconds. The men burst into a song as they tightened the ropes.

'Was you ever in Dundee;

Donkey riding, Donkey riding'

Where the girls they are so free etc.'

Humpage, white knuckled, was at the helm, to steady her as the sails filled with a crack like a pistol shot. Over she went, her one hundred and sixty foot masts describing a perfect arc. "T'gallants and royals next," Mr Baguly roared. The men, used to the procedure were already there. Then Mr Baguly's next order. "Lee fore braces – look out aloft. Haul steady men, handsomely now." This had to be done carefully and without any jerk – there were men one hundred feet up hanging on with one hand. "Right now lads – sheet home for England and home."

The men on deck were on to the halyards:

'Away, haul away from Calais unto Dover

Away, haul away, haul away Joe.'

Clarissa and Mr Penaluna watched this well drilled group of men going about their work so quickly and Mr Penaluna noted that the two soldiers he had rescued from Colonel Price's wrath on St Helena were high up the masts and knew their work.

"Fish the anchor," Bo'sun shouted.

"Keep her full and by Humpage," Mr Penaluna said.

"Could do with the spanker and the head sails, she's yawing a bit Sir."

"Have patience Humpage, there's plenty room to yaw."

"Yes Sir. Sorry Sir."

Mr Baguly came to Mr Penaluna who was by the binnacle, "She responds well Sir."

"She does indeed and carrying six hundred tons too. I fancy the main courses will take her forward a few knots – we'll try them, if you please Mr Baguly."

"Main courses lads. Handsomely now. Let the bunt out slowly we don't want no rips – let her fill gently." Over she went, the lee rails under water, the bows cutting through pure cream and hurling it yards either side. The seas were leaping into the fore riggings and all the ropes and rigging were humming from tension and speed of the wind.

"Heave the log please Mr Baguly," Mr Penaluna asked politely.

The leather cup vanished over the side, followed by the piece of rag and then the knots.

"Thirteen," came the answer.

"Spanker and head sails if you please Mr Baguly." They were in place and filled within seconds. Mr Penaluna looked round and saw Humpage's smile, at least a yard wide.

"Satisified?" Mr Penaluna asked.

"She goes beautiful Sir – Just beautiful."

Mr Penaluna turned to Clarissa who had deliberately been unobtrusive as all these delicate manoeuvres were completed. "That is how we'll keep her going – if the winds are kind to us and with luck they will be, we'll cover over three hundred miles a day." Clarissa tightened her grip on Mr Penaluna's arm which was intended as an indication that she had every confidence on the 'North Star's' safe and speedy arrival in Poole Harbour. With such a man, how could it fail?

Clarissa looked up and there was George in the cross trees, eighty feet up, swaying about and enjoying an enormous sandwich. She didn't wave, because she was not quite sure that he was firmly and securely up there, and he might be using his putative waving hand to grip something solid.

Big seas slammed on to her weather sides and then burst into hissing missiles of spray. The main deck was torrents of water rushing to the bulwarks and scuppers. It was thrilling for everyone on board, and they were all on their way home.

Next morning Mr Penaluna rose early and went to the helm where the board was kept – the mileage was chalked on – somewhat smudged, but the news was there, over two hundred miles in fourteen hours, and the wind was coming at them at exactly the best angle for speed.

"Ha. There you are Mr Baguly," Mr Penaluna began. "Send Steward here if you please."

"Steward, ask Mr Eefamy to do large bacon sandwiches for all the crew and coffee with milk too."

"Supplies won't last if you do that – we've vittled for four weeks and you're givin' it away wholesale."

"With this wind Steward, we'll be in Poole Harbour in four or five days, never mind weeks – so feed 'em and I'll find work for them to do."

"What work is that Mr Penaluna – if you don't mind me askin?" Mr Baguly said.

"Backstays and stun'sails all round, with this wind, I want sixteen or even eighteen knots and I know she'll do it."

"You'll have the sticks out of her Sir, she won't take that, no how."

"Yes, she will, or my name's not Theodore Penaluna."

Mr Baguly looked at his Skipper in astonishment - he had known him for fifteen years and never heard mention of his Christian name.

"Theodore, Eh Skipper. That's a fine name."

"That's right Mr Baguly. Theodore was my father's name and my Grandfather's – yes – I know what you are thinking – were they awkward old buggers too, and the answer is – yes, they were, so I'll maintain the family tradition, and I'll be selling my oranges in Poole before the week is out."

"Is this where the wire ropes come in then Sir – for back stays?"

"Exactly, Mr Baguly, ask Bo'sun to get a team ready, and as soon as they have breakfasted we'll really crack on."

The wind continued to come at the 'North Star' at the most favourable angle and she responded like a true thoroughbred, slamming her way through fifteen foot high waves and sending spray backwards for half the length of the decks. The weather was fine, very few clouds were about, no threat of rain, and the crew spent as much time as they possibly could on deck enjoying the experience. All seamen of that time knew about the great races which had taken place with the tea clippers like 'Cutty Sark' and 'Thermopylae', and now the crew knew what it was like to 'crack on'. Just for a short period it was possible to think that they were actually mastering the seas. Usually the sea had a way of countering an attack of hubris, but this time it did look as if confidence in their ability to rule the waves was justified.

Mr Penaluna stood next to Humpage who was at the helm. Their feet and legs moving and pressing down to give them balance, sea legs in fact. Both wore heavy waterproofs and sou'westers, both were happy, indeed exultant. Mr Penaluna had a word with Humpage and then waved to Mr Baguly.

"Humpage here admits that this is a 'two man sea' – he needs someone on the wheel with him."

"Aye Aye Sir – I'll put one of them soldiers with 'im – this is a passage to remember Sir."

"Enjoy it Mr Baguly – and remember it too, when we are tacking and weaving and making no headway, I'll remind you of this trip – keep on this line Humpage, and you'll be with your wife and children before the weekend."

"Thank you Sir – I'm looking forward to that."

George brought his breakfast out of the galley and Bo'sum spotted him looking up at the cross-trees.

"Not today young man – not today – have your breakfast down 'ere – or better still give me that bacon sandwich and coffee and go and make yourself another one."

Bo'sun went aft where the spray was not quite so fierce and as he sank his teeth into the barm-cake his thoughts turned to his lady friend in England and though he would never have admitted it, he was hoping she hadn't found anyone else in his absence.

The crew sensed that this passage was going to be of the very rare type when there was actually very little to do. The Skipper or Mr Baguly might tell them to tweak a sail this way or that way just slightly, but the wind was so constant and the ship so perfectly made that there was at most nothing to do. The watch on watch system which meant only four hours sleep at a time, gradually disintegrated and neither Mr Penaluna or Mr Baguly intervened.

The 'going home' enthusiasm spread throughout the ship. They had been away for the best part of twelve months and now they were on their way home at high speed. The bows cut through the water like a knife and the rigging twanged and hummed – it was sweet music.

There was the occasional job when a stun-sail broke loose because of the strain, but the men jumped up the rigging like children, laughing and joking as they went.

The look out shouted that there was a steamer ahead. They were soon up to it, as it clanked and rattled along at about seven knots. Humpage was having a spell away from the wheel and was stood aft near the rudder. As they approached the steamer Mr Baguly motioned to the men on the wheel to bring her to port a point or two to make sure they passed the steamer with fifty yards of sea between them. Once they were level with the groaning monster, Humpage offered a rope to the crew of the steamer – as if to give them a tow, they were not pleased, but the 'North Star's' crew enjoyed the joke, and to a man swore they would never leave sailing ships and work on a steam ship.

CHAPTER 20

Clarissa finds out about Thurza

The Isle of Scilly came into view early one morning and it was George who spotted it first from his breakfast position sixty feet up the main mast. It was a calmer day, and he had gained Bosun's permission for the ascent.

"Land on the port bow," came the call from above.

"I thought so," Mr Baguly said. "I could smell it – I knew we was there."

Soon there was the Lizard and the Bishop Lighthouse – the farthest west light of England. And the St Agnes Lighthouse. Mr Penaluna came on deck to check on progress, and began to walk about with a look on his face of suspicion, almost of apprehension.

"What's up Mr Penaluna?" Mr Baguly asked, sensing that all was not as it should be.

"Fog, we are in for a fog – it drifts across from France."

"Nothing good comes out o' there," Mr Baguly said.

"You're right. And unless I'm very much mistaken this will be a thick 'un." He saw Bo'sun hovering and said, "You thinkin' what I'm thinkin'?"

"Yes – I am – this is just about the busiest part of the Channel and if we are in a pea-souper and those big steamers comes rattling along – blind as bats – we're gonners."

"You are right. Fetch the fog horn and tell Steward to bring up my shot gun and some cartridges."

The temperature fell and so did the wind. There was a moan from an invisible lighthouse – it was a fog signal.

"Put men all around as look outs Mr Baguly, and sound our own fog horn every few minutes. The air changed to raw and damp, and moisture clung to the sails and rigging, at first as drops, but as they accumulated, streams of water dripped everywhere. The spars creaked and the sails began to flap uselessly – they were loosing way, and soon would be just drifting.

"Go round and check the ropes Bo'sun, tell the men to slacken off any that are too tight – this kind of damp shrinks 'em and they'll part if we aren't careful."

Mr Penaluna looked up and saw only as far as the cross-trees sixty feet up, beyond that the masts and sails were shrouded in fog. The men were all quiet now, all ebullience gone, replaced with worry and uncertainty. Only an hour before they were laughing and joking about arriving home and getting their pay, getting drunk and having a few weeks off work. Now they were cold, damp and afraid: a sailing ship drifting in the busiest waters in the world with visibility down to twenty yards.

Clarissa came on deck and sought out George who was standing by the rail watching Mr Baguly prepare to take soundings. Mr Penaluna had Steward to bring a table on deck and this was now covered with charts.

"How can they use charts to tell us where we are?" Clarissa asked.

George had seen his done before and was able to tell his mother exactly how it helped. "On the bottom of the line Mr Baguly is holding a heavy lead cylinder which is cupped. They will fill the cup with tallow or soap and throw it over the side and make it bounce on the sea bed two or three times."

"Why do that? – what will they learn?"

"When they pull up the lead cylinder they check the depth and examine the kind of sand, pebbles or shells stuck to the soap. Then Mr Penaluna will look at his charts which give details of depths and sea beds, and after six drops of the rope he can calculate exactly where we are."

"So we are safe?"

"I think so Mama – I always feel safe if Mr Penaluna and Mr Baguly are in charge."

The two gentlemen concerned leaned over their charts learnedly and went to the side to look at the water.

"About three knots I'd say Skipper."

"Yes I think so too, so cast the lead every hour and let me see the sample." He then approached Clarissa. "I think the worst is over my dear, we are away form the busiest part of the Channel – there is little likelihood of steamers here."

The fog lasted another day, but at last a wind came with slightly more strength. The crew, who were on deck to a man, sleepless now for thirty-six hours, looked at each other and nodded. The 'North Star' gathered speed.

Mr Penaluna who like his men had not left the deck for over a day, held his hand up to feel the breeze – he turned his hand this way and that, in case the palm had lied. A tired smile came to his face, he looked at the sails, they were filling and some of the rigging creaked.

"Two hours sleep now for the crew Mr Baguly, and then it will be our turn."

"Aye, Aye, Sir."

Clarissa was still on deck with George and as the fog cleared they could see nine ships. George carefully pointed out to an attentive mother exactly what they were.

"That one there, the big one is barquentine, and it is followed by a schooner and a snow."

"And the little one?"

"Oh! They are just fishing trawlers, not proper deep sea ships." George threatened to continue with his list, such was his enthusiasm.

"Do you think Steward could manage to make coffee?"

"No probably not – but I can and I will – would you like it on the cross-trees Mama?"

"You would find it difficult to get two cups of coffee up there and if I were to go up, you would find it quite impossible to get me down again – so we'll have them right here please."

When the crew had slept, Mr Penaluna told Sweeting and Bo'sun exactly where they were: "Now I want you to go South East from here," he said pointing to the charts, "until you are well clear of the Eddystone rocks and then and only then, will you head due East. We are about one hundred miles from Poole and with this wind we could make it by nightfall, but I don't want that, so once the men are all up and about, reef up the main course and stow for harbour. We'll go along nice and slow and go into Poole on the early morning tide."

With that he signalled to Mr Baguly to get his head down and shouted, "Steward – wake us in two hours – with coffee." Steward grunted.

Next morning everyone on board the 'North Star' was up and alert. The men were reckoning up how much pay they had to come and were vying with each other in expressing just how mad they were going to go with all that money in their pockets.

"I want a big beef stew and as much cider as I can swallow," one said. Another man boasted about what was going to happen to his girl friend. "She'll be for it, I can tell you," he shouted. Bridgetower said nothing. He had drawn no pay at Cape Town nor at St Helena. He was due over six months pay and he would be heading straight for Marie. The men went about their work jigging, dancing and singing and the wind seemed to catch their mood as it freshened and the 'North Star' went over to leeward and picked up speed.

A pilot cutter came towards them at sun up and the pilot climbed aboard, took a drink as was the usual custom, and spoke to Mr Penaluna.

"I've asked a tug to come to us in an hour – it can be tricky getting a big 'un around Brown Island at this time of the year."

"That's in order" Mr Penaluna replied.

The tug duly arrived and the usual procedure was gone through as regards haggling over the price, but the bargaining was by no means bitter and the tow-rope was soon around the bitts.

"Rig in the jib-boom," shouted Mr Baguly and the ship was quickly reduced in length by some seventy feet.

The pilot signalled to Mr Baguly to cast off the tug-boat's rope, and just using the way, he put her alongside the wharf as neatly as could be. Mr Penaluna had telegraphed to Fothergill and Jones his time of arrival and all the occupants of No 18 Wellington Terrace were there waving madly. Mr Fothergill was first up the gangway with a leather bag containing the men's wages and a tarpaulin wallet full of documents. George ran down the plank into the arms of Polly, Marie, Ann, Caroline and Rose. Marie, eager to welcome George, was also looking keenly to catch a glimpse of Bridgetower. He was ready with his dunnage over his shoulder – no unloading duties for him, someone would have to do it, but not Bridgetower. Once George was released, the girls were able to welcome Mrs Eefamy.

Mr Penaluna and Mr Baguly looked on, then Mr Penaluna said to Bo'sun, "Tell 'em it's ten bob extra if they stay with the ship to unload – we need ten or twelve – do your best." He then turned to Mr Fothergill – "Now perhaps we can enjoy a glass or two of Madeira."

"Splendid idea Penaluna, quite splendid."

Thurza was not with the little party from Number 18 who had assembled to meet the North Star and Clarissa asked why this was. Caroline answered.

"She always stays late on Thursdays to balance her books, so that she can bank the money on Friday." Mentions of working late and banking money appealed to Clarissa.

"Right. I'll go round to the Works before I go home and I'll see how she is getting on."

Tom was with the party. He had brought the girls to the docks in a carriage.

"Tom, you can drop me off at the Works, then take the girls home." Clarissa said, and then added, "George are you coming too?"

"Yes, I am coming with you as well, because Bo'sun has got Nelson out of the hold, and I can bed her down for the night."

Tom joined in. "Tie her to the carriage, she'll follow alright if she sees you are in there with the girls."

So the little procession made its way through the streets of Poole, and duly dropped Clarissa and George off. George then led Nelson over to the yard where the stables were. He was intent on finding a vacant one for his beloved pony, and he was making up his mind to sleep nearby for the first night.

Thurza was hard at work balancing up the cash and making what had become for her, standard deductions for her own purposes and the papers were on her desk. Tremblett came into the office and said to Thurza, "Your young policeman is outside, he says he can't come in because he had got something urgent on, but he wants to see you for a minute."

Thurza looked down at her paperwork, guessed that even if he looked at it, Tremblett would not realise the weight of mischief, indeed crime, which lay there on the desk, and went out to see what was so urgent about P. C. Shorrock's visit. As she left, and went into the yard, Clarissa came in by another door, saw the desk and spotted Tremblett, "Where is Miss Paxton – is she still here?"

"Yes Ma'am, she is, welcome back, she is in the yard talking to her young policeman friend."

"Oh well, don't rush her on my account, I'll wait here and look at the books."

The conversation in the yard lasted ten minutes and that was all the time needed for the dreadful truth to be revealed. Clarissa knew all there was to know about invoices, discounts, Bank statements, receipts etc. Her mind could calculate ten per cent or add figures or spot deductions with unerring accuracy. The two sets of books were there open and they revealed all of Thurza's attempts at embezzlement. Clarissa opened a drawer wide and saw a plump little leather draw-string bag and guessed that it contained the 'difference'. She placed this in a conspicuous position on the papers, and sat there smouldering.

Thurza returned from her tryst and P. C. Shorrock was with her, as she entered the office. Clarissa said quietly, "Very appropriate – you have committed these crimes, AND you have brought in your very own policeman."

Thurza's beautiful face acquired the expression of an ancient witch; it was contorted with hatred. Young

Shorrock stepped away, horrified by the transformation and stunned by what he had heard. And there was more. Clarissa pointed to the papers.

"These are not errors nor are they miscalculations, this is systematic theft." Thurza looked at Clarissa with loathing and made a dart for the drawer where the pistol was kept. Her hand was inside the drawer when young Shorrock slammed it shut. Thurza held her very painful wrist as Shorrock opened the drawer to reveal the gun. He placed it carefully in front of Clarissa, as if adding to the pile of damming evidence.

George had witnessed all this. He was up above the office where the oats and fodder for the horses was kept. Clarissa, out of the corner of her eye, spotted him and said, "George, please bring Mr Tremblett here." She studiously avoided looking at Thurza and sat there trembling and boiling with indignation.

"Ah, there you are Mr Tremblett, kindly escort this young person off my premises, and take her to the railway station, she is leaving Poole."

Tremblett touched his forelock, and stepped aside from the door. Thurza hesitated for a moment. Even her quick brain could think of nothing to say. Without looking at P. C. Shorrock, her former admirer, she left with Tremblett for the station.

Clarissa looked at the young policeman, guessed that he was greatly smitten by Thurza and said, "Well young man, this is a big lesson for you in your chosen career – trust no one. I do know Inspector Martindale, I'll think about this matter for a day or two, and decide if I am going to set the law into motion."

"If it is theft ma'am, there it is out of your hands, theft is a crime and that is for the law to decide what to do next."

"Yes. You are probably right – but there are ways, so we'll leave it there."

Clarissa then called out George's name.

"George I think we'll go to Number 18 now, and have some supper." And turning to young Shorrock said "I'll be in to see your Inspector tomorrow or the day after."

Clarissa began the walk home by putting her arm into George's.

"You're trembling," George said.

"I'm alright, the fresh air will steady me up." And slowly they made their way through the quiet streets of Poole towards Wellington Terrace.

The house was full: Caroline, Anne, Polly, Marie, Rose, Tom and Mr Penaluna were all there, and judging by the way the table was laid, the evening meal was ready to begin. Mr Penaluna went over to Clarissa's side.

"Are you alright my dear, you look quite exhausted?"

"It's all been a great shock, George will tell you the rest. He heard the whole disgusting business", and she guided Penaluna into the parlour. There, she told him the sordid details of the whole affair, and gave way to floods of tears. Penaluna was quite out of his depth, but struggled manfully and with great affection to help as best he could. His devotion for Clarissa was as unswerving as his love of the sea, and that was beyond words. Clarissa threw

427

herself into his arms, and gained great comfort from his gentleness.

George meantime related the story to the gathering in the kitchen. It was punctuated, indeed frequently halted by such helpful remarks as "I never liked 'er", "I told you so", "the little madam, and after what Mrs Eefamy did for 'er". But slowly the story unfolded, and warm-hearted little Rose said, "Mrs Eefamy must be very upset, I'm going to take her something." She remembered once before, when her mistress was distressed; that a large cup of tea with whiskey in it seemed to do the trick. She prepared one for Mr Penaluna as well, and took them into the parlour. Mr Penaluna signalled to Rose, to put them on the table, as he continued to gently pat Clarissa's shoulder and to murmur the reassuring "there theres", so efficacious in these circumstances.

Gradually, Clarissa regained her composure, and took little sips of the tea and the appropriately named water of life, and was able to tell Penaluna the whole story.

"It was the same with Strange. Do you recall I bought 'the North Star' off him? Took him on board as a clerk and he diddled me."

"You never said."

"No. I was too ashamed to tell you. He did it under my nose."

"This one I took into my home, dressed her, fed her. Treated her like my own family. It really is unforgivable."

"And they end up thinking they have a grudge, I'll bet she does, and I'm sure Strange thinks of himself as badly done to."

"She will go through some process of self justification, and within a week, according to her, I will be in the wrong – you'll see."

"You are quite right my dear," said Penaluna, gently putting his arm around his beloved lady friend. "The human mind is a very complex mechanism which is mainly devoted to thinking up the thoughts which give us the most comfort."

"You are a great comfort to me, Theodore."

"And you are my chiefest joy in life."

"Not your boat?"

"It's a ship," said Penaluna laughing. "You said 'boat' to annoy me."

"Ship, boat, it is all the same to me, just as long as you are the captain and you are steering it."

"I'd like to steer you off to bed."

Clarissa pushed him away. "You men are all the same, I am upset and you think of bed." Clarissa then opened her arms and welcomed him in "But you'll have to find somewhere else to sleep tonight – you can't sleep here."

"Don't worry, I'll be very brave."

Clarissa said suddenly "Come on we'll to back into the kitchen, let's see what is for dinner."

Thurza was taken to Poole Station by Bert Tremblett in a little pony and trap. She assured Bert that she had money (Clarissa's money) and she bought a ticket for the next train out, which as it happened was to Weymouth. She had much to think about. Her life at Number 18 was completely ruined and her putative life as the lady friend and possibly the wife of Edward Shorrock was wrecked beyond recall, or so she thought. What she did not know was that Shorrock was so smitten by Thurza that he would have forgiven her anything. She alighted from the train at Weymouth and went in search of an inn. Her main thoughts during the two hour journey were centred on accommodation and making a living. The right inn for her would offer a roof over her head, three meals a day and the possibility of employment. She walked up and down the main streets of Weymouth for over an hour and finally decided that the Falcon Inn was the one for her.

At Number 18 during breakfast the morning after their return from their travels, and Thurza's summary exit, all the girls, George and Mrs Eefamy were enjoying their ham and eggs when Captain Penaluna turned up. He did not like the breakfast he had been offered at his hotel, or so he said. He was really quite worried about Clarissa because of all the upset of the contretemps with Thurza, and made the poor breakfast an excuse for his early visit. He joined in at the toast and marmalade stage of the meal, just in time to hear what Clarissa intended to do.

"I want her room cleared out. I want no trace of that person left in my house," Clarissa began. She turned to Rose and said "Tell Tom to give her clothes to a charity, and to take all the furniture, carpets and curtains to the poor end of Poole and find a deserving family. Then, turning to Caroline and Anne said, "I want you to find a good decorator, and I want the room completely re-beautified."

"Isn't that all just a bit extreme?" Caroline said.

"No, it isn't extreme at all. We have had a thief, and

someone capable of calculated deceit, living with us and enjoying our affection as well as our hospitality. It is not the money – oh, yes, I nearly forgot. Rose, tell Tom there is a little leather bag of money in her drawer at the office. I do not know how much there is, nor do I want to hear. Tell Tom to take the little bag and to give it to the Sailors Benevolent Society, I believe they have an office near the docks."

"But it could be a pretty penny," Captain Penaluna butted in.

"Tainted money – I don't want it." Clarissa had really got worked up and was smouldering with indignation, as the unworthiness of yesterday's revelations came back to her. "The thing I cannot forgive is the ingratitude, we took that creature in as a penniless orphan and she saw my absence as an opportunity to rob me, us. That is our works, our money. She lived among us and robbed us. Ingratitude of that proportion is vile and I want everything of her's out of our home. Marie, let's have another pot of tea."

As Marie got up Penaluna took her seat next to Clarissa, and held her hand.

"You have been dreadfully treated my Dear, quite dreadfully treated. You need a quiet three or four days, in a country hotel, and I know just the place, where you will be well looked after."

"What I need is work – if I hadn't gone away, none of this would have happened. I am going to the works just as soon as I can. I want to see what else she has been up to. I must call at the Bank too. I'll never go away again, do you hear, never again. Oh. This is too much."

Tears flowed and Penaluna continued his ministrations. Penaluna was glad that anger had given way to tears, soon Clarissa would be her old determined self again, and after another cup of tea, would be off to work with her mind as sharp as a razor.

Two weeks after these events Tom was delivering orders and he had to go to Weymouth, and he spotted Thurza, and he stopped his rig and had a few words with her. She was settled at the Falcon Inn, helping in the kitchen and keeping the bedrooms tidy. Tom hoped for the owner's sake that she was kept away from the office. Upon his return to Poole he found young P. C. Shorrock and told him the news. Shorrock had a word with his Sergeant and got two day off and went to Weymouth to see if he could rescue the situation. He was convinced that Thurza's misdemeanours were just a one off aberration and was determined to forgive and forget. Thurza was glad to see young Shorrock, and during the two days spent as much time with him as she could. Things were often arranged quickly in those days because distances, even one as short as Poole to Weymouth, a mere thirty miles, were seen as a great obstacle and they agreed to marry. Shorrock hurried back to Poole to see his Sergeant, who arranged a meeting with Inspector Martindale.

"So you want a transfer to Weymouth?" the Inspector began.

"If that is possible Sir, I am getting married."

"Not my business really, I know, but Mrs Eefamy has told me the whole story. This girl is not trustworthy from what I hear. If she could deceive her employer could she not equally deceive you? She sounds a bad lot to me."

Inspector Martindale looked up at this point and looked straight into young Shorrock's face. Inspector Martindale was a man of some experience, an observant man, and a keen student of human behaviour, and one glance at the young man's face told him all he needed to know. He smiled and said "Carry on with your work here. I'll write to Weymouth today and I'll see what I can do for you – but watch her lad, watch her, or she'll lead you a merry dance."

Four weeks later he was transferred to Wyke Regis, a tiny village near Weymouth, and he married Thurza, but he never knew if his meals would be ready when he came home from his work. The house was always untidy and periodically Thurza would go missing for two or three days at a time.

"Been to Weymouth to see a few friends," she would say. "Nothing wrong with that is there?"

Shorrock had Thurza as his wife but her spirit was never tamed and she remained a constant source of delight and worry to poor Shorrock all his life.

Back at Number 18, Penaluna was becoming like one of the family. Never a mean man and always of an independent spirit he took to doing the shopping and would arrive at the door carrying great parcels of meat from Mr Wilkinson's shop or a crate of fine wine and something nice for the ladies. He had been ashore for about four weeks and he was beginning to feel the wanderlust coming on him. Clarissa arrived home from work one evening to find the kitchen table covered with maps and charts. Polly was busy making tea for Mr Baguly and Mr Fothergill, George was there too and the conversation was very animated.

"How are we to eat with the table like this?" Clarissa began.

"Don't worry my Dear, I have booked a table for us all at the Talbot for seven o'clock. Polly and Marie are going to Rose's for tea, so we are all provided for."

"But why so many charts and maps – these cover all the World surely?"

"Yes they do. I have always wanted to follow Drake's journey. I intend to go round the World – yes all of it, trading as I go. It has always been an ambition of mine and I intend to do it."

Penaluna's enthusiasm and exuberance were palpable. Mr Baguly's response to the news was a little less enthusiastic. Mr Fothergill was a bit worried that some legs of the journey would not be quite as profitable as he would have wished. Clarissa knew she would be without Penaluna and George for at least twelve months.

Clarissa's contribution, knowing that the trip was now inevitable, was to offer to make the trading part of the expedition a reality by offering to clear her warehouses of all the surplus unsold pots.

"What weight are we talking about my Dear?" Penaluna asked, brightening to the suggestion.

"Many tons – I don't know how many, but I have thousands of pieces. Some are seconds sure enough, but I can't see people in the colonies arguing over the odd blemish."

"Right. I'll have Bos'un contact your warehouse man, and 'Chips' will come and crate them up" Penaluna was already 'reckoning'. Sailing and reckoning were among his favourite occupations.

George stood near the maps and traced with his finger the magical names Ecuador, Chile, Bangkok, Jakarta, Honolulu, New York, India, Pinang, but most of all Trincomalee, his face glowed with anticipation, as he repeated the name 'Trincomalee, Trincomalee."

GLOSSARY

Most of the information for the Glossary came from "Two Years Before The Mast" by Dana. Also I obtained many facts by reading the Hornblower books by C S Forrester, 'First Voyage' by Commander Frank Worsley and 'The Voyage of the Cap Pilar' by Adrian Seligman.

ABACK	A situation when the wind changes suddenly and begins to push the ship backwards
AFT	Near the stern of the ship
A-LEE	Is when the helm is put in the opposite direction to that in which the wind is blowing
ALOO	When the rigging is in disarray, perhaps after a storm, things are said to be all aloo
ARM,YARD ARM	The extremities of the horizontal pole used to hold the sail in position
ATHWART	Across the ship
AVAST	An order to stop whatever is going on
AWNING	A shelter of canvas over a ship's deck, or over a boat to provide a shelter from rain or sun
BACKSTAYS	Strong supporting ropes leading from one mast to another, or down to some part of the ship to strengthen up the masts
BALLAST	Heavy material such as lead, iron or stone placed at the bottom of the hold to keep the ship steady. All sailing ships need ballast to bring down the centre of balance
BARK or BARQUE	A three masted ship with fore and main masts equipped with square sails but the rear or mizzen mast is rigged like a yacht
BATTENS	Thin strips of wood used to tighten the tarpaulin around the hatches
BEATING	Going against the direction of the wind by tacking
BEND	To bend a sail is to secure it to the yard
BILGE	Is the floor of the ship beneath the hold. Any

436

water which leaks into the ship, perhaps in a storm, settles in the bilge

BINNACLE	A box near the helm in which the compass is kept
BITTS	Perpendicular pieces of timber secured through the deck to tie anything to firmly, e.g. A tow rope
BLOCK	A wooden pulley wheel
BOATSWAIN	(pronounced Bosun) - a kind of seagoing foreman
BRAILS	Ropes used to haul up fore and aft sails
BRIG	A square rigged ship with two masts
BULK-HEAD	A temporary wooden partition
BULWARKS	A wooden structure (like a fence) which surrounds the ship
BUM-BOATS	Rowing boats used for errands, to and from a ship
BUNT	The middle portion of a sail
BUNT-LINES	Ropes used to haul up a sail
CANVAS	The cloth used to make sails. The lighter textured variety was used where the winds were gentler, e.g. In the Mediterranean, and the heavier ones for say rounding the Horn or crossing the Atlantic
CAULK	To caulk is to fill the seams where timbers join with oakum, to prevent leaking
CLEW	The lower corner of the square sails, and the after corner of a fore and aft sail
CLOSE-HAULED	This is a term used to describe the ship when she is sailing with her sails so braced as to take maximum advantage of the winds. 'Full and By' and 'On a bowline' (pronounced 'bolin') means the same thing

COAMINGS	Raised work around the hatches, to stop water going below decks
COMPANION-WAY	The staircase down from the deck to the cabins
COURSES	The sails which hang from the lower yards
COXSWAIN	(Pronounced cox'n) The man who steers the jolly boat or other rowed boat, and is in charge of it
CROSS-TREES	Complicated wooden structure usually of oak to join the lower mast to an upper one
CUTTER	A small sailing ship usually of sloop formation
DAVITS	Apparatus projecting over the side of a ship, used to hoist boats out of the water and onto the deck
DEAD-RECKONING	A system to aid navigation whereby the results of heaving the log and noting the changes in steering are carefully calculated
DRAUGHT	The depth of water a ship requires to float her
DUNNAGE	A sailor's luggage or personal belongings usually kept in a sea-chest
FORE	The forward part of the ship, or item kept there, e.g. Fore-mast, or fore-hatch, as opposed to aft
FORE-AND-AFT	Lengthways with the ship, as opposed to alwart which is across the ship
FORECASTLE	(Pronounced Focksle) The forward part of the ship, under the deck where the quarters are for the sailors
FORE-MAST	The mast nearest to the front of any ship
FOUNDER	A ship founders when she fills with water and sinks
FULL AND BYE	Sailing close hauled on a wind. It is the order given to the helmsman to keep the sails full and close to the wind. See also 'Bowlinee'
GALLEY	The place where the cooks work

GANGWAY	The means whereby passenger or crew can walk on or off the ship. Usually place amidships
GUNWALE	(Pronounced 'gunnel') the upper rail which runs all around a ship
HALYARDS	Ropes used for hoisting or lowering yards and sails
HANDSOMELY	Slowly, carefully. Used as part of an order where the men are handling expensive cargo
HATCH or HATCHWAY	An opening on the deck to give the opportunity to go below or to come from below on to the deck level
HAWSER	A rope of very thick gauge
HELM	The machinery which steers the ship
HOLD	The interior of the ship where the cargo is stored
HOLY-STONE	A stone about the size of a family bible (hence its name) It is used for scouring the decks of a ship
HOME or SHEET HOME	Sails are said to be home when they are firmly secured and at the desired angle to give the best results
JIB	A small sail position in front of the fore-mast and attached to the jib-boom
JOLLY BOAT	A small boat, usually kept aft
JURY MAST	A temporary make do mast, rigged at sea to replace a broken one
KEDGE	A small anchor used for warping
KEEL	The lowest and the principal timber of a ship running fore and aft, for the full length
LAND-FALL	The sighting of land when it has been out of sight for some time. Making a good land-fall is arrived arriving at a spot on the map exactly as planned

439

LARBOARD	The left side of the vessel, looking forward
LEE	The side opposite to that from which the wind is blowing. If the wind is on the starboard side that is the weather side and the starboard or portside is the lee side
LEE-SHORE	This is a shore towards which a wind is blowing. A situation greatly feared by sailing ships, because they could be blown aground or against rocks if quick action is not taken
LOG or LOG BOOK	A journal kept by the Captain of all daily events, winds, weather, courses, distances and everything of importance regarding the crews, accidents, injuries etc
LONG BOAT	The largest boat on a Merchant vessel
MATE	An officer under the Captain
MISS-STAYS	To fail in going about, from one tack to another, usually because of incorrect timing
NAUTICAL MEASUREMENTS	Fathom = 6 feet Cable = 200 yards League = $3^1/_2$ miles approx. Nautical mile = 2000 yards
OAKUM	Is old boat rope picked to pieces and used with melted tar to seal gaps in the woodwork of a ship
PAINTER	A rope fastened to a boat so that it can be made fast
PENNANT	A long narrow flag used in the Royal Navy of Nelson's time and flown by Commodores and above
POOP	A raised deck
PORT	The same meaning as larboard and the opposite to starboard
RATLINES	(Pronounced ratlins) Rungs running across the shrouds, like the rungs of a ladder

REEF	To reef a sail is to reduce its depth which in turn reduces the speed of a sailing ship
RIGGING	A general term for all the ropes used on a sailing ship
ROYAL	The sail higher up than a top gallant
RUDDER	The steering mechanism at the rear of the ship
RUNNING RIGGING	The ropes which are used through pulleys to haul sails into position. As opposed to standing rigging which is permanently in place, e.g. The shrouds
SCUPPERS	Holes cut into the side timber-work to allow water to run off the decks
SEIZE	To fasten or rope something securely
SHEET	A rope used to set a sail and to keep it in its correct place
SHROUDS	A set of ropes secured to the masthead and down to the sides of the ship to help support the mast
SNOW	A kind of brig, with square sails as well as fore and aft sail
SOUND	To obtain the depth of water with a lead and line
SPANKER	A fore and aft sail set behind the mizzen-mast
SPAR	A general term used for all masts, yards, booms etc
SPLICE	To join together two ropes by interweaving their strands
STARBOARD	The right hand side of a ship, looking forward - opposite to port or larboard
STAYS or IN STAYS	Is when a ship is about to be changed from one tack to another, and is not going anywhere until the sails are adjusted to the new position
STERN	The after end of a vessel

STUDDING SAILS	(Pronounced stun'sls') Light sails set high up outside the square sails to give that little extra if a ship's Captain wants to 'crack on'
TACK	To bring a ship to another direction so that the wind comes to it from the portside instead of the starboard - it is done to maximise the chances of the ship going forward AGAINST the wind
TAFFRAIL	The rail around a ship's stern
TOPGALLANT	(Pronounced To'gallant) The third mast above the deck and the sail it carries is also called the top gallant
WEAR	To change direction in order to take advantage of a more favourable wind, similar to tacking but weaving is done by carrying round the stern instead of the bows
WATCH	On a merchant ship like Mr Penaluna's all the men would be divided into two gangs or watches: the larboard and the starboard, with a mate in charge of each gang or watch. They would work four hours on and four hours off all day everyday, except from 4-6 in the afternoon and from 6-8 in the evening, these watches were of two hours duration each and were called the dog-watches. Work on board a sailing ship and in the Royal Navy aboard fighting ships were tremendously arduous, and a four hour shift, up to the waist in cold sea water, wrestling with ropes, climbing the rigging and making repairs was thought to be the maximum anyone could expect
YARD	A long length of timber tapered at each end from which a sailing ships sails are hung
YARD-ARM	The ends of a yard
YAW	The motion of a vessel when she goes off the desired direction

Appendix of ships rigs

(use this key in conjunction with the following ships illustrations)

Stay Sails

1. Flying Jib
2. Outer Jib
3. Inner Jib
4. Fore Topmast Staysail
5. Fore Staysail
6. Jib Topsail
7. Jib
7. a. Genoa Jib

Yard Sails

8. Skysail
9. Royal
10. Topgallant
11. Upper Topsail
12. Lower Topsail
13. Course
25. Cro'jack

Named after the mast on which the sail is set.
i.e. 10. Fore Topgallant.

14. Royal Staysail
15. Topgallant Staysail
16. Topmast Staysail
17. Staysail

Named after the masts abaft the sail.
i.e. 16. main Topmast Staysail.

Boom Sails

18. Foresail
19. Mainsail
20. Mizzen
24. Spanker

Gaff Sails

21. Fore Topsail
22. Main Topsail
23. 23. Mizzen Topsail

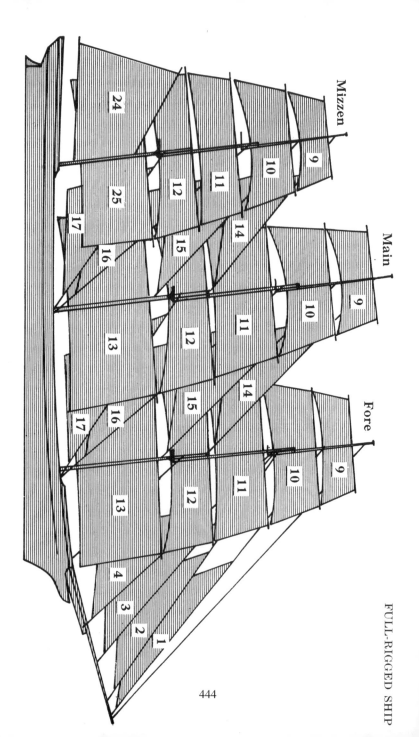

FULL-RIGGED SHIP

444

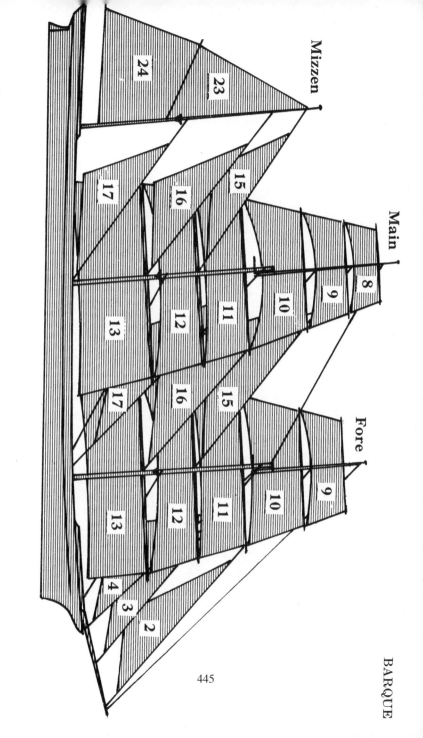

BARQUE

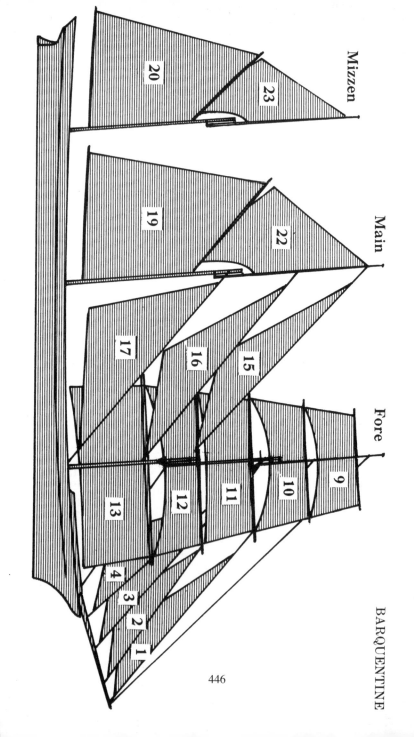

Mizzen

Main

Fore

BARQUENTINE

446